"The King
and
"The Freckled Shark"

TWO CLASSIC ADVENTURES OF

DOC *SAVAGE*

REG. U.S PAT. OFF.

by Harold A. Davis and
Lester Dent writing as Kenneth Robeson

with new historical essays
by Will Murray

Published by Sanctum Productions for
NOSTALGIA VENTURES, INC.
P.O. Box 231183; Encinitas, CA 92023-1183

ISBN: 1-934943-07-X   13 Digit: 978-1-934943-07-6

First printing: July 2008

Series editor: Anthony Tollin
P.O. Box 761474
San Antonio, TX 78245-1474
sanctumotr@earthlink.net

Consulting editor: Will Murray

Copy editor: Joseph Wrzos

Proofreader: Carl Gafford

Cover restoration: Michael Piper

The editors gratefully acknowledges the contributions of Jack Juka and John Gunnison in the preparation of this volume, and William T. Stolz of the Western Historical Manuscript Collection of the University of Missouri at Columbia for research assistance with the Lester Dent Collection.

Nostalgia Ventures, Inc.
P.O. Box 231183; Encinitas, CA 92023-1183

Visit Doc Savage at www.shadowsanctum.com and www.nostalgiatown.com.

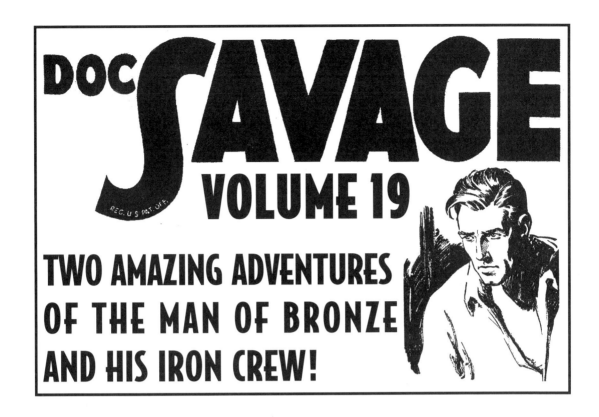

DOC SAVAGE
VOLUME 19
REG. U.S PAT. OFF.

TWO AMAZING ADVENTURES OF THE MAN OF BRONZE AND HIS IRON CREW!

Thrilling Tales and Features

**Cover art by Walter Baumhofer and Emery Clarke
Interior illustrations by Paul Orban**

Doc Savage refuses a crown, and saves a throne as he and his men battle

THE KING MAKER

A Complete Book-length Novel

By KENNETH ROBESON

Chapter I
RICHES, RAGS, AND TERROR

SIXTY or seventy pedestrians probably saw the silk-hatted gentleman get out of his resplendent town car in front of New York's finest skyscraper. Out of the sixty or seventy, nobody seemed to catch the significance of the man's pale face and lips drawn so tightly that they were blue.

"The lucky stiff," some onlookers possibly reflected.

Taking snap judgment on the silk hat and costly town car, most of the onlookers would have swapped places willingly with the top-hatted personage. In New York, such trappings signify an individual of importance, a somebody.

Had they known the truth, no amount of money would have inveigled an onlooker into changing places.

Maybe some of the spectators noted that the man's face was pale and grim. If so, they may have decided he was a business magnate with pressing responsibilities.

The truth was that the gentleman in the topper was scared. He was in the grip of an awful terror.

This frightened, very-much-dressed-up personage stalked rapidly into the vast and ornate lobby of the cloud-piercing building.

His town car waited. On its door was the coat-of-arms of the ruling house of the kingdom of Calbia, one of the Balkan countries of Europe. Probably nobody in the crowd knew it, but the uniform of the chauffeur designated him as no less than a general in the Calbian army.

Now there is something about ragged clothing and shabby attire that seems to label the wearer, the world over, as a person of lowly station.

This was why those rubbering at the swanky car and the silk-hatted man paid little attention to the old woman who entered the building at the same time.

She was very short, broad and stooped. There were wrinkles in her face, in which one could almost hide a lead pencil. A shawl was tied over her head, knotted under her chin. A rent in the top permitted a glimpse of gray hair. Her dress looked as if she had made it herself. Her shoes were shabby.

The man and the old woman—riches and rags, as it were—entered the same elevator.

"Call your floors," said the elevator operator.

"Eighty-six," came from the man in the silk hat.

"Eighty-six," the old woman echoed, somewhat shrilly.

The two passengers looked at each other. There was nothing in their expressions to indicate that they had met before.

"The eighty-sixth is Doc Savage's floor," the elevator operator offered, apparently by way of information.

The cage shot upward and stopped. Both passengers stepped out into a plain, yet rich, corridor. It was evident, from the way they looked around, that neither had ever been here before. They found their way to a door.

The door bore a name outlined in very small letters of bronze. They read:

DOC SAVAGE

Grasping the knob, the man in the silk topper tried to walk in. But the door was locked. He knocked with a brisk impatience—and the door opened.

The gentleman in the silk hat made a mistake which later cost him his life. He elbowed into the room ahead of the old lady. This act was anything but chivalrous.

SO unusual was the appearance of the man who had opened the door, that both visitors jerked to a stop and stared.

The individual was little taller than a half-grown boy. He came near being as wide as he was high. His hands swung on great beams of arms well below his knees, and they were covered with hairs which resembled rusty shingle nails. This gorilla-like fellow's face was phenomenally homely. He frowned at the gentleman in the silk topper, showing dislike of the way the man had shoved in ahead of the old lady.

"Doc Savage?" the silk-hatted one demanded imperiously.

"I'm Monk," grunted the apish one. "I mean—I'm Andrew Blodgett Mayfair."

His voice was tiny, childlike, a ludicrous tone for such a mountain of hair and gristle.

"Tell Doc Savage that Baron Damitru Mendl wishes to see him at once," commanded the pompous man.

"Monk" did not seem impressed. He glanced past the silk hat, frock coat, and morning trousers to the shabby old lady.

"You wanta see Doc Savage, too?"

"Please, sir," she quavered.

She appeared to be overawed by the magnificence of the office, with its sumptuously comfortable chairs, its impressive safe, and a huge, finely inlaid table.

"Just a minute," said Monk, tiny-voiced. He crossed to a door, opened it and stepped through, closing the panel behind him.

He was in a great room, which held literally hundreds of huge bookcases. These were crammed with tomes.

Monk advanced. He stopped when he could see the bronze man.

This man of bronze occupied a chair under a reading lamp. The chair was massive, yet it seemed small, so Herculean were the proportions of the man sitting in it.

The muscular development of the bronze man was something to arrest attention. Like great cables, sinews wrapped his frame. Their size, and the way they seemed to flow like liquid metal, denoted a strength bordering on the superhuman. These sinews, in repose, were not knotty, but were more like bundled piano wires on which a thin bronze skin had been lacquered.

"Two persons to see you, Doc," said Monk. "One is a guy in a silk hat who seems to think he's somebody. He shoved in ahead of the other one, a kinda ragged-lookin' old lady."

Doc Savage glanced up. This movement emphasized the most impressive thing about him—his eyes. The orbs might have been pools of fine flake-gold. The gold flakes, appearing to be always in motion, caught little lights from the reading lamp.

"The gentleman has bad manners, eh?" The bronze man's voice was pleasant and low, but obviously capable of great volume and tonal change.

"You said it."

"Use your own judgment, Monk."

Monk ambled back into the outer office, furry hands brushing his knees. He executed a polite bow in the direction of the shabby, elderly woman.

"Doc'll talk to you first," he said kindly.

"Thank you." She started for the door.

Baron Damitru Mendl snapped, "I am the Calbian ambassador to the United States. My business is important!"

Monk frowned. "You could be the king, and it wouldn't make any difference around here."

WHEN she entered the ample library and saw Doc Savage, the old woman's mouth sagged open. She was more than a little impressed by the bronze giant.

"Doc Savage?" she quavered. "I've heard a great deal about you and the wonderful things you do. You help poor people who are in trouble, don't you?"

Doc Savage's nod and the tone of his reply were calculated to put her at ease. "Something like that," he said.

"My poor son," said the visitor rapidly. "He's crippled. The doctors say they can't help him. I've heard that you can do many things better than any other man. I read in the paper that you are one of the greatest chemists in the world, and that nobody knew as much about electricity as you do. But, above everything else, is your skill as a surgeon. I want you to help my boy!"

Doc Savage said nothing. The tiny lights flickered in the flake-gold of his eyes.

"I know you can help him," quavered the elderly lady. "You see, his legs—"

"It will be better to make the diagnosis myself," Doc Savage put in quietly.

"Then you'll help him!" The elderly visitor sounded as if she were about to burst into delighted tears.

"Where is he now?"

"In my room at seventy-eight thirty-two East Fourteenth Street."

The tiny lights in the bronze man's eyes seemed to grow a bit more brilliant.

A box of apparatus, replete with knobs and dials, stood on a stand at his elbow. A microphone was attached to this. Leaning over, the bronze man flicked the switch, then spoke into the microphone.

The elderly woman seemed startled when she heard his words. To her, it was plain the syllables were not understandable. They were in some weird, not unmusical, guttural language.

Doc Savage switched off the apparatus, then glanced at his guest.

"The matter of your son will be looked into," he stated.

"What did you say into that box of a thing?" the old woman asked, surprisingly enough.

Doc Savage seemed not to hear the inquiry. He bowed her politely to the door.

The success of her mission seemed to have moved the elderly woman to an ecstasy of delight. Once she was in the outer office, she appeared unable to control her pleasure. She hobbled to Baron Damitru Mendl, kneading her hands together.

The baron glowered at her.

"Doc Savage is helping me!" squealed the crone.

Then she opened the hands which she had been kneading together. The homely Monk was behind her. Doc Savage was still in the library. Hence, neither saw what the old woman's cupped palms held.

Baron Damitru Mendl saw it, however.

The object was a small red marble.

AT the sight of the red marble, Baron Damitru Mendl became starkly pale. He actually trembled. His eyes protruded.

"Doc Savage is helping me!" shrilled the old woman.

Repetition of these words had a startling effect upon Baron Damitru Mendl. He whirled, grabbed up his silk hat and fled the office. Once in the corridor, he thumbed an elevator button furiously, and when the cage arrived, literally dived inside.

The elderly woman took a second cage a moment later.

Doc Savage appeared in the door which connected outer office and library. The size of the door emphasized his giant proportions.

"Thought we had another visitor, Monk."

Monk scratched the bristles atop his bullet of a head. "We did have, Doc, but I guess the guy flew into a rage because we interviewed the old woman first. He walked out on us."

Monk was an intelligent, observing individual. He was, in fact, conceded to be one of the greatest of living chemists. His reputation in that field was worldwide.

But Monk had not seen the red marble.

Down in the lobby, the old hag was hobbling toward the street. Chuckles came from her wrinkled face.

"*Ce frumos!*" she cackled. "How beautiful! That Doc Savage is not the mental wizard these Americans seem to think he is."

The words were spoken in the language of the Balkan kingdom of Calbia.

Outside the crone scampered down the street. More muttered words came.

"*Ma bucor!* I am pleased. I very cleverly made Baron Mendl think I had enlisted the aid of Doc Savage. The fool! He now believes Doc Savage to be against him."

Chapter II
EXPLOSION IN THE NIGHT

BARON DAMITRU MENDL climbed into his costly town car and sank back nervously on the rich cushions.

"Ce plictisitor!" he groaned in Calbian. "How vexing! General, look! See that old hag?"

The town car had the most modern of equipment. One could not yell at the chauffeur; there was a microphone in the rear, which actuated a loudspeaker beside the driver.

"I see her," said the chauffeur, who wore the uniform of a Calbian general.

"Follow her!"

The town car crept forward. But the trail was a short one. The crone ducked suddenly into a crowd about a subway entrance and lost herself thoroughly although Baron Damitru Mendl got out and searched.

Returning to the town car, Mendl perched on the cushions and tangled and untangled his hands nervously.

"I have heard a great deal about this man, Doc Savage," he said. "They say he is a muscular marvel and a mental wizard who devotes his life to the strange business of helping those who are in trouble."

"Doc Savage has a remarkable reputation, your highness," agreed the general, who seemed to be a confirmed "yes-man." "But who was the old wench?"

"I went to Doc Savage to enlist his aid in preserving my own life," replied Mendl. "In Savage's office, the old hag ran up to me and cried out, 'Doc Savage is helping me!' Then she exhibited a red marble."

The general in the driver's seat started violently. "A red marble."

"Exactly, general! The red marble proves that the old crone is a secret agent—one of my enemies."

The general wiped a slight dew of perspiration off his forehead. "I suggest we leave this vicinity at once, your highness."

"An excellent idea!" Baron Mendl nodded vehemently. "Drive to my hotel. I must send a radiogram, then take all possible measures to protect myself."

The long town car went into motion without a jar.

BARON DAMITRU MENDL had a suite of rooms in the hotel which was conceded by almost everyone to be New York's most fashionable hostelry.

The national flag of Calbia was displayed in front of this hotel, alongside the United States colors. The presence of the Calbian emblem had a meaning. It indicated that an important diplomatic personage was a guest of the hotel.

The flag was out in honor of Baron Mendl, Calbian ambassador to the United States.

Baron Mendl went directly to his room, secured a radiogram blank and wrote out a message. He addressed it simply to a stateroom number on a liner which was now crossing the Atlantic from Europe. The communication read:

FIRST-CLASS CABIN 36
LINER S S MONTICELLO, AT SEA
AGENT FROM CALBIA HAS ENLISTED AID OF DOC SAVAGE AGAINST US STOP HAVE OBSERVED OTHER SECRET AGENTS WATCHING ME STOP BELIEVE MY LIFE IN DANGER STOP LEAVING CITY STOP WILL ADVISE YOU MY WHEREABOUTS LATER.
BARON DAMITRU MENDL.

As an afterthought, Baron Mendl drew a small brown code book from a pocket and converted the message into a secret cipher. He burned the first copy painstakingly, crushed the ashes, and threw them out of the window. Then he went down to the hotel wireless telegraph office and filed his coded missive.

His movements marked by an apprehensive haste, he packed his luggage. Bellboys, made unusually spry by the prospect of handsome tips, loaded his bags into the town car.

"We are going on the yacht, general," Baron Mendl informed the driver.

Along the upper shore of Manhattan Island, on the Hudson River side, are a number of swanky yacht clubs. To one of these, Baron Mendl went. The town car was left in the yacht club garage.

Baron Mendl and his chauffeur boarded a seventy-foot, Diesel-engined, seagoing palace. The boat had lines of speed, while mahogany woodwork and brass fittings lent an air of luxury to it. Native Calbians composed the crew, with one exception—the first mate, who was a freckled, red-headed New England Yankee.

"Mr. Lacy," Baron Mendl addressed the red-headed mate. "Put all hands to searching the yacht. Look for bombs, or stowaways."

TWENTY minutes later, the red-headed mate made his report. "No bombs. No stowaways," he stated.

"You are positive, Mr. Lacy?" persisted Baron Mendl.

"Plumb certain. We even probed the water tanks."

Baron Mendl surveyed the sky. The sun was just dropping below the horizon. A profusion of clouds promised an extremely dark night.

"Cast off," directed the Calbian ambassador. "Head southward through the bay, and straight out to sea."

The trim vessel got under way, took the middle of the river, picked up speed, and swept past the warehouses and wharves which fringe the Hudson's banks. The sun disappeared entirely, and after a brief dusk, black night came.

The yacht was just nosing into the open sea as complete darkness fell.

"Extinguish all lights," commanded Baron Mendl.

"That's agin' the law, sir," the mate, Lacy, protested.

"Lights out!" snapped Baron Mendl. "Otherwise my enemies, using an airplane or a speedboat, might spot me."

The red-headed Lacy had been holding his curiosity fairly well, but now it got the better of him.

"What's going on here, anyway?" he demanded.

"You were hired to take orders, not to ask questions," he was informed sharply.

Lacy grumbled, and departed to switch off the lights. Masthead lights, running-lights—even the illumination in the cabins was turned off. A silent wraith in the thick murk, the yacht ran out to sea.

Lacy, consumed with curiosity, and still smarting from Baron Mendl's rebuke, stood in the bows with binoculars jammed to his eyes. He had appointed himself as extra lookout.

Lacy was in the bows when he heard the hissing sound. It was shrill, that hiss, and unlike anything he had ever heard before. He could not tell exactly from where it came.

He started to turn, got half around—and the whole Atlantic ocean seemed to go to pieces. There was a flash—so brilliant that its lights ran into his eyeballs as if it were molten metal.

Lacy had a split-second impression that the yacht and the surrounding sea were both going to jump high into the sky and that the yacht had separated into many pieces for its jump.

Then an explosion-hurled timber slammed against Lacy's red-thatched head, and he became unconscious.

Chapter III
DEATH TIES A TONGUE

DOC SAVAGE, in his headquarters on the eighty-sixth floor of New York's most impressive skyscraper, saw the flash which marked the destruction of Baron Damitru Mendl's yacht. The bronze man's windows faced toward the lower bay and the sea. Moreover, his flake-gold eyes missed little that transpired about him.

At the moment he observed the flash, Doc Savage was nearing the end of his daily two-hour exercise routine. It was rather late for the exercises, but the unusual man of bronze never allowed a twenty-four hour interval to elapse without taking them.

When he saw the bright flash out at sea, Doc Savage called a suggestion to Monk, the homely chemist.

"Tune in the radio, Monk, and see if you can pick up something that will tell us what that flash was."

The pleasantly ugly Monk was engaged at the moment in painting a small, crimson flag on the side of Habeas Corpus.

Habeas Corpus was as uncouth a specimen of his kind as Monk was of the human race. Their kinship extended farther than that. Both Habeas and Monk would be classed as very intelligent members of their species.

Habeas Corpus was Monk's pet pig. Habeas was lanky and razor-backed, with legs like a dog, and phenomenal ears. His ears seemed large enough to serve as wings.

Monk dropped the brush he was using into the can of crimson paint, went to a radio receiver, turned it on, and tuned.

Later, he let out a yell.

"Doc! Doc!" he barked excitedly. "That flash was a yacht blowing up! A coast guard cutter just reached the wreckage! I picked up the cutter radio report."

Doc Savage approached the radio. The flowing ease of his movements conveyed a striking impression of tremendous muscular strength. "Any survivors?" he queried.

"One—the mate of the yacht, a guy named Lacy. He's all banged up, but was able to tell 'em who was on board."

Monk paused and squinted his small eyes at the giant bronze man. "Listen, Doc—you remember the guy in the silk hat who came in here this afternoon, then walked out? He told me he was Baron Damitru Mendl."

Doc Savage said nothing, but the flake-gold in his strange eyes seemed to swirl faster.

"Baron Mendl was on that yacht, and the explosion killed him," Monk concluded.

THE closest inspection of Doc Savage's lips would have showed no movement, yet a weird trilling sound came into being and permeated the vast room. It defied description, this trilling, being possessed of no tune, roving the musical scale aimlessly. It might have been the product of some wayward breeze through the array of massive bookcases, or the night song of an exotic jungle bird.

Monk blinked. He knew this sound. The eerie trilling was a characteristic exclusive to Doc Savage—a tiny, unconscious thing which he did in moments of stress.

"We'd better get at the bottom of this," Doc said sharply. "Something queer is going on!"

"Wonder what's back of it?" Monk pondered.

"No telling." Doc moved for the door. "Come on."

Monk scooped Habeas up by an ear—the over-

DOC SAVAGE'S EXERCISES

Doc Savage's amazing faculties—his terrific strength and the acuteness of his five senses—are the result of intensive exercises from early youth. Each day, regardless of his surroundings, Doc Savage puts himself through a stiff two-hour routine. He tenses his muscles, making one play against the other, and in this way strengthens them.

To keep his sense of hearing at an acute pitch, Doc has an instrument capable of sending out sound waves far below and above the average hearing range. Yet Doc can distinguish these sounds.

A case holding many bottles of varied scents and odors keeps Doc's sense of smell at the keenest, allowing him to identify, in case of necessity, any smell.

All throughout the exercise period Doc juggles many figures in his head, working out abstract mathematical formulas, taking a number and extracting the square and cube roots, carrying the results to many decimals.

All these exercises help to make Doc Savage the superman he is.

---

sized ears served very nicely as handles, and Habeas did not mind—and cried, "Where we goin'?"

"To the explosion scene."

The Hudson River lay only a few blocks to the west. It did not take them long to reach the waterfront.

The warehouses were great gloomy hulks in the pale light cast by street lamps. Signs were barely decipherable in the dimness. One of these read:

HIDALGO TRADING COMPANY

A door in the shoreward end of this warehouse opened to Doc Savage's signal, and it became evident that walls and roof of the structure were remarkably thick. The place, in fact, was virtually a huge vault. Darkness gorged the rear, and just what this huge building held was not immediately discernible. A hooded bulb illuminated the forward portion. This light stood on a workbench.

Affixed in a vise on the bench was a long, thin, razor-sharp blade of Damascus steel. The sheath for this, reposing near by, disclosed that the weapon was a sword cane, innocent-looking but deadly.

A man who had opened the hangar door looked at Monk and said sarcastically, "The world's homeliest man, and ugliest hog!"

Monk leered. "Hello, Ham, you shyster!"

Ham—his Alma Mater, Harvard, knew him as Brigadier General Theodore Marley Brooks, the most astute lawyer ever to pass its portals—was a slender man with a waist like a wasp, the dark, piercing eyes of a listener, and the large, mobile mouth of an orator. Ham's dress was sartorial perfection. Good taste kept his clothes from being flashy, but he was a man who gave his physical appearance close attention.

Ham and Monk glowered at each other.

An uninformed observer would have thought fisticuffs, if not something worse, imminent. The truth was that these two were good, if quarrelsome, friends.

Doc clicked light switches, and electric radiance whitened the hangar—for that was the real purpose of the vast building. Housed inside were a number of planes. These ranged from small gyros to a gigantic tri-motored speed ship with wonderful streamlining. All were amphibians, capable of berthing on land or water.

"We'll take the big plane," Doc announced. "It is more efficient for a landing in the open sea."

THE coast guard cutter, which had been first to reach the spot where disaster had overtaken Baron Damitru Mendl's yacht, kept in more or less continuous radio communication with its base. The operation of this radio transmitter guided Doc Savage to the scene. The bronze man employed a sensitive radio direction-finder, with which his fast amphibian plane was equipped.

The direction-finder amplifier fed into a loudspeaker, so that Monk and Ham could hear the cutter's transmission. This was in continental code, but both the chemist and the lawyer understood it. They were skilled operators.

"The cause of the explosion seems to be a profound mystery," Ham remarked.

"I wonder what we're gettin' mixed up in," Monk muttered. The homely chemist leaned over to scratch one of Habeas Corpus' winglike ears. "What does this thing smell like to you, Habeas?"

"Trouble!" said Habeas.

HAM

MONK

MONK, HAM AND THEIR PRIVATE WAR

They always squabble, these two. To listen to them when they are together, a stranger would think them on the point of slaughtering each other. One would well believe, from the sharp-tongued Ham's talk, that nothing would give him more pleasure than to run the keen sword cane which he carries through Monk's anthropoid form.

Monk and Ham's squabble dates back to the Great War, to an incident which gave Ham his nickname. As a joke, Ham taught Monk some French words which were highly insulting, telling Monk they were the proper things with which to curry the favor of French generals.

Monk tried the words out on a French general, and that worthy promptly had Monk clapped in the guardhouse for several days.

But within the week after Monk's release, Ham was hailed upon a charge of stealing hams from the supplies. Somebody had taken the hams, and Ham's—he was Brig. Gen. Theodore Marley Brooks then—billfold, with his private papers inside, was found upon the scene. A search of Ham's quarters turned up the missing pork.

Ham's agile tongue finally got himself out of the scrape, but not before the whole army knew about it, and had a good laugh.

Somebody stole the hams and planted the evidence. Just who it was, Ham had his suspicions. But he had never been able to prove it, and that still irked him, for the nickname of "Ham" had stuck, and he did not care for the cognomen.

Monk had always been entirely too innocent about those stolen hams.

When the pleasantly unlovely pig made this intelligent reply—or seemed to make it—Ham started violently. The phenomenon gave him a shock, although he had witnessed it numerous times before, and knew very well that the pig did not have a voice.

Monk was a proficient ventriloquist, and frequently exercised his dexterity in the art on Habeas Corpus.

At an altitude of two thousand feet above the cutter, Doc Savage ran a bronze fingertip over a row of buttons on the dashboard of the plane, selected one and pressed it. Mechanism clicked, and from a wing compartment a parachute flare was launched. This was like a small sun, as it settled slowly toward the sea.

Doc Savage pointed. "Wreckage—evidently from Baron Mendl's yacht."

The flotsam consisted of deck chairs, life preservers, portions of lifeboats, and a few torn timbers.

Before the parachute flare fell into the sea, Doc Savage dropped his big amphibian on the surface and taxied alongside the cutter. The sea was rough, the landing a dangerous one, requiring great skill. The man of bronze, however, showed with no expression that he considered the descent anything but ordinary.

The cutter was a drab, businesslike vessel with a keel length of approximately a hundred feet. Three-inch guns fore and aft had their breech mechanism swathed in weather coverings.

Doc turned the amphibian controls over to Monk, then clambered out, balanced adroitly, and ran to the tip of the wing.

Monk, an expert airman, jockeyed the wing tip close enough to the cutter to enable Doc, with a tremendous leap, to board the coast guard craft.

"This fellow Lacy," Doc demanded of the cutter skipper. "Where is he?"

"In the fo'castle," replied the officer.

"Let's see him."

Lacy was a still, slack shape on a bunk. His ordinary ruddy color had ebbed until his skin about matched the battleship-gray paintwork of the cutter. He was senseless, and barely breathing.

Doc made a quick examination. The strange bronze man was skilled at many things—he knew more chemistry than Monk, more law than Ham; but above all was his knowledge of surgery.

"There's a fracture of the squamous portion of the occipital," he stated. "In other words, a fractured skull."

The cutter skipper strained his hair with his fingers. "He must be pretty bad. He was unconscious when we found him, revived enough to talk some, then passed out again."

"Did he give any hint as to what caused the blast, or why the yacht was destroyed?" Doc asked.

"No."

"I want to take him to a hospital. That is his only chance."

The commander shrugged. "That'll have to be O.K.'d by my commanding officer."

The cutter captain went to the radio cabin and communicated with his headquarters. Orders to cooperate fully with Doc Savage came crackling back with a rapidity that gave the officer rather a shock. He had heard of Doc Savage, of course, but he did not know the bronze man had such influence with the coast guard.

Guardsmen transferred the seriously injured Lacy to Doc's speed plane.

The small boat, which had been lowered to pick up Lacy, still bobbed alongside the cutter. Entering this, Doc Savage directed that he be rowed through the floating wreckage of Baron Damitru Mendl's yacht. The casual strength dominant in his unusual voice had its effect on the sailors, and they rowed about briskly.

The bronze man picked up a shattered hatch, inspected it closely, then discarded it. He did the same with a life preserver, two deck chairs, the stem of a lifeboat, and miscellaneous spars and timbers.

His examination was short, for he wanted to get Lacy to the hospital. He soon boarded the plane.

"You sized up the wreckage, Doc," Monk said. "Whatcha' make of it?"

"The manner in which those timbers are shattered indicates that the force of the explosion came *not* from within the yacht, but from the top of the superstructure."

"You mean like a dropped bomb?"

"It might have been a bomb."

Doc Savage was moved to alter his surmise shortly after he reached the hospital with Lacy.

THE hospital to which Doc took Lacy was not especially large or ornate, but it was acquiring an increasing reputation for good work, and, moreover, handled an unusual number of charity cases.

Probably not more than a dozen people in New York City knew that Doc Savage had financed the construction of this institution and was furnishing the money which kept it in operation. The building stood near the river, and Doc was able to taxi his plane almost to the door.

Appearance of the bronze man with the patient created something of a flurry among the surgeons, and it was not because their salaries were paid out of Doc's pocketbook. They did not know that. What excited the surgeons was the prospect of seeing a master of their profession perform.

The main operating room, scene of the most delicate work, was circular, with a glass ceiling, through which spectators would observe operations. Every surgeon who could find a free moment posted himself above this glass with a pair of strong binoculars, hoping to see Doc Savage's skilled fingers perform new miracles of surgery.

They were not disappointed. Exactly how Doc revived Lacy was probably understood by only those with the necessary technical knowledge. Certainly it was beyond Monk and Ham, who were present. The attention of those on hand, the rapt intensity of the observers above, told them that Doc was doing something far beyond the ordinary.

An hour later, Lacy talked a little.

"Have you any idea what caused the explosion?" Doc queried.

"Nope," said Lacy, in a fairly strong voice.

"It was apparently something in the nature of a bomb."

"You mean dropped from an airplane?"

"Yes."

"Nix. It couldn't have been that. I was on lookout. I didn't hear a plane."

"A plane motor can be efficiently silenced."

"There weren't any lights on the yacht," Lacy insisted. "I'm plumb certain of that. I tell you, it couldn't have been an aerial bomb. A plane couldn't have seen us."

"How about planted explosive?" Doc suggested.

"Nix again." Lacy managed a slight grimace. "We searched the yacht ahead of time. Baron Damitru Mendl's orders."

The lights played in the flake-gold of Doc's eyes. "What was Baron Mendl afraid of?" he asked.

"I don't know, and that's the truth," Lacy said earnestly. "I was just one of the yacht's crew. I tried to question him, but he told me I was hired to take orders and keep my mouth shut."

"You had better not talk any more now," Doc informed him. "Later, we will discuss the affair in detail. There may be some minor point which you overlooked, but which will give me a clue."

"Am I gonna pull out of this all right?" Lacy asked.

"You are," Doc told him.

Chapter IV
THE PRINCESS

DOC SAVAGE was wrong, but due to no misjudgment of his own.

The spectacular nature of Doc Savage's career had made him excellent newspaper copy. Almost any of his feats were good for a front-page story. One of the surgeons who had observed the operation forgot that there was an order standing which directed that newspapermen were to be given no information concerning Doc Savage. This specialist called a friend—a reporter on a tabloid paper—and gave praise of the extremely delicate nature of the operation which Doc had performed upon Lacy's shattered skull.

The tabloid appeared with two-inch headlines, scooping all its rival sheets.

An hour later, the hospital attendants heard a single shot. It came from the private room where Lacy lay.

They rushed to the room. Nurses are supposed to be inured to unpleasant sights, but two of them screamed when they saw Lacy.

A pistol bullet had entered Lacy's left temple, tunneled through his brain, and all but torn off the ear of the opposite side in leaving his head.

An open window and a fire escape indicated the route by which the murderer had come and gone. At the foot of the fire escape was found a copy of the tabloid newspaper which carried the story of Lacy's operation. The story had furnished the killer with both the name of the hospital and Lacy's room number.

Extremely pale, and staggering a little as he walked, the surgeon who had given the newspaper the yarn went to the phone and called Doc Savage. He told the bronze man exactly what had happened. Then he tendered his resignation.

"Your resignation will not be accepted," Doc Savage advised him.

"But the story I gave the newspaper resulted in the man's death," the surgeon groaned. "It furnished the killer with Lacy's whereabouts. I murdered that man just as surely as if I had done it with my own hands."

"It was unfortunate," Doc agreed. "But your resignation will not help matters. In you there is the making of a great surgeon. You can do more to atone by going ahead with your work."

"I—am very grateful—to you," the other said weakly, and hung up.

DOC SAVAGE had received the call in his skyscraper office. When the conversation had terminated, he advised Monk and Ham of what had occurred.

"For the love of Mike," Monk muttered, small-voiced. "Lacy was killed to shut his mouth. Somebody was afraid he might know things. Doc, there must be something infernally big back of this."

"Lacy told us all he knew, I'm sure," Doc said slowly. "But, in later questioning, he might have given us some clue. And it was to prevent us getting that clue that he was slain."

The bronze giant, of such titanic proportions that the massive furniture about him was dwarfed in comparison, swung into the library. He went to the chair in which he had been seated, reading, when the elderly hag visited him that afternoon. He switched on the apparatus which stood beside the chair—the device into which he had spoken in the weirdly unintelligible tongue when the crone was present.

"Renny—Johnny—Long Tom!" Doc called into the microphone appended to the contrivance.

When there was no answer, Doc called again.

Monk and Ham looked on, their perpetual quarrel for the moment forgotten. They knew that the apparatus was a radio transmitter and receiver. It operated on a short wave-band.

Doc Savage possessed several other transmitter-receiver outfits which operated on this same wavelength. The sets were kept turned on continuously in the spots frequented by his five aides—their apartments, their automobiles and their private planes.

"What's the idea of tryin' to raise the other three of our gang?" Monk queried.

"Remember the old woman who visited us at the same time that Baron Damitru Mendl was here?" Doc countered.

"Sure, and was she a homely old heifer!" Monk grunted.

At that, Ham snorted and eyed Monk's homely features meaningfully.

Monk ignored the dig. "What about the old woman, Doc?"

"When she was present, I spoke a few words of the Mayan language into the radio. Close watching of her face convinced me she did not understand the language. Hence, she does not know that the words directed Long Tom, Johnny and Renny to trail her."

Monk's big mouth sagged open. Ham almost dropped his sword cane.

"You mean the old lady was a phony?" Monk exploded.

"Exactly! Her story about an ailing son was a pack of lies."

Monk blinked incredulously. "But how'd you catch on?"

"The address she gave me, where her son was supposed to be, was seventy-eight thirty-two East Fourteenth Street. There is no such number. Moreover, her manner gave her away. She was somewhat too glib."

Doc Savage now shifted his attention to the radio. "Johnny—Long Tom—Renny!" he called again.

He secured no answer, and left the apparatus turned on.

"The three of them are trailing the crone," he said, settling back in the chair. "I directed them in Mayan to pick up her trail when she left the building. I gave them the description. They were downstairs in our secret garage."

Monk grinned. His grin was remarkable, for it puckered all of his homely face, persimmon fashion. Ham withdrew his sword cane a few inches from its sheath and clicked it back. Both were excited.

The fact that Doc was quiet in the chair, his metallic features impassive, did not deceive them. He was already moving to unravel this tangle of murder and mystery. If events of the past were any criterion, there would be danger ahead, plenty of action—adventure!

Monk and Ham were not mournful about the prospects. To them this sort of thing made life worth living.

A click came from the radio—a microphone being cut into the voice circuit.

"DOC SAVAGE!" called a rather scholastic tone from the loudspeaker.

Doc leaned close to the transmitter. "Yes, Johnny," he called.

"The superannuated crone has terminated her meanderings," advised Johnny.

Johnny—William Harper Littlejohn, as the realms of geology and archaeology knew him—never used a small word where he could think of a big one.

"Where did she go?" Doc demanded.

"She promenaded the metropolis for an interval," explained the master of big words. "In her peregrinations, she tarried to indulge in three telephone calls. To our vexation, we could not overhear the telephonic discussion."

"Where is she now?"

"In a hovel. I think that term fits the habitation adequately."

"Is it on Fourteenth Street?"

"In Brooklyn—87 Mervin Street."

"All right," Doc said quietly. "Watch the place, you fellows. Monk, Ham and myself will be right out."

"You desire to interview this crone?" questioned Johnny.

"Right. We are getting mixed up in an infernally big plot. As yet, we have no idea what it is all about. But the ambassador of a Balkan nation and the crew of his yacht have been murdered entire—"

The telephone rang, interrupting the conversation.

Monk clamped the receiver to an ear, blinked once, then barked, "Doc! Quick!"

"Just a minute, Johnny," Doc said into the radio set, and swung to the telephone.

"It's a girl," Monk breathed, and surrendered the phone.

"Savage speaking," Doc said.

From the telephone receiver came a series of dull thumps.

"Well?" Doc said sharply into the transmitter.

"They're breaking the door down!" The whisper was feminine, husky, hasty.

"What is this?" Doc demanded.

Apparently she did not get his words, for her whispered exclamation poured on in a frenzied rush.

"*Ajutor!* Help! I got away from them and into this room, and got the door locked. They'll break in soon! They don't know this phone is here, and I'll hide it. Quick! Help me, Domnule Savage!"

"Who are you?" Doc demanded.

Again his words went unheeded, as the girl's rushing whisper continued.

"*Ce rusine!* They come! *Ajutor! Help!*"

A clatter came from the phone receiver, as if the other instrument was being shoved into some place of concealment. Either from accident or deliberate design, the receiver had not been replaced.

Listening intently, Doc Savage got an idea of what was going on. A crashing of wood might have been a door going down, and a loud rattle of feet followed—after which the girl cried out and there were gasps, blows, and some sharp ejaculating in the Calbian tongue.

"*Ma bucur!*" a man exclaimed. "Good! Now we will tie her up securely." His tone was resounding, pleasantly boyish.

"*Da domnule!*" another grunted. "Yes, sir! And we had better take her away from this place in a hurry!"

"Why?"

"Because her screams or the struggle may have been heard."

Nu! declared the man with the exuberant voice. "No! This home is empty. No one will have heard. We will merely take her into the next room."

There was footstep clatter, muttering voices, the slam of a door—then silence.

DOC SAVAGE swung into the next room, where there was a second telephone line, and used that instrument to summon an operator and start a trace on the connection over which the girl had called.

While the call was being traced—he had no other way of learning from where the girl had phoned—the bronze man went back to the radio transmitter.

"Johnny—you and Long Tom and Renny close in on that old woman and grab her. If you get into a jam, call the office. Monk and Ham will be here."

As they heard these words, Monk and Ham blinked, then looked as if they had stepped into puddles of cold water. They did not fancy playing reserves.

"You can stay by the telephone wire over which the girl talked," Doc advised them. "But do not leave this office unless Johnny's party or myself calls."

"O.K.," Monk muttered, and picked up the phone.

Doc Savage got the results of the traced call a moment later. The address from which the girl had spoken was on the upper west side of Manhattan Island.

Monk and Ham registered gloom as they watched Doc's exit. The pig, Habeas Corpus, sat at Monk's feet, big ears waving slowly, fan fashion.

At Doc's expense, certain remodeling had been done on the skyscraper, fitting it to the bronze man's requirements. There was, for instance, an elevator of special design which operated at tremendous speed—its descent for sixty stories was almost a free fall, and the shock of its halt was quite appreciable.

The cage let Doc out in a basement garage which held his collection of cars. The machines ranged from a large limousine to roadsters, small coupés, and three trucks of assorted dimensions, none of which were especially flashy, but all fitted with engines of unusual power.

Doc selected a roadster, long and sombre, with an engine which, running at moderate speed, could hardly be heard. Tooling this car out into the street, he headed northward.

Many a pedestrian stopped and twisted his neck to stare after the remarkable-looking bronze man, for there was much that was arresting about his appearance.

Traffic cops fell over themselves to open a way for him, and this was not entirely because of the low license numeral which the roadster bore, itself a symbol of influence in New York City. Almost every cop on the force had heard of Doc Savage, and was aware that he bore a high honorary police commission.

The house from which the girl had called was on an unprepossessing side street. Doc did not drive past it, but parked around a corner a block distant. Here he left the machine.

A cigar store on the corner was lighted. Other stores were dark. At the moment, no one was in sight.

The bronze man walked to a store awning, which was rolled up. He grasped the frame and, with a lithe ease, climbed hand over hand until he reached a shelf of ornamental masonry. There were grooves between the bricks, which furnished grips for the tips of his corded fingers. The building was four stories high, and he mounted it as easily as another would climb a ladder.

No one saw him.

A ghostly silence marked Doc's passage across the roof tops. He reached the house which was his objective. These houses were in reality not houses at all in the sense in which the term is accepted outside the metropolitan centers. The block was really one long building, partitioned.

Doc tested a roof hatch, found it locked, and moved back to the rear. A thin silk line, a grappling hook attached to one end, came out of his clothing. Hooking the grapple behind a chimney, Doc dangled the cord down into the courtyard in the rear and slid down it.

He came to a window. Trying to open it, he found it locked.

A diamond-pointed glass cutter—and a suction cup to grasp the pane and keep it from falling after it was free—disposed of the window with silence and celerity.

Like some nebulous liquid of bronze hue, Doc seemed to flow inside the house.

DOC SAVAGE lowered the cut square of glass to the floor. The feel of the floor, together with the shimmering effect of the moonlight which penetrated the window, told of varnish recently applied. The air smelled of paint. The house had been redecorated recently. There was no furniture in it.

With quick tugs, the bronze man removed the custom-made oxfords which shod his feet and drew off silk socks. His coat pockets were spacious enough to accommodate the footgear. Then he went forward.

Included in the two-hour ritual of exercises which Doc had taken daily from childhood was a series of calisthenics intended to develop his toes. These toes were not the comparatively useless appendages of an ordinary man. They were sensitive, possessed of a prehensile strength.

Many individuals bereft of their arms earn a livelihood on the vaudeville stage and with circuses, demonstrating how they have learned to shave, drive nails, and turn the pages of a book, using only their toes. Doc Savage could do all of these things, and was master of feats which few of these armless wonders could equal. For instance, he could take a string in the toes of one foot and, using that foot exclusively, tie a knot in the cord.

This pedal facility, developed by careful exercise, was handy in searching out solid footing, as Doc now descended the none-too-substantial stairs.

He heard sound—a mutter, a grunt. They came, he decided when he had gone down farther, from the ground floor.

"Ba gati deseama!" a man growled. "Take care! Not so much noise!"

"No one will hear us," said the boisterous young male voice which Doc had previously heard over the telephone.

The words were couched in the mother tongue of Calbia. Doc understood this language, for his mastery of worldly knowledge was particularly thorough on the matter of foreign languages.

The speakers were in a room to one side of the front door. Doc went on—rapidly, stealthily.

The corridor was itself unlighted by any bulb, but was made faintly luminous by the rays which slanted through the partially open door of a room to one side of the entrance.

From his clothing Doc produced a periscope of his own construction. The barrel of this, black in color, and scarcely larger than a match, could be telescoped out. He used the little contrivance to inspect the room, furtively.

Eight men were in sight.

Seven of the men were attired exactly alike, in the rough dungaree outfits which steamship concerns supply to their deck hands. They did not wear uniform caps, and nowhere was there a sign of the ship to which they belonged—if they were really sailors. Round faces, dark eyes, and slightly full lips—they all had these characteristics—were partial proof that they were Calbians.

They all wore gloomy expressions.

"Rusime!" said the man with the young, hearty voice. "For shame! Cheer up, gentlemen, we are in no danger!"

"I hope you are right, Captain Flancul," mumbled one of the group.

Captain Flancul—he of the boisterous voice—resembled a movie director's idea of a European military officer. His height was near six feet, and he stood as stiffly as if there had been a ramrod strapped against his spine. He wore a neat gray business suit. His hair was close cropped and dark, his forehead high, his eyes brilliantly intelligent, his mouth thin and grim. Small scars on his features indicated to the informed that he was not a stranger to the Calbian national custom of settling minor disputes with saber duels.

DOC SAVAGE shifted his periscope. In the portion of the room into which he could see, there was no sign of the girl.

Doc shoved a hand into a pocket and brought out several objects which, at first glance, might have been mistaken for glass marbles. These were in reality thin-walled glass containers holding a liquid. Some were marked differently than others—with a tiny colored speck.

Doc selected one which bore a green dot, and flipped it into the room. It burst with a sound not unlike that of a dropped bird egg.

Doc Savage held his breath.

The occupants of the room stared at the spot where the unusual missile had burst. Not having seen the thing, they were at a loss to understand what had occurred.

"Bagati deseama!" rapped lusty-voiced Captain Flancul. "Take care—" Without bending his ramrod back, Captain Flancul tilted forward. He hit the floor full-length, with a resounding crash.

Except for the slight rebound of his body, he did not move afterward. A long, irregular snore fluttered his lips.

He had been nearest to the glass ball when it burst.

The other men collapsed almost as suddenly. Only two of the party managed to stir so much as a step before they went down. Without exception, they seemed to sink into a deep slumber.

Doc Savage continued holding his breath.

The glass ball held a powerful anaesthetic gas, the vapor from this particular container producing an unconsciousness which lasted some ten to fifteen minutes. The other balls in Doc's pocket were charged with a stronger gas, inducing, when used, a stupor which lasted two hours or more.

The gas had a peculiar quality. It mingled with the air and became ineffective after the passage of perhaps a minute.

Doc allowed the minute to elapse, and then, breathing freely, stepped into the room.

He saw the girl.

Ordinarily, feminine beauty left the bronze man untouched, for he had schooled his tastes carefully so that they did not run in that direction. But now he stared, and his strong lips, parting a little from amazement, showed even white teeth.

Her traveling suit, trim and expensive, was obviously a Paris creation. The trim hat was small, chic. A skilled manicurist had worked recently upon her slim-fingered hands. Her feet were small—expensively shod; her ankles shapely in silken hose of an elaborate open network design.

Her features might have been the work, in warm marble, of a great sculptor. Her hair was honey-blonde; her nostrils thin; her lips exquisitely molded.

Altogether, the picture she presented was entrancing.

The girl occupied a chair, to which she was strapped with several belts which the men apparently had contributed. She was sleeping from the effects of the anaesthetic gas.

Doc Savage freed her, then began a search of the house. In an adjacent room, which had been recently painted and varnished so that the floors were still covered with brown protective paper laid down by the painters, he found the telephone. It was concealed under a pile of the paper in a corner.

The receiver was off the hook. Doc lifted the instrument.

"Monk, Ham!" he called.

"We're still in the office," Monk's childlike tones replied.

"Things are going all right at this end," Doc assured him. "Has Renny, Long Tom, or Johnny called in?"

"Not a word."

Doc hung up.

BACK in the front room, Doc proceeded to search Captain Flancul and the other sleeping men. Their pockets yielded numerous small Calbian coins, but there were no identifying papers.

Doc noted that each man had close-cropped, bristling hair—the haircuts were all of the same style. Around the left wrist of each man there was a slight groove, a mark which might have been made by the band of a wrist watch, except that it was narrower. To Doc, this meant the presence of military identification wristlets, recently removed.

These men were soldiers.

With the belts which he had removed from the girl's ankles and wrists, and augmented by strips torn from the dungaree garments, Doc bound the men securely. He also wedged a gag between the jaws of each.

The next five minutes he spent in a further examination of the unconscious individuals and in a short scrutiny of the house.

The girl was the first to recover consciousness, due probably to the fact that she was farthest from the anaesthetic ball when it burst. Her eyes, which had been closed, now opened. They were dark and long-lashed, under thin, trained brows.

She did what few persons would have done—she remained perfectly quiet until she could speak coherently.

"You are Doc Savage?" she asked when she could control her voice.

Doc nodded. "And you?"

"Princess Gusta Le Galbin."

Included in Doc's fund of knowledge was an understanding of the European political layout. He knew the names of the members of each imperial household. He drew on his memory now.

"You are the daughter of King Dal Le Galbin, monarch of Calbia?" he queried.

The tall, exquisitely beautiful young woman nodded. *"Da,* that is right." She nodded at the door. "Let us step into another room, where we can talk without being overheard by this riff-raff."

Politely, Doc Savage offered the young woman his arm. She took it, swaying a little, and they moved out of the room.

As they did this Princess Gusta Le Galbin, breathing rapidly as if she were short of breath, put a hand to a pocket in her frock. Her fingers explored there a moment. She eyed Doc furtively, seeking to learn whether he had noticed this action. Apparently, he was unaware of her move.

When the young woman's hand dropped to her side, there was concealed in its palm a small hypodermic needle which had been hidden in her frock.

"Listen!" she breathed sharply. "Do you hear anything?"

Doc Savage half turned on a heel, apparently to learn what his ears could detect.

The young woman struck with the hypodermic needle. Its point penetrated the bronze man's forearm.

Almost at once the giant man of bronze grew unsteady on his feet, and sinking slowly, became limp upon the floor.

Princess Gusta Le Galbin eyed him.

"Buna!" she exclaimed. "Good! He was easily deceived."

She went back to Captain Flancul and his men and began untying them, first removing the gag from the mouth of the captain himself.

"You overpowered him?" Captain Flancul demanded anxiously in Calbian. His voice was weak, for he had just revived from the gas.

Princess Gusta nodded. "It was simple."

Captain Flancul shuddered. "Not so simple, princess. He overcame us before we even knew what had happened. Suppose we had been less cunning in our arrangements to receive him here?"

"In that case he might have evaded our trap."

"It was your planning, princess—first myself and my men to attempt to capture Doc Savage when he came; then you, our pretended prisoner, to use the hypodermic needle upon him if he did overcome us.

"Let us"—Captain Flancul made a grim face—"go into the other room and attend to this Doc Savage."

Chapter V
THE "OLD WOMAN"

DOC SAVAGE'S three men who were trailing the old crone had been watching for some time the house into which she had gone.

Johnny, the big-worded archaeologist and geologist, was a very tall and an almost incredibly bony man. Monk had once described Johnny as looking like the advance agent for a famine. Due to the bony nature of his frame, Johnny's clothing never fitted him well. Attached to a lapel by a dark ribbon, was a monocle—actually a powerful magnifying glass which Johnny needed in his business and carried as a monocle for convenience.

"We are indulging in unproductive inaction," insisted Johnny.

"Keep your hair on," Long Tom rumbled. "Renny is scoutin' the place. When he gets back we'll go in."

Major Thomas J. "Long Tom" Roberts easily seemed the physical weakling of Doc Savage's group of five aides. He was not tall, and only moderately well-knit. He had the complexion of one who had lived much of his life where the sunlight could not get to him.

Long Tom's appearance was slightly deceiving for, in a fight, he could probably whip ninety-nine out of the first hundred men he would meet walking down a city street.

Long Tom's work in the field of electricity had earned him something of a reputation, his name being mentioned in connection with such terms as "wizard of the juice" and "electricity shark."

"I wonder what motivates this enigmatic procedure of ours," pondered verbose Johnny.

"You mean—what is Doc's idea?" Long Tom shrugged in the gloom of the shrubbery where they were crouched. "Search me. Doc wants this old heifer, so we'll bring her in. *Ps-s-st!* Here comes Renny!"

A tower of gristle and bone reared out of the darkness. Renny—Colonel John Renwick—was well over six feet tall and weighed in excess of two hundred and fifty pounds. His face was extremely long, and wore the expression of one who had just attended a funeral. This was Renny's characteristic look when he was embroiled in trouble. He loved trouble.

The outstanding thing about Renny's appearance, however, was his hands. These, when squared into fists, made somewhat less than a gallon of a gristle and bone composite which rivaled granite in hardness. It was Renny's boast that he could knock the panel out of any wooden door with either fist.

He was also one of the greatest of modern engineers, although he seldom mentioned that fact.

"It's a roomin' house." Renny's usual tone was a great roaring, and he now experienced difficulty in whispering. "The old woman seems to have a room on the second floor rear. Come around to the back here and you can see into the window."

Using all stealth possible, they wormed through the shrubbery to the back of the house. Only one window was lighted.

"Watch it!" Renny breathed hoarsely.

A telephone stood on a table near the window. Even as they watched, the old woman hobbled to this.

"Hey!" grunted Long Tom, "I'm gonna listen in on that talk."

THE electrical wizard darted forward, wrenching to free a small metal case which was planted in an inside pocket. Once out and opened, this proved to hold an electrical device with dials and switches, and a small recess which contained a watch-case type receiver.

Johnny clamped the receiver to an ear, turned switches and adjusted dials. Then he walked along the rear wall of the house, holding his device close to the wooden clapboards.

"Chances are that the phone wires lead from a conduit strung down the alley underground," he whispered. "I'm tryin' to get my pickup device in the neighborhood of the lead-in."

He succeeded a moment later. Long Tom's device was one which simply utilized that troublesome inclination of old-time regenerative radio receivers to pick up the conversations on nearby telephone wires. Long Tom had designed the apparatus in the box specifically for this purpose.

By crowding their ears close to the watch-case receiver, all three could hear what was being said.

The old woman had evidently called a number and was waiting for an answer. They could hear the regular buzz of the automatic ringer. Then there was a click as a distant receiver lifted.

"*Da,*" said a harsh voice. "Yes."

"This is Muta," came the shrilly querulous tones of the crone. "I have called three times in an effort to get further orders, but our chief was not there."

Big-fisted Renny nodded soberly. "That explains the calls the old battle-ax made while we were trailing her."

"Keep still, or we'll miss some of this," grunted Long Tom.

"Is the chief there now?" demanded the hag, Muta.

"No," said the harsh voice. "He is away—on business of his own."

"What shall I do?" queried Muta.

"What is the matter, ugly one? Are you lonesome?"

"Cainele! Muta snapped. "Dog! Answer my question."

"You might join us and await the arrival of our chief."

"I will do that," Muta decided. "Watch for me. I will soon arrive."

Clicking denoted the severance of the telephonic hookup.

Long Tom and the other two exchanged whispered words in the darkness.

"What we heard proves that the old bag of bones is small fry," the electrical wizard pointed out. "She gets her orders from a big shot. What do you say we trail her—and grab the big guy?"

"Not a bad idea," muttered Renny.

Johnny agreed. "Supereminent."

Renny remained at the rear, to watch. Long Tom and Johnny took the front of the house. They waited near the entrance.

The front door opened and a man came out. He was a short fellow, extremely wrinkled—a dwarf. This individual reached the corner, where there was a streetlight.

"I'll be superamalgamated!" exploded Johnny. "That is the old woman!"

"She ain't a woman at all!" snorted Long Tom. "Muta is a man—a dwarf!"

THEY hastily summoned Renny from the rear, then ran for their cars. The two machines they were employing in their detective work were of a type calculated to attract the least notice. One was a taxicab, its outward appearance differing little from thousands of other cabs in the city. The other conveyance was a small delivery truck, bearing the name of a prominent milk concern.

Renny drove the taxi. Long Tom and Johnny dived into the delivery truck.

Starting the engines, they went ahead and managed to catch sight of their quarry shortly before the dwarf reached the next streetlight.

Muta's actions indicated he was hunting a taxicab. Accordingly, Renny rolled forward.

Swinging to the curb, Renny called hopefully, "Hack, sir?"

Muta veered over. He was so short that it was necessary for him to lift on tiptoe to peer into the cab.

Renny got a close look at the fellow's countenance, and was unfavorably impressed. True, he had never seen a more bland, peaceful-looking bundle of wrinkles. But this in itself was an incongruity which bordered on the hideous.

Removal of the gray wig, the shawl, and the ragged dress, which had been Muta's disguise, had worked a stark change. There was something fiendish about the fellow. A barrel of a torso hinted at no small strength.

Muta showed snaggled teeth in what was supposed to be a grin, but which Renny considered more of a snarl. He got into the hack, and gave an address.

Renny, endeavoring not to show his huge fists too prominently, put the machine in motion. The address he had received was near the waterfront.

Well to the rear, Long Tom and Johnny trailed along in the milk truck.

It was the custom of Doc Savage's men, when engaged in a mission which might be dangerous, to communicate their whereabouts to Doc's headquarters at frequent intervals, if convenient.

The milk conveyance was fitted with a portable radio receiver-transmitter. While Johnny drove, Long Tom switched this on. In a moment he was in communication with Monk and Ham in the skyscraper office.

"That old woman was really a man—a dwarf," Long Tom explained. "He's working for somebody. Name is Muta. We're trailing him, hoping to grab the boss."

The fact that Doc had directed Muta to be seized was not mentioned. They were using their own judgment, something which they did frequently. They knew this was the course that Doc would want them to follow.

The street sloped downward and the air became saturated with the faint, always-present smell of the waterfront—brine, fish and rotting wood. Buildings needed painting. Many of them were ramshackle.

The bay came into sight. A fleet of tugs, their whistles bleating, were conveying a departing liner toward the open sea. Somewhere a bell buoy ding-donged.

Above the bay, Manhattan skyline was an array of vertical splinters against the heavens—black, freckled with the white of windows. Overhead, clouds and moonlight made a jumble of sepia and silver.

Johnny and Long Tom observed Muta alight from Renny's hack. They swung around the next corner and stopped. A moment later Renny, having circled the block, joined them. They all hurried forward.

Muta approached a small wharf. Alongside this was moored a dark, seagoing speedboat, perhaps sixty feet in length.

A small warehouse stood at the shoreward end of the pier. Affixed to the side of this was a box which evidently held a telephone.

As Muta strode on to the wharf, the phone on the side of the warehouse rang noisily.

MUTA halted.

Aboard the seagoing speedboat several men appeared. It was too gloomy to make out the details of their appearance.

One of them called to Muta in the not unmusical language of Calbia—evidently directing Muta to answer the telephone, since the dwarf turned back.

Johnny and his two companions were close enough to hear what was said.

"Hello," said Muta. "Ah, it is you, chief! What orders do you wish?. . . You have what?. . . Doc Savage has been overpowered? *Ma, bucur!* Excellent!"

There was a pause, during which Muta listened—and Johnny and the others could not overhear what was said.

"Da, domnule!" Muta grunted at last. "Yes, sir, I understand. I am to remain here with the others, because you can handle Doc Savage without further assistance."

Muta hung up, wheeled and strode down the wharf toward the speedboat. He clambered aboard, and with the other men disappeared below deck.

"Holy cow!" Renny muttered in the shadow of the warehouse. "Doc is in a jam!"

"I don't believe it!" grunted pallid Long Tom. "Doc never has failed to take care of himself."

Johnny wrapped his monocle carefully in his handkerchief and stuffed it in his coat pocket, as if he feared there would soon be danger of its being shattered. "I advocate precipitous action," he said. "What say you we invest yonder craft by force?"

"You mean grab this dwarf Muta and see if he knows where Doc is?" demanded Renny, whose grammar gave no hint that he was as highly educated as the big-worded Johnny.

"Right! Make 'im tell what's behind all this, too!"

"Let's go!" grated Long Tom.

By way of preparing for action, each man plucked a unique weapon from a special armpit holster. Resembling oversized automatics, these guns were supermachine pistols designed by Doc Savage. A compact curled magazine was attached to each.

They were charged, not with ordinary lead missiles, but with mercy bullets—slugs which produce quick unconsciousness instead of fatal injury.

The three men advanced, crouching close to the planking to keep out of sight of the speedboat deck, which was lower than the wharf.

Long Tom, loitering in the rear, dipped his hands into his pockets several times and transferred small objects to the wharf planking. Then he went on with the others.

They crouched near the speedboat and prepared to leap down upon its deck.

"We'll give 'em a chance to surrender," Renny rumbled grimly.

"O. K.!" Long Tom snapped. "Let's—Hey! Look out!"

A manifold clatter and running drew their eyes toward the shoreward end of the wharf.

"Holy cow!" Renny thumped.

Several shadowy men were rushing them, guns in hand.

"They had lookouts posted on shore!" Johnny yelled, forgetting his large words for once.

Chapter VI
THE RIVER STYX

ONE of the charging group yelled, *"Opriti!* Stop! Get your hands up!"

Renny poured a rumble out of his cavernous chest and started to swerve his supermachine gun.

"Wait! Wait!" Long Tom barked. "Drop your gun! Hold your breath!"

Renny and Johnny, comprehending, obeyed. All three men charged their lungs with air, and held it there.

Yelling triumphantly, the rushing men came close. It was possible to see their round, dark faces and to ascertain that all looked like native Calbians. Their weapons were automatic pistols of the type supplied to the Calbian army.

Unexpectedly—to the victim, at least—the foremost Calbian caved down and flopped end-over-end like a rabbit shot on the run. In rapid succession the others followed him to the wharf boards. They spread themselves out, lay motionless, and began an even, deep breathing, which here and there became a snore.

Long Tom chuckled. "I spread some of Doc's glass balls of anaesthetic on the wharf. These monkeys ran over 'em and broke 'em."

"The boat!" Renny thundered.

With sprawling leaps, they gained the deck of the seagoing craft.

A man popped out of a hatch, an automatic in hand; his gun came up.

There came a roaring sound from Renny's huge fist, as if a Gargantuan bullfrog had opened up with a short, deep croak, and the ejector mechanism of the engineer's supermachine pistol spouted empty cartridges.

The gunman at the hatch melted down, rendered senseless by the mercy bullets before he could fire or cry out.

Howling, Renny plunged for the hatch. Johnny, a gangling animated skeleton, dived for the cabin companion.

Johnny found the cabin door locked. It resisted his slamming shoulder. Long Tom, trying another hatch, found it secured also.

"Only that one hatch open," the electrical wizard rasped. "We'll go in with Renny."

Renny dropped through the hatch; Long Tom and Johnny piled after him. They found a metal ladder,

Several shadowy men were rushing them, guns in hand.

Both Long Tom and Johnny were more than ordinarily agile. They proceeded to grasp Renny and climb him as though he were an oversized rope. Renny's belt snapped when Johnny seized it, but a moment later all three were on deck.

Up forward, hatches and companions had spewed armed men. Their guns began to bang and lip flame. Moreover, two more men were running down the wharf. These had evidently been among the lookout group on shore, and had remained behind to take care of an emergency.

which led into a deep hold compartment. This was dark, but a bulkhead door in the rear made a rectangular panel of light. They flung toward this.

The light panel blotted out suddenly as the door closed.

"Trap!" Renny thundered, and pitched backward.

He grasped the metal ladder. There was a click, and it dropped off the bulkhead.

"Trick ladder!" Renny howled, dodged the descending rungs.

"I'll be superamalgamated!" groaned Johnny. "What have we got into?"

RENNY crouched slightly, then leaped. He grasped the hatch edge and pulled himself up.

A swarthy man with an automatic was just stooping to peer into the hold. Renny's huge fist drifted out of the black recess and collided with the fellow's jaw. Head and fist did not differ greatly in size. The dark man skittered across the deck, and hung like a rag over the rail, senseless.

Renny chinned himself, got his elbows over the hatch edge, then rumbled to those below: "Grab my legs and climb up."

"Down!" Renny rapped, and flattened behind the hatch coping.

Somebody threw a hand grenade, but with bad aim, so that it hit the deck, bounced and landed in the water before it exploded. The wave it kicked up washed over the deck, drenching Renny and his two companions, and the boat rolled.

Long Tom's superfirer moaned, and two Calbians went down, reeling.

Renny raised his head, lowered it as a bullet snapped past.

"They're passin' up more grenades from below!" he boomed. "Blast 'em, they'll blow us to pieces! Lets take to the water!"

With a concerted leap and dive they cleared the sea speedster's rail. Long Tom squawked painfully as he collided with a pier piling. Then, stroking rapidly, they were in the forest of vertical timbers under the wharf.

"They'll have a swell time gettin' us out of here," Renny rumbled.

Their enemies cursed and yelled in Calbian. They threw grenades, but the explosions only tore the piling—one grenade even bouncing back and opening a sizable cavity in the boat deck.

Next, the Calbians tried turning on a searchlight. Johnny shot this out, and also drilled two men in the legs with mercy bullets.

Comparative silence fell over the wharf.

"It's up to them to think fast," Renny chuckled. "This shootin' and the grenades will attract the police."

The Calbians did think fast, and efficiently. A bustling sound came from the boat Then there was a loud hissing—and liquid sprayed through the wharf piling. A strong odor accompanied it.

"Gasoline!" Renny groaned. "They've connected a fire hose to their fuel tank. They got us! They'll burn us outa here and shoot us when we show up."

Muta's shrill, querulous voice came to them.

"You three—you have one chance!" he snarled. "Come out and surrender, and we will not put a match to the gasoline."

"Holy cow!" Renny mumbled. "We'd better take him up. We're lucky at that."

"Coming out!" Long Tom called.

THE three men paddled to the speedboat, first dropping their machine pistols into the water. With no gentleness at all, they were hauled aboard.

"Where are your weapons—the strange guns which shoot so rapidly?" Muta demanded.

"We dropped 'em in the bay," Renny growled.

"Take them below decks," Muta gritted to his men. "We must get underway quickly. The police may come."

Hedged in by gun muzzles, the three captives were conveyed below.

Powerful engines were started. The moorings were cast off, and the big seagoing racer backed out into the harbor, away from the growing wail of police sirens enroute to the scene of the fight. As Renny had surmised, the uproar had drawn the officers.

The harbor night swallowed the boat. For such a large and fast craft, its engines were unusually

silent. There was little but the moan of disturbed water, the slam of waves against the bows, as it streaked not toward the mouth of the harbor, but northward, up the Hudson River.

On deck there was much tramping about, clattering of mechanism, and low orders. Renny and his two companions overheard enough to tell them what was going on.

"They're putting a couple of boats overside," he muttered. "Wonder what they're gonna do?"

He found out shortly. Muta and others came below carrying chains, padlocks and wire. Using these, they fastened Renny and the other two men securely, padlocking the ends of the chains around hull braces.

Muta stood back, admiring the job. Absently, his hand drifted into a pocket and brought out a small red marble. He juggled this from one hand to another.

When Renny stared at the red marble, it was hurriedly pocketed.

Muta made an elaborate gesture of consulting his watch. "You gentlemen will have possibly five minutes in which to live, after we abandon this craft. Perhaps a little longer, but not much."

"You won't get away with it!" Long Tom snorted. "The police will grab the guys who were overcome by our gas on the wharf. They'll be made to talk."

"Nu!" Muta corrected. "No! We brought those

men along. We will take them off with us in the small boats."

Long Tom could think of no retort to that.

Muta teetered on his heels, a grotesque, misshapen gnome in the fitful light of the hold compartment.

"It is too bad that you will not be on deck to see what happens to you," he jeered. "It is my understanding that Doc Savage's assistants are men of considerable learning. You should be most interested in what will happen to you."

"Whatcha mean?" Long Tom demanded. "Say, what's back of all this?"

Muta bent forward, and in his ugly eyes the light of a zealot flamed. "Something big! The most far-flung plot of the century, my friend!"

"Yeah?"

"You will be killed by a weapon such as the world has never before seen!" Muta said shrilly. "It comes from nowhere. It cannot be avoided. Darkness, fog, smokescreens are no defense against it!"

Long Tom thought that over, and only one retort occurred to him. "Doc Savage will take care of you birds," he growled.

Muta sneered. "Savage has already been seized. Very soon, he will be killed."

With that, Muta and the others clambered out on deck. The speed of the engines decreased, but they did not stop. Then there came the noise of the collapsible boats being laid overside, and loaded.

Shortly after, the seagoing speedboat, abandoned except for the three prisoners below decks, was wallowing sluggishly in the Hudson River. Its headway had stopped completely.

The engines still ran. They had been declutched from the propeller drive shaft.

Chapter VII
THE FAT RESCUER

IN the house with the newly varnished and painted rooms, on New York's Upper West Side, Princess Gusta Le Galbin, of the reigning family of Calbia, stood and tapped an impatient toe on the floor.

Captain Flancul stood nearby, and from time to time favored the young woman with a glance which was nothing if not admiring. Once he indicated the prone and motionless form of Doc Savage.

"You did excellent work, my dear," he remarked.

"You will please abstain from the use of affectionate terms," Princess Gusta said shortly.

"A thousand pardons, your highness!" Captain Flancul bowed. "May I suggest that your highness depart, and leave me here alone to question this man Savage?"

They were conversing in Calbian.

"Nu," replied the young woman. "No. I will handle this myself."

"But—"

"Silence!" commanded Princess Gusta, exercising one of those imperious airs which is supposed to be the exclusive property of royalty. "You, Captain Flancul, are merely a wealthy industrialist of Calbia, who happens to be advisor to my father, the king. Please remember that, and do not be so free with your orders."

Captain Flancul clicked his heels, executed a stiff-backed courtesy, and said, "Yes, your highness. And if you will excuse me, I will see that my men are maintaining a proper lookout."

Then he walked out.

Princess Gusta fell to studying Doc Savage. Some men lose their personality when they are asleep, becoming somewhat flabby and dowdy looking. But not this bronze man. Motionless there on the floor, he was as striking a personage as he would have been if he were erect and moving about the room.

The extremely attractive princess of the Calbian royal family was impressed.

"Minunat!" she exclaimed, this being a very expressive Calbian word for "wonderful!"

Shortly, Captain Flancul returned to the room with word that his men were on guard.

For lack of anything else to do while they waited for Doc Savage to regain consciousness, Princess Gusta produced a case which had held her hypodermic needle, and recharged its magazine with a drug which brought unconsciousness.

Captain Flancul nudged Doc Savage's frame with his toe. "How much longer will it be before he awakens?"

"At least half an hour," the young woman assured him. "The effect of this drug should wear off by then."

Captain Flancul paced around the room several times. His stride was marked by the spectacular goose step which was part of the Calbian army training.

Suddenly, in the next room there was a yell, then blows, a scuffle. The door opened with the force of an explosion.

A man popped through, leveled a revolver and snapped dramatically: "The hands very high, please!"

HE was a man of bubbles. His stomach was a bubble, his chest another smaller bubble swelling out of it. And his head was still another bubble. His skin was olive, but at the same time ruddy, as if it had been rouged. He had a pleasant mouth and pleasantly wrinkled eyes, and there was a certain amiable jauntiness in his slightly flashy attire. He looked like a soft, cheerful man of some three hundred pounds.

There was nothing soft or cheerful about the two big spike-snouted automatics nor the rock firmness with which he held them.

"*In sus!*" he rapped. "Up!"

He had a strange, laughing voice.

Captain Flancul threw his arms above his head as if he had been menaced by something of incredible deadliness.

Princess Gusta was, at the moment of the newcomer's appearance, holding the hypodermic needle in her hand. She had had presence of mind enough to turn her hand, and the needle being small, had escaped notice. Now she palmed the needle and lifted her hands in such a fashion that its presence was not noticeable to the fat man.

"Wonderful!" beamed the fat man. He smirked in the direction of Captain Flancul. "Your men, my dear Captain Flancul, are not very efficient. I had merely to knock out the watchman in the rear, and I walked right in. A few blows laid out the dogs in the next room. You should have fighting men."

Angry-eyed, Princess Gusta faced the fat man.

"Conte Cozonac!" she snapped. "You will be shot for this outrage!"

"My dear princess, we are not in Calbia."

After saying that, plump Conte Cozonac began to laugh, his mirth pouring forth in bubbles and trills and hearty squeaks. It was strange laughter, as unusual as the man's mirthful voice.

Finally, when his glee had subsided, Conte Cozonac indicated, with a slight gesture of one gun, the prone form of Doc Savage.

"What have you done to my friend?"

"So he *is* working with you!" Princess Gusta clipped. "That is what we wanted to question him about."

"On the contrary, he is *not* working with me," Conte Cozonac assured her, chuckling. "However, I have hopes of enlisting his aid."

"Liar! He's already assisting you!"

"You do not believe me, your highness?"

"I would not believe you under any circumstances, Conte Cozonac," the girl assured him.

The fat man drew himself up with a dignity he purposely made elaborately absurd. "An insult! Or perhaps, coming from one of the parasites who rule Calbia, it is a compliment."

Princess Gusta nipped her lip. "The compliment we should have paid you years ago was a firing squad at dawn."

This sent the fat man off into a fresh gale of twittering, squeaking laughter. Strangely enough, he seemed to enjoy the insult—if reference to the firing squad did anything but amuse him, he failed to show it.

When his joyful giggling had subsided, he struck an attitude. "I," he said, "am the King Maker!"

"You," the girl retorted, "are the biggest rogue Calbia has ever seen!"

At this point Captain Flancul made a slight move. Apparently, he entertained ideas of drawing a gun.

Plump Conte Cozonac jutted forward both of his long-nosed automatics menacingly. "Be careful, my good advisor to the King of Calbia!"

The words had hardly left his lips when Princess Gusta whipped an arm downward and threw the hypodermic needle. It flew accurately, needle point forward, and struck Conte Cozonac in the neck, two inches below an ear.

The fat man cried out once, then fell to the floor, squirmed a little, and relaxed. The impact as the hypo needle struck had been sufficient to inject some of its contents.

CAPTAIN FLANCUL sprang for the fat man.

"No!" said Princess Gusta. "He is helpless, and will remain so for more than an hour."

Drawing himself up, Captain Flancul clicked his heels, saluted. "May I tell you, princess, that you are one of the most remarkable young women I have ever known?"

Princess Gusta Le Galbin seemed not to hear.

"There has been too much fighting and shouting in this house," she said quietly. "Some of the neighbors may call the police. The purpose for which we rented this house—the seizure of Doc Savage—has been accomplished. I suggest that we depart."

"What about the prisoners?"

"We will take them."

Captain Flancul hesitated. "There is another way, your highness—the way all traitors should go."

Princess Gusta nodded. "That is true."

"Then it is settled," Captain Flancul said, grim-faced. "I will leave two of my men here. They will use knives."

"No! It is not settled! They will not be executed!"

Captain Flancul became somewhat red. "But princess, these two men are—"

"No arguments, please!" the young woman said with imperial dignity. "We will simply hold them until affairs in Calbia are adjusted. I do not think the adjusting will take long, now that we have this Conte Cozonac."

Captain Flancul saluted again. "Very well."

He swung over, apparently with the intention of picking up Doc Savage and carrying him outside.

There was a blur of bronze. Captain Flancul tried to scream, but the sound ended abruptly as Doc's metallic fingers trapped his throat. The Calbian officer tried to strike blows, sought to wrench free, but in those great, corded bronze hands he experienced a feeling of helplessness such as he had never felt before.

Loosening one hand from the man's neck, Doc searched him quickly and disarmed the fellow. Then he flung him away.

Captain Flancul sprawled out helpless, partially paralyzed by the terrific pressure which had been exerted upon his neck.

Princess Gusta ran for her hypodermic needle.

Arising, moving with a speed which the young woman found hard to credit, Doc reached the needle ahead of her and scooped it up.

"Oh!" gasped Princess Gusta, and recoiled.

"You at least were not going to allow me to be killed," Doc said dryly.

The young woman seemed bewildered. "But the drug in that needle—you should still be unconscious," she gasped.

The bronze man's features had remained inscrutable throughout.

"If it will interest you, there was no drug in that needle when you used it upon me."

Surprise caused the girl to show white teeth. "You mean—you have not been unconscious at all?"

"Correct," Doc assured her. "The hypo needle in its case came to my attention while untying you. Emptying it was merely a precaution on my part."

"But why—"

"There are two ways of securing information," Doc continued. "One—by questioning; the other—by ruse. It seemed convenient to use the latter method."

The girl shrugged, somewhat fearfully. "And I thought I was clever!"

CAPTAIN FLANCUL had ceased his squirming as it dawned upon him that Doc Savage had tricked them. He sat up, but did not attempt to get to his feet.

Doc eyed the two guns which he had taken from Captain Flancul, then ejected the cartridges and struck the weapons together sharply. Sparks flew from impacting steel, and the gun mechanisms were shattered, rendered useless. He snapped the point off the hypo needle, then tossed all the weapons aside.

Princess Gusta had been eyeing Doc. The ease with which he had mutilated the pistols, the tremendous strength he had displayed, caused her to grow a little pale.

"What are you going to do with us?" she queried.

"Ask you questions," Doc told her. "And let us hope that you both make truthful replies."

"Is that a threat?"

"Merely some good advice."

Unexpectedly, Captain Flancul lifted to his feet. He walked toward Doc Savage. His eyes held a queer light.

Only for a fractional moment did Doc wonder what was behind the man's actions. Then he understood.

The bronze man whipped backward, twisting and ducking as he did so. The room quaked with the roar of a shot, and a bullet, blasting through the space Doc had vacated, chopped newly painted plaster off a wall.

One of the men in the other room, knocked out by fat Conte Cozonac, had regained consciousness and had come to the door, a gun in hand. Captain Flancul, glimpsing him, had sought to hold Doc's attention.

Doc's leap carried him to one of the guns which he had broken. In scooping it up and throwing it he seemed to use but a single gesture, and that so swift that there was no time for the gunman in the door to dodge. The gun smashed against his face, tipping him over backward.

Captain Flancul and Princess Gusta moved together, leaping headlong for the room where the gunman stood. Doc's lunge had carried him some distance from them, and even his tremendous speed could not head them off. They hurtled through the door, Captain Flancul going down and grabbing the gun of the man Doc had struck.

Flinging in pursuit of them, Doc perceived that he could not get to Captain Flancul in time. Veering over, he used the solidity of the door jamb to stop himself, drove out a hand, grasped a doorknob and wrenched the panel shut.

Captain Flancul's bullet tore a splintery hole high up in the panel.

Doc, springing back, scooped up fat Conte Cozonac, bounded to the stairs, and went upward. He carried Conte Cozonac's three hundred pounds under one arm, bending sidewise to balance the weight, and seeming not greatly hampered by the burden.

Behind him, several shots thundered. At least three guns were firing. Probably more of Captain Flancul's men had revived.

In the second-floor hall, Doc tried a door which led to a front room. It was locked, but splintered open under his tremendous shove.

In the street in front, a police whistle blared shrilly. The shooting had attracted a cop.

DOC, realizing those below would attempt to escape by the rear, backed out of the front room and broke down a door which led into a court chambers. Crossing to a window, he shoved the glass pane out with a quick pressure.

He twisted back, the ugly *whack* of an automatic

coming simultaneously with his move. Some of Captain Flancul's men were already in the court. They kept up steady fire.

Under cover of the barrage, Captain Flancul, Princess Gusta, and the others made their escape. Those not able to run were carried.

Doc Savage waited only long enough to ascertain that they were going to get away. Then, carrying huge Conte Cozonac, he mounted flights of stairs to the roof, unbarred the hatch and clambered out.

He retrieved his silk line with the grapple on the end and ran to the northern extremity of the block of buildings. The street there was dark. The cord was extremely strong, and Doc, still carrying Conte Cozonac, slipped down it to the sidewalk. An expert flip freed the grapple from its lodgment on the roof coping.

There was excitement in the street in front, people running. Two blocks away a car engine burst into life, and the machine roared away, until its sound was absorbed by the traffic mutter of the New York night.

Doc Savage carried Conte Cozonac to his roadster, dropped the fellow into the seat, got behind the wheel and drove toward his skyscraper office.

Chapter VIII
MYSTERY EXPLOSION

IN the skyscraper headquarters, Monk and Ham were quarreling. The fact that no observers were around detracted no whit from their enjoyment of the good-natured fracas.

"You baboon!" Ham yelled, gesturing with his sword cane. "You blunder of nature! This is the last straw!"

Monk was engaged in assembling his portable chemical laboratory. This device was something he always took when accompanying Doc Savage on an expedition. It occupied little space, yet it contained an unusually complete assortment of chemicals.

The homely chemist eyed Ham and sighed. "What's in your hair now?"

For answer, Ham lunged and struck a hearty blow with his sword cane. The object of his attentions was the pig, Habeas Corpus. But Habeas was intimately acquainted with Ham. He jumped, and was a yard away when the sheathed cane landed.

"Hey!" Monk howled. "Take your spite out on me if you gotta. But let that hog alone!"

"I'll assassinate both of you!" Ham promised. He pointed at the crimson pennant which Monk had painted on Habeas. "You put that on the freak just to devil me!"

It was hardly likely the ordinarily observant Ham had failed to previously discover the scarlet pennant. More likely, he had delayed to the present

moment to make a fuss about it.

"I didn't paint that flag there to pick a fuss with you," Monk disclaimed innocently. "The hog likes red flags."

"Harvard is a great university," Ham snapped. "Painting its colors on the side of that hog is an insult."

Monk grinned. "How was I to know crimson was a Harvard color?"

"You're gonna use some paint remover on that hog!" Ham promised ominously.

Monk, showing no great concern, moved to a case which held a teletype machine. This was connected with the police circuit and furnished Doc with a copy of all alarms broadcast.

Ordinarily, Monk did not pay much attention to the teletype, but just now he was somewhat worried because Renny, Long Tom and Johnny had failed to report for a time.

The pleasantly ugly chemist took one look at the copy roll and let out a yell. "Ham! Come here!"

Ham peered over Monk's shoulder, and read:

ATTENTION WATERFRONT PRECINCTS MYSTERIOUS SHOOTING ABOARD SEAGOING SPEEDBOAT ON BROOKLYN WATER FRONT. CRAFT FLED INTO HARBOR. LONG BOAT, NARROW BEAM, PAINTED BLACK. REPORT PRESENCE OF SUCH CRAFT.

TAXICAB, LICENSE S3, AND MILK DELIVERY TRUCK, LICENSE S4, FOUND ABANDONED NEAR SCENE.

"S3 and S4!" Monk exploded. "The S on them licenser means they're Doc Savage's cars! Them's the two machines Renny, Long Tom and Johnny were using!"

Ham reached for his hat. "We'd better look into this."

They rushed for the door. Habeas Corpus, squealing, scampered after them. In the corridor they encountered Doc Savage, carrying Conte Cozonac. The fat man was still senseless.

"DOC!" Monk yelled. "Renny and the others are in a jam!"

His small voice an excited squeak, Monk told about the message over the teletype.

Doc Savage said nothing, but he went to the library with his plump burden. Conte Cozonac was planted in a chair, his wrists positioned carefully on the arm rests. At Doc's touch, steel bands flashed up, encircling the wrists and locking there. Other bands, hidden in the legs of the chair, appeared and secured the portly man's ankles.

Nothing less than a steel-cutting torch would now free Conte Cozonac.

Doc locked all doors. They were of thick steel, though they did not look it.

"We want this fellow to be here when we get back," the bronze man explained. "He can tell us a great deal."

Monk and Ham in his wake, Doc entered the speed elevator and was dropped to the basement garage. All three piled into the roadster. The machine raced them toward the waterfront hangar which masqueraded as a warehouse.

"Got any idea what this is all about, Doc?" Monk demanded.

"You've heard of Calbia?" Doc suggested.

Monk nodded. "It's a Balkan kingdom, one of the few remaining monarchies where the king actually runs things. It has a population of ten or twelve million."

Doc nodded. "One point you forgot—Calbia is now in the throes of a revolution."

Monk blinked. "Huh? I didn't know that. There ain't been much about it in the papers."

"Censorship," Doc told him. "The Calbian government prevents news of political disturbances from getting abroad. Calbia's not the only one. The others do the same thing."

"Why?"

"Any hint that the government may be unstable affects foreign credit, the value of their bonds, and that sort of thing. Naturally, no one wants to buy the bonds of a government which may be out of business tomorrow."

"This Calbian revolution is something serious?"

"It is," Doc assured him. "Long ago, I arranged with certain men, closely in touch with the political situation in each European country, to keep me informed by cable of developments. That is where my information came from."

Monk gave one of Habeas Corpus' ears a thoughtful tug. The porker was riding on his knee. "You think this business is connected with the Calbian revolution?" he asked.

Instead of answering that, Doc countered with a question. "What would you say if Princess Gusta Le Galbin, only daughter of the ruling King of Calbia, and Captain Henri Flancul, wealthy Calbian and chief advisor to the king, were here in New York, and had made an attempt to capture me?"

"Did they?"

"They did."

Monk scratched his red-bristled nubbin of a head.

"We're mixed up in somethin' big, Doc," he declared.

THEY reached the hangar, drove the roadster inside, and entered the big speed plane. A moment later the craft was moaning across the river surface, and quickly lifted into the air.

In the soundproof cabin, conversation in ordinary tones was possible.

"Who was the fat guy we left in the office?" Monk queried.

"He is Conte Cozonac, commander-in-chief of the revolutionary forces seeking to overthrow the King of Calbia," Doc answered.

Monk and Ham were surprised, but they did not ask the bronze man how he knew all of these facts. Doc was a student of political affairs of all nations. It would have been no shock if Doc had told them the names of all of the obscure plotters seeking to overthrow the government of, for instance, Germany. He probably had that information. His fabulous knowledge seemed to touch on all things.

"Baron Damitru Mendl, who was murdered when the mysterious explosion demolished his yacht, was Calbian ambassador to the United States," Doc offered further. "Yes, brothers, this whole thing smacks of political intrigue for big stakes."

The bronze man now switched on the radio apparatus and tuned it to the wavelength of a police radio station. He asked for further information concerning the seagoing speedboat. He secured only one additional morsel worthy of attention.

"The speedster headed for the mouth of the bay and the open sea, according to persons who were attracted by the shooting," said the operator of the police radio station.

Doc promptly banked the big tri-motored plane around and headed it in the opposite direction.

"We're going the wrong way," Monk grunted.

"There's a chance that they doubled back and went up the Hudson," Doc pointed out. "Anyway, if they took to the sea, we would stand little chance of finding them until daylight."

The motors of the big ship were well muffled, their sound being only a powerful hiss. As the craft climbed to a thousand feet and raced northward, it was doubtful if pedestrians on the street or such sailors as happened to be on the decks of ships in the harbor heard it.

Shortly after taking off, Doc touched a lever and released a parachute flare. With Monk and Ham he used binoculars to sweep the river surface, but he discerned no sign of the boat they sought.

Three miles further on, they dropped another flare.

Monk's squeak, Ham's shout, and Doc's abrupt gesture were simultaneous. They had sighted the craft.

"It's standin' still in the middle of the river," Monk offered unnecessarily.

MANHATTAN ISLAND, the Bronx, Yonkers, made a bank of lights to the right. Hoboken and the Jersey shore north toward Englewood was a patchy glow on the left. The river, whitened by the flare, was a slightly rippled ribbon of steel-blue beneath.

Doc stood the plane on its nose and bored down for the boat.

"No sign of life aboard," Monk reported, and Ham nodded agreement. Both were using binoculars.

The plane landed close alongside the black, slender speedster, and long before it lost headway, Doc dived overside, and struck out with driving strokes. He could hear Diesel engines idling in the slim black craft.

Monk and Ham brought the plane to a quick stop—the propellers were fitted with a reversing device—then yanked a collapsible boat out of its locker.

Doc kept high in the water and was careful that his arms, in stroking, did not get before his eyes and obstruct his view. However, there was no movement, no sound from the black boat.

Doc reached the stern. There were no dangling ropes or chains, a circumstance which might have delayed a man of lesser strength and agility. To the corded bronze arms and hands, the rudder post offered a quick means of getting aboard.

Listening, Doc heard only the mutter of idling Diesels.

"Renny—Long Tom—Johnny?"

His call brought a faint rattling of chains from somewhere below. Doc darted forward, came to a hatch and descended. A flash appeared in his hands and spouted light. The flash was of a type which used no battery, current being supplied by a generator operating from a spring motor which was wound by twisting the rear portion of the barrel, the whole being waterproof.

Outside, the flare that had been dropped from the plane settled into the river, fizzed, sent up a cloud of steam and went out.

Doc found his three men, gagged, and secured by chains. Planting the flash on the hull floor, Doc wrenched out the gags, then went to work on the padlocks with a slender metal probe which came from his pocket.

"Holy cow!" rumbled Renny. "Step on it!"

"What's up, Renny?"

"They told us we'd croak in ten minutes after they left!"

"The interval has been substantially longer than ten minutes," put in big-worded Johnny.

"They wasn't kiddin'," Renny thumped.

"That dwarf, Muta, spouted a lot of stuff about a mysterious weapon that was a world-beater," Long Tom added.

Doc did not speak, but worked steadily upon the padlocks. He got one open, a second, then another—and Renny was free.

The big-fisted engineer swung his arms to limber them. "We got a chance to see this infernal weapon work," he said.

"I hope we don't see it at too close range," Long Tom mumbled.

"Say, strange they left the motors running. Reckon that's got somethin' to do with their murder plan?"

Doc did not comment, but continued his frenzied work upon the padlock. "Get off, Renny. Dive overboard and swim."

Renny seemed not to hear. He grasped the chains securing Johnny, wrenched at them, and succeeded in snapping one. There was amazing strength in the engineer's huge fists, strength probably exceeded only by Doc's remarkable development.

Doc got Long Tom loose, then Johnny. They ran to the hatch, vaulted out, and plunged overboard.

"I tell you Muta wasn't foolin', Doc," Long Tom declared, and raised a great splashing with his overhand stroke.

They were some fifty yards from the black speedboat when Doc abruptly stopped swimming and breathed, "Listen!"

The others, listening, could hear nothing.

"What is it, Doc?" Renny queried.

"A strange whistle, so shrill that it is probably inaudible to your ears."

"What is the thing?" demanded Renny.

RENNY'S question was answered in cataclysmic fashion.

The sky and the river seemed to turn suddenly to white-hot flame. It blinded them. Then the air slammed against their eardrums and the water smashed their bodies with excruciating force.

Where the black boat had been, wreckage spouted into the air. River water split apart, and a wave of foam, debris and water rushed upon the men and engulfed them.

Doc, stroking heavily, regained the surface, and soon the other three men appeared. They stared at the spot where the dark craft had been.

Nothing remained but bubbles, demolished timbers, and boiling river water.

"That's the same way Baron Damitru Mendl's yacht went, I'm bettin'!" Long Tom gulped.

"Holy cow!" Renny thumped. "What was it? I mean—it was an explosion of some kind, but where did the explosive come from? And how was it set off?"

"Possibly a time bomb," Johnny suggested.

Somewhere in the darkness the pig, Habeas Corpus, was squealing and Monk and Ham were shouting at each other.

"You danged near upset this tub!" Ham accused Monk.

"Listen, if I hadn't balanced it, it would have upset!" Monk shrilled back at him.

The pair were not far distant, judging by their voices, and apparently had put off from the seaplane in the collapsible boat. They paddled up when Doc called to them, giving his whereabouts.

"What in blazes happened?" Monk demanded, helping them aboard.

"A bomb on the boat," insisted Johnny.

He was badly mistaken—as he found out a moment later.

"Listen!" Doc said sharply. "There's that shrill hiss again, that whistle!"

This time also the others were unable to hear it. Doc's long use of the exercise device, which made sound waves above and below the audible frequency, had given him hearing more efficient than their own.

"Hang on," Doc ordered. "The thing may get us this time, or it may not—"

The white-hot flash, the ear-splitting roar, the mountainous rush of water repeated itself. The collapsible boat capsized, throwing them all into the river. Spray spattered about them.

Doc had retained a clutch on his flashlight. Regaining the surface, he played its beam about.

Monk came up beside him, stared, then exploded. "Our plane!"

The tri-motored speed ship had been demolished. Only an aileron was visible, and this bobbed about and soon sank, after which bubbles ceased to rise. The river became calm.

"No plane in the darkness could drop a missile, or rather two missiles, with such accuracy," Doc stated.

Renny paddled about with his big hands until he found the gaunt Johnny in the water.

"I ask you, gentleman of big words," he inquired, "do you still think it was a bomb?"

"I'll be superamalgamated," was the best Johnny could answer.

Chapter IX
THE MAKER OF KINGS TALKS

AN hour later, Doc Savage and his five men entered the huge building which housed their headquarters.

"It might have been a bomb," Johnny was insisting stubbornly. "Maybe a plane dropped it, a plane equipped with some new type of sight."

"There was no sound of a plane," Doc reminded him. "Just that strange, faint whistle."

"Yeah," Renny thumped gruffly. "I've been in a few wars in my time, and anything that can find and destroy a target as small as our plane or that boat on a night as dark as this—whatever the thing is, it's quite a weapon."

They entered the library with its impressive array of bookcases holding volumes of massive scientific works. Through an open door was visible the enamel, the glass, and the shiny metal glitter of the laboratory.

Conte Cozonac, a more or less shapeless mound of fat, occupied the chair into which he had been fastened. He eyed Doc Savage and the other five, alert-eyed. He had revived.

Strangely enough, one watching the portly revolutionist would have secured the impression that he considered his predicament highly humorous. There was a sort of bubbling humor in his eyes, and when he shifted, his paunch jiggled as if he were laughing. But whether the jiggling was from suppressed merriment or not, it was hard to say.

"I tried yelling," he said blithely. "The walls seem to be soundproof."

Doc Savage advanced and touched buttons inaccessible to the occupant of the chair, which released the steel wrist and leg bands which imprisoned Conte Cozonac.

The fat man did not arise.

"If you do not mind," Cozonac asked. "What happened back at that house?"

Doc told him.

"So the girl did not lay you out with her needle, after all!" Conte Cozonac ejaculated. For a moment, his laughter squeaked and twittered. "Then, Mr. Savage, my attempt to rescue you was so much superfluous effort."

Doc's flake-gold eyes fixed themselves upon the fat man. "You entered the place to rescue me?" he asked.

"Assuredly!"

"And why the great interest in me?"

"I will tell you." Conte Cozonac shed his mirth and became surprisingly dignified. "Prepare yourself for a shock."

"I fail to comprehend."

Conte Cozonac bowed stiffly.

"You, Doc Savage, *are the future King of Calbia.*"

DOC'S five men reacted in various fashions to this statement. Monk grinned unbelievingly and continued his diversion of scratching Habeas Corpus behind the ears. Ham twirled his sword cane slowly. Long Tom and Johnny exchanged glances.

"Holy cow!" Renny grunted.

"Quite a few offers come my way," Doc Savage said slowly. "Usually they are in the nature of bullets, knives, or other forms of sudden death. This is the first throne proposition."

"The offer is made in entire seriousness," Conte Cozonac announced.

"Suppose we go into details."

The fat man nodded briskly. "I presume you are sufficiently posted on the Calbian political situation to know that a revolution is now in progress—and I, Conte Cozonac, am the leader of the rebel forces."

"I knew that," Doc stated quietly.

"And with how much more are you familiar?"

"Very little."

The bulky man eyed Doc. "How does the idea of being a king strike you?"

"Preposterous, in the first place. Furthermore, kings are out of style. A republican government is much more desirable."

Conte Cozonac shook his head slowly.

"I hardly thought it would be necessary to sell you the idea of a throne. Listen—let me tell you of some of the atrocities committed by the present regime in Calbia. Did you know that within the past year the King of Calbia has ordered many men shot by firing squads? Furthermore, there are thousands of political prisoners in Calbian jails."

"Political difficulties in the Balkans are usually bloody affairs," Doc replied.

"Especially when a tyrant like King Dal Le Galbin is on the throne," Conte Cozonac pointed out. "The king is supported and advised by a ring of arch rogues. That fellow, Captain Flancul, is one of the worst."

"Princess Gusta applied that same designation to you," Doc pointed out dryly.

Conte Cozonac indulged in birdlike laughter for a moment. "If I had not been very careful indeed, they would have planted me in front of a firing squad long ago. You see, I am the gentleman who is going to chase those grafters out of Calbia."

"Yes?"

"Exactly. I am the King Maker," Conte Cozonac boasted.

"While we are on the king-making subject, it might be well to point out that kings are usually natives of the country over which they wield a scepter," Doc said.

"Which leads up to the fact that you are no Calbian, eh?"

"Exactly!"

"I can make a king," Conte Cozonac chuckled, "and he does not have to be a native of the country, either."

DOC SAVAGE was silent for a time, as if considering this. Monk and Ham, their perpetual quarrel for the moment a minor matter, watched Conte Cozonac intently. Extreme quiet held the room, and the ticking of at least three watches was audible, all jumbled together.

"The Calbian people will be glad to accept you as their sovereign," Conte Cozonac told Doc earnestly. "Your reputation has penetrated even to Calbia. My mere word is sufficient to assure many thousands that you are the man for the throne. And the work which you will do in Calbia, thrashing King Dal Le Galbin and his corrupt satellites will, I am sure, mold public opinion in your favor."

"We don't just go to Calbia and take over the throne, eh?" Doc asked.

Conte Cozonac made a grim mouth, the rest of his face retaining its mirthful expression. "Frankly, Domnule Savage, you will have to win the revolution first."

"So that's the catch!"

"I came from Calbia to do two things. The first was to enlist your aid." Conte Cozonac hesitated, then continued: "My other purpose was to have Baron Damitru Mendl draw up a new set of plans and make a working model of the devilish weapon which he invented."

Doc leaned forward slightly.

"Baron Damitru Mendl invented the device, which causes the mysterious explosions?" he asked quickly.

"Correct!" Conte Cozonac put the tips of fat fingers together over his chest. "The weapon is a terrible one. Blueprints of it have been in the Calbian war department flies, Baron Damitru Mendl having surrendered them before the government became so corrupt. He understood that his device was to be used only in the event of war."

"Who is using the infernal contraption now?"

"King Dal Le Galbin and his clique. Their spies must have learned that I was coming to America to see Baron Damitru Mendl, who was in sympathy with my revolutionary efforts. So they murdered Baron Mendl. But I was fortunate enough to get on their trail and follow them to that house."

The fat man paused to give emphasis to his next words.

"They tried to murder you, Doc Savage, and there is not the slightest doubt but that they will endeavor to do so again."

"Do you have any conception of the nature of this mystery weapon?" Doc queried.

"None."

The fat man separated his fingertips, straightened slightly in his chair, and his plump face became grim, questioning, anxious.

"What is your decision, Mr. Savage? Will you help us, and accept the throne of Calbia after things are straightened out?"

Doc said nothing.

Conte Cozonac moistened his lips. "Later, of course, you can abdicate the throne in favor of some worthy person. That is entirely up to you."

"This will take some thinking over," Doc Savage told him.

Chapter X
THE "SEAWARD" TROUBLE

THE time was one week later.

The passenger ship *Seaward* of the Calbian-

American Line, was in the Mediterranean. The *Seaward's* trip from New York had been uneventful, except that the craft was in a fair way of breaking its own record for the trans-Atlantic run. This did not mean that the *Seaward* was in a class with the fastest American, Italian, and other ocean greyhounds. She was slower, though not exactly a sluggish boat.

The sun overhead was hot, the decks almost blistering to the feet of such passengers as were using the deck swimming pool. The salt water in the pool, pumped fresh from the sea, was cool enough to offer relief.

Monk, his ungainly form sprawled in a chair in the sitting room of a suite, mopped perspiration and squinted at big bronze Doc Savage.

"Doc, for a future king, you're sure leading a secluded existence," he grumbled. "We haven't been out of this suite all the way across the Atlantic."

"No need of inviting trouble," Doc reminded him. "In tentatively accepting this king proposition, we took hold of something big. This is a Calbian ship. We may have enemies aboard."

Monk, fanning himself, got up and moved over to where Habeas Corpus dozed. He tried to aggravate the shoat with a tickling finger. Habeas opened one eye, then resumed his sleep, ignoring Monk.

The chemist ambled to the porthole and glanced out, then pointed. "There's Conte Cozonac."

The individual whom Monk indicated looked like a large, much too-well-fed Chinaman. A pigtail dangled down the fellow's back. His blouse resembled a robe, and reached to his ankles, and his feet were shod in embroidered slippers. He shuffled along with hands tucked inside his sleeves. The disguise was remarkable. A close acquaintance would scarcely have recognized Conte Cozonac.

"Doc did a good job, disguisin' him," Monk declared.

Renny, Ham, and Johnny got up and crowded around the porthole. They had been shut in long enough that any type of diversion, even observing disguised Conte Cozonac, was welcome.

Long Tom, the electric wizard, was not present. This was unusual, for Long Tom had never before deliberately passed up a chance to accompany Doc Savage.

"Think I'll stay behind in New York and work on my insect eliminating device," Long Tom had declared, some hours before sailing time.

Long Tom's interest in this device, an apparatus which would be of inestimable value to farmers, although profound, had not before exceeded his love of adventure.

Among Monk and the others, there had been considerable discussion of Long Tom's changed attitude. Doc Savage had not joined in these discussions.

DOC now joined the group watching Conte Cozonac through the porthole.

Conte Cozonac was sauntering aimlessly along the rail, seeming to watch the waves. Sternward an orchestra was playing, and the fat man began to sway his hands in accompaniment; his lips moved. A casual observer would have thought he was keeping time and repeating the words of the song to himself.

Doc Savage watched Conte Cozonac's lips intently. Among the bronze man's accomplishments was that of lip-reading.

Conte Cozonac was singing the words of no song. He was speaking sentences soundlessly.

"I have done considerable roaming around the boat," he said. "I have seen none of our enemies. Probably there will be no trouble if you show yourself on deck. Incidentally, we land at the Calbian seaport tonight. The city of San Blazna is seventy miles inland from the port, over the mountains. There is a railroad to the capital."

Doc Savage moved a hand in front of the porthole to indicate that he understood. This act was the first intimation the others had that Conte Cozonac's lip movements had conveyed a secret message.

"I'll be superamalgamated!" Johnny gasped. "What was the subject matter of the clandestine dissertation?"

"Nothing of importance," Doc replied. "He had been able to find no enemies aboard—and we land tonight."

Johnny polished his monocle thoughtfully with a bony thumb. "This hermitageous sequestration is abominable," he said.

"Well, you can get out and walk around," Doc told him. "Of course, there's the chance that somebody may take a shot at you."

The gaunt Johnny thought this over, and evidently concluded to take the chance.

"I will promenade," he decided.

"Better let me disguise you," Doc advised.

The bronze man selected a makeup box from his luggage and proceeded to ornament Johnny with a cropped white mustache, a clipped Vandyke, and a pair of spectacles with plain glass lenses.

Ingenious shoulder and torso pads gave the geologist the appearance of a much plumper man.

Johnny tried to borrow Ham's sword cane, insisting that a stick was a necessary accoutrement for the type of individual he was playing.

Ham refused the loan. The dapper lawyer rarely let his valued sword cane out of his hands.

Leaving the suite, Johnny strolled along the deck. The *Seaward* was a liner large enough that the appearance of a new face did not attract attention. Enjoying the breeze, such as it was, and drawn by the hilarious shouting of bathers at the pool on the rear deck, Johnny moved sternward.

He was approximately even with the after funnel when he snapped to a stop, and his protruding eyes threatened to push the spectacles off his nose.

Scuttling along the deck ahead of him was the dwarf—Muta.

TWO things moved Johnny in his next act. He loved excitement. Furthermore, he had been cooped up in a suite of cabins so long that it did not take much to touch him off. Without thought of consequences, he darted forward to seize the bland-faced midget.

Muta did not hear Johnny coming. The under-sized rogue had his attention fixed on something ahead—an individual who was strolling down the deck—a bulky gentleman in Chinese garments.

Muta contemplated some violence toward Conte Cozonac, for the one in celestial garb was he. Or thus Johnny reasoned.

Johnny descended upon Muta, wrapping the squat fellow in his long arms.

Muta squawked in surprise, then reached up and managed to grab Johnny's hair with both hands, and yanked.

The gaunt geologist discouraged the hair pulling by casually inserting a thumb in Muta's left eye. The dwarf bit like a dog, and his teeth snapped barely an inch short of Johnny's throat. Johnny retaliated by grasping an ear and endeavoring to twist it off. Judging from Muta's squawk, he nearly succeeded.

The dwarf kicked Johnny's shins with such violence that the bony geologist's feet went from under him, and he clattered down on the deck with a sound like falling stovewood.

The fight was not uneven, although Johnny was fully twice as tall as his antagonist. The pair were probably not far apart in weight.

The two rolled on the deck. They kicked, gouged and bit, making the fray a steady parade of free-for-all brawling tactics. Muta seemed to know an endless string of foul tricks.

Johnny, scarcely resembling the tall gentleman who had once headed the natural science research department of a famous United States university, returned each vicious act of his foe, usually with a little interest.

Conte Cozonac whirled when the brawl started. He gaped, pop-eyed, and his hands untucked themselves from his sleeves to dangle limply at his sides.

"Don't mix in this mess!" Johnny yelled, using what, for him, were very small words. "I'll take care of this sawed-off squirt!"

The geologist's yell was intended to advise Conte Cozonac not to take a hand in the affair. It accomplished its purpose. Conte Cozonac merely stood and stared, as any fat, easy-going Celestial might be expected to do.

Johnny seized his chance, and landed a punch. The dwarf dropped. Another blow subdued him.

A small red marble came out of Muta's pocket and rolled on the deck.

Johnny mopped perspiration. He eyed the red marble curiously, wondering what its significance could be.

The captain of the *Seaward* and two other ship's officers came running from the direction of the bridge. They shouted questions in Calbian.

"This runt!" Johnny indicated Muta. "He tried to kill me in New York!"

The captain picked up the red marble. "Who does this belong to?" he asked.

Muta pointed at Johnny. "It is his!"

"Liar!" Johnny growled. "What is that marble, anyway?"

There was a commotion in a nearby doorway. Johnny turned his head.

Johnny had not previously seen Princess Gusta Le Galbin or Captain Flancul, but Doc Savage had described the two. The geologist recognized the pair now.

Princess Gusta and Captain Flancul had stepped through the door. Princess Gusta gasped, and leveled an arm at Johnny.

"Arrest that man!" she snapped. "He is an enemy of Calbia!"

Chapter XI
CASTAWAYS

THE captain of the *Seaward* and his officers gaped, astounded.

"Cum!" gulped the skipper. "What?"

"This is one of Doc Savage's men!" said the girl.

Johnny jutted an angry jaw. "I'm an American citizen!" he cried.

"Seize him, captain!" Princess Gusta directed.

Johnny rapped, "Nix! Nix!"

The officer advanced.

"You pinch me, and it'll be just too bad!" Johnny threatened. "I'm an American, I tell you!"

"Small difference that makes!" the *Seaward* commander growled. "This is a Calbian vessel, and I am a loyal subject of King Dal Le Galbin. You are in custody."

Conte Cozonac, hands thrust into the sleeves of his oriental gown, hovered on the crowd outskirts. There was a suspicious bulge in the sleeves, as if his hands held guns.

"I'll take care of myself," Johnny shouted—for the benefit of Conte Cozonac.

It was better for Conte Cozonac to avoid betraying himself, if possible.

Johnny started retreating. Seeing him, Muta seized his chance and scuttled away.

"Grab that bird!" Johnny yelled.

But no one paid him any attention.

Captain Flancul snapped an automatic from his clothing.

"*Cainele!*" he snarled. "Dog! We will waste little time on him." He aimed deliberately at Johnny.

"*Nu!*" shrilled the Princess Gusta, and grasped his arm. "No! It might cause international complications."

Johnny took advantage of this squabble to lunge suddenly and seize Captain Flancul's gun. They wrestled for a moment.

Princess Gusta swung a small, hard fist at Johnny's head, missed him when he ducked, and knocked the breath out of Captain Flancul.

This action allowed Johnny to get the automatic. With it he menaced the *Seaward* officers. "Get back! Elevate your hands!"

They hesitated, glaring wrathfully, then obeyed.

Retreating to the first doorway, Johnny dived through. He found himself in the foyer which gave entrance into the main lounge. He crossed the lounge in a series of ungainly leaps, raced down a passage, descended and dived into Doc's suite.

"I have managed to complicate the situation, Doc," he imparted. "In fact, I've played hell!"

IN a tumbling procession of many-syllabled words, Johnny told of what had occurred, finished with, "Conceivably, I acted hastily."

"Grabbing Muta was a natural move," Doc assured him.

Renny banged his huge fists together, making a flinty sound. "They're sure to try to pinch us, Doc. And if they do, we're sunk."

"D'you think they'll use a firing squad on us?" Monk demanded.

Doc answered that. "Probably not, after we exert some influence, but their interference will cramp our style."

It became apparent that excitement was sweeping the liner. There was shouting, and much scampering about. Doc, watching the deck through the porthole, noted the appearance of numerous men with rifles, some of these being *Seaward* sailors, but a far greater number male members of the passenger list.

"Say; how come the passengers are joinin' in this?" Monk pondered, over Doc's shoulder.

"They must be Calbians, formerly residents of the United States, going back home to help their country out of the present crisis," Doc replied.

"A fine lot of bums!" Monk snorted. "You'd think if they was livin' in the United States, they'd stay there instead of rushin' home to fight."

"If you were in Calbia," Ham put in sarcastically, "and a war broke out in the United States, what would you do?"

"Take the first boat home to get into the scrap, probably," Monk admitted grudgingly.

Doc watched preparations for a time.

"They're going to rush us," he decided.

"Imagine that tigress, Princess Gusta, and Captain Flancul being on this liner," Johnny groaned.

Monk nodded. "Yeah, it's—"

"Ultra unpropitious," Johnny supplied.

Doc deserted the porthole, whipped to their luggage heap, and began sorting the stuff over. The containers for his equipment were metal boxes, light, strong and waterproof, each bearing an identifying numeral.

He sorted out a number of these and clamped several in his arms.

"Get the rest," he directed his four men.

Then he opened the corridor door. Shots roared out, and lead planted itself noisily in the woodwork.

Lowering the cases, Doc opened one, extracted grenades holding his anaesthetic gas and flung two into the corridor, one in either direction. They detonated with mushy *plungs!*

The men held their breath for a minute, then went out, carrying the boxes of equipment. Those who had fired upon them—sailors and passengers of Calbian extraction—slumbered in the passage.

The five men worked downward.

"The engine room is our objective," Doc announced.

Monk, Habeas Corpus perched on a box carried under one arm, grinned widely. "Long Tom would enjoy this," he said. "Too bad he stayed behind in New York to fiddle with his coils and vacuum tubes."

They reached the engine room, and a single-anaesthetic grenade was ample to render engineers and firemen unconscious.

THE *Seaward* was an oil burner. Hurrying forward, Doc Savage adjusted the fuel valves and set several levers, so that there would be no danger of unattended boilers exploding. Then he shifted levers which caused the propellers to cease turning.

He took up a position at the speaking tubes which communicated with the bridge, and whistled in them until he attracted attention.

Strangely enough, it was Captain Henri Flancul who answered from the bridge.

"You have exactly one minute in which to leave the engine room," snarled Captain Flancul.

"We cannot afford to be carried to Calbia—" Doc began.

"You will be. *Da!* And for this outrage, you shall

Concealed entirely by the smoke ... Doc and his men entered the launch.

most certainly go before a firing squad. You have committed piracy."

Doc did not comment on the dire prediction. "Put the commander of the *Seaward* on the speaking tube," he demanded.

"You have one minute—"

"The commander of the *Seaward* on the tube!" Doc repeated.

There was such a crackle and snap of authority in the bronze man's tone that Captain Flancul was shocked into complying with the demand. No doubt the hollowness of Doc's voice as it came through the speaking tube helped.

"Well?" said the *Seaward* captain shortly afterward.

"We are willing to make terms with you," Doc told him.

"What terms?"

"Lower your largest launch, put plenty of fuel in the tanks, then drop a landing stage and lower the boat alongside, the engine running. We will then leave your liner undamaged."

"Nu!" came the snapped reply. "No!"

"I am making no threat," Doc replied with brittle terseness. "But let me point out that we have control of the engine room, and in our possession are weapons other than that gas. Think it over."

There ensued a wait of two or three minutes, during which Doc, an ear to the speaking tube, could hear voices in consultation. Captain Henri Flancul seemed to be doing some vehement objecting, but the master of the *Seaward* eventually shouted him down.

"You will leave my liner unharmed?" the commander queried.

"Yes."

"We accept your terms. The launch will be at the stage in a few minutes, engine running."

Doc moved away from the tube and gathered up his equipment boxes.

"But Doc," Monk protested. "When we get into the launch we'll be swell targets for those bums with rifles. I know something of these political fanatics. The captain of the *Seaward* may mean well, but I'll bet Habeas Corpus here against Ham's necktie, which is my idea of something no man should own, that some of those fellows will shoot at us."

Judging by his lack of response, Doc might not have heard Monk. He led them out of the engine room and down a passage which smelled of grease. They were not molested. Ascending a companion they turned left, and, after waiting a time, advanced and found a hatch in the hull had been opened and a landing stage set in place.

The launch, engine muttering, was snubbed to the stage.

Monk began again, "But, Doc, them rifles—"

The bronze man opened one of his cases. It held spheres of metal fully as large as Monk's nubbin-like head. Doc flipped levers on three of these and tossed them out into the sea. They spouted a pall of black smoke.

"FOR the love of Mike!" Monk chuckled. "That'll take care of the rifles."

The smoke bombs continued to pour vapor. The dark cloud grew and grew until it enveloped most of the *Seaward*. There was a breeze, which pulled the smoke away in a long, black serpent which rolled its sepia belly against the surface of the Mediterranean.

Concealed entirely by the smoke, and making no noise, Doc and his men entered the launch. At the loudening roar of the engine as they pulled away, numerous rifles did discharge from the *Seaward*. Only two bullets hit the launch, however, and these sank themselves forward on the decked-over bows.

ON the deck of the *Seaward* the commander swore and dashed about, searching for those who had used the rifles. The skipper was a man who believed in keeping his word.

Captain Henri Flancul muttered under his breath. "Clever devils! I never thought they would use a smoke screen."

Princess Gusta, at his side, gasping in the smoke, exclaimed, "You put those men up to using the rifles?"

"No!" Captain Flancul disclaimed. "But I knew what they would do."

"Sometimes," the young woman said thoughtfully, "you seem very bloodthirsty, Captain Flancul."

"I have the welfare of the ruling house of Calbia deeply at heart," Captain Flancul told her solemnly.

"And you are a wealthy man who stands to lose much if the revolution is successful," Princess Gusta retorted.

After a time, the breeze blew the smoke away from the *Seaward*. But before the last of it was wafted off an unexpected thing occurred.

The sound of the launch engine was still audible, although the craft was lost in the smoke.

Whu-r-o-om! A terrific explosion occurred, from the spot where came the sound of the launch engine. The white flash of the blast was brilliant enough to penetrate even the smoke screen. The shock caused the big *Seaward* to list a trifle, and water carafes danced on the dining saloon tables.

After that, the launch engine was heard no more.

The wind carried the smoke away. The black pall did not disperse, but rolled along like dark cotton upon the water.

The *Seaward's* engines were put in operation and the liner cruised over toward where the explosion had occurred. Lifeboats were lowered. The crews found a few splintered timbers, scarcely a one larger than a man's hand—and that was all.

"Some mysterious explosion killed Doc Savage and his men," was the verdict rendered when the lifeboats had returned.

PRINCESS GUSTA LE GALBIN, remarkably enough, became quite pale when she heard the news which confirmed the destruction of the launch. She excused herself and went hastily to her cabin. Then she locked the door, and flung herself upon the ornate bed.

After a while she began to sob uncontrollably.

The *Seaward* resumed its course. Behind the liner, and off to one side, the smoke screen still hovered, a wide-flung fog of black. Somehow that black mass was strangely like a shroud covering a coffin.

Chapter XII
THE PLANE

THE *Seaward* sailed for three hours before she got out of sight of the smoke pall. On the bridge of the liner an earnest conference was held, during which the bits of the wrecked launch were displayed. The subject under discussion was what medium could have destroyed the small craft.

There was, the skipper of the *Seaward* declared, no bomb concealed aboard the small boat. The explosion had been one of almost incalculable violence; but beyond that they could determine little.

Shortly after the *Seaward* was lost to view, a plane appeared in the sunny Mediterranean sky. The craft spiraled slowly at an altitude of nearly twenty thousand feet, and it was to be suspected that this height was maintained for the purpose of escaping detection. It would take a sharp eye, looking up from the sea, to discern it.

The plane was a large one, tri-motored, fast, and obviously new. It was of English manufacture, a very modern type.

Upending its tail abruptly, the plane screamed downward in a long dive. When it pulled level, the sea was only a few hundred feet below, and the mass of black smoke a slight distance to one side.

The ship was an amphibian. As it banked to come down on the sea, an observer interested in aeronautics would have noted that the motor exhaust stacks bore a silencer of unique design—a type not in use in Europe, although the plane itself was manifestly a British product.

The plane taxied close to the smoke pall. The pilot shoved an arm out of the cockpit window, gripping a revolver. He throttled his engine, then fired three slow shots. He counted carefully to twenty-five, then discharged three more bullets. The lead went into the sea beside the hull float. He was signaling.

A collapsible boat, driven by an outboard motor of extreme smallness, scooted out of the remnant of the smoke screen.

The boat held Doc Savage and his four men.

Monk, carrying Habeas Corpus by an ear, stood up and stared at the plane, particularly at the pilot.

"For the love of Mike!" he cried, amazement on his face.

"Holy cow!" Renny jabbed oversized hands at the plane. "Long Tom!"

Ham, turning his sword cane slowly in his hands, eyed Doc.

"You had the foresight to transfer to this collapsible boat a moment after we left the *Seaward*." Then he pointed at the plane and its pilot, Long Tom. "But where'd our invalid pal, the electrical wizard, come from?"

"I thought he remained in New York to conduct his experiments," Johnny added.

"A blind," Doc explained. "Long Tom crossed to England on a fast liner, bought that plane and came south."

The bronze man paused to touch one of the metal equipment boxes. "There is a portable radio in here," he said.

"I heard you working with it a couple of hours ago," Ham admitted.

Doc nodded. "I was summoning Long Tom."

A WIDE grin was on Long Tom's pallid countenance as he helped them transfer their equipment, then the collapsible boat, to the plane.

"Why keep the cat in the bag, Doc?" Monk grumbled.

"Sorry," Doc told him. "But Captain Flancul and Princess Gusta are clever. They might've done some eavesdropping."

"Yeah," Monk admitted. "We would've talked it over, probably, if we'd have known. They might've overheard."

Long Tom seated himself at the control wheel, opened the trio of throttles, and maneuvered the plane off the water. He set a course east and north, toward Calbia, climbing rapidly to some twenty thousand feet.

Renny pulled thoughtfully at his long jaw. "You figured on such an emergency as this, Doc?"

"Not exactly this."

"Well, it worked out neat. Them guys on the *Seaward* think we're dead."

Monk chuckled. "Are they gonna get a shock!"

Westward, off in the direction of Italy and Spain, indications were that the sun would shortly descend. Already the Mediterranean had begun to change color. Ahead, over Calbia, clouds were wadded profusely in the sky.

Doc opened the portable radio and prepared it for operation.

"Whatcha gonna do?" Monk wanted to know.

"Get in contact with the revolutionary forces," Doc advised him. "They have radio equipment. Through them, we will notify Conte Cozonac that we are safe."

"Then what?"

"We will land before we reach the coast, wait for darkness, then visit Conte Cozonac and concoct a definite plan of operation."

Chapter XIII
BAT SHIP

IT was night.

Clouds over Calbia shut out the luminance of moon and stars at a height of nine thousand feet, so that only sepia murk lay below. The cloud formation was nimbus—a dark and shapeless layer with few openings. From this type of cloud rain usually falls, but there was no downpour now, although the clouds themselves were saturated, and gave promise of a slow, steady precipitation later in the night.

Doc Savage's plane kept in the clouds. The party had landed on the sea far out of sight of anyone ashore, and had waited until the night was well along before again taking off. They were fairly sure no one had observed their presence, nor was the passage of the plane likely to be detected, for the exhaust silencers—they were the type developed by Doc, which Long Tom had brought from New York—were highly efficient.

Renny was navigating, and gaunt Johnny had the controls. Frequently, both looked over their shoulders into the cabin.

Doc Savage was engaged in a task which interested them all, intrigued them the more so since the bronze man was more than usually reticent about the purpose of the thing.

Doc had been working upon his contrivance for some little time before his activities had come to their notice. When they had discovered him, he was just closing one of the metal equipment boxes.

What had gone into the box, they did not know.

"That thing—what is it?" asked Monk, who was always full of questions.

"That's an experiment," Doc replied, and that was all they got out of him.

Employing some steel piano wire from a large spool, Doc fashioned a secure cradle for the metal box, so that it would dangle at the end of the wire. Then he lowered the receptacle through the door and began playing out wire. The spool was large, and he unreeled all of the wire.

The metal box was now towed along at least a quarter of a mile behind the plane. Doc extinguished the flashlight which had illuminated his operations.

Monk wrinkled his flat nose in the gloom of the plane cabin. Curiosity was literally oozing from his pores, but he did not attempt to question Doc further. He knew that it would get him—nothing. The man of bronze would only exercise his habit of appearing not to hear the inquiries.

Whatever the significance of the object they were towing, Monk felt that it was important. Doc had done strange things on other occasions which had turned out to be of no small significance.

Ham announced, "I'm going to eat my share of those sandwiches Long Tom brought. You fellows gobbled up yours, but I'm going to eat mine slowly. A gentleman gets some enjoyment out of his food."

The lawyer moved to his seat. An instant later, he emitted a yell.

Habeas Corpus exploded a pained grunt.

"Dang you, Ham!" Monk howled. "I told you to quit kickin' my pig around!"

"If I catch him, I'll throw him out of here and see if those big ears are really any good as wings!" Ham gritted. "And if you open that big mouth of yours, I'll let you go with him."

Monk tried to keep the glee out of his voice. "Aw, what ails you now?"

"That infernal hog," Ham snarled, "ate up my sandwiches!"

HALF an hour later, the plane lifted above the clouds.

Renny scrutinized the stars, consulted the compass, the airspeed meter, and scribbled figures on a paper pad by the light of a flash.

"We're about twenty miles north of the Calbian capital city of San Blazna," he vouchsafed. "That's the spot you wanted, ain't it, Doc?"

Doc Savage had been making sure that the end of piano wire was securely fastened to a fuselage cross-piece. They were still towing the mysterious metal box behind.

"Twenty miles north of San Blazna is the location," the bronze man agreed. "As you fellows know, I was in communication with the revolutionary forces before we landed on the sea to kill time. They gave us the location of their headquarters. Conte Cozonac will hurry there by plane as soon as the *Seaward* docks. He is probably there now."

"All right," Renny told Johnny, who had the controls, "stand her on her nose, big words."

The plane upended and went down.

"Take it easy," Doc suggested. "We want to keep that box on the piano wire as far behind us as possible."

Johnny flattened the plane out slightly and their descent took the form of a great spiral, slow swings with a radius of nearly a mile.

Binoculars in hand, the other man opened the cabin window and hung outside. This was strange country below, and just how he would make a landing was puzzling Johnny.

"Want to drop a flare when the altimeters show we're close to the ground, Doc?" the gaunt geologist and archaeologist called.

"They have a landing field of sorts, they advised by radio," Doc told him. "We are to signal with a flashlight, and they will mark the field with lanterns. The signal is the letter C in the Continental Code."

"C standing for Cozonac, maybe," Monk suggested absently.

"C meaning cooked, which is what your goose is

going to be, if you don't teach that hog to leave my stuff alone," Ham growled.

"Habeas is just playful," Monk explained.

"Sure, sure," Ham gritted. "But he never plays with anybody's stuff but mine. And do you know why?"

"I can't imagine," Monk disclaimed innocently.

"Because you've taught him to work on me!" Ham said angrily.

Monk opened his mouth to make some retort—instead, he grabbed wildly for the handiest support.

A crack, cataclysmic in its loudness, slammed through the roar of air about the open cabin windows. Reverberations followed, like something monstrous and hard rolling down vast steps, or thunder romping through the clouds. A scintillating light-burst made visual accompaniment to the sound salvo.

Convulsing air pummeled the plane, heaved it over on a wing tip.

Johnny, juggling the wheel, treading the rudder, nursed the ship to an even keel.

In the sky behind them, a mammoth skyrocket might have opened a ball of fire. Blazing fragments sank, swirling slowly, shedding bright sparks.

"Another explosion!" Monk gulped, his small voice almost lost in the air roar.

"It destroyed the box we were towing on the piano wire," Doc agreed.

"Holy cow!" Renny squinted at the spot which Doc occupied in the darkened cabin. "Was the box a decoy?"

"It was."

"Then, Doc, you know what is causin' the explosions!"

"WHAT'S makin' the blasts?" Monk demanded.

"You're too optimistic," Doc advised. "There is no definite proof of what the thing was. Towing that metal box behind was merely an experiment."

Monk pondered this. He knew from long experience that Doc was not in the habit of putting theories into words. The bronze man made no wild conjectures. Therefore, unless he knew the exact nature of the mystery, knew with such certainty that he could recreate the device himself, Doc would avoid any statement.

"What was in the metal box?" Monk persisted.

"Remember the alcohol stoves we brought along in case we might have to camp out?" Doc said.

"Sure. Designed 'em myself. Four of 'em, and they give off a lotta heat for their size."

"All four of the stoves were in that metal case—lighted."

"Lighted!"

"Right. If you had used binoculars on the box before it was destroyed, you might have noticed that it was almost red-hot."

The discussion was interrupted.

Two searchlights suddenly poked up white, exploring rods from the ground. Another beam appeared. The trio swayed, crossed and uncrossed, somehow remindful of stiff, reeling white ghosts.

On the ground, an anti-aircraft gun winked a red eye. A flare shell ripened a brilliant fruit high above the plane. Light bathed not only the plane but the earth as well.

A woods lay below, a furry carpet of trees. In the center was a clearing. It seemed comparatively level.

As the flare shell sank, the earth grew more brilliantly lighted. Remarkably enough, a casual glance could discern no living being below.

Renny, who had been in the engineering corps dining the war, was familiar with camouflage.

"A lot of the trees are just green paint on tents," he declared. "There's a military force camped below us."

"How many?" Monk demanded.

"Ten or fifteen thousand men, I should judge. Man, they've got some up-to-date war machinery!"

A green hut which resembled a treetop spurted flame—and an anti-aircraft shell opened off the left wing tip.

Johnny hurriedly changed course. Doc untied the end of the trailing piano wire and cast it overboard in order that it might not hamper their maneuvering. Then, thrusting a flashlight from a window, he blinked it rapidly.

He made a dash-dot-dash-dot combination—the letter C of the Continental Code.

"That'll tell us if they are Conte Cozonac's men."

The reply to the signal was prompt. Searchlights went out. The anti-aircraft guns did not fire again.

Shortly afterward, a string of lights appeared, evidently electric lanterns. They marked the position of the landing field.

"I AIN'T so sure about this," Renny rumbled pessimistically.

"Aw, you're suspicious of everything," Monk told him. "They turned out their searchlights and quit shootin', didn't they? They're Conte Cozonac's outfit."

"Yeah, but the thing that exploded—who turned it loose on us?"

"The Royalists, of course. They're usin' the darn thing."

Renny snorted. "But how'd they know we was comin'?"

"Ever hear of spies?" Monk queried sarcastically. "The Royalists may have agents in Conte Cozonac's radio station."

"O.K., O.K.," Renny muttered.

Doc Savage now took over the controls of the plane. The others, expecting him to land immediately, received a surprise. The bronze man swung the big ship far wide of the copse of wood which harbored the military encampment.

"Monk! Ham! Come here!" he called.

Monk and Ham hurried forward. For several seconds, they consulted with Doc in the control cockpit.

Renny, Long Tom and Johnny, being in the rear, did not hear what was said.

Monk and Ham left the control compartment and hurriedly strapped on parachutes. Then they opened the cabin door. Monk scooped up Habeas Corpus and tucked the pig under an arm.

"Here goes!" he grunted, and stepped out into black space.

Ham followed him, hand on his 'chute ripcord ring.

The darkness below swallowed the two plummeting forms.

Renny lumbered to the control cockpit. "Holy cow, Doc! Why'd Monk and Ham go overboard with 'chutes?"

"Come here, all of you," Doc suggested.

All three crowded about the bronze man.

"We'll employ a somewhat different policy than usual on this Calbian job," the bronze man explained. "Each man is going to be assigned a definite job. None of you will know what the others are doing, except in the case of two of you working together."

"What's the idea?" Long Tom wanted to know.

"Nobody, in case of capture, can give information about the others."

"Say, we wouldn't talk—"

"Wait! Any man can be made to talk," Doc explained. "Truth serums or hypnotism will do the trick, for instance."

"Yeah. That's right, too," Long Tom agreed.

"The same thing applies to me," Doc stated.

"You mean—"

"You will not let me know where you are except when you make reports. In other words, if captured, I do not want to be able to give your whereabouts."

"Everybody works separate, eh?"

"That's it, except when two are on the same job."

Long Tom considered. "Not a bad idea, after all."

"Monk and Ham evidently landed far enough from the military encampment to escape discovery," Doc announced, after watching the ground below for a time with binoculars. "There is no excitement."

"Were they to signal a safe landing?"

"No. Too much chance of a light being seen," Doc advised.

He sent the plane back toward the encampment where the landing field was marked by electric lanterns.

Chapter XIV
THE BRONZE MAN PLANS

DOC Savage planted the big plane in the clearing without great difficulty. Use of the landing lights on the wingtips simplified the descent. Wheel brakes brought the bus to a stop. He loosened one brake, gunned the motors on that side, and turned the ship, so that it was ready for a quick take-off, should an emergency arise. He did not switch the engines off, but left them idling.

Gripping the tiny supermachine guns charged with mercy bullets, the party dropped out of the cabin.

Men approached. They came in squads, walking with military precision, automatic rifles ready in front of their chests.

Johnny dashed the beam of a flashlight over them, augmenting the glow of electric lanterns which marked the landing field.

The rebel soldiers wore olive-green uniforms. The regalia was sprightly, and showed the liking of these Balkan peoples for ornate attire. Even the privates wore snappy Sam Browne belts. The officers carried swords.

On the sleeve of every soldier—the right sleeve just above the elbow—was sewed a circular piece of red cloth. Obviously these red balls were the insignia of the revolutionists.

"That's funny," Renny rumbled.

"I see nothing conducive to joviality," Johnny retorted.

"Remember the little red balls them fellers on the black ocean speedboat in New York carried?" Renny countered. "And I believe you said when you grabbed Muta on the *Seaward* one of them red balls fell out of his pocket."

"True." Johnny fingered his monocle magnifier. "Hm-m-m!"

"Well, these soldiers are wearin' red balls on their sleeves. I was just wonderin', that's all."

The squads of soldiers came to a stop, at the Calbian command, of *"Otriti!"*

"Cine este acolo!" called an officer. "Who is there?"

"Doc Savage," Doc replied.

"Comandantul sef, Conte Cozonac is awaiting you," the officer replied gravely.

COMMANDER-IN-CHIEF Conte Cozonac's quarters proved to be a round tent, the outside of which was painted to resemble a *fagul,* a Calbian tree. Inside the tent were tables which supported numerous telephones, modern metal filing cabinets, and numerous maps in which many pins were stuck, evidently designating the position of military forces. There was also a desk.

Conte Cozonac bounded from behind the desk when Doc and his men appeared. The fat fellow had donned a resplendent uniform, the tunic of which was arrayed with glittering medals. An automatic was holstered on his right hip; a rapier, the hilt jewel-inlaid, dangled on his left. A dagger thrust into the belt completed the warlike display.

On Conte Cozonac's right arm, above the elbow, was a round, red ball insignia.

"I am delighted at your safety," he said in excellent English. "After that terrific explosion in the sky, I feared something had happened to you. What was it?"

"It was rather mysterious," Doc said dryly. "One of those devilish blasts occurred some distance behind our plane."

"You mean—they used their weapon on you and it missed you?" The fat man seemed bewildered.

"It failed to touch us, all right."

"Strange, indeed strange. Their infernal device is supposed to be infallible. How do you account for its missing you?"

If Renny and the other two expected Doc to explain about the four lighted alcohol stoves towed in the metal case behind the plane, they were disappointed.

"There are many mysterious aspects to these explosions," Doc said slowly. "Particularly this one. For instance, how did the men who turned that weapon loose upon us know we were coming here tonight? We figured that they thought us out of the way."

Conte Cozonac twittered sudden, squeaking laughter.

"It wasn't funny!" Renny thumped.

The fat man straightened his face. "I was laughing because they failed to get you. This is the first time, to my knowledge, that their infernal contrivance has not proven effective."

"Well, how'd the Royalists know we were coming?" Renny pondered. "Maybe they've got spies in your camp."

"Perhaps they did not know," Conte Cozonac said, considering. "Perhaps they heard your plane, knew none of their own ships were in the air, and reasoned yours was a revolutionist craft. Then they used their strange weapon, and missed. But I do not believe there are spies here. You see, I have chosen my men most carefully."

"Yeah, maybe," Renny agreed doubtfully.

Conte Cozonac surveyed his visitors, then his bulbous form shook as he started in surprise. "Where are your other two men—Ham, the lawyer, and the chemist Monk, who has the pet pig?" he asked.

"They have been sent on a mission," Doc told him.

"What was its nature?"

DOC SAVAGE was silent for a while. He seemed to be debating the words which would best fit the explanation he wanted to make.

"In order to guarantee the safety of my men, no one but myself is to know what work they are doing," he finally said.

Conte Cozonac reddened. "You mistrust me?"

"Not at all. I, myself, will not know where they are most of the time."

"But why?"

"In case the enemy should capture one of us, there will be no chance of betraying the others."

Conte Cozonac considered this. After some thirty seconds, he smiled widely.

"Safety first, eh?"

"Exactly."

"You do not take many chances, Savage," the other chuckled. "Of course, I will ask no questions. After all, you are the future king of Calbia."

If he was intrigued by the prospect of becoming the *Regele,* the King of Calbia, Doc exhibited no outward elation.

Several officers now entered the tent. Their uniforms and the flamboyance of their trappings indicated they were of high rank.

"My staff," Conte Cozonac explained.

The bony Johnny noted that the right sleeve of all the uniforms bore the red ball insignia. This moved him to put a question: "I say, what significance has the erubescent circumferentiation?"

Conte Cozonac mulled over the big words for a moment, then laughed in his strange fashion.

"That is the symbol of liberty—the insignia which my revolutionary party has adopted."

Johnny was thoughtful. "Do your men carry red marbles?"

Conte Cozonac nodded. "Our secret agents do, yes. They use them as badges."

"Badges!"

"Why do you ask?"

"Muta carried a red marble," Johnny said grimly.

The fat man sprang to his feet. "What?"

"I saw it twice."

The chief of the revolutionists sank back into his chair. Perspiration appeared upon his bulb of a forehead, and he produced a silk handkerchief and slowly blotted the moisture.

"Intr'adevar!" he muttered. "Indeed! That is valuable information. It proves that the Royalists

have tipped their men off to carry the red marble, undoubtedly for use in tricking my own followers."

"You think that's why Muta had one?"

"Da!" The fat man's full jowls shook with the vehemence of his nod. "Yes! There is no explanation."

Doc Savage put in quietly, "Suppose we consider ways and means."

Conte Cozonac settled back. "Well spoken! Have you a plan?"

"The present regime in Calbia is probably the nearest thing to an absolute monarchy that exists in the world today," Doc stated. "The government is entirely in the hands of three persons—King Dal Le Galbin, Princess Gusta Le Galbin, and Captain Henri Flancul. Is that right?"

"Da," said one of the staff officers. "You are correct."

"Seizure of those three would leave the Royalist forces leaderless, would it not?"

"Da."

"Loss of the three chieftains should cause the Royalist army to become demoralized."

Conte Cozonac nodded vehement agreement. "It would."

"Then we will seize the trio," Doc stated.

THE giant bronze man's suggestion that they kidnap the two principal members of the Calbian royal family and their chief advisor gave the revolutionist staff officers a shock. They traded blank looks.

Having grown up under a monarchy, probably having been taught from childhood that the *regele,* or king, was only a little short of a sacred personage, Doc's suggestion undoubtedly struck them about as the kidnaping of the president would strike a citizen of the United States.

Conte Cozonac also showed evidences of being stunned, but he came out of it quickly—not enough, however, to start trilling his weird laughter. His round face was solemn.

"You know, Doc Savage, that is an idea worthy of the man of bronze," he declared earnestly. "It is perfect. If you need men, I can supply them—any number up to two hundred thousand. About that number of able-bodied men have enlisted in the revolutionary cause."

"In work of that kind," Doc told him, "a very few men have a better chance of success, while a mob would be defeated by its own inability to strike with swiftness and without discovery."

Conte Cozonac indicated Johnny, Long Tom, and Renny. "You mean that only yourself and your men are to seize King Dal Le Galbin and the other two?"

"That is the idea."

There was silence in the tent, broken occasionally by the tinkle of one medal against another as the staff officers shifted, or the guttural challenge of a sentry posted nearby in the darkness.

Abruptly, far-off in the night, rifles crackled. The moan of machine guns joined in, then the heavy thump of artillery and the reverberations of exploding shells. Although the war sounds were miles away, the very ground under the tent seemed to tremble.

"Makes me think of old times." Renny said thoughtfully.

A phone rang. Fat Conte Cozonac went to it, listened, spoke in Calbian, then hung up.

"A Royalist raid on one of our positions," he said. "Our revolutionists are managing to hold them back."

The warlike noises subsided after a time.

Doc Savage had been waiting, no change visible upon his metallic countenance, and now that the distant raid seemed to have played out, he spoke.

"About this mystery weapon which is in the hands of the Royalists—have they been using it upon you?"

Conte Cozonac looked as grim as a man of his fatness possibly could. "They certainly have," he said firmly. "On three different occasions planes carrying my staff officers have been literally blown to smithereens, as you Yankees describe it. Motor cars have been wrecked. Once a moving train was demolished. The force of the blast centered on the locomotive."

"It is always moving machinery that suffers, eh?" Doc questioned.

"Not always, although usually a moving object. Two men who helped me organize this revolution were killed while cooking their supper over a camp fire in the woods."

"Did loss of those men cripple your force badly?"

Conte Cozonac shook his head slowly. "Not greatly. The opposition must have only a few of the mystery weapons. Once they have time to manufacture them, it will be terrible!"

Doc Savage had been occupying a folding camp chair. Now he stood erect.

"We want that infernal machine, whatever it is. It must be rendered harmless."

The fat man nodded. "Everything is in your hands."

Doc eyed his three men. "Come on. We have a lot to do before morning."

Chapter XV
THE CHINESE BUZZARD

DAWN saw the sun come up pale and red

behind the clouds. Rain had started a few hours before daylight, a slow drizzle, which was little more than a fog, but produced infinite discomfort.

Renny had turned into a camouflaged barracks tent to get some sleep. The prospect of excitement did not interfere with his slumber, except for one nightmare in which he was a Brobdingnagian giant walking around in a land peopled by wee kings, princesses and Captain Flanculs. A sack was part of Renny's equipment in the dream, and into it he continuously stuffed kings, princesses, and Captain Flanculs.

Doc Savage's bronze hands shook him awake.

"Holy cow!" Renny grunted, rubbing his eyes with fists almost as large as his own far-from-small cranium. "Did I have a dream!"

He listened to the thunderlike thump and rumble of cannonading in the distance. "You know, those field guns are bound to be killin' a lot of people."

"We want to stop this thing as soon as possible," Doc agreed. "Come on, Renny. I've been working through the night, and have things ready for you."

"Didn't you sleep?"

"No. Time for that later."

"Where're Johnny and Long Tom?"

"They've already departed on their mission."

"Huh?" Renny thumped. "What's their job?"

"Remember that none of you was to know what the others are doing," Doc reminded him.

"Sure, I forgot." Renny fished about for his clothes, failed to find them, and boomed, "Hey! Where'd my duds go?"

"I took them," Doc advised. "Wrap a blanket around yourself."

The big-fisted engineer complied with the command. He followed Doc out of the tent and across the encampment to the clearing. On the edge of this, a large, camouflaged canvas cover had been rigged over Doc's tri-motored amphibian, to keep off the rain.

Renny peered at the aircraft.

"Holy cow!" he exploded.

The amphibian was now painted an entirely different color, being a particularly garish purple. Nor was that all. Coiled around the fuselage was a flame-spouting Chinese dragon, done in practically every color of the rainbow. There were numerous characters of the Chinese alphabet emblazoned on the wings, hull and tail structure.

In large letters on each side of the hull a name was painted:

CHAMP DUGAN
THE PURPLE TERROR

Renny squirmed in his rain-sodden blanket "Say, what's this mean? Who's Champ Dugan?"

"You," Doc said.

"Huh?"

The bronze man now withdrew from a pocket a sheaf of yellow papers—cablegrams both sent and received.

"Read these over and you'll get the idea," he said.

RENNY consulted the messages which had been sent and received by Doc Savage from his powerful private radio station atop the New York City skyscraper before they sailed on the *Seaward*. The messages had gone to men in China, India, Persia, and Turkey.

The names of most of these men were strange to Renny, but he did recognize a few of them as individuals he happened to know were deeply indebted to Doc Savage and would do anything to oblige the bronze man. Hastily, Renny went through the rest of the messages.

"The way has been paved for you, as you can see," Doc told him. "A man in China, a gentleman who is under the impression he owes me a debt of gratitude, was to radio the King of Calbia, using the name of Champ Dugan.

"According to the wire my friend sent from China, the imaginary Champ Dugan was a world-beater as a fighting airman. Several references were given, and as you will note from the wires there, the references were men who were also glad to help further our deception. The upshot of that was that King Dal Le Galbin hired the mythical Champ Dugan."

"And you thought of all this in New York," Renny muttered.

"The mythical Champ Dugan is supposed to be on his way to Calbia," Doc continued. "Radiograms have been sent from India, Persia and Turkey with his name signed to them. Champ Dugan, in fact, is due to arrive at the capital of Calbia today."

Renny rarely allowed a grin to decorate his long, sober face. However, he now permitted himself the luxury of a wide smile.

"This is the real reason you sent Long Tom via England, to buy this plane, eh?" he asked.

"Exactly. You will notice that Champ Dugan is to receive a high command in the Calbian Royalist air force. King Dal Le Galbin evidently has a good opinion of Yankee free-lance airmen. Notice the salary he's paying you."

Renny consulted the telegrams. "A thousand dollars a week! Not bad!"

"Except that you usually make that much a day at your trade of engineer," Doc added dryly. "Now as Champ Dugan, flyer extraordinary, you should be able to get close to King Dal Le Galbin and Princess Gusta."

"The idea is to grab 'em if I can?" Renny rumbled.

"Even more important, get a line on the thing causing the big explosions," Doc suggested.

"Yeah. That's the main job, after all."

"With a few suggestions as to how Champ Dugan is to act, you'll be ready to go. I'll disguise you, also."

THREE hours later the Chinese dragon plane with the name "Champ Dugan" lettered on its side dived out of eastern clouds and descended on the Calbian capital city of San Blazna. It was from the east that a plane from China would be expected to arrive.

Due to the drizzling rain, few people were in the narrow streets of San Blazna when the grotesquely decorated plane first appeared. Here and there squads of soldiers marched. Automobiles were few, far outnumbered by the mule carts of peasants.

The noise of the plane brought San Blaznites from their houses like hornets out of a disturbed nest. They stared upward. Evidently they were no strangers to air raids, and feared the weirdly colored ship might be an enemy plane.

Steam plumes spurting from locomotive whistles and power houses told Renny an alarm was being spread. He had removed Doc Savage's remarkable silencers from the plane exhaust stacks, and the ship was making a great deal of noise, completely drowning out the sound of the whistles below.

From a military airport on the edge of San Blazna, a squadron of fighting planes appeared and climbed upward. There were nine of them, holding formation triangles of three craft each.

Renny watched their flying closely. To a layman, it might have appeared that Calbians were skillful fighting buzzards, but to Renny's experienced eyes, they were doing a ragged job.

"Kiwis," opined Renny.

Renny's accomplishments did not end with the field of engineering, where he was among the greatest, but included, among other things, many hours of flying time, a portion of them under the highly efficient tutelage of Doc Savage. Doc possessed the facility that goes to make great teachers—he seemed able to convey some of his own uncanny skill to those whom he instructed.

Not many fliers were more skillful than Renny, and he proceeded to give a demonstration of that fact.

The nine Calbian pursuit planes spread into a duck flight line in the drizzle and approached. Pilots craned their necks from cockpits to study Renny's weirdly bedizened chariot.

Renny flew straight forward.

Probably by way of warning, two of the pursuit craft discharged machine gun bursts. The tracer lines threaded over Renny's head, and not far distant from it either. The fighting crates came on arrogantly.

Renny let them get quite close. Abruptly he stamped the rudder and wrestled the controls. One of the planes which had used a machine gun was the object of his maneuver. The big amphibian literally pounced upon this craft.

The pursuit pilot's face, glistening wet in the rain, became starkly white as the great ship cannoned toward him. He was, in fact, more stunned than Renny had expected, and the big-fisted engineer was forced to battle the controls again to prevent a collision.

The pursuit pilot dove out of his way, oozing a cold sweat. He had been scared badly.

Renny booted his big bus around and hung onto the tails of the pursuit squadron.

The Calbian flyers, not sure whether he was an enemy, sought to jockey clear. They found that impossible. Their fighting craft were smaller, much faster than Renny's lumbering amphibian, yet such was the engineer's skill and knowledge of aerobatics that he succeeded in making the Calbian army pilots look like rank amateurs.

Diving at them fiercely, keeping away from their machine guns with an uncanny facility, Renny literally chased the pursuit ships into the clouds.

Then Renny dived down and proceeded to raise the hair on the heads of the inhabitants of San Blazna.

A RIVER snaked through the center of San Blazna. A large stream, it bore the name of River Carlos, after King Carlos Le Galbin I, the founder of the present dynasty of Calbia. At one point, two bridges spanned this stream, and nearby, on the left bank, stood the great castlelike structure which was King Dal Le Galbin's palace.

Renny flew under the arch of both bridges, apparently with but inches to spare on either side. He chased a squad of highly uniformed Royalist soldiers into the king's castle. Then he thundered around the castle, a wing tip almost scraping the masonry.

Sentries tried to shoot at him from the walls. He cranked down the landing gear of the amphibian, swooped at the riflemen, and sent them scuttling to cover.

The Calbian flag and the king's personal colors fluttered on a flagpole above the castle gate. Renny, calculating beautifully, flew close enough to the pole to carry away both flags on his landing gear. He looped and barrel-rolled arrogantly over the castle.

Untangling both flags from his wheels, he yanked the undercarriage up, landed on the river, and beached his craft under the castle walls.

The Renny who got out of the amphibian hardly

resembled the sober-faced gentleman the engineering profession knew. For one thing, Renny's hair had been dyed a particularly gaudy red. His face was freckled. Most startling change of all was the enormous grin which had displaced his usual funeral-going expression.

His garb was a Chinese blouse, with enormous sleeves which ordinarily hung down over his hands, concealing the proportions of his enormous fists with surprising effectiveness. He wore baggy Turkish trousers, soft Russian boots.

With Doc's aid, Renny had disguised himself to look the part of "Champ Dugan," the daredevil Yank buzzard from China. His arrival in San Blazna had been in Champ Dugan's style.

Once, in medieval times, the river waters had been diverted into a moat which encircled the castle. A walk along the edge of this moat now served as a promenade. Renny clambered up the river bank and strode along this esplanade.

A platoon of guardsmen, each in a high fur uniform cap, swung toward him on the double-quick. Their uniforms were most eye-filling. Renny concluded this was a part of the castle guard.

Playing Champ Dugan to the fullest, Renny greeted the guardsmen with a wide, freckled grin. "Hi, soldiers!" he called.

"You are under arrest," he was informed in Calbian.

"Yeah?" Renny snorted. "Listen—you mugs start with me, and you'll get them pretty uniforms mussed!"

The officer in charge stepped forward and grabbed at Renny's arms, evidently with the idea of pinioning them.

There was a whack of a big fist on a jaw and the officer sprawled on his back.

"I can whip the king's guard as well as the Calbian air force," boasted the pseudo Champ Dugan. "You palookas don't know so much about fightin'."

The arrival of a courier interrupted what might have developed into a first-class scrap.

"Are you Champ Dugan, the Yankee flier from China?" asked the messenger.

"So somebody in Calbia has heard of me, eh?" Renny made a big freckled grin.

"King Dal Le Galbin will give you an audience at once," said the other.

"An audience—oh, you mean he wants to talk to me? O. K., let's go."

Chapter XVI
THE CALBIAN TOUGH GUY

KING DAL LE GALBIN had a tangled mass of snow-white hair. His eyes were blue, his jaw strong, his mouth grim. The handsome lines of his features explained where his daughter, Princess Gusta, got her exquisite beauty.

The monarch of Calbia had powerful shoulders and a lean waist, and although his age must have been near fifty, indications were that he was still very much a man.

He wore an extremely plain uniform, tailored snugly to his strapping physique. He affected no medals, gold braid, swords, or pistols.

"Give me one good pursuit plane, and I can whip your whole air force," Renny declared loudly. "They're not so hot."

The ruler of Calbia, the man who was at present the world's nearest approach to an absolute monarch, produced a plain gold case of monogrammed cigarettes, and offered it.

"Do you smoke, Champ Dugan?" he asked.

Renny shook his head. "Fightin' and braggin' is my only dissipation."

To his surprise, Renny was discovering that he rather liked King Dal Le Galbin.

King Dal permitted a court flunky to dash forward with a patent lighter and ignite his cigarette.

"You seem to be a rather unusual individual, Champ Dugan. In your opinion, what is wrong with my air force?"

"Judging from the samples I've seen, they're not fire-eaters. Too, they're a little shy on combat training. What you need is about fifty free-lance fliers, professional swashbucklers."

"My air force has not been very effective against the rebels." The king drew slowly on his cigarette.

"Who has charge?" Renny asked.

"One of my advisors is air minister—Captain Henri Flancul. I will summon him."

Renny would willingly have postponed confronting Captain Flancul. It was possible Flancul had seen him, either in New York or on the liner *Seaward*, and might recognize him. But a meeting was inevitable, and he might as well have it over with now.

Captain Flancul, a resplendent figure in uniform, entered.

Princess Gusta also came in to the audience chamber. The young woman's frock was plain, cut on military lines. She was, Renny reflected, one of the most ravishing beauties he could recall having seen.

The ruler of Calbia performed the introductions.

"This is Champ Dugan, Yankee aviator who is going to see what he can do with our air force."

Captain Henri Flancul flushed. "What does that mean?" he demanded. "I thought I had control of the air force?"

"You are not being displaced," the monarch told him. "Champ Dugan is merely an advisor. But I might suggest that you take his advice."

Renny was watching Captain Flancul and Princess Gusta intently. They gave no sign of not accepting him, in his fictitious personality of Champ Dugan, buzzard from China. Doc's disguise was effective.

DURING the remainder of the day, Renny behaved in a fashion calculated to elevate himself in the graces of the king.

The most discerning eye could have observed nothing in Renny's actions to indicate that he contemplated kidnaping the King of Calbia and, if possible, the king's daughter and chief advisor as well.

Renny kept alert for some word of the mystery device which had caused the explosions. He even sounded out officers of the king's guard on the subject. They obviously knew nothing—which surprised Renny somewhat.

Renny borrowed a pursuit plane that afternoon and led a Royalist patrol into revolutionist territory.

"If we meet any rebel ships, you kiwis stay in the background," Renny directed, before the take-off. "Don't give a hoot how many there are. I'll show you guys a real sky brawl."

They met rebel planes—eleven of them. Two were bombers, and the rest pursuit jobs. Alone, Renny dropped out of the clouds upon the flight.

For a few minutes planes whirled in the rain-soaked sky like leaves in a mad wind. Streams of tracer bullets raced here and there, like cobwebs invisibly spun.

The Royalist fliers circled above, obeying the command to stay out of the "dog fight." The blustering, freckled Yankee had said he would show them how it was done—and he kept his word. King Dal's fliers saw four enemy planes go spinning down at the end of squirming smoke plumes.

Just what happened to the rebel pilots they did not see, due to a fog which blanketed the ground. The presence of the fog was a fortunate circumstance. Otherwise, someone might have discovered that none of the planes actually crashed, and that the smoke was coming not from flaming gasoline tanks but from ordinary smoke bombs hidden in cockpits.

Conte Cozonac's fliers were cooperating with Renny, helping him build up a reputation.

Renny led his Royalist squadron back to San Blazna, after he had apparently, single-handedly, defeated the rebel airmen and shot down in a few minutes more revolutionist planes than King Dal's fliers had been able to bag since the outbreak of hostilities.

Renny became a hero. King Dal personally complimented him.

Princess Gusta was also extremely friendly, listening with interest to hair-raising tales of some of Champ Dugan's aerial accomplishments in China and elsewhere.

Among other things, Renny had a fertile imagination.

Later, Princess Gusta offered to ride Renny around the town in one of the royal limousines and show him points of interest. Renny was not acting when he grinned from ear to ear. He was making excellent progress, and it was only a question of time until an opportunity would present itself for the kidnaping.

Furthermore, Renny could not imagine a more charming and desirable guide than the king's daughter.

ON that sightseeing ride, there occurred an incident which wiped out some of Renny's satisfaction.

The royal limousine which they used was long and sleek, plain black in color, except for the ornate coat of arms of the Calbian ruling family, encrested on either door.

The chauffeur was a meek individual whose vocabulary seemed to be limited to, "Yes, Your Highness."

There was no escort, Princess Gusta having ignored her sire's suggestion that they take one.

In the course of their sightseeing, they visited the ancient stone house—now a museum—where the first King Le Galbin had been born, some generations ago. Renny gathered that this first Le Galbin had been born a lowly peasant, and had made himself king by using his brain and fighting ability.

The street outside was deserted, except for the meek chauffeur in the limousine, when they left the old house. Secretly, Renny debated whether this might not be a good time to kidnap Princess Gusta.

A shabby-looking beggar hobbled around the nearest corner. The fellow's left leg dragged, and he used a crutch. He approached, doffed a greasy hat from tangled hair that needed combing, and offered it hopefully for alms.

Renny, feeling expansive at the moment, used both bands to fish in the pockets of his voluminous trousers for a coin.

With stunning speed, the mendicant whipped up his crutch and crashed it down on Renny's head.

Stunned, the big-fisted engineer sank to his knees.

"Grabiti-va!" shrieked the panhandler. "Make haste! Help me seize them!"

Nearby doors banged open. Shabby men poured out and rushed to the attack. They swarmed over Renny, seized Princess Gusta.

The chauffeur tried to run, but was knocked unconscious.

Princess Gusta managed to shriek once, but the sound was not loud, and brought no aid.

"Long live the revolutionists!" howled a thug.

Renny, half unconscious, and squirming under a

blanket of bodies, rumbled weakly his disgust. These men must be some obscure band of revolutionist sympathizers. Under the impression that they were doing a great thing, they were about to ruin Renny's carefully laid plans.

Renny and Princess Gusta were hauled to their feet and shoved toward the limousine.

"Wait!" cried the fellow who had wielded the crutch. "Kill the tyrants here!"

"Da!" agreed another, and produced a knife.

There came an interruption to upset the plans of the killing. An enormous apparition of a fellow appeared around a nearby corner.

"Plecati!" he rumbled savagely. "Go away!"

RENNY caught a glimpse of the newcomer, and decided he had never seen a more fearsome individual. The fellow towered well over six feet, and his bulk was tremendous. His skin was dark, almost black, and his straight jet hair was combed down at the sides and down over his forehead and eyes, after the fashion of the Calbian peasants of the more remote hill sections.

The dark giant wore a loose, ragged blouse, and tight breeches which came only to his knees. He was bare footed.

The big one descended upon the fight, his fists bowling two attackers over. He jumped like a fighting rooster and kicked another in the chest. The fellow went down hard.

"Plecati!" the huge stranger bawled again. "Go away!"

One revolutionist fanatic flashed a knife, lunged at him and missed. He was sent reeling by a big scarred fist.

"Go away!" rumbled the stupid-looking giant, with an almost childish vehemence.

The gang who had seized Renny and Princess Gusta began to exhibit a great willingness to do as they were told. The swarthy giant was a tremendous fighter. He floundered around, great arms swinging, occasionally wrenching a gun out of the hands of some fanatic who sought to use it.

That this monster was no stranger to physical combat was indicated by the number of scars on his rather puffy features, and the pronouncedly flaring nose which looked as if it had been broken numerous times.

Renny, his head clearing, reared up and joined the fray. Renny was no mean scrapper himself, but this individual with the hair over his eyes was a battling prodigy.

The would-be assassins finally fled.

Renny wiped perspiration out of his eyes and peered at the dark giant.

The big fellow ignored Renny. He dropped to all fours in front of Princess Gusta and planted his forehead against the damp cobbles. He remained in that position of obeisance, saying nothing.

"What is your name?" Princess Gusta asked the kneeling monster.

"Botezul," said the huge dark one.

He had a coarse, roaring voice, more boisterous even than Renny's own.

"And who are you, Botezul?" asked the young woman.

"Me mountain man, Your Highness," Botezul explained. "Me hear about revolution and come to join army of King Le Galbin. Me walk along street and see fight."

The fellow spoke the dialect of the Calbian mountaineers, and seemed to have but a limited command of words.

"Get to your feet," directed Princess Gusta.

Botezul arose, but kept his head bowed. He was so huge that Renny suddenly felt quite small.

"So you want to help the king, Botezul?" the young woman queried.

"Yes, Your Highness."

Princess Gusta considered a moment, then smiled slightly. "How would you like to be my personal guard, Botezul?"

Botezul promptly got down again and planted his forehead on the cobbles. He did not say so, but it was evident that the idea of being bodyguard to the beautiful princess suited him perfectly.

"Very well," said Gusta: "from now on you are my guard."

Renny smothered a groan. He had visions of future trouble with this stupid Botezul. Renny was a discerning individual, and he felt quite sure that Botezul could, barehanded, thrash two big-fisted engineers such as himself.

DURING the rest of that day and the one following, Renny's dislike of Botezul grew more acute. The dark giant acquired a habit of scowling blackly at Renny, and expectorating in a most annoying fashion when Renny, playing the part of Champ Dugan to its utmost, began bragging about what a great fighter he was in the air and on the ground.

Renny got a heavy monkey wrench from a mechanic's kit at the military airport and tucked it inside his ample Chinese blouse. When the chance presented itself, he was determined to ascertain what effect the wrench would have on Botezul's thick skull.

Renny dispatched a number of cablegrams to professional free-lance fliers in different parts of the world, offering them good pay to fight for the Calbian government. Doc Savage had furnished a list of such fliers. Summoning them was necessary for the part Renny was playing. The aerial swashbucklers would lose nothing, since their salaries would be paid when the revolution was over.

Renny continued to seek surreptitiously some trace of the weird weapon Baron Damitru Mendl had invented. He found absolutely nothing.

On his third night in the capital city of San Blazna, Renny decided he saw his opportunity to accomplish the purpose for which he was there—the seizure of King Dal Le Galbin, and possibly Princess Gusta and Captain Henri Flancul. Once captured, they could be forced to reveal the secret of Baron Mendl's invention.

It was King Dal's custom, Renny had observed, to seclude himself in a wing of the castle during the early part of each night, there to consider reports, sign official papers, and make plans. Except for the presence of the ruler, this wing was usually untenanted.

Furthermore, Renny had observed that the royal motor cars passed unchallenged through the gates. If he could seize King Dal and the other two, bind and gag them and place them in the rear of an automobile, he might leave the castle without being challenged. It was worth trying.

Accordingly, near the hour of midnight, Renny crept to the palace wing where the monarch was at work. In the big engineer's clothing were some of Doc Savage's anaesthetic grenades, small smoke bombs, and some boxes of tacks. The latter were to sprinkle behind the fleeing car, in case there should be pursuit.

Renny was in high spirits. He had seen enough of the Calbian government to feel quite sure that with King Dal, Princess Gusta, and Captain Flancul out of the way, things would go to pieces. These three were absolute dictators of both civil and military affairs. No one of less authority was accustomed to giving important orders.

To Renny's notion, there were no others with outstanding ability, certainly none who could grasp the reins of government in a hurry.

Capture of the dominating trio would also put Baron Mendl's secret in Doc Savage's hands, Renny felt sure. Doc would find a way of making the three talk.

WITHOUT difficulty, Renny reached the king's chamber. The door hinges did not squeak when he entered furtively—he had oiled them secretly that afternoon.

The dark giant, Botezul, had not been in evidence for an hour or two. The big fellow would be on guard outside Princess Gusta's door, Renny reasoned.

Renny advanced swiftly. A slight sound—perhaps the noise of his feet on the floor—warned King Dal Le Galbin of Renny's presence.

The king wheeled quickly.

"Quiet, or you'll get hurt!" Renny growled.

"What—"

Without finishing his startled query, King Dal struck out with a fist. He was a powerful man, but Renny, with his infinitely greater strength, easily turned the blow aside. Before the ruler could cry out, Renny's tremendous fist landed on his jaw.

King Dal Le Galbin collapsed.

"We'll soon have Baron Mendl's contraption," Renny grunted to himself.

Producing cords and a gag which he had brought with him, he trussed up the monarch and rendered him incapable of making any sound. Some of the cord was left over, and Renny pocketed this.

Shouldering the white-haired sovereign, Renny strode to the door. Not believing anyone was in the wing of the palace, he stepped through boldly. That was where he made his mistake.

Botezul, gigantic, darksome, had been concealed outside. He lunged, and his huge arms enveloped Renny.

The struggle was short—shorter than any fight in which Renny had ever before engaged. The big-fisted engineer discovered himself entirely helpless. He was flung to the floor. The cords were wrenched from his pocket and used to bind him. He was gagged with a sleeve plucked from his own Chinese blouse.

Chapter XVII
BOTEZUL TAKES CHARGE

THE lumbering Botezul, saying nothing, untied King Dal Le Galbin, who had already regained his senses. Then Botezul got down on all fours and put his forehead against the floor.

"Me suspect this man, Your Highness," he mumbled. "Me watch him."

King Dal Le Galbin bent over shakily and plucked at Botezul's shoulder, indicating that he was to get to his feet.

"You shall be amply rewarded for this, my good man," he said earnestly. "I did not have the slightest suspicion of this fellow."

"Him no good," muttered Botezul.

"So it seems. Will you please summon my daughter and Captain Henri Flancul?"

Botezul went away, but was back shortly, trailing like a big, good-natured black dog behind the excited Princess Gusta and Captain Flancul.

In a few words, King Dal explained what had happened; finishing: "This Yankee flier was obviously attempting to seize me."

Botezul lumbered forward abruptly, rumbling, "Look, Your Highness!"

The dark giant rubbed briskly at the freckles on Renny's countenance. These began to come off. Then he secured a handkerchief and rubbed at Renny's hair. Color on the handkerchief indicated Renny's red hair was dyed.

"See?" said Botezul. "Him got makeup on."

Captain Henri Flancul cried out and darted forward. He scrubbed the rest of the freckles off Renny's face, then covered Renny's red hair. Kneading and twisting the engineer's face, he made it assume its habitual expression of unutterable gloom.

"I know this man!" Captain Flancul snarled. "He is one of Doc Savage's five assistants!"

The words had a remarkable effect on attractive Princess Gusta. At first she paled slightly, then color swam over her face; her lips parted, and she gasped, "This man was with Doc Savage—when they put off in that launch from the *Seaward*."

"That is right," Captain Flancul told her.

"Then Doc Savage may be—alive?"

"I hope not," Captain Flancul gritted.

This remark caused Princess Gusta to give Captain Flancul a stare of unutterable loathing.

Renny interrupted proceedings by stirring and groaning, endeavoring to sit erect. Botezul loomed over the engineer and jammed him back to the floor.

"This man, him belong to gang of men you no like?" Botezul queried, indicating Renny.

"Yes, Botezul," explained King Dal Le Galbin. "This fellow is one of a group of five men who assist an American known as Doc Savage. This Doc Savage is helping the revolutionists to fight us."

Botezul pushed Renny back on the floor again as the engineer sought to arise.

"Why not make this feller tell how we can get hands on Doc Savage?" questioned the dark-skinned giant.

"Ma bucur!" exploded Captain Henry Flancul. "Excellent! A good suggestion. We can make this spurious Champ Dugan tell us whether Doc Savage is alive, and if so, force him to reveal how we may trap the bronze man."

"I DO not approve of that suggestion," Princess Gusta said abruptly.

Captain Flancul frowned. "Why not, Your Highness?"

"I do not like the idea of torturing this man. He will not talk otherwise."

"You need not concern yourself about the dog!"

"Yes, Gusta," King Dal put in. "There is too much at stake to be squeamish. The man will not die, I promise you, until he has stood trial, but we may have to use a certain amount of violence to make him talk."

"Me make him talk!" muttered Botezul.

Princess Gusta included Botezul in a glance of disapproval.

"What is the matter, Gusta?" the elder Le Galbin demanded sharply. "Don't you want this Doc Savage captured?"

The young woman flushed slightly.

"What a question!" she snapped, then pointed at Renny. "How do you propose to loosen his tongue?"

Captain Henri Flancul answered this. "The old citadel on the outskirts of the city has, in its dungeons, a number of devices which we might use."

Princess Gusta shuddered. "That horrible place! They are medieval torture chambers!"

"The citadel, Your Highness," Captain Flancul reminded her, "was built by the first Le Galbin to be a king of Calbia. I suggest that we load this man in a car, take him to the citadel, and let Botezul work upon him."

"Da!" rumbled Botezul, eagerness in his voice.

Renny, glowering at Botezul, resolved to settle with the swarthy, ugly giant if it was his last act.

"We will go to the citadel," King Dal Le Galbin concluded finally.

"I will go along," the young woman asserted.

There was some argument about that, but Princess Gusta was adamant in her insistence and won out.

Renny was carried down to the castle garage, in another wing of the building, securely bound and gagged, and placed in a large sedan. The car curtains were drawn.

Captain Flancul drove, and Botezul occupied the front seat beside him. King Dal Le Galbin and Princess Gusta stayed in the rear with Renny.

Two towing cars, filled with palace guardsmen, formed an escort.

THE night was not especially clear. The rain, which had started on Renny's first night in Calbia, had continued intermittently, and judging from the overcast condition of the sky, there would be more of it.

The headlights of the sedan slammed whitely against the houses which walled in the narrow San Blazna streets. The engine seemed unusually noisy. After numerous turns, the machine left the city limits and turned onto a rough road.

Renny lay motionless on the rear floorboards; there was nothing else he could do. He recalled having seen the citadel numerous times before.

The structure was round, of graystone, and from a distance might have been mistaken for a water tank. It was hundreds of years old, however, and the huge-fisted engineer did not doubt but that its dungeon held hideous instruments of torture. Medieval times in Calbia, if he remembered his history, had been extremely productive of such devices.

Moreover, Renny had heard a report that political prisoners were confined to the citadel, where they were subjected to treatment that was far from kind.

Perhaps Baron Mendl's invention was even kept there. That was a thought. The truth was that Renny had seen nothing during the last few days to prove that the ruling house of Calbia was in control of Baron Mendl's device.

Furthermore, it had struck Renny that King Dal Le Galbin was as well-liked as the average monarch could be. Certainly there had been no evidence of cruelty in his character.

But perhaps what was to transpire at the citadel would show the other side of the sovereign's character—a side which Conte Cozonac had insisted was existent.

Renny never did learn what treatment his captors contemplated handing him at the citadel—for, in the front seat, things suddenly happened. Huge Botezul leaned forward abruptly, switched off the engine and yanked on the emergency brake.

Captain Flancul snarled, "What are you—"

Botezul's enormous fist in Captain Flancul's mouth stopped the words. The blow not only silenced Captain Flancul, but it also rendered him senseless. He slouched over, unconscious.

The car, momentum snubbed by the brakes, slewed crosswise on the road, and stopped with the front wheels resting in a shallow ditch.

The huge Botezul whirled, smashed the window which separated the driving compartment from the rear, and swung a fist at the king's jaw.

The ruler of Calbia ducked, got his jaw out of the way, but took the force of the blow on his forehead. He sagged back, stunned.

Princess Gusta wrenched at a handbag which she was carrying, got it open and hurriedly put a hand in it. But Botezul, grasping, tore the bag out of her hand.

Noting that the bag held a small pistol, Botezul threw it out of a window.

THE escort cars had stopped the instant they saw something was wrong. Nattily-clad guardsmen piled out and, guns in hand, raced to the aid of their monarch.

Botezul leaned out of the car. He had some small objects in his right hand, but in the darkness their exact nature could not be ascertained. He flung these toward the approaching guardsmen.

The latter promptly began collapsing. Once down, they lay still, showing every indication of being in a deep sleep.

Botezul watched until he was sure the last guardsman was out of commission; then he got up, hauled Renny from the rear of the car, and began untying him. The gag was removed from his mouth.

"Dang you!" Renny snarled. "I dunno what your game is, but it's gonna be too bad for you if I get any kind of a chance to fight!"

Princess Gusta, whipping out of the machine on the opposite side, tried to run away in the darkness. Botezul overhauled her with great leaping strides, gathered her up and brought her back, kicking and squealing. The young woman's strength, not inconsiderable, had no effect on the huge fellow.

With Princess Gusta clamped tightly in his arms, Botezul looked at Renny. The glow from the automobile headlight illuminated him faintly.

Renny did not look at Botezul; he was staring at the recumbent guardsmen. Being on the sedan floorboards during hostilities, he had not seen what had occurred.

Suddenly, coming from all the darkness, its source traceable to no particular spot, there drifted a low trilling sound. It filtered up and down the musical scale, melodious but without tune. The quality of ventriloquism it seemed to possess was eerie.

"Doc!" Renny howled, astonished.

The big-fisted engineer knew this sound was peculiar to Doc Savage alone—the small, unconscious thing which the bronze man did at various times. Just now the strange trilling probably meant that Doc was elated.

For Botezul, the swarthy giant, was Doc Savage in disguise.

DOC waved a dark-dyed hand in the general direction of the guardsmen. "Anaesthetic balls," he explained. "The wind blew the stuff away from us and over them. They'll be unconscious for an hour, at least."

"Holy cow!" Renny got to his feet. "That brawl, in the street, when you stepped in and made a hit with Princess Gusta—"

"Was deliberately staged," Doc explained. "The beggar who hit you with the crutch and the others were agents loaned to me by Conte Cozonac. They were members of the Revolutionary party."

Princess Gusta, still in the grip of Doc's corded arms, stopped struggling. Doc planted her on her feet.

"You—are Doc Savage!" she gasped.

By way of answering her, Doc removed a black wig, the coarse hair of which had hung down and concealed the unchangeable flake-gold of his eyes. From either nostril he removed a metal shell which had given a flatness to the whole nose. Wax padding came out of his mouth.

"The skin dye," he told her, "has to be removed with a chemical."

"Oh!" gasped the young woman. "You are really—Doc Savage!"

Then she burst into tears, just as she had done aboard the liner *Seaward* upon learning of Doc's supposed untimely demise when the mystery blast destroyed the launch.

Renny rubbed his wrists where Botezul—Doc—had tied him.

"What was the idea of grabbin' me?" he asked ruefully. "I figured I was gettin' along pretty good."

"You were," Doc assured him. "But did you know that Captain Flancul had a heavy guard posted at his door?"

"Heck, no!"

"There was one. By grabbing you, I believed it possible to get the king, Princess Gusta, and Captain Flancul in a group."

"It worked out that way."

Doc nodded. "It was my idea to use anaesthetic gas on them. But Captain Flancul suggested this trip to the citadel, so I merely postponed seizing them until we had left town."

Renny sighed. "Well, we've got our three prizes, Doc. That means the trouble in Calbia is just about over."

"You may be a little optimistic," Doc told him.

"Whatcha mean?"

"Johnny and Long Tom are doing a little scouting quite a few miles from this spot," Doc explained. "You see, I've been keeping in touch with them. Their report may give you quite a shock, Renny."

"Shock! What kind?"

Doc nodded toward the sedan. The scars on his features, put there with makeup, did not seem nearly so fearsome as they had before.

"We'd better get out of here with King Le Galbin, Captain Flancul and the princess. Time for explanations later."

Princess Gusta Le Galbin climbed meekly into the machine when told to do so. With Doc at the wheel, the car moved away, leaving the vicinity of the unconscious escort of guardsmen.

Chapter XVIII
THE TERROR CACHE

LONG TOM, the electrical wizard, had a face so pale that it was inclined to show up in the darkness like the features of a ghost. To get rid of this undesirable phenomenon, he had rubbed the end of a burned cork over his lineaments, darkening them. As an added precaution, he wore dark clothing.

Johnny, the gaunt geologist and the man of big words, also wore dark attire.

The two men were picking their way furtively down a Calbian mountain road. Fir trees were thick along the way, their branches almost interlacing overhead. This, coupled with the cloudiness of the night, made it very dark.

Somewhere in the distance, a dog barked. Long Tom and Johnny both came to a prompt halt. They knew that a man, prowling through the night, is prone to stop and listen to such sounds, especially if his nocturnal mission is of a sinister nature.

The electrical wizard and the geologist were following such an individual. It was Muta they trailed.

Long Tom and Johnny had been assigned their task before Renny flew away from Conte Cozonac's camp to play the part of Champ Dugan, the daredevil Yankee air man from China. Doc Savage's instructions to them had been simple.

"Just hang around, wandering over the countryside, letting no one see you—and turn up whatever you can," the bronze man had suggested. "Do not go near the revolutionist army or Conte Cozonac."

"Look for some sign of Baron Mendl's doo-dad, eh?" asked Long Tom.

"That's it. And anything else interesting."

For two days, it had seemed to Long Tom and Johnny that they were going to unearth nothing of value. Then, only a few hours ago, they had discovered Muta. The ugly dwarf had apparently been in hiding near the camp of the revolutionists.

Muta's lurking place was in a rather substantial farm house which, among other things, was equipped with a telephone. Whether or not Muta had received orders over this phone and was now on his way to comply with them, Long Tom and Johnny did not know. But they were certain that Muta was bent on some mission which boded no good.

The dog stopped barking and the footsteps ahead resumed. The dwarf was moving onward. Doc's two men trailed him.

"My hypothesis is that yonder renegade is a spy," offered big-worded Johnny in a wispy whisper.

"Yeah," Long Tom agreed. "He's probably been scoutin' the revolutionist forces. Man, I sure favor crawlin' that sawed-off runt!"

"Doc advocated that we refrain from apprehending him," Johnny said regretfully.

Slung in a knapsack on his back, Long Tom carried a portable radio outfit. It was with this that he had informed Doc Savage—who was playing the part of Botezul, the swarthy Calbian mountaineer—that Muta had been discovered. Doc had returned instructions to follow Muta, noting every move the thick, squat rascal made.

THE road which Long Tom and Johnny trod became narrower, rough, and more steep. Rocks underfoot, scattered at first, grew more plentiful.

"Wait!" Long Tom breathed. "We're liable to step on a rock and make a noise that the runt will hear."

From the back pack which held the radio set, Long Tom produced a pair of headphones and another apparatus which, when assembled, bore likeness to nothing so much as a college cheer-

The dwarf ... sprawled in the chair ... seemed almost as large as a normal man ...

leader's megaphone. This latter was actually a highly sensitive microphone which, connected to the audio-amplifier in the radio receiver and certain supplementary coils and tubes, was set into the headphones.

With this contrivance Long Tom could pick up faint sounds over a long distance.

The two trailers dropped back nearly a hundred yards, and followed Muta by the aid of Long Tom's electrical "listener" alone. Even if they would inadvertently turn a pebble, Muta was unlikely to hear it.

"I wonder what's become of Monk and Ham?" Long Tom pondered.

"Problematical," murmured Johnny.

"We haven't seen 'em since they jumped out of the plane with parachutes before we landed at Conte Cozonac's camp," Long Tom breathed. "Monk had the pig, Habeas Corpus, under his arm. I hope they got down all right."

"You have my concurrence in that wish," returned Johnny.

"Blast it!" Long Tom whispered. "We don't even know what mission Doc sent 'em on. I guess it's just as well. If the Royalists should grab us, we couldn't tell 'em where Monk and Ham are. That was a good idea of Doc's—all of us workin' separate."

"What about our nefarious quarry?" Johnny queried.

"Muta? He's still goin' straight ahead."

Then they fell silent, since it was not particularly diverting to conduct a conversation in whispers. They dared speak no louder, lest they be heard.

The clouds parted overhead momentarily, allowing silver moonlight to flood down, and this illuminated the roadway which they were traveling. It was a strange sort of a thoroughfare.

What they had thought merely a profusion of pebbles they saw now was actually the remains of a cobblestone pavement, which exposure through countless years had caused to separate, the mortar disintegrating. The road did not show signs of having been used much. Certainly, no wheeled vehicles had traveled this way for a long time.

There was timber about them, a thick tangle of woods. The ancient road twisted through this, mounting steadily upward.

Long Tom moved to one side, climbed atop a great boulder and strained his eyes to peer through the moonlight.

"*Pss-st!*" he hissed softly, summoning Johnny. "Look up on the mountain above us. You can just make it out. Quick, before a cloud comes over the moon."

Far above them was a ragged hump, unmistakably manmade in its contours. They could tell little about it, except that the edifice was of stone.

Clouds shuttering out the moonlight allowed no further inspection.

"Wonder if that's where we're headed for?" Long Tom pondered. His guess was correct. Muta led them directly to the place.

LONG TOM and Johnny had thought at first that the shapeless structure was a ruined castle or an ancient fortress. It turned out to be neither of these.

The building was a great, rambling stone house, surrounded by a high wall. This wall had been torn away in places, apparently by Calbians who wanted to use the stone in other structures, and this had given the ragged outline as viewed from below.

The house itself was not abandoned, but in a fair state of repair. The wall must have been torn away long ago, during a period when the place was untenanted.

Back of the house, Long Tom and Johnny perceived, as the shifting clouds let through more moonlight, a stretch of flat country which, in the western United States, would have been called a mesa. The lighted windows of a few farmhouses glowed on this plain.

Windows of the rambling old house were also alight. An opening door made a rectangular panel in the darkness, and Muta, entering, was silhouetted in it.

"This is where he was headed for!" Long Tom darted forward. "Come on! Let's see what's up."

They ran forward, glancing frequently upward to make sure no telltale moonlight was likely to break through the clouds. When the clouds did part, the two men dropped flat in the grass which, luckily, was knee-high.

The stone house had wide eaves, and these offered a shelter. They crouched close to the cold stone and shifted sidewise to a window. The room beyond was empty, so they tried another. Then they saw Muta.

The dwarf had sprawled in a chair. Sitting thus, he seemed almost as large as a normal man, due to his tremendous torso.

Three other men were present in the room. They wore the uniforms of Conte Cozonac's revolutionary party, complete even to the red-ball insignia on the right sleeve.

Long Tom and Johnny studied these men intently.

"Say, I've seen them before," Long Tom breathed, softly. "They were in the revolutionist camp the night we landed. Blast it, one of 'em is a member of Conte Cozonac's staff."

"Spies!" Johnny whispered.

"Sure, imagine that! Say, the fat Conte Cozonac is gonna have a spasm when he learns one of his own staff is a Royalist."

The two prepared to listen in, having acquired by now a slight understanding of the Calbian language. They did this simply by creeping to the door and clamping the mouth of Long Tom's supersensitive pickup microphone to the keyhole. The lock of this door had been made for a medieval iron key, and the keyhole was large.

MUTA was speaking.

"I tell you we must find how Doc Savage caused the explosion to occur a quarter of a mile behind his plane that night," the dwarf shrilled.

"I have put many questions to different soldiers in the revolutionary army," said a voice which Long Tom and Johnny recognized as belonging to the member of Conte Cozonac's staff. "When he landed, Doc Savage would offer no explanation. No one could give any information."

Muta swore fluently, and said, "This matter is of vital importance. If Doc Savage has a defense against our weapon, we must know what it is."

"An effective defense against the device might conceivably defeat our cause," agreed the staff officer.

Long Tom put his lips close to Johnny's ear and breathed, "They're discussin' the contraption that causes the mysterious explosions—the mystery weapon that Baron Damitru Mendl invented."

"We must dispose of that bronze man," Muta grated. "He is entirely too dangerous."

"That should be simple," replied the member of the revolutionist staff. "We have merely to tip King Dal Le Galbin that Doc Savage and that engineer who has the enormous hands are both in the royal castle at San Blazna."

"True," admitted Muta. "But Doc Savage was tricked into coming from the United States to do certain work for us. We must not interfere until it is completed. He suspects nothing. It will be a simple matter to slay him when the time comes."

"I hope so," mumbled the other, "but this Doc Savage is more clever than it seems possible for any man to be."

These words were giving Long Tom and Johnny something to think about. Muta, so they had thought, was one of the men of King Dal Le Galbin, yet the fellow knew Doc Savage was in San Blazna, knew Renny was there, too—and he had not divulged the information to the Calbian monarch.

"This is gettin' me dizzy," Long Tom breathed.

"Doc tricked into coming from New York!" Johnny whispered, forgetting his large words. "I don't get it, either!"

Inside the stone house, Muta resumed speaking.

"There is another point which worries me. What has become of the rest of Doc Savage's men?—the homely chemist, Monk; that lawyer, Ham; and the other two, the geologist and the electrical expert?"

"They seem to have disappeared completely," said the staff officer.

"I do not like that!" Muta growled. "Those men are all clever individuals far above the ordinary in intelligence. Working with that bronze man who is actually a mental wizard and a muscular marvel, as the Americans claim, they form an extremely dangerous combination."

"But Doc Savage does not suspect the true situation," the staff member reminded.

"And lucky for us that he does not," Muta agreed.

THERE was a brief pause in the conversation. Long Tom and Johnny spent the interval wondering just exactly what it was all about. Their theories were completely upset.

Instead of Doc Savage simply coming to Calbia to remove a tyrant king from power so that he himself might assume the throne until the country was peaceable, there seemed to be more mysterious ramifications. Doc, it appeared, instead of being completely in command of the situation, had been out-guessed, was being used as a tool by the sinister dwarf and whoever was associated with him.

"Blazes!" Long Tom breathed. "I'd better try to raise Doc by radio and warn him."

"Wait," Johnny whispered back.

Voices within the house had resumed.

"How is the work progressing?" Muta inquired.

"In excellent fashion," said a voice—it was not the staff officer this time, but one of the others. "Nearly one hundred of the devices are ready for use. As you know, we were awaiting certain ingredients necessary for the mixing of the explosive. The last complete machine we wasted in a futile attempt to destroy Doc Savage's plane."

"The materials for the explosives came?" Muta demanded.

"Last night. They were brought by plane."

"Nearly a hundred of them ready, eh?" Muta laughed harshly. "They will make short work of this revolution. It is to be regretted that we will have to use them, though. They should have been held in reserve for the future war—the war which we will wage once we have control of the government of Calbia."

One of the other men made a tongue-clicking sound of sympathetic agreement, and said, "If we use them now, the countries adjacent to Calbia will learn of this terrific weapon which we have in our possession."

"That might be an advantage, after all," Muta replied. "Knowledge of the existence of this weapon will play upon the minds of the people of those countries, and perhaps make our conquest much easier."

Long Tom, whispering close to Johnny's ear, advised, "What we've heard gives us the motive behind all this. The ring is tryin' to seize the throne of Calbia. Then they plan to gobble up the surroundin' countries, using their infernal machine as the power."

"The villain at the head of it must have a Napoleonic complex," Johnny replied.

In the house, Muta grunted, "I think I'll look at the machines you have ready."

There was a scraping of chairs, a clatter of feet, then a thump, the nature of which Long Tom and Johnny failed to comprehend immediately.

Long Tom scuttled to the window and looked in. The room was empty.

Chapter XIX
THE SHOCK

JOHNNY joined Long Tom, and together they swept the room with their eyes. They did not discern a sign of the late occupants.

"Let us invade the premises," the bony geologist breathed. Long Tom said, "We oughta get Doc on the radio an' tell him—"

"Later," said Johnny, who had spent the last few days in wearisome scouting, and who now craved action. "I'm going in."

"I'm with you, guy!"

They tried the door; it was not locked, and opened without undue effort. On tiptoe they crossed the floor, then circled, searching.

"That thump we heard—it must've been a secret door," Long Tom whispered.

The electrical wizard sank to his knees and began to scrutinize the boards of the floor. Johnny, using his monocle magnifier, inspected the thick stone walls. It was he who found the concealed door.

Cleverly made, the panel resembled the stone of the walls. He grasped rough ends of the rock, tugged, and only succeeded in breaking his fingernails.

Long Tom rapidly thrust and yanked at other flinty projections, one of these proving to be a catch. Pushing it, the panel flew open. It was perhaps two feet wide and about four high.

A man was standing on the other side of the panel—the staff officer. He had a gun in one hand, and the instant the panel opened he shot Johnny at a spot six inches above the belt buckle. Johnny grunted loudly, folded his bony frame in the middle, jacknife fashion, and fell to the floor. He rolled, kicking and squirming.

The staff officer then swerved his gun at Long Tom.

The electrical expert hurled the megaphonelike pickup mike which he was carrying. Hitting him squarely in the face, the device upset the fellow. His arms flailed out, and he fell backward down a flight of narrow, steep steps, which descended from the secret opening. He screamed once on the way down, and his gun discharged twice.

With a flying leap, Long Tom went after him. He landed on the fellow, feet-first; but there was no need of that. The officer had cracked his head on the way down, and was out cold.

Johnny appeared at the top of the steps, still doubled over. He wobbled half the way down, fell the rest of the distance, and, remarkably enough, hit on his feet.

"Oh-h-h!" he groaned, both skeleton-thin arms wrapped across his chest. "I've got on one of Doc's bulletproof vests, but darned if it feels like it helped much."

"You should have some flesh under the vest for a pad," Long Tom snorted.

Leaning down, he cracked the staff officer over the head with the fellow's own gun to prolong unconsciousness. Then he lunged down a passage which angled away to the left.

UNBENDING himself a little, Johnny followed Long Tom. They ran twenty feet, turned a corner, came to a stop.

A wall of mortared stone blocked their progress. Outwardly, the place seemed a blind panel.

"There must be another hidden door somewhere!" Long Tom rapped.

While his words still echoed, the floor dropped from under their feet. With a wild spring, Johnny sought to reach solid footing. He failed. For the whole length of the passage, the floor simply folded like a dropped leaf.

They fell no more than six feet, and hit water. Down they went, well over their heads. When they came up, sputtering and splashing, it was to find themselves in intense darkness. The trap door of the passage had closed over their heads.

Soon afterwards, there was a loud splashing—a roar of incoming water near by. They could plainly feel the swirl of the current.

"They got this thing fixed so they can flood it with water!" Long Tom yelled. "Man, are we in a jam!"

"Come!" Johnny barked. "Let's get to the far end of this thing."

They stroked furiously.

"You've got—a grenade?" Long Tom puffed.

"Right," said Johnny. "Maybe we can blow the floor out of this pit."

Gaining the extremity of the rapidly filling pit, they flattened against the wall. Grasping rough edges of stone, they hauled themselves up as far as possible out of the water, reasoning that the shock of the air would be less violent than the concussion made by the water. Handkerchiefs were ripped in half and stuffed into their ears.

Then Johnny threw his grenade. The concussion from the explosion was so terrific that their ears temporarily ceased to function, despite the precaution of the handkerchief. Their bodies felt as if numberless axes, chopping simultaneously, had tried to remove their flesh.

The water shoved up over their heads. With what strength they could muster, they stroked forward.

The trap door floor at the far end had been ripped open. Grasping the shattered edges, they clambered through, stumbled to the stairway, trampled over the unconscious form of the staff officer, and mounted.

"We're gonna—make it!" Long Tom gulped.

They staggered out into the upstairs room.

Two tear-gas bombs landed in front of them and opened with a sound which they barely heard, due to the effect of the grenade on their ears.

Muta had thrown the gas missiles from the door.

Long Tom and Johnny had no defense against the tear gas. Blinded, they tried to find the door.

Since they were without the use of their eyes, they failed to put up much of a fight, as Muta and his companions, protected by gas masks, seized and bound them.

THIRTY MINUTES elapsed before Long Tom and Johnny could use their eyes with any degree of success. The tear gas was not of the efficient type used by the American police, but seemed to contain ingredients other than the usual xylyl bromide. It made them violently ill for a time.

The staff officer had been revived. He stood with the stunted, evil Muta and the others, and scowled at the two prisoners.

Muta, puffing out his over-developed chest, jeered, "It seems that we meet again, and—"

"Dry up, you freak!" Long Tom gritted.

Muta's tone changed to a snarl as he continued where he had been interrupted: "—and I am to have one more try. I am disposing of you gentlemen. Listen, I will make you a proposition."

Long Tom blinked. "What?"

"If I fail to get rid of you this time, I will place my person in your hands, to do with as you see fit."

"Yeah," Long Tom sneered. "You'd do that!"

Muta shrugged.

Long Tom winked his still-aching eyes rapidly for a time, then for lack of anything else to say growled a threat. "It isn't lucky for yahoos like you to crack down on Doc Savage's friends."

"I am stricken with terror!" Muta laughed, and shivered dramatically.

"Which shows you don't know Doc Savage well enough yet," Long Tom told him grimly. "Furthermore, Conte Cozonac and this rebel army will also start huntin' for you if anything happens to us. You aren't liable to get away from 'em."

At this, Muta went into a gale of laughter. His mirth spread to the staff officer and the others. They all cackled like guineas.

"What's the joke?" Long Tom demanded.

"Wait," Muta suggested, and consulted a large turnip of a watch he drew from a pocket. "Yes—wait about five minutes."

No more was said during the interim. It was raining again. The drops pattered on the roof, and streams running from the eaves made sobbing and gurglings which, under the circumstances, struck Long Tom and Johnny as altogether unpleasant.

A rumble, hollow and reverberating, broke out in the distance. It was not thunder, but the noise of cannonading, as the revolutionist army and Royalists fought.

Footsteps splattered moistly outside. Muta himself opened the door.

Conte Cozonac walked in.

LONG TOM and Johnny stared at the fat leader of the revolutionists with popping eyes. Conte Cozonac was probably the last person they had expected to appear.

"Look what we have here," Muta grinned, and waved a short arm at the two captives.

"What happened, Muta?" Conte Cozonac demanded.

Long Tom gazed blankly at Johnny. The skeleton-thin archaeologist returned the look.

Conte Cozonac and Muta were co-conspirators!

In staccato Calbian, Muta told Conte Cozonac what had occurred.

The bulbous rebel chief scowled blackly throughout the recital. Then he stamped over and stood, various of his bulges shaking with rage, over Long Tom and Johnny. His usual trilling and cackling laughter was markedly absent.

"I want certain questions answered," he grated. "First, where are Doc Savage's other two men, Monk and Ham?"

"Blessed if we know," Long Tom retorted—truthfully.

The fat man teetered on his heels. His face was a study in rage and villainy.

"I am not going to try any melodramatic deceit," he said grimly. "You two fellows are to be shot; but first, you are going to tell me where my men can get Monk and Ham."

Long Tom wet his lips. "So you think."

With a swift gesture for such a fat man, Conte Cozonac kicked the electrical expert in what is probably the tenderest part of the human body—the throat.

Long Tom moaned and made hacking sounds, and groveled on the floor, but could do nothing because of his bindings. He was tied with braided cotton cords.

"Take them into the underground room," Conte Cozonac commanded.

Muta and the others lifted the two prisoners and bore them to the concealed door, through it, and down the narrow steps.

Conte Cozonac, following, snarled, "They must be disposed of, but first they must answer my questions."

Chapter XX
TALE OF DECEIT

A FEW miles from the Calbian capital city of San Blazna, Doc Savage was making a statement which did not differ greatly from the latter half of Conte Cozonac's speech.

"First, you had better answer some of my questions," the bronze man was telling Princess Gusta Le Galbin. "Then I will put your mind at rest about your present position."

King Dal Le Galbin and Captain Henri Flancul had regained consciousness, although both were still slightly dizzy from the effects of Doc's blows.

"You have seized us and are going to turn us over to the revolutionists!" the Calbian ruler shouted wrathfully.

Doc Savage ignored him. "Why did you and

Captain Henri Flancul come to New York, princess?" he asked.

The young woman studied the bronze man by the glow which the car dashlight diffused backward. The machine was nosing down a little-used country thoroughfare. The rain on the top made sounds like dozens of mice scampering, and the twin windshield wipers *swick-swucked* in concert. Water was pooled in the road, and flew away in lazy sheets from the impact of the wheels.

"Some years ago, Baron Damitru Mendl invented a fearsome weapon of warfare," the young woman stated. "The plan for that weapon—there was only one in existence—was locked in the vaults of the Calbian war department."

"Conte Cozonac told us that," big-fisted Renny put in.

"There was an understanding with Baron Mendl," continued the young woman. "This weapon was not to be used, or manufactured, except in the defense of Calbia."

"Baron Damitru Mendl had retired from the inventing business?"

Princess Gusta nodded. "He was given his title of baron as a gesture of appreciation for his scientific works. He grew interested in politics and became Calbian ambassador to the United States. He was very efficient."

"In what particular branch of science did Baron Mendl specialize?" Doc asked abruptly.

"A study of light."

"Hm-m-m. The science of light, I thought so. Well, go on with your explanation of why you went to New York."

Big-fisted Renny, listening, would rather have delved deeper into the relation of Baron Damitru Mendl's study of the physics of light to the mystery weapon which he had invented. Renny smelled the beginning of an explanation of the nature of the weird, terrible explosions which destroyed airplanes, boats, automobiles, railway engines, and even men cooking around a campfire.

"Some weeks ago the plans of Baron Damitru Mendl's invention vanished from the Calbian war department vaults," said Princess Gusta.

"HAVE you any idea who stole the plan?" Doc questioned.

Captain Henri Flancul took it on himself to answer that. "No idea whatever," he stated.

Doc's golden eyes, shifting briefly from the milky mixture of headlight glare and raindrops ahead, rested upon Captain Flancul.

"So you and Princess Gusta came to New York to get duplicate plans from Baron Damitru Mendl. Is that it?" he inquired.

"Da," agreed the young woman. "Yes. We

cabled him, and he said he would give us duplicate plans."

"Holy cow!" Renny rumbled abruptly. "The fat guy, Conte Cozonac, said Baron Damitru Mendl was with the revolutionists."

"Conte Cozonac," Doc said dryly, "was a remarkable liar."

"Before Captain Flancul and myself reached New York—while our liner was still at sea—we received a radiogram from Baron Mendl," Princess Gusta went on. "It informed us that you were aiding the rebels."

Doc watched the road, his metallic features immobile.

"Baron Mendl was wrong. That dwarf, Muta, visited my office disguised as an old lady. He must have deceived Baron Mendl into thinking I was an enemy."

King Dal Le Galbin kept an attentive ear upon the conversation, but was saying nothing.

Captain Henri Flancul occupied a corner of the rear seat, scowling.

"Baron Mendl was murdered before we reached New York," the young woman stated. "We did not get his secret. We determined to seize you, Doc Savage, and hold you. We did not want one of your ability aiding the rebels."

Doc wheeled the car into a side road, guided it carefully through a hundred yards of bad mud, and stopped before a dilapidated hut. The profusion of tall weeds, the lack of beaten paths, indicated that the shack had been abandoned for some time.

"We stop here," he said.

Renny had been thinking things over. Now he emitted a rumble of comprehension.

"I'm beginnin' to see how this stacks up. Holy cow! That lardy lug, Conte Cozonac, and the midget, Muta, must belong to the same gang!"

THEY got out of the car in a rain that beat their shoulders and ran wetly against their faces. Doc's bronze hair—he had discarded the black wig which he had worn when disguised as the giant, Botezul—seemed impervious to the moisture.

"But Doc," Renny continued, "what was the idea of Conte Cozonac tellin' us that string of lies about wantin' our help?"

"He had two reasons, it would seem," Doc replied. "First, by getting into our confidence and making us think that he wanted our help, he was in a position to know our every move, and therefore stood a better chance of disposing of us. Secondly, the clever rascal saw where we could actually be of assistance to him—he wanted us to seize King Dal Le Galbin here, Princess Gusta, and Captain Henri Flancul."

"That fat guy ain't no slouch as a schemer,"

Renny boomed. "When did you get wise to him, Doc?"

"The first definite clue was the attempt to destroy us with the mystery weapon, just before we arrived at the revolutionist military camp. Only Conte Cozonac and his men knew we were coming."

They moved on toward the rickety shack.

King Dal Le Galbin, the previous rage now entirely absent from his voice, put a question. "Just whose side are you on in this affair?"

"You might call it my own side," Doc said quietly. "I am here to get this mystery weapon and render it useless."

"You mean—destroy it?"

Doc ignored that. "My other purpose is to stop the bloodshed of this revolution. That can best be done by eliminating the ringleaders."

"Conte Cozonac and Muta?" the ruler of Calbia queried.

Doc opened the door of the shack. "And possibly some others," he said in answer.

"Others?" the king insisted.

"Conte Cozonac is not a wealthy man, as an investigation of his past life shows," Doc said. "Muta, the dwarf, is a plain criminal, and not rich."

"I fail to see what you mean."

"These revolutionists have fighting planes and other modern weapons of war. Did they capture them from your Royalist forces?"

King Dal Le Galbin's vehement headshake was visible as Doc thumbed on a flashlight. "They have captured very few weapons," he answered.

"There you are," Doc told him. "Their equipment cost money, a great deal of money. Some man, or men, of wealth are backing them. That man, or men, we must identify and seize."

"Holy cow!" Renny thumped. "Then Conte Cozonac and Muta ain't the big shots behind this!"

ALTHOUGH extremely ramshackle, the hut possessed a waterproof roof, and the interior was fairly dry. The woodwork had been torn out. In one end hay was stored, old and brown hay.

Doc Savage went to this, moved a portion of it aside, and exposed a portable radio outfit.

"I have been coming to this shack at certain hours each day," he advised. "At those times, Monk and Ham make their reports."

"Monk! Ham!" Renny rumbled. "I ain't seen 'em since they left our plane by parachute!"

"They have been keeping undercover."

"Doing what?" Renny asked.

"Trailing Conte Cozonac. That is, they've done it as best they could while keeping themselves out of sight."

Captain Henri Flancul stepped forward, and executed a precise military bow.

"May I," he said, "offer sincere apologies for my past attitude toward you, Mr. Savage? It would seem that in my zeal to aid Calbia I have been opposing one of her best friends."

King Dal Le Galbin drew himself up as if to follow the same procedure as had Captain Henri Flancul, but a thought moved him to pause.

"Why, in view of your knowledge of Conte Cozonac's deceit," he asked, "did you go through with the kidnaping of my daughter, Captain Flancul, and myself?"

Doc was working over the radio set. "That, you will understand later," he replied.

"You mean that the three of us are actually still your prisoners?" the king ejaculated.

"If the fact that you must remain in my company makes you prisoners—yes."

Renny's great voice vibrated in the shack. "Say, Doc, I don't see—"

The bronze man held up a hand, a gesture for silence. Then he flipped a switch which put the radio loudspeaker into circuit. Low, monotonous words came from the speaker.

"Calling Doc Savage—calling Doc Savage—calling Doc Savage."

It was Monk's childlike voice.

Doc cut the transmitter in circuit, adjusted knobs until the radiation was satisfactory, then spoke into the compact mike.

"All right, Monk," he said.

"Been tryin' to get you for five minutes," Monk stated excitedly over the airwaves. "We been keepin' our eyes on Conte Cozonac. Tonight, he sneaked away from the rebel camp and went to an old stone house on top of a mountain. He met Muta there."

"Yes," Doc said, "but why the excitement?"

"Under that old house somewhere, there must be hidden rooms," Monk explained. "We been eavesdroppin'. This old house is the plant where them infernal machines are bein' manufactured."

"Give me the location of the place," Doc directed.

"You ain't heard the worst yet, Doc. They've got Long Tom and Johnny." Then Monk rapidly gave the location of the old house.

Doc reached for the master switch, which controlled the radio. "Their lives in danger, Monk?" he queried.

"Conte Cozonac was goin' to question 'em first—"

"Monk, you and Ham do what you can," Doc directed. "Try to hold out, if it won't put Long Tom and Johnny in too tough a spot, until I get there."

"You're coming out, Doc?"

"Right out."

Doc switched off the radio.

Chapter XXI
THE DEATH STEEPLE CHASE

RENNY, long face set, jaw out, lumbered for the door. "My plane—at the airport, Doc! We can use that!" he cried.

"Fine!" Doc snapped the lid down on the radio case, then began tearing at the pile of hay in the end of the shack. "It's only a few minutes' run from here to the airport."

From the hay, he withdrew one of his metal equipment cases. Renny looked for the identifying number on the case. He knew the numerals on most of them, and the contents each number signified. Number 4, for instance, was gas bombs, and 13, fittingly enough, was the one which always held Doc's little supermachine pistols and ammunition drums—these were bad luck for anyone.

But the number had been painted out on this case, the case Doc now held.

King Dal Le Galbin demanded, "Do you wish us to go with you?"

Captain Henri Flancul said, "I prefer to tackle this thing side by side with Mr. Savage, from now on."

"My sentiments also," said the ruler of Calbia. He made a fighting jaw. "It has been a long time since I had any real excitement. I believe I shall get a kick out of this."

They ran toward the car, Doc Savage carrying his two boxes—the radio case, and the metal equipment container which bore no identifying numerals.

"We will leave Princess Gusta in the car at the airport," he said. "Some of the Royalist army pilots will escort her back to the palace."

"You will do nothing of the kind," the young woman declared. "I shall see this thing through with the rest of you."

Doc slid under the car wheel, clicked on the lights, then extinguished his own flash, which had been giving illumination. Then he turned in his seat to eye the elder Le Galbin.

"You had better convince her that she should remain behind," he suggested.

There was argument in the back seat as the car wallowed and moaned through the mud. Rain sheeted the windshield, and the wipers raced until it seemed they would tear themselves off.

The machine topped a hill, a sharp little rise, and for twenty feet beyond all four wheels were off the ground. They traveled over black asphalt pavement, which had probably come from Calbian oil wells, there being rich petroleum fields in certain sections of the little kingdom.

The car alternatingly lunged and slackened speed, as straight stretches and curves were traversed.

"You, Gusta, are a young lady, and as such have no business with us tonight," the King of Calbia was insisting in the rear.

"Rats!" Gusta retorted. "Less than a month ago I heard you say in a speech that women should be allowed to do anything that men do."

"That was just a speech," snapped her parent. "Furthermore, it was spoken before the Calbian National Women's Suffrage League, and was just to make them feel good."

Doc applied the brakes, and tires shrieked on the wet pavement. The machine skidded, careened into the airport, and excited sentries popped out of their boxes, shouting; *Opriti! Cine este acolo?* Stop! Who is there?"

Renny barked half a dozen orders, assuming the character of Champ Dugan, the Yankee buzzard from China who was going to do big things with the Calbian air force.

Mechanics ran to wheel his plane out of a hangar.

Doc and the others got out of the car. The bronze man indicated Princess Gusta. "Is she going?"

"It seems she is," her royal parent sighed. "She out-talked me."

RENNY'S big plane, with the Chinese dragon painted upon it, was, fortunately, fueled. A horde of Calbian mechanics wheeled it out into the drizzling rain.

Doc took the controls. The engines were equipped with electric starters, operated by dash buttons, and he thumbed the latter. Exhaust stacks spat sparks, then lipped blue flame as the cylinders warmed.

The Calbian Royal Air Force mechanics stood around, staring and whispering, no doubt trying to tell each other what it was all about.

Princess Gusta scrambled into the plane, as if apprehensive of being left behind after all.

While the engines were warming, Doc clipped the radio telephone headset over his ears, tuned the transmitter to the wavelength of Monk's outfit, and sent out a call.

"Yes, Doc," came Monk's small voice through the ether.

"We're taking off in a plane and should be with you before long," Doc advised him. "How are things up there?"

"Ham is inside the house and down underground somewhere," Monk replied. "We're using Habeas Corpus to carry messages back and forth between us."

"What about Long Tom and Johnny?"

"Conte Cozonac and Muta are questionin' them tryin' to find out where Ham and I are. Long Tom and Johnny are stallin'."

Doc Savage signaled with an arm thrust through the cockpit window. Mechanics grasped short ropes tied to the wheel clocks and yanked the blocks out. Doc advanced the three throttles, and the engine clatter became a banshee howl.

The plane rolled and the tail lifted. The undercarriage jarred for a while; then that ceased. They were in the air.

The big amphibian headed directly for the mountains. The metal propellers, colliding with raindrops, made a wild note. There were no lighted windows in San Blazna, due to the fear of a rebel air raid. There was only blackness where the capital city lay.

Speaking into the radio mike, Doc queried, "Are you sure Johnny and Long Tom are to be killed eventually?"

The motor roar caused Monk's reply to sound very faint. "Sure. Conte Cozonac and Muta have said so half a dozen times, according to the notes Ham is sending me by Habeas."

"Don't let the thing get too far along before you interfere."

"We won't. I'm behind the wall near the house. Don't dare get any nearer, or they might hear me usin' this radio outfit."

Doc discerned a light in a farmhouse window below, and used it to check the side drift of the plane, after which he consulted the compass, the altimeter, and then corrected their course slightly.

"Can we land near the place, Monk?" he asked over the radio.

"Yeah," Monk replied. "The top of this mountain is flat, kind of a mesa. There's a barley field or somethin' about a quarter of a mile away. We found it when we trailed Conte Cozonac here."

"I'll show a light when we're over the spot," Doc told him. "Return the signal with your flash, indicating the direction of the field."

"Sure."

THE plane pointed its baying nose at the heavens and climbed rapidly. The altimeter needle ran past seven thousand feet, ten, twelve. Doc studied the air speed, then the dash clock, calculating their progress.

"Here's something new," came Monk's wee voice. "The pig just brought another note from Ham. Long Tom and Johnny are trying to pump Conte Cozonac. They got the fat guy mad, and he admitted he's not the real brains behind this."

"Did he let slip who his boss is?"

"No."

Once more, Doc Savage eyed the air-speed indicator and instrument board clock. The markings were in luminous paint, readable with the lights off. Doc cut the ignition switches, and all three motors went silent. The plane tilted in a gentle dive.

"We'll glide down, so they won't hear us," he announced loudly, for the benefit of the others in the plane.

Leaning close to the radio mike, he called, "Monk!"

"Yeah!"

"I'm going to blink the plane lights now—the landing lights. Look up and see if you can—"

"Doc! Doc!" Monk yelled. "There was a shot in the house! Something's happened! I'm goin' in!"

After that, no more words came over the radio.

Doc stood the plane on its nose. The gentle hissing of its descent became a mad scream of air past struts and flying surfaces. The altimeter needle retreated so swiftly that its movement was plainly discernible.

"Pitch out a parachute flare, Renny!" Doc called.

Renny boomed, "But I thought—"

"We had bad luck," Doc interrupted. "The thing didn't hold. Monk heard a shot in the house and has gone in to join Ham."

"O. K.." Renny got a 'chute flare out of a rack, wrenched the sliding window back, twisted the flare igniter and tossed it out. An instant later they flew through a rain-streaked glare.

The earth was only a few hundred feet below; falling rain made it hazy, unreal. Doc let the altimeter crawl back a bit more, then flattened and swung in a tight, moaning bank.

The flare, following them down, made lustre enough to show the barley field which Monk had mentioned.

The big amphibian all but turned sidewise in the sky as Doc fish-tailed away speed. His passengers gripped the seats to prevent being thrown into the aisles, and they hardly had time to straighten themselves before the ship slammed down, bounced, settled, and, wheel brakes squeaking, slowed to a stop.

DOC cut the engine ignition.

Above the rattle of rain on the skin of fuselage and wings they could hear shots, the rappings drifting from the stone house.

"Out!" Doc commanded.

Renny was first through the cabin door. Captain Henri Flancul followed him, then Princess Gusta and her father.

Before he left the amphibian, Doc Savage scooped up the metal case which carried no telltale numerals. He opened it, worked with the contents, then closed it and took the case to the rear. He thrust the box far back in the fuselage.

It was very dark, for the flare had dropped and extinguished itself. The others had not seen what he was doing.

Renny, curious about the delay, began, "What are—"

"Let's go!" Doc ran forward.

Such was the bronze man's speed that he left the others behind almost immediately. He had his flashlight out, the beam leaping ahead, spotting obstacles.

Its radiance was hazy in the rain, a nebulous elongation that might have been a will-o'-the-wisp.

Doc vaulted a fence, tore through brush, then waded through knee-high grass.

The stone house lunged up out of the darkness like an immobile monster. The windows were shapeless red blotches, the door a longer smear of brightness. Doc, aware the sounds had ceased, veered through the door.

No men were in the room. And Doc, looking, saw that all doors were closed.

The pig was reared up against one wall, squealing, sniffing and pawing like a dog. His performance was full of meaning.

Doc went to the spot in which the pig was interested. He took only a split second to locate the secret door.

When the panel was opened, Habeas grunted loudly and dived through. The impact of his feet on the stone steps was a staccato rattle which blended as almost one sound.

Doc raked his flash beam along the passage. At his feet were lumps of rent masonry. Planks had been spread over a hole in the floor—a hole opened by Long Tom and Johnny's grenade, although Doc had as yet no way of knowing that.

The bronze man stepped over the boards bridging the aperture, and went on, coming to the blank end. One glance told him what Long Tom and Johnny had failed to realize: there was no secret door in this end. The stone wall was solid.

Stooping swiftly, Doc grabbed Habeas Corpus by the handiest projection—one winglike ear. Carrying the shoat, the bronze man started back toward the steps.

Somewhere in the passage, there must be a hidden aperture, he thought. Habeas' action had shown that Monk must have gone down the stairs.

Doc eyed the plank-covered hole in the floor, intending to investigate it first. He had taken only a few steps when the hinged floor went down.

Chapter XXII
LOCKED ROOM

PRECEDING the folding of the trapdoor floor, there was a faint click and grate of machinery. Slight this was, but coupled with Doc's quick reasoning that the blind passage had some significance, it was sufficient to warn him.

The passage was narrow. Doc twisted, jumped, and planted his feet against one wall. His shoulders slammed against the other wall. The stone was rough, and he managed to wedge there.

When the trap was down, his flashlight showed the water pit beneath.

He began to work for the stairs. It would have been a slow, laborious task for ordinary muscles, but the bronze man was not in that category. He gained the solidity of the steps just as a slab of stone, ostensibly part of the passage wall, hinged back.

Conte Cozonac looked out. It was doubtful if the fat man even saw Doc, for a bronze mallet of a fist, lashing against his face, was large enough to cover mouth, nose and eyes completely. The revolutionist leader was driven backward so forcibly that his arms whipped around and stuck out straight in front of him.

He went down heavily, and momentum lifted his heels into the air. They came back to the floor with a distinct crack. Crimson seeped from Cozonac's pulped lips and unshaped nose.

The big-bodied dwarf, Muta, was standing behind Conte Cozonac, but managed to dodge with a terrier alacrity. He held a gun, fired it while still in the air. It was an unaimed bullet, and went wild. The report was ear-splitting in the confines of the narrow stone corridor which led, at a gentle slope, downward.

Muta's leap carried him forcibly against the wall, and this ruined his second shot. There was no third. The midget was scooped up, held with a steel-banded efficiency, and the gun was literally milked from his clutch by bronze fingers.

Carrying the hideous little dwarf, Doc charged forward. He held Muta's gun ready. The bronze man rarely employed firearms in personal combat, his reason being that he considered reliance on a gun bad policy.

The passage veered and opened into a large room. A man in the uniform of a revolutionist waited there, with a pistol. He had the weapon ready, but did not fire at once for fear of hitting Muta, who was clamped in front of Doc's chest, a kicking, screeching, rather ineffective shield. The soldier shifted his pistol, endeavoring to get a bead on Doc's skull.

The gun Doc had taken from Muta whacked an earsplitting thunder. The soldier's arm folded as if it had acquired an extra joint between wrist and elbow. The pistol slipped from between his fingers.

Doc, lunging on into the room, swept him aside. He glimpsed Monk, Johnny, Long Tom and Ham arrayed along the wall, each bound securely.

TWO men in the regalia of the rebel forces—the officer who belonged to Conte Cozonac's staff, and one other—were running forward. They grasped automatics which had barrels almost as long and thin as pencils.

The subterranean chamber convulsed again as Doc's captured gun drove lead. The weapon was small in his mighty hand, almost hidden, and its muzzle flame was a maroon spark that jumped out of his fist.

The foremost of the two soldiers screamed, went weak in the knees, and quite pale. Doc's bullet had mangled the fellow's hand against the grip of the automatic. The rebel's pistol hit the floor at his feet, bounced, and spun like a top. The man, interested only in his agony, and goggling at his shattered hand, made no effort to secure the firearm.

The survivor—the staff officer—lost his nerve. The beating he had taken from Long Tom earlier in the night probably helped. He dropped his gun and jutted his arms overhead. The mad desire to get his hands very high caused him to raise up on tiptoe.

"*Nu!*" he shrieked. "No! Do not shoot!"

Doc Savage hurriedly searched the prisoners, relieving them of weapons.

Renny lumbered into the underground room, which was lighted from the ceiling by fairly efficient gasoline lanterns. King Dal Le Galbin, his daughter, and Captain Henri Flancul followed.

Captain Flancul glanced over the scene.

"*Buna!*" he exclaimed. "Good! You have captured them. I will go back outside and see if there are others."

He whirled and vanished down the passage toward the exit.

Doc and Renny hurriedly untied Monk and the others.

"Blast it!" Monk growled. "There's another exit from this place. They used it to get around behind me and Ham. That's how they grabbed us."

"Where is this other exit?" Doc demanded.

Monk pointed. "Over there."

The bronze man moved across the room. Around the walls, long work benches were arrayed. These held metal working machinery and many tools. Some boxes were stacked in a corner, a few of them empty; but some held wire, others metal in the shape of thin sheets and hollow, light tubes.

This stuff, Doc decided, was part of the raw material from which the mystery weapons were being manufactured. But there was no sign of the weapons themselves.

Doc found the rear exit. This was in the form of a ladder which led up to a trap door that opened silently under his shove. He clambered out and found himself in a rear room of the old stone house. The trap was in the floor.

Crouching there, Doc listened. He heard steps—one man.

"Captain Flancul," Doc called.

"Yes?" came Flancul's voice.

"Find anybody?"

"No one. I shall search outside, though."

USING his flashlight, Doc went over the house rapidly. The furniture was ancient, worn. Some of the pieces possibly possessed great value as antiques.

A cramped chamber held a thin-legged, elaborately carved desk which Doc opened.

Pigeon holes contained numerous papers and letters. More documents were weighted down by a telephone.

Doc moved the instrument aside, and scrutinized the papers. The Calbian language he read fluently. The documents were of an innocent nature, being bills and social letters, but the addresses they bore were interesting.

Every missive was addressed to Conte Cozonac. It appeared that Conte Cozonac owned this house.

Doc's scrutiny was very rapid; he seemed only to glance over the letters.

Then he lifted the receiver from the hook and listened. There was the usual wire humming sound. Another sound, too! Low and regular, it was not unlike the note of a wind blowing past a transmitter at the other end of the wire.

A man was listening at the other end. The hissing was his breathing.

Doc was immobile a moment. Then the tendons enwrapping his throat tensed, and he began to speak. From his lips came an exact imitation of Conte Cozonac's bubbling voice.

"Yes?" he said in Calbian, mimicking Conte Cozonac's voice.

With this trick, he had thought to get some information of value from the person on the other end of the wire. Instead, he got a gust of harsh, ugly laughter.

"Stop that!" Doc rapped, using Conte Cozonac's tones of rage. "What do you laugh at?"

The mirth died. There was silence; then the other spoke.

"A score of pardons, Domnule Cozonac. The laughter had nothing to do with you. Is everything all right?"

"All satisfactory," Doc replied. "Have you a report?"

Again, there was pause. During the wait, Doc heard, some distance from the other instrument, the faint challenge of a military sentry.

Then: "No report, Domnule Cozonac," said the voice.

Doc prepared to put more questions, but a click came over the wire. The other had hung up.

Doc hesitated, then replaced his own receiver and went back toward the underground room.

He had recognized the voice on the end of the line. It was another of Conte Cozonac's rebel staff officers. No doubt the man had spoken from the rebel encampment—the challenge of the sentry, faintly overheard, had told Doc that.

The staff officer, Doc reflected, must have been on the wire awaiting a report from his chief.

HAD Doc Savage been present at the other end of the phone line when the staff official hung up, he would have received something of a shock. The staff man was excited. He waved his arms at the others in the headquarters tent.

"The bronze man!" he barked. "Savage must have imitated Domnule Cozonac's voice!"

Outside, weapons rattled and feet tramped. A squad of men was assembling.

"Come!" snapped the staff officer.

He ran outside, the others following him. Three motor trucks rolled up, large, open affairs intended to accommodate troops.

"How do you know it was Savage's voice you heard?" demanded someone.

"It had to be Savage speaking," retorted the other. "Conte Cozonac and Muta and the others are prisoners. It is not likely they escaped."

"But how did you know—"

"No time for talk now, my friend!"

"Load!" crackled a command.

The soldiers clambered into the trucks; the staff officer and his aides followed. Truck engines moaned; wheels threw mud and water; the machines lumbered forward.

They took a road which led toward the old house on the mountain top.

"Hurry!" the staff man snarled repeatedly. "We must reach the place before Savage takes Conte Cozonac away."

The truck engines labored; the vehicles bounced over rocks.

"Can it be that Doc Savage suspects our coming?" demanded a man.

"He does not suspect," grunted the staff official. "We will take him by surprise."

WHEN Doc Savage entered the underground room in the stone house, Long Tom, the electrical wizard, asked, "Learn anything, Doc?"

"This is Conte Cozonac's house."

"Hm-m-m."

"There is a phone upstairs, a direct line, it seems, to the revolutionist camp."

Long Tom squinted. "The phone help you any?"

"No. There was a staff officer at the other end. But I didn't have much luck pumping him."

Ham was roaming among the work benches and packing cases, apparently in search of his sword cane. Usually dapperly clad, the lawyer was now something of a wreck. His coat and shirt were almost torn off; his knuckles were skinned. One eye was in the process of turning black.

"Blast it!" he growled. "What'd they do with my sword cane?"

The homely Monk called, "Come here, Habeas!"

The grotesque-looking shoat trotted up.

"Help the shyster hunt his sword cane, Habeas," Monk directed. "Savvy sword cane? The thing he's all the time tryin' to wallop you with. Go find!"

Habeas trotted off.

King Dal Le Galbin stood nearby, keeping an eye on the prisoners. Attractive Princess Gusta was at his side, but her attention was not on the captives. She was watching Doc Savage—when she could do so without the bronze man noticing.

There was in Princess Gusta's eyes, when they rested upon Doc Savage, an unusual warmth. It was barely possible that this was simple gratitude. But the young woman herself was not sure. From the moment of her first glimpse of the remarkable bronze man, she had been in something of a state of mind.

Princess Gusta Le Galbin, without being aware of it, was a pleasurable victim of the unique attraction which the big bronze man exerted upon members of the opposite sex. This magnetic charm for femininity was one quality Doc had not developed by careful exercise. It came from his personality, unusual physique, and his undeniable handsomeness. It was, in fact, a power which Doc would gladly have gotten rid of. It frequently caused him embarrassment.

There was no provision for any woman, however desirable, to play a part in his perilous career.

CAPTAIN HENRI FLANCUL came down the stone stairs and into the workroom.

"Buna!" he said. "Good! There is no one lurking outside. I have searched thoroughly."

"Fine," rumbled big-fisted Renny. "We can look this joint over without bein' interrupted."

"The mysterious weapons are stored here somewhere," gaunt Johnny reminded them.

Captain Henri Flancul clicked off a precise military salute and a deep bow before Doc Savage.

"Conte Cozonac and Muta are prisoners. The mystery weapons are almost in our hands."

"The job is not done, by any means," Doc reminded him.

Captain Flancul saluted again. "True. The mastermind must be trapped. But I have confidence that you will seize him."

Doc surveyed the workroom. The walls of stone were broken in the rear by a wooden door of ponderous timbers. A metal bar crossed this, the end being slotted and fitted over a thick steel staple. A padlock, looped through the staple, made a stout fastening for the door.

Long Tom, following Doc's gaze, stated, "I think the infernal machines are behind that door."

At his words, Doc swung to the panel.

Ham, moving to follow him, jerked to a halt and stared. "Well, that pig finally did something worthwhile," he said.

Habeas Corpus, the grotesque shoat, had succeeded in locating the lawyer's sword cane. Ham secured it hastily.

Doc Savage inspected the lock on the door.

"It won't be difficult to open," he decided.

Chapter XXIII
THE HUNDRED PERILS

DOC got a hammer from one of the benches and went to work on the lock. He struck rapidly; sparks flew; then the steel began to give.

The lock surrendered. Doc removed the bar and gave the door a shove.

"Who's gonna guard the prisoners!" Renny boomed.

Nobody volunteered to stand watch. They were all too desirous of seeing the mystery weapon.

"Monk, Ham," Doc said, "it's up to you."

"Aw," Monk grumbled. "O. K., Doc."

He and Ham stayed behind, scowling blackly at the prisoners. The latter were all conscious by now, but had wrapped themselves in a great silence, except for an occasional frightful groan from the pair who had been hit by Doc's bullets.

Doc led the way through the opened door.

The chamber beyond was long and low of ceiling. Extensive racks had been hastily assembled with crude lumber. These were in the nature of cradles—and they held the mystery weapons.

For some seconds, Doc and the others surveyed the place in silence.

"Holy cow!" grunted Renny.

Skeleton-thin Johnny echoed his pet ejaculation, "I'll be superamalgamated!"

"Nearly a hundred of 'em!" Long Tom calculated aloud.

King Dal Le Galbin and Princess Gusta said nothing, but stared at the devices blankly, as if not fully comprehending their nature.

"Cum—!" Captain Henri Flancul began, then changed to English. "What are they?"

"They look like little airplanes," Renny offered.

"They are," Doc said.

"Huh?"

"Aerial torpedoes."

The bronze man stepped close to make an inspection. The tubular bodies of the aerial torpedoes possessed a length of several feet, and were made of some thin, light alloy metal. Attached to the rear were control fins which did not differ greatly from the conventional airplane type.

The wings were not in place, but were bound securely with cords to the torpedo-shaped fuselages.

"Partially dismantled for convenience in moving," Doc decided. "Wings can be attached in a hurry."

Renny began fumbling with one of the devices.

"Careful!" Doc warned.

"Think I want to set it off?" Renny snorted.

He got a small lid open and examined the inside. "These babies run with tiny silenced gasoline motors," he called.

Doc bent over the aerial torpedo.

"Motors such as these were in use as far back as the World War days. Exhaust is conveyed into mufflers, from which it escapes with comparative silence. In this case there is only a shrill whistling, a sound which your ears failed to detect when the infernal things were sent against us in New York."

"But how are they directed at a target?" Renny demanded. "By radio?"

"Not radio," Doc decided. "The secret of their uncanny accuracy is Baron Damitru Mendl's invention."

His movements careful, the bronze man delved deeper into the sinister contrivance.

THE explosive came to light. The stuff was in a metal container, insulated against vibration by spring suspension.

"Compressed trinitrotoluene," he decided.

"What is that?" Princess Gusta asked curiously.

"T.N.T."

"Oh!" the young woman shivered. "Is there much of it?"

"Enough to scatter this end of the mountain over a good deal of Calbia," Doc told her. "But don't worry; the stuff has to be touched off. In the case of these things, that happens when they strike a solid body. There is a simple percussion detonator arrangement."

Doc explored further into the innards of the torpedoes. Intricate apparatus came to light. The mechanism was electrical in nature, but its construction was unlike anything the bronze man had ever seen before. There were vacuum tubes, coils, batteries, amplifying transformers.

Mounted on the belly of each torpedo was a long metal tube. This faced forward and was open at one end. Wires ran from it to the apparatus.

Doc probed in the tube. "Pretty ingenious," he remarked.

"How are the things guided, *Domnule* Savage?" questioned Captain Henri Flancul.

Doc straightened. "Well—" He went silent. Then his weird trilling note came into being, ranged the musical scale briefly, and ebbed away.

"What is it?" Renny boomed.

"Footsteps!" Doc rasped. "Sounds like forty or fifty men!"

Quickly Doc lunged for the steps.

Monk waved at the captives. "I'm gonna tie these cookies up. Then Ham and me can help in the scrap."

"Tie 'em tight."

Monk grinned fiercely. "Won't I, though?" he grated.

Doc mounted the steps, the others trailing him. They got upstairs, then came to a halt.

The night outside was ablaze with flares. Through the rain they could see nebulous, fast-moving figures.

"Got us surrounded!" Long Tom groaned.

Doc reconnoitered briefly.

"They were careful!" he said, sober voiced. "I did not hear their approach in time."

Long Tom breathed, "You mean—"

"We haven't a chance of getting out of here undiscovered," Doc told him.

"They're creeping up on all sides," Johnny imparted, after peering into the rain.

Renny, with the forethought of a man who had been in tough spots before, lunged for the nearest light, intent on extinguishing it.

"Let it burn," Doc told him.

"But it'll show us up!" Renny boomed.

"Dousing the light will tell them we know they are coming," Doc corrected. "Let them get close. We'll use some of these."

From inside his clothing, Doc Savage produced several metal bulbs not quite as large as hen eggs—gas.

"But these devils may have gas masks," Captain Flancul pointed out.

"Their masks will be no protection against this," Doc told him. "The vapor has merely to come in contact with the skin to produce an agony which will render them helpless, although it will do no really serious damage."

Chapter XXIV
THE FIRE

PRINCESS GUSTA said, "Give me a gun, someone!"

Renny passed her one of the pistols which had been taken from the captives below.

"We'd better scatter, and watch from the windows of the rooms that are dark," the big-fisted engineer boomed softly.

He and Captain Henri Flancul scuttled through a door.

Ham and Monk came up the narrow stone steps from the subterranean region.

"Quiet!" Doc warned them. "Keep out of sight."

"How'd you reckon they got tipped that we had grabbed Conte Cozonac and Muta?" Monk breathed.

"That," Doc replied grimly, "is a mystery."

Princess Gusta, standing close beside the bronze man, asked, "Is there—much danger?"

"Enough that you had better go below," Doc breathed back.

The girl shuddered. *"Nu!* And get near the explosive in the torpedoes? No!"

"If the stuff should detonate, we would be no better off here. A single one would blow this house to bits."

Then, as a partially reassuring afterthought, Doc added, "But they're not going to explode—let us hope."

For a time there was nothing but the sob and gurgle of the rain. A gusty breeze carried a fine spray inside, and it was like a cold, ghostly touch on their bare skin.

From outside, a voice called in Calbian.

"We know you have discovered our arrival!" the fellow shouted. "You will surrender at once!"

The shout moved Doc to cyclone action. He flashed backward, dived into one of the darkened rooms. Renny was at the window there. Doc went on to another chamber, and found Captain Henri Flancul.

"The devils!" Captain Flancul snarled. "Something warned them that we knew of their arrival. What was it?"

Without answering, Doc went on to the other rooms. King Dal Le Galbin occupied one, Monk and Ham another. All expressed puzzlement.

Returning to the large chamber, Doc extinguished the lights.

"This," he said quietly, "is going to be tough."

BEFORE many moments had elapsed, the voice outside called out again.

"You have no chance! Messengers have gone back to the revolutionist camp to get field guns! We will blow that house to pieces!"

Doc answered him in Calbian. "Are you forgetting that we have your aerial torpedoes here? They will make short work of your field guns."

The other laughed harshly. "They might, if we used motor trucks or tractors to pull the guns. But we will do nothing so crude as that. The messengers have orders to bring the guns with horses."

Monk, fingering a captured pistol, hopefully inquired, "How about tryin' a shot at his voice, Doc?"

"Sounds as if he were behind the wall, and you won't hit him," Doc replied. "But go ahead. Shooting has got to start some time."

"I also shall try my marksmanship," gritted Captain Henri Flancul.

Monk and Captain Flancul fired together. Their answer was a jeering yell from outside, then a drumming volley of rifle, machine gun, and pistol fire. The stone walls stopped many of the bullets, but others jangled the glass out of the windows, chewed at the door frame, and made dull poppings as they tore through the roof.

The fusillade gave no indication of subsiding.

"Long Tom!" Doc called.

"Over here!" answered the electrical wizard from below a window.

"Get on to that portable radio transmitter and contact the Calbian army station at San Blazna," Doc directed. "Have them send planes to chase these birds off. Your Highness"—to the king—"you'd better help him. Your fliers will be more speedy if they know you are in trouble."

Captain Henri Flancul murmured, "The portable radios that are a part of the listening devices! I had forgotten them. Our position is not so bad, after all."

"Everybody else scatter to the windows," Doc suggested. "Keep under cover, and give an alarm if they try to rush us. We'll save the gas grenades as a last resort."

Several minutes dragged away, the firing continuing its mad rattle. Occasional bullets ricocheted in the room, screaming shrilly. But the defenders were well sheltered, and no one was hit. A portion of the roof, weakened by the leaden hail, caved in.

Monk fired twice through a window.

"No," Doc told him. "Let me do the shooting, unless things get too bad."

From an underarm holster, padded so that its presence was hardly noticeable, the bronze man drew one of his tiny superfiring pistols, the magazine charged with mercy bullets. He chose his time, and fired quickly through a window.

A rebel machine gun promptly went silent.

Princess Gusta, finding herself beside Monk, breathed curiously, "Why did he tell you not to shoot?"

"He doesn't want anybody killed," Monk explained.

"But he is shooting—"

"Mercy bullets," Monk finished for her. "They don't kill anybody—just lay 'em out."

"But they are trying to—"

"Massacre us?" Monk snorted. "Sure, I know. But things never get bad enough to make Doc deliberately kill. I'll say this, though—guys who mix with him kinda have a habit of windin' up as victims of their own traps."

Long Tom and King Dal Le Galbin had found a windowless cubby—a closet off the kitchen—where they could use the radio without danger of getting shot. The pair approached Doc after a time, crawling along the floor.

"We contacted the Royalist army air station," Long Tom imparted. "A flight of bombing and pursuit planes are gonna take off right away."

"Excellent!" exclaimed Captain Henri Flancul from the darkness nearby.

DOC SAVAGE began shifting from one room to another. Choosing moments when the barrage slackened slightly, he discharged sharp bursts from his superfirer. Almost every burst silenced a besieger.

Coming upon Monk in the room where the trap door led to the subterranean rooms, Doc directed, "Better tag me around, Monk."

"Huh?" Monk was dumbfounded. "Leave here?"

"Right"

"But the prisoners might get away."

"Monk, I have been thinking," Doc said dryly. "The result is a great suspicion. Let's try something."

Together, they worked toward the front of the house. Monk was puzzled, wondering why Doc wanted him to leave the trapdoor room.

"What gets me is why they don't charge the place," he grumbled. "You'd think they knew about the gas grenades."

"They probably do."

"For the love of Mike! You ain't kiddin'?"

On the echo of Monk's words all gunfire suddenly ceased.

"What's this mean?" Monk grunted.

"Stand still!" Doc breathed. "I believe my ruse is going to work."

For once, the bronze man's tone held emotions, tension.

"You're talkin' riddles," Monk groaned. "What'd leavin' the room have to do—"

"Wait!"

They did not have long to wait, perhaps a minute. Then Renny's great voice roared. "Conte Cozonac—Muta—the others! They've all got away!"

Doc Savage seemed to have been waiting for that. He pitched immediately for the other room. His flashlight came out and darted luminance. No one was in the big room.

Doc ran on and wrenched open the door of the chamber which held the trap door—the room which Monk had occupied a few minutes before.

Leaping flames confronted them. The whole floor was afire.

Monk howled, "Where'd they go?"

"Out the back window!" Renny shouted. "That's why the shooting stopped. Their pals were givin' 'em a chance to get away."

Monk started for the door, as if intent on pursuing Conte Cozonac and the other culprits. He changed his mind when the barrage of machine gun and rifle fire suddenly resumed.

Flat on the floor, the homely chemist snarled, "But I tied them birds myself. They couldn't get loose!"

"Well, they did," Renny thumped. "I heard 'em runnin' away."

Monk scuttled toward the secret door which led into the underground regions. "I'm gonna look for myself," he said.

Doc trod at his heels.

Behind them flames crackled and roared. Smoke billowed, and mingled with it was a distinctive odor—a tang of gasoline. The floors of the flaming room must have been drenched with the stuff. That explained the rapid spread of the blaze.

Monk and Doc reached the workroom.

"Look!" Monk gritted, pointing.

The ropes which had bound the late captives were heaped on the floor. They had not been untied.

"Cut!" Monk rumbled, excitement making his usually small voice almost as loud as Renny's roar. "Somebody used a knife on the ropes!"

Doc Savage went on to the storeroom which held the aerial torpedoes. He moved along the racks supporting the contrivances, scrutinizing each one closely.

Then he sighed an audible relief—something he very seldom did—and said, "Was afraid they might've left a time-fuse connection on one of the things. They didn't."

Monk, gaping at the arrayed instruments of death, failed to share Doc's cheerfulness.

He pointed at an empty rack. "Hey! Wasn't there a torpedo on here?"

"There was."

Monk's jaw sagged, and his hairy hands made nervous gestures, as he asked, "The prisoners took one of the torpedoes with 'em when they escaped?"

"They did," Doc replied.

Chapter XXV
THE PLOT MASTER

MONK was in anything but a happy frame of mind, and Doc Savage's next words did nothing to cheer him.

"The chances are that they took the torpedo with the idea of sending it back at us," offered the bronze man.

Monk experienced difficulty in swallowing. Then events of the last few minutes, upstairs, took on significance.

"Doc, you got me out of the room where the fire is! You did that deliberately, so that they could escape."

"Something like that."

"But why?"

"It looked like the simplest solution of this whole mess."

The chemist groaned audibly. "You're way out of my depth. If this is a solution, well, I—hope it *is* a solution."

Doc studied the ceiling. It was of concrete, steel reinforced, and the storeroom being rather far underground, several feet of earth lay between themselves and the burning room above.

"The heat won't explode these," the bronze man decided, and touched one of the aerial missiles.

"Maybe not," Monk muttered. "But I know dugouts and how explosives work on 'em. This ain't deep enough to protect us from the T.N.T. in that infernal machine they took away with 'em."

Doc moved toward the stairs, ascended them, and found Renny and Ham endeavoring to extinguish the gasoline fire, but without noticeable success. The hail of lead from the besiegers was a handicap.

"No use!" Renny said hollowly. "The floor is dry, and the gasoline set the stuff off like tinder."

Doc demanded, "Where are the others?"

"Some of 'em are watching from the windows. That crew outside may try to rush us."

From the kitchen Princess Gusta Le Galbin called, "Here are pots and pans and a bucket or two. We can carry water from that trapdoor pit underground."

Doc and Monk ran to get the receptacles.

"You," Doc informed the young woman, "are what Americans call a brick."

Monk tried to chuckle, produced an eerie croak instead, and put forth a second effort which was moderately hearty. The chemist was visioning imminent arrival of the missing aerial torpedo. He had seen enough of the things to know what the result would be.

"Doc doesn't pass out many compliments, Your Highness," he told Princess Gusta.

"So I have noticed," she said dryly.

Monk caught her double meaning, but did not feel like remarking upon it. Young women, especially those as attractive as this one, were usually accustomed to flattery of the sort sometimes called "sweet nothings." Doc did not go in for that sort of thing. Monk decided the princess was piqued.

They filled the buckets and kettles in the water trap from which Ham had rescued his sword cane, using the aperture opened by Long Tom and Johnny's grenade for the purpose. Transferring the water to the fire was a ticklish, dangerous procedure.

In another part of the house, more of the roof, rent by machine-gun slugs, collapsed. Shot sounds were steady thunder out in the rain.

"We can keep the fire from spreading beyond the gasoline-soaked area," Doc concluded, after watching the effects of their first bucket-brigade effort.

"Wonder why they started the fire?" Monk pondered. "Trying to burn us out?"

"No," Doc told him. "They did it to furnish what you might call a magnet for their aerial bomb."

Monk dropped his kettle. "Huh?"

"The aerial bombs are attracted by heat."

LONG TOM appeared in time to hear the last statement. The pallid electrical wizard strained fingers through his hair and shook his head slowly.

"But Doc, I supposed the torpedoes were guided by some radio adaptation."

Doc was silent, seemingly listening.

"Baron Damitru Mendl's invention is an 'eye' which, in connection with the usual relays and mechanism employed in radio-directing, sends the aerial torpedoes toward objects emitting heat," he offered. "You will recall that all of the objects struck in the past were giving off heat—airplane motors, boat engines, motor cars, even a camp fire."

Monk shuddered. "We can't get this fire out. Let's clear outa here before the bomb strikes."

In the pause which followed, the clamor of machine guns and the squeal, rip and bite of striking bullets, appeared to take on a more deadly loudness.

"We couldn't make it," Doc declared quietly. "The gunners are too far away to reach with our grenades."

"Holy cow!" Renny boomed. "How can you take this so easy, Doc? When that thing hits— *blooie!* It's curtains!"

Doc said, "Take it easy."

"Blast it! I ain't got your nerves!"

Long Tom, his voice strained and shrill, managed a gurgle that was meant for a laugh.

"I'd like to go out knowing more about this 'eye' that Baron Damitru Mendl invented, Doc."

The bronze man knocked shut the door of the room, from which the flames were coming, so that the light from within might not betray them.

"The secret of the 'eye's' ability to literally see and guide the torpedoes to any hot object in darkness, fog or even a smoke screen is found in a well-known scientific principle."

King Dal Le Galbin came crawling in from one of the other rooms, shouting, "They seem to be moving back farther from the house!"

"Gettin' out of the way of the blow-up," Monk groaned silently; then aloud: "What is that scientific principle, Doc?"

"Any object that is warmer than its surroundings gives off beams of radiant heat," Doc stated. "The heat from an ordinary radiator is an example. These rays penetrate darkness and smoke."

The ruler of Calbia snapped, "This is a fine time to be discussing scientific principles!"

"Dry up!" Monk grunted, their danger making his temper short.

Doc continued as if there had been no interruption.

"The heat rays are invisible to the naked eye, although you can detect them by other methods. Holding your hand near the source of heat—the radiator for instance—is the simplest way."

"Hurry it up, Doc!" Long Tom groaned. "I know my hair is turning white!"

"Baron Damitru Mendl's 'eye' for detecting these heat rays is simply a photo-electric cell of remarkable sensitivity," Doc finished. "The mechanism which causes the 'eye' to point, like a compass needle, at the source of the rays, is too complicated to explain without illustrative drawings. But it is not new in principle. The 'eye', due to its astounding sensitivity, will *sight* a hot object from a considerable distance."

"I know why you pulled that box of lighted stoves along behind our plane," Monk grunted. "The heat was greater than that given off by our plane engines, and thus decoyed the torpedo."

Doc began, "Yes. That—"

He went silent.

Through the gunfire, the hungry bullet noises and the rain came a mutter that all recognized instantly.

A plane motor had started.

"MY army fliers!" King Dal Le Galbin gasped.

"Nix," Monk discouraged him. "It's somebody takin' our plane up."

The motor sound drummed, ebbed, rolled out again as the motors were warmed; and after a while it took on a changed note, shriller, more forceful.

"They're in the air!" Renny rumbled.

The multiple bawl of exhausts went faint, then began to grow rapidly louder.

"They climbed for some altitude," Doc decided aloud. "Now they're coming back, probably to turn the aerial torpedo loose."

Renny knocked his big fists together, and that noise was audible over the other uproar.

"Run for it, eh?" he cried. "Maybe we got a chance?"

Doc's one word was an emphatic crash. "No!"

They waited. Doc was motionless, saying nothing more. His five men, having before been in peril as great as this and having seen the amazing man of bronze extricate himself with some bit of master strategy, were not entirely without hope.

But there was always a chance of a slip. Doc, for all of his fabulous ability, was no supernatural personality. This might be the one time his plans would go wrong. The five were undeniably scared.

The plane roar was a thing approaching thunder.

Princess Gusta gripped Doc's arm.

"I guess I'm not a brick, after all," she breathed thickly. "I'm—scared. Awfully scared!"

This was the psychological moment to drop an arm around the young woman's shoulder, and that was conceivably what she expected. Doc disappointed her.

"Cover your head with your arms," he directed. "The blast may knock the roof down on us."

The explosion did do exactly that, but it was a lead-shattered section of the roof which did fall, not the entire covering.

The very air itself took on the aspect of white-hot flame that blinded. There was shock against their eardrums, a slam of air that almost split the membranes. Raindrops, coming downward by the gallons, sheeted on the house and through the holes.

The part of the roof collapsed, its drop a crack and roar.

The shooting stopped as if some magic had caused every gun to run out of ammunition at the same instant.

Silence followed. Probably the flames crackled and some rain fell, but the force of the blast had rendered their ears insensitive to such minor noises.

Ten seconds, twenty, the pause lasted. Then: *Thump!* The sound of a fall was heavy, and not far off.

"The plane motors," Doc said.

There came a crash; then lesser clatters.

"That will be the rest of the plane," surmised Doc.

AFTER a time, the rain grew steady in its washing downpour, but the gunfire did not renew.

Habeas Corpus, the pig, grunted a few times, as if in complaint, until Monk promised audibly to pull off his oversize ears and make Ham a present of them. Monk sounded like a man enjoying one of the happiest moments of a lifetime, or maybe the most relieved moments.

"The aerial torpedo backfired on 'em, eh, Doc?" Monk asked. "How come?"

"There was," Doc enlightened him, "a metal box in the tail portion of the plane, far back."

"The one you brought from the shack—the case without any numbers on it?" mallet-fisted Renny interjected.

"That's it. It held apparatus which emitted rays that attracted the photo-electric 'eye' in the aerial torpedo."

"Holy cow! But wasn't it hot enough to attract attention?"

Doc shook his head. "The business of these rays is complicated. They go *through* solids—they're possibly a form of atomic stream. Science really doesn't know much about them. But the rays can be created and sent out without a great deal of heat."

Renny made a long face. "Too complicated for me!"

"Consider these heat rays and X-rays as having somewhat the same qualities. Does that make it simpler?"

"Sure."

"All right. The box in the plane emitted the rays in great quantities. I left it there to draw any aerial torpedo which might be launched at us."

"I getcha."

"But wasn't they afraid the plane motors would draw the torpedo after it was launched?" Monk put in.

"The fire here in the house would be the stronger attraction, especially since the 'eye' was pointed at the fire. But the device in the box was powerful enough to turn the contrivance back."

No shots had come from outside. Doc thumbed a flashlight and ranged its beam over those assembled in the room.

"Notice one of our party is missing," he said grimly.

The others stared about.

"Captain Flancul!" gasped Princess Gusta. "Where is he?"

"I didn't see him through the last half of the scrap!" Monk muttered.

"Maybe he was caught under a piece of the roof when it fell!" Renny boomed, and wheeled as if to search.

"Captain Flancul was caught—but not under the roof," Doc said quietly. "The explosion overhead got him."

Princess Gusta brought a hand up and pressed it tightly to her eyes. "Then Captain Flancul—"

"Telephoned from here tonight, while pretending to search, and summoned the party of rebels who are outside," Doc finished.

Renny rumbled rage. "Captain Flancul was the ringleader?"

"Apparently. It was he who freed the prisoners."

"But, Doc, if you suspected—"

"There was no proof against him," Doc explained. "When the rebel party came, it seemed certain that someone had summoned them. Captain Flancul was the logical one to suspect."

"But you let 'im escape!"

"Let him give himself away," Doc corrected. "We know he is guilty. Our job now is to get him."

THE task of getting Captain Henri Flancul proved to be a nearly impossible accomplishment. Nor was it any simpler to seize Conte Cozonac and Muta.

True, enough of their bodies was found to identify each. The trio had been in the death plane. There was not much more to it.

The Calbian Royal Air Force pilots arrived in a dozen pursuit planes and dispersed the revolutionist besiegers, shooting a few and chasing the others into the thick woodland.

A wounded rebel verified what Doc had surmised. Captain Henri Flancul was the instigator of the revolt. He had stolen Baron Mendl's secret from the Calbian war department archives. It was Captain Flancul's wealth which had financed the purchase of rebel arms. He had fancied himself as a modern Napoleon, this Captain Flancul. He had hoped to make himself King of Calbia, then, with Baron Mendl's weird secret as a weapon, had contemplated conquest of surrounding countries.

The injured rebel told something else, too—he explained the fact that the aerial torpedo had been used against certain members of the revolutionist force. The victims had been men who disliked Captain Flancul, men who disagreed with his Napoleonic ideas. The torpedoes had been employed to put them out of the way.

DOC SAVAGE did not become King of Calbia.

King Dal Le Galbin, with fine trustfulness, did offer the bronze man a dictatorship by way of reward. He was even insistent that Doc accept. But, since the revolution collapsed almost as soon as it was left leaderless, Doc declined with fitting ceremony.

Princess Gusta Le Galbin, especially entrancing in a creation of San Blazna's finest dressmaker, was on hand and heard Doc's decision. She went away somewhat tight-lipped, and was secluded in her quarters the rest of the day, with not even her favorite lady-in-waiting admitted. That night, at the royal banquet tended Doc and his men, even a heavy application of mascara did not hide her red eyelids.

"Doc sure slays 'em," Monk, looking more apish than ever in evening clothes, told Ham.

"It's too bad, you ape," Ham, very natty in like regalia, retorted. "She's a swell girl."

Doc Savage did ask one boon before leaving Calbia—which was granted. A sample of the aerial torpedo was sent to the war department of every country in Europe, together with detailed information as to how objects emitting suitable heat could be used as a decoy for the devices, and thus serve as a defense.

"That gets rid of the terror of the thing," Doc declared.

Terror! The bronze man called the menace of the uncanny aerial torpedoes that, not knowing of the thing which he was next to encounter. Had he been a clairvoyant, he might conceivably have looked at what he was to meet within a few weeks, and consider the menace of the air missiles of comparative mildness.

It began in London. A man came to Doc Savage. He brought with him terror, death, awful mystery—and a story.

Several hundred years ago, there had been a great city in the jungles of Indo China, a populous city, with much wealth. One day, terror walked the streets—a thing so frightful that all the inhabitants fled in frenzy, and no single one ever returned, so that the city stood yet in the jungle, very much as on the day it was abandoned, except for the encroaching creepers and plants.

The terror was still there—and something else.

That was the man's story. It led Doc Savage and his five aides to the mysterious horror of *The Thousand-headed Man.*

Monk naturally knew nothing of the unpleasantness ahead when he suggested, "Say, Doc, how about takin' sort of a vacation for a few weeks, here in Calbia?"

Ham, overhearing the remark, snorted loudly. Princess Gusta, Ham had noted, had turned to the pleasantly homely Monk for comfort.

Monk was doing very well as comforter. Giving up the job did not appeal to him.

THE END

THE MEN BEHIND DOC SAVAGE

Lester Dent (1904-1959) might be called the father of the superhero. Writing under the house name of "Kenneth Robeson," Dent was the principal writer of *Doc Savage,* producing over 150 of the Man of Bronze's thrilling pulp adventures between 1933-1949. The formative influence of Doc Savage on important pop culture heroes including Superman, Batman, the Fantastic Four and the Man From U.N.C.L.E. is undeniable. Dent was also a contributor to the legendary *Black Mask* during its golden age, for which he created Miami waterfront detective Oscar Sail. A real-life adventurer, world traveler and member of the Explorers Club, Dent wrote in all genres for magazines ranging from pulps like *Adventure, Argosy* and *Ten Detective Aces* to prestigious slick magazines including *The Saturday Evening Post* and *Collier's.*

Harold A. Davis (1902-55) worked alongside AP telegrapher Lester Dent at the Tulsa *World,* and served as assistant telegraph editor at the New York *Daily News* before being hired as the first managing editor of Alicia Patterson's *Newsday.* Davis ghosted twelve Doc Savage novels beginning with *The King Maker* and concluding with *The Exploding Lake* in 1946.

INTERMISSION by Will Murray

Doc Savage's unorthodox relationship with the opposite sex drives the adventures in this volume.

Like Nick Carter before him and Superman after him, the Man of Bronze kept a respectful distance from the ladies. Doc's thinking was that because his life's work was that of a modern Galahad, he had too many enemies to ever safely marry.

His editors also reasoned that, since Doc Savage was written with 15-year-olds of all ages in mind, encumbering Doc with a girlfriend, fiancée or wife would detract from the escapist nature of his adventures. Not to mention turn off the literal 15-year-olds who hero-worshipped the Man of Bronze.

Additionally, Street & Smith's institutional memory—in the person of Doc Savage co-creator Henry W. Ralston—no doubt recalled the dime novel era and the ill-fated marriage of the company's star hero, detective Nick Carter. He wed Ethel Dalton in 1887. No sooner had the couple had their first child, than she was kidnapped. In 1904, after the character had been semi-retired from active participation in the Nick Carter series, they abruptly killed her off.

Being unattached meant that in every adventure Doc Savage encountered fresh female faces. The girls he met usually made a play for the handsome bronze man. That was part of the wish fulfillment of the Doc Savage mystique. The social mores of the 1930s required that the big bronze hero not take advantage of their interest—which of course sets Doc apart from modern action heroes, who freely bed their heroines.

In the world of Doc Savage, the 1934 adventure Lester Dent called *The King Maker* reverberated for years to come. Doc Savage turns down a throne, discarding a lovestruck princess in the process. This is not the first princess the Man of Bronze cast aside, of course. In his first exploit, Doc had to untangle himself from Princess Monja of the Valley of the Vanished. That Mayan enclave remained unknown to the outer world, so the general public never learned about that.

But in Doc's reality, his refusal to marry Princess Gusta made headlines. It was remarked upon in the next adventure, *The Thousand-Headed Man,* and from time to time afterward, well into the years and stories to come.

Every Doc Savage plot emerged from a conference between author Lester Dent, editor John L. Nanovic and Henry W. Ralston. No doubt Dent took notes on these occasions, but few survive. *The King Maker* notes do repose among Dent's papers. An examination sheds a great deal of light on the thinking processes that produced each Doc adventure. One sheet appears to be a record of the three-way exchange through which the bare plot bones were agreed upon:

Situation = LOCALE = Balkan country

VILLAIN WANTS = Control of government, ostensibly.

Actually, control of war secret which is in archives of country. What is war secret? Gas? Gun? Guided bomb? Guided death machine?

Dent underlined "Guided death machine" to signify that he and his editors had arrived at an agreement. Then he wrote:

Guided Death Machine is: utilizes "warmth rays" given off by warm bodies to guide shells.

SITUATION: Revolution has started. Doc goes into it, unbidden.

1 = Doc starts to work; this fact reported to enemies.

2 = Doc opposed; meets girl; enemy.

3 = Trouble on high seas.

4 = Doc set adrift on high seas; rescued.

5 = Doc has trouble at army air field; lands.

6 = Doc's man gets to work.

7 = Doc's man learns.

8 = Doc's man trapped.

9 = Doc goes to work.

10 = Doc works; opposed.

11 = Doc gets in deeper; men caught.

12 = Doc makes bold stab.

13 = Doc in deep.

14 = Doc's wise move got him out.

Chapter I

The Man Kindness Killed

1 Prince Graul Le Galben, a pompous man, comes to visit Doc Savage.

2 An old woman comes, too, and Prince Mendl is piqued when Monk admits old woman first to see Doc.

Writing in longhand, Dent developed the story over nineteen chapters. He struggled with the name of the Balkan nation, ultimately settling on Calbania. Nanovic shortened that to Calbia, to avoid suggesting Albania. From this, Dent typed up a chapter-by-chapter outline of about ten pages, submitting it to John Nanovic for his and Ralston's approval.

Appended to one of Dent's handwritten notes was a question evidently directed at Nanovic:

What motivates this enigmatic procedure of ours?

Under this, Nanovic scribbled "Not here," circling it. Evidently Nanovic did not want draw Ralston's attention to Dent's irreverent comment.

Dent later put his question into Johnny Littlejohn's mouth in Chapter V.

The King Maker was written in December 1933, one year after Dent penned *The Man of Bronze.* It was a busy and hectic time. Recovering from nervous exhaustion, Lester had just begun scripting the *Doc Savage* radio program slated for airing during the coming winter.

Concerned over his workload, he brought in his old Tulsa *World* co-worker, Harold A. Davis, who had landed in New York City to work for the *Journal American,* as a collaborator. Davis' involvement in *The King Maker* is not clear. But the latter chapters show signs of his simpler style. Dent of course revised the story to give it that Kenneth Robeson flair. It was their first collaboration.

The origins of this story may have more than one source. Dent was a huge fan of Dashiell Hammett's stories in *Black Mask.* One of Hammett's Continental Op stories, "This King Business," took the San Francisco detective to Europe to sort out political intrigue surrounding a Balkan throne. No doubt Dent read and was inspired by the 1928 tale.

Equally likely is the inspiration for the character of Conte Cozonac. Dent often created "heavies" who were themselves heavy. And the count was among Dent's heaviest. He was no doubt borrowed from Caspar Gutman, the memorable soundrel of Hammett's *Maltese Falcon.*

A decade before, a situation identical to the one Doc Savage faced in *The King Maker* happened in real life. In 1921, a kingdom was offered to Jerome Napoleon Charles Bonaparte, great-grandson of the King of Westphalia. He was asked to assume the throne of Albania by the regents who controlled that nation. The regency feared the return of William of Wied, who fled his throne at the onset of World War I. Bonaparte declined. Later Ahmet Zogu was named president, becoming King Zog of Albania in 1928.

Undoubtedly this was the springboard for *The King Maker*—and the reason Lester Dent coined the term Calbania.

When dealing with fictitious nations, every attempt was made to obscure the real-life model. Calbia appears to be based on the Kingdom of Serbs, Croats and Slovenes, known as Yugoslavia, then ruled by King Alexander I. The national flag painted in Walter Baumhofer's striking cover appears based on the Albanian flag. The language Dent put into the mouths of the Calbians, however, is guidebook Roumanian.

The King Maker appeared in the June, 1934 issue of *Doc Savage Magazine.* That October, while visiting France, King Alexander was assassinated by a Bulgarian revolutionist allied with Croatian separatists. It was the first political assassination to be captured on film.

By contrast, 1939's *The Freckled Shark,* turns the tables on the usual Doc formula. Instead of the hero resisting the romantic overtures of the girl involved, this time the mighty Man of Bronze is the lovestruck one.

As Lester explained to his editor in his outline:

Nanovic: Think might work in new type of love angle in this one; wherein Doc…finds it necessary to associate with girl; who is brainy and swash-buckling type, and toward end of yarn has difficulty keeping from falling for her.

How Dent handles this while keeping Doc Savage in character cannot be revealed here, but for this tricky tale, "Kenneth Robeson" took a leaf from the pages of *The Shadow.*

The outline for this story is unremarkable, except that originally Lester Dent planned to include Doc's adventure-seeking cousin, Patricia Savage. Apparently he or Nanovic concluded that the Man of Bronze would have his hands full with the female fire-eater named Rhoda Haven, and Pat would only overcomplicate the plot.

Once more Dent sets an adventure in his familiar haunts in the Florida Keys, which he scoured for pirate treasure back in the days he lived on the schooner *Albatross.* Mention is made of the Labor Day hurricane of 1935—the most powerful in U. S. history—which decimated the Keys. Dent visited Lower Matecumbe in its aftermath, wandering through a tangle of wind-twisted railroad ties and discovering a boat which had been pushed a half mile inland. He searched for the remains of missing World War I veterans who had camped there—but found nothing. The awesome destruction inspired his 1936 *Black Mask* story, "Angelfish."

Finally, the fictitious character of Señor Steel seems to be based on Bolivian leader Gérman Busch Becerra, a former war hero of the Chaco War—which served as the backdrop of the 1935 Doc adventure *Dust of Death*—who repeatedly rose and fell from power throughout the latter 1930s, ultimately declaring himself dictator in 1937.

Lester Dent had an uncanny way of anticipating world events, both big and small, through his Doc novels. As pulp scholar Rick Lai has pointed out, not only does Dent's descriptions of Señor Steel closely match that of Becerra, but like Steel, the Bolivian strongman secretly imprisoned his political enemies on an island—although a different island than the one named in *The Freckled Shark.* Remarkably, this fact did not become public until after Dent's story was written.

The Freckled Shark appeared in the March 1939 issue of *Doc Savage.* Only weeks after publication, Becerra abolished the Bolivian constitution and was branded the first totalitarian dictator of the Western Hemisphere. With his ties to Germany (the Bolivian army was trained by Germans), it was feared that he might ally himself with Adolf Hitler. That never came to pass. By another strange coincidence, the mercurial Becerra, balked by Bolivian political realities, in frustration committed suicide in August 1939—only a few months after *The Freckled Shark* appeared in print.

Sometimes it was not healthy to be the model for a Doc Savage character. •

THE FRECKLED SHARK

Jep Dee Went Fishing and Hooked Himself a Whale of Trouble!

Complete Book-length Novel

BY KENNETH ROBESON

Chapter I
THE TOUGH LUCK OF JEP DEE

MATECUMBE is one of the largest of the string of islands extending south from the tip of Florida and called the Florida Keys.

Jep Dee came to Matecumbe. He stayed two weeks and nothing out of the ordinary happened, except that he did a lot of crawdadding—every day, once in the morning and once in the evening, Jep Dee went hunting crawfish.

That is, he pretended to go for crawfish.

The Caribbean lobster—called crawfish—really looks much like a crawdad from a Missouri creek, although it is served in restaurants and cafeterias and called "Florida lobster," and there are recorded instances where these tropical lobsters have weighed fifteen pounds, which is fully as large as the regular Northern lobster. But it is always called by the natives, crawfish. Properly cooked, the tropical lobster, or crawfish, makes a very savory, succulent and appetizing viand.

True, Jep Dee never ate any of the crawfish he caught.

As a matter of fact—but that was a secret—he never caught any crawfish. He bought them from an old cracker who lived on a nearby island. The old cracker made a living, such as it was, by crawfishing for the market.

Jep Dee never made any effort to catch a crawfish.

He did tell a lot of lies about how he caught them. He would tell how he reached into coral holes and under ledges in the daytime and pulled the big ones out.

He told how he sculled his boat over the reefs at night with a gasoline lantern burning in the bow, until the eyes of the crawfish gleamed like the eyes of cats in automobile headlights along a road at night, after which he gigged them with a little three-tined spear. He was a liar. All he ever gigged was his leg, by accident, one night.

Jep Dee had a nose and fists that looked as if they'd had accidents in the past. He had a mouth that never said much; it had thin lips. Suns had burned him. Sea brine had turned his hide to leather. He was about a foot shorter than an average man, also a foot wider.

One night Jep Dee got drunk and said he could whip his weight in wildcats. There were no wildcats available, but he did very well with four tough crackers and three big yacht sailors who got tired of his chest-beating and tied into him. They still talk about that fight on Matecumbe; it's the main topic of conversation. The main topic used to be the big hurricane of 1934.

Jep Dee paid fourteen dollars and ninety-five cents for the boat—twelve feet long, cypress-planked, rusty iron centerboard, two oars, a ragged, dirty sail—in which he went "crawfishing."

He came to Matecumbe, and every day for two weeks he went out and came back and said he had been crawdadding, until finally he found what he was looking for.

Jep Dee went out on one of his usual nightly crawdad hunts, and found what he sought, and never came back.

A COLLEGE boy in a yawl was the next person to see Jep Dee. This was weeks later.

At first, the college boy thought he was seeing a wad of drifted seaweed lying on a beach, and his second opinion was that it must be a log. Fortunately, he put the yawl tiller over and went in to look.

The college boy was sailing down to Dry Tortugas to see the flock of flamingos, birds that are getting about as scarce as buffaloes. He was on vacation. He was just passing a tiny coral island about sixty miles from Key West, Florida. The island had no vegetation—it was almost as naked as Jep Dee.

Jep Dee could not talk enough to give his name. So he became, in the newspapers, "an unidentified man."

The only thing Jep Dee wore was a rope about four feet long and an inch thick. It was tied to his neck. Not with a hangman's knot, however. From head to foot he was a mass of blisters and sores, the result of exposure to terrific tropical sun and salt water, and the fact that the crabs had not waited until he was dead before starting to eat him.

He had no hair, no eyebrows, no eyelashes, no fingernails. These items had been plucked off.

Also, Jep Dee seemed to be insane.

He had just enough strength to kick the college boy in the face; and while the astonished young alumnus sprawled on his back, Jep Dee got up and ran. His sense of direction was bad, and he dashed into the sea, where he floundered until the college boy caught him.

They had quite a fight. Jep Dee had no strength, but he knew all the evil tricks of brawl fighters, many of which didn't require much power.

Jep Dee did much yelling during the struggle. Most of it was incoherent, but now and then a phrase was understandable. Once he screeched:

"Damn you, Horst! You go back to the island and tell Señor Steel—"

Just what he wanted a man named Horst to tell one named Señor Steel was unintelligible. The fight went on, in water about waist-deep. Once more, Jep Dee spoke understandable words.

"I've seen men being tortured to death before," he screamed, "but the way these—"

He did not finish that sentence, either.

The college boy got him overpowered, rolled him into the dinghy and rowed out to the yawl and spread him under the cockpit awning. Jep Dee lay limp and sucked in breath, making weak whistling sounds. It seemed remarkable that he should be alive.

"Hey, fellow," the college boy said, "you have had some tough luck, haven't you? How are your eyes? Can you see me?"

As the doctor explained, later, Jep Dee couldn't see anything. He was temporarily blinded.

"Who is this Horst?" the college boy asked. "And who is Señor Steel?"

No answer.

"What about men being tortured to death?" inquired the young man. "What did you mean by that?"

Jep Dee went on breathing with whistles.

"You're pretty far gone, old boy," the college boy said kindly. "I'll untie that rope from your neck, and you'll feel better."

The college boy took hold of the rope, and Jep Dee began to fight again. He fought with a whimpering desperation, wildly and unceasingly, as long as the other made any attempt to get the rope loose.

Jep Dee wanted to keep that rope around his neck more than he wanted to keep alive.

THE yawl sailed into Key West, and they put Jep Dee in a hospital that stood in a nice part of town in a grove of palm trees.

"Exposure," the doctors said. But this was before they looked more closely at Jep Dee. After a better examination, they stared at each other in bewilderment.

"Hair, eyebrows and eyelashes have been—pulled out," one doctor said.

"And fingernails plucked off," another stated.

"Take the rope off him," said the head doctor.

So Jep Dee began to fight again. He struck at them, and although his eyes were swollen shut, so that he couldn't see, his hands managed to find a tray of medicines; and he threw bottles at the spots where he imagined doctors would be until he grew so weak that his most furious heaves barely got the bottles over the edge of the hospital bed.

"Mental trouble," the head doctor said. "Thinks he has to keep that rope around his neck."

"What'll we do about it?"

"Humor him. Let him keep it for a while. The man is in very bad shape, and there's no need of exciting him by taking away his rope. I doubt if he lives."

But Jep Dee did live. He lay on the cot on his back, and during the hours when he was awake, he stared fixedly at things in the room, as if he were trying to see only them, and not something that his mind kept trying to resurrect.

For days, he did not sleep. Sleep-producing drugs seemed to have no effect. And when, finally, he did sleep, a nightmare seemed to come upon him at once and he kept making mewing sounds of horror.

He got better.

"Now," the head doctor said, "we can untie that silly rope from his neck."

Three doctors and a nurse got messed up in this attempt before it came to an end with Jep Dee still in possession of the rope, which he kept tied around his neck. It was a thick rope, and when he slept he kept it coiled neatly on his chest, like a snake.

They had not yet identified Jep Dee.

Off a drinking glass they took his fingerprints, distorted prints, because his fingertips had swollen and festered as a result of the plucked-off nails. They sent these to the Key West police, also to the headquarters of the State police at Tallahassee, and to the department of justice in Washington, and

from the latter place they got a telegraphic answer that read:

OUR RECORDS SHOW MAN'S NAME JEP DEE. RECENTLY SENTENCED TO BE SHOT IN CENTRAL AMERICAN REPUBLIC OF BLANCA GRANDE. SAVED BY INTERVENTION OF AMERICAN CONSUL. UNDERSTAND PRESIDENT-DICTATOR OF BLANCA GRANDE HAS STANDING OFFER OF TWENTY-FIVE-THOUSAND-DOLLAR REWARD FOR DEATH OF JEP DEE. IF REWARD OFFER IN ANY WAY RESPONSIBLE FOR PRESENT CONDITION OF JEP DEE, AMERICAN GOVERNMENT IS GOING TO BE INTERESTED BECAUSE IT IS ALREADY NOT ON GOOD TERMS WITH PRESIDENT-DICTATOR OF BLANCA GRANDE.

After this telegram came from the department of justice, they questioned Jep Dee. He could now talk. That is, he had been asking for food and swearing at the doctors.

"Go to hell!" he said.

"If the president-dictator of some South American country ordered you tortured," the doctor said, "they want to know about it in Washington."

"You heard me!" Jep Dee snarled.

"But you should tell—"

"It's none of your damn business," Jep Dee said.

"But—"

"G'wan away!"

"You might at least let us remove that rope—"

"Scram! Vamoose!"

IN the dark and quiet hours of that night, Jep Dee reached under his pillow and got a pair of scissors—small scissors which a nurse had used to snip off his innumerable bandages when dressings were changed and which Jep Dee had stolen and hidden. With the scissors, Jep Dee carefully cut the rope loose from his neck.

He did not cut the knot in the rope. He untied it. With infinite care—and pain too, because of his missing fingernails. The untying took almost an hour. Just before he finished untying it, he listened intently and looked all around, taking great precautions not to be observed.

Twisted between the rope strands, in that part of rope which had been tied in the knot, where it could be discovered only when the rope was untied and untwisted, was a piece of dried shark skin.

The shark skin was freckled.

Whether the shark which was original owner of the skin had been freckled, or whether the freckled aspect of the shark skin came from some other cause, was impossible to ascertain at a glance.

Jep Dee was still quite blind. He fingered the

"I doubt if he lives."

piece of shark skin carefully and caressingly, as if he enjoyed feeling of it.

He did something which no one had heard him do before. He giggled. Not hysterical giggling, nor mad; just the elated chuckle of a man who had put something over.

He got out of the white bed. He was stronger than anyone had thought. He went to the window and dropped the scissors outside, listening carefully to see how far they fell, and by this, concluded that the window was on the first floor. He crawled out, dropped to the ground and felt his way through the grove of palms until he fell over a low hedge, beyond which was a sidewalk.

Jep Dee wore white hospital pajamas. He walked two blocks, feeling his way. Because Key West, Florida, was a winter resort, it was not unusual for people to be seen on the streets in beach pajamas, or suits of slacks that looked very like pajamas. The white hospital pajamas of Jep Dee attracted no attention.

He walked until he heard footsteps approaching, when he stopped and listened. Heavy footsteps. A man's.

Jep Dee said, "I'm not walking in my sleep. I'm a blind man. Will you help me to the post office?"

"The post office is closed at this time of night," reminded the man Jep Dee had met.

"I know," Jep Dee said. "I want you to stop me at a drugstore and loan me a dime for an envelope, a sheet of paper and a stamp."

The man laughed pleasantly, said, "Sure, I'll accommodate you," and took Jep Dee to a drugstore, where he got paper, envelope and stamp, then to the post office.

Jep Dee could write legibly without the aid of his eyes, but it must have been agony without his fingernails. On the paper he scrawled:

SHARK SKIN TELLS EVERTHING

He folded the piece of freckled shark skin inside the paper, inserted it in the envelope, and addressed the missive to:

Miss Rhoda Haven
Tower Apartments
New York City

While Jep Dee was licking the stamps and sticking them on the envelope and putting the envelope in the mail slot—the letter went air mail—the good Samaritan who had led him to the post office went out and called a policeman, because he could see that Jep Dee was the next thing to a dead man, and had no business up and running around. The cop came.

Jep Dee got the idea the cop intended to retrieve the letter which he had mailed, so there was a rousing fight there in the Key West post office, before they got Jep Dee back to the hospital.

News of the mêlée got to the papers, and a reporter came and took a picture of Jep Dee.

Chapter II
THE WAMPUS-CAT

BY the barest margin, the story—picture included —caught the final edition of the morning newspaper, the one that the newsboys sold on the streets around eight o'clock, to people who were going to work.

However, one newspaper was purchased by a man who did not happen to be going to work. He had been up all night raising hell, as a matter of fact, and was going out to a drugstore—before he went to bed—to buy a box of aspirin, experience having taught him how his head might feel when he awakened.

He looked at the Jep Dee story and forgot all about aspirin.

"Damn!" he croaked.

He put his head back and ran like a pickaninny who had been walking through a lonesome graveyard at dark midnight when he heard a deep groan. He got out in the street and ran, because people were in his way on the sidewalk. He bounded aboard a ritzy, streamlined cabin cruiser moored to one of the yacht docks.

He fell down a companionway into the cruiser cabin in his haste.

Half a dozen men were in the cruiser cabin. They began laughing.

"Horst is seeing things!" one man chuckled.

"After the way he drank last night, I don't wonder," said another.

The man who had been in the market for aspirin—Horst—lay on the cabin floor and panted and glared.

Horst had the look of being twin to the devil. Twin to the pictures that depict the devil, at least. Horst was a little heavier than the devil, thicker through the neck, possibly not so tall, and did not have quite the same pointed dog ears with which artists equip their devil pictures. He was a rather brown devil.

"Stop that laughing!" Horst snarled.

The mirth died. Suddenly. As if ice water had been dumped on the chucklers.

Horst got up and took a gun out of his clothing, a large gun that was as black as the murder-mood in Horst's eyes.

"Who thinks this is funny?" he asked gutturally.

No one said anything. For a minute, terror walked around and around on feather-light feet.

At last a man took hold of his courage and said, "We came to Key West to throw a party and celebrate the last of Jep Dee. Nobody meant anything when they laughed, Horst."

The men had been a little drunk. They were shivering sober now.

Horst said, "Listen to me."

He didn't need to tell them to do that.

"Jep Dee is alive," Horst said.

TEN minutes later, the occupants of the cabin cruiser had scattered to check on the newspaper story. None of them had slept, for they had caroused the previous night through, but now there were no thoughts about sleep. Some went to the post office where they stood around looking innocent and asking casual questions.

Horst and another man went to the hospital, where Horst told a glib story about a pal of his who resembled the published picture of Jep Dee, a ruse that got him a close look at the blind castaway whom the college boy had found on a desert island.

Horst stood looking down at Jep Dee, and he put a hand in his pocket, resting it on the black gun. But there were too many doctors around. Not to mention two policemen who stood out in the hall. The cops were asking a doctor when Jep Dee would be able to answer questions. It seemed that Jep Dee had fainted and not yet revived.

Horst went back to the big, sleek, fast cabin cruiser.

His men joined him.

"It's Jep Dee, all right," Horst snarled. He looked more devillike than ever. "The sharks didn't get him. He must have made it by swimming."

One of the men who had gone to the post office reported, "I talked to the guy who led Jep Dee to the post office. Jep Dee mailed something in an envelope."

"Mailed what?"

"It looked," the man said, "like a piece of freckled shark skin."

"Like what?"

"A chunk of hide off a freckled shark. That's the best description I could get, and this guy who led Jep Dee to the post office had a good memory."

"Oh, damn!"

Horst made unpleasant faces while he thought.

"You say the guy that led Jep Dee had a good memory," he continued. "Good enough to remember the address on the envelope? Or did he see it?"

"He saw the address."

Horst scowled. "Well?"

"The piece of freckled shark skin," the man explained, "went to Miss Rhoda Haven, Tower Apartments, New York City."

Horst acted as if he had taken a hard hammer blow between the eyes. His mouth fell open slackly, his arms dropped, and he sank on a transom seat.

Small waves hit the boat hull and made the sounds of a kid with an all-day sucker, sea gulls circled around outside and gave their rather hideous I-feel-like-I'm-going-to-die squawks, and inside the cabin the boat clock clicked steadily.

"Damn, this is bad!" Horst croaked.

Suddenly he bounded to his feet.

"Call the airport," he yelled. "Reserve places for all of us on the first plane to New York."

"But what about Jep Dee?"

Horst said, "He's helpless. He won't be leaving the hospital. We'll leave a man to watch him. Hutch, you do that."

"Any preference about how I watch Jep Dee while you're gone?" Hutch asked.

"Use your judgment," Horst snapped. "Call the airport, somebody."

"You have to go to Miami," a man reminded him, "to catch the regular air line."

"Then charter a fast private plane!" Horst yelled.

WHILE one of his men was finding a plane and chartering the craft, Horst paid a visit to the cable office. He spent some time composing a cablegram, which he dispatched.

The cable was in code, and there was almost two pages of it.

The plane they rented was fast, so they ate dinner that evening in the restaurant at the airport where they landed on the outskirts of New York City. The dinner was grim. All of them were worried, Horst most of all.

They were dressed in dark, discreet business suits, the coats of which were cut full under the armpits so as not to reveal the firearms that rested in shoulder holsters. They spoke little.

Two of them, who had a distinct accent that marked them as South Americans, spoke not at all when there was any stranger near enough to overhear. Horst and the other two spoke excellent English, so much so that it was difficult, even after a conversation with them, to say whether they were native Americans.

There was an air of viciousness about almost everything they did. They did not have to act vicious. They *were* vicious.

From the airport, Horst went to the main New York cable office. He asked for a message for Jerry Shinn, stated convincingly that this was his name.

There was a cablegram, and it was in code; had been sent from the South American republic of Blanca Grande, was in answer to the message Horst had sent from Key West.

Riding uptown in a taxicab, Horst translated the cablegram. It said:

GET THAT FRECKLED SHARK SKIN, THEN WIPE OUT THE HAVENS AND EVERYONE CONNECTED WITH THEM.

STEEL

The men gazed at the message dubiously.

"Get the shark skin, eh?"

"And wipe out the Havens."

"That last order," Horst said grimly, "may be easier to give than to carry out." He leaned back and thought in silence for a few moments, and what he was thinking about must have been unpleasant, because he shivered.

"That Tex Haven," he said, "is an old wampus-cat."

Chapter III
THE DIRTY TRICK

THE "wampus-cat" being an imaginary creature, its exact measurements and specifications and qualities are necessarily indefinite. It may be long or short, high or low; and it may bark or mew or squall, as the circumstances require. But generally the qualifications state that it is an eat-'em-up kind of an animal.

But it was hard to look at Tex Haven and imagine a wampus-cat of any kind.

The man looked mild. He had a long face that was as benign as the countenance of a village parson. He had a long body that looked as if it had been constructed to fit inside a judge's robes. His teeth showed a lot, his brownish hair was always tangled, the light of sunny Ireland was always in his blue eyes; and one looked at him and naturally expected him to laugh and chuckle more than he was silent. In truth, he rarely spoke a word; and when he did, it was a low-voiced one.

Tex Haven spoke gently to men, spoke loudly and pleasantly to babies, and hardly ever spoke to women. He kept away from

high windows, looked four or five times each way before he crossed a street. He never drank. He swore terribly. He smoked a corncob pipe.

He did not get a letter during the time—six weeks—he had lived at the Tower Apartments, until the missive came from Jep Dee. Tex Haven got it out of the mail box.

"Rhoda!" he called gently.

His daughter came.

She was a tall girl, as long and gentle-looking as her father; but whereas old Tex Haven's construc-

Tex Haven fired once with his right hand and once with his left.

tion ran a bit too much to bones, the daughter was streamlined. Her hair was deep and coppery and always perfectly waved, her eyes were gentle, her mouth sweet and kind. There was a Madonnalike gentleness about her face. She dressed well, but with almost nunlike severity. She never drank. She swore only when it was necessary. She did not smoke, and whenever she got hold of one of old Tex Haven's corncob pipes, she invariably took a hammer to it—then threw away the pieces.

"Jep Dee," Tex Haven said, and extended the letter.

Rhoda Haven read Jep Dee's letter.

Rhoda Haven had degrees from four of the world's greatest universities. She had explored the Inca country of South America, and written a book which was used as a text by archaeologists. She had nearly lost her life in experiments with a terrible tropic fever, and had come out with a cure for the fever, something that had previously baffled scientists. She had written a treatise on governmental administrative science that would probably win a Nobel prize.

A great sculptor had said that her head was the perfect type of patrician beauty.

The president-dictator of the South American republic of Blanca Grande had offered one hundred thousand dollars to anyone who would bring him Rhoda Haven's head—without body attached.

"FROM Key West," Rhoda Haven said of the letter, "with no name signed."

Tex Haven sucked thoughtfully on his corncob pipe.

"Be from Jep Dee, figures like," he said.

"I think so, too."

They examined the shark skin. It was thin, so it must be the skin off a very young shark. It was also stiff, and had a tendency to curl. The freckle spots were not regular, but scattered; some of them were rather large and others were small. All freckles were shades of deep-brown or black.

Tex Haven said, "Mean anythin' special to you?"

"Not a thing."

"Here, neither."

"But the note," Rhoda Haven pointed out, "says that the shark skin explains everything."

Tex Haven took his corncob pipe out of his teeth and gave it a look of mild reproach.

"Kinda looks like there might be a headache comin' up," he said.

The telephone began to ring. It rang steadily. Tex Haven went over to it, an ambling, peaceful-looking tower of a man, picked up the instrument, said, "Hello, hello?" several times, then stood holding the instrument and looking mild and patient.

"Tarnatin' thing just goes on ringin'," he said.

The telephone rang and rang. About five minutes later, knuckles tapped the door politely.

"Yes," Rhoda Haven said.

A voice outside the door said, "Telephone man. There's something wrong with your phone that makes it ring steadily. May we come in and fix it?"

Gentle-looking old Tex Haven started to open the door.

His daughter grabbed his arm, breathed, "No!"

To the man on the other side of the door, the girl said, "Just a minute, until I get into a robe. I'm taking a bath."

Tex Haven knocked the fire out of his corncob, poured the smoldering tobacco into a tray, put the pipe in his pocket.

"'Twould have fooled me," he said in a voice so low that it was hardly audible.

Rhoda Haven said, "I may be wrong. But I think trouble of this kind only originates in the mechanical ringer at the switchboard. I doubt if it would be our instrument."

Each day since coming to the Tower Apartments, one of their first morning acts had been to carefully pack all their belongings in two handbags.

Tex and Rhoda Haven moved swiftly, got the two bags, whipped to a window and went down a fire escape. From the bottom of the fire escape, they dropped into a garden where the shrubbery was thick and where pigeons fluttered and cooed.

Three men stood up in the bushes. They held guns.

One gun-holder said, "We figured the phone gag might not work, in which case you'd maybe be going this way."

Tex Haven eyed them mildly.

"You-uns downright serious about this?" he asked.

"What do you think?" one said. "Horst sent us. We want that piece of shark skin."

Tex Haven said, "Waal, in such case—"

QUITE a number of people had seen old Tex Haven go into a gun fight at one time or another, and not many of them had ever been able to explain where he got his guns. There was apparently some kind of magic about it. One minute the mild-looking old codger's hands would be empty—next they were full of spouting iron.

Tex Haven fired once with his right hand and once with his left. One man barked and turned around from the force of a bullet in his shoulder. A second man stood for a moment very stiff and dead, hit between the eyes, before he fell.

Rhoda Haven doubled down, scooped a handful of soft dirt, sent it toward the face of the third man. He snarled, tried to turn his head from the flying dirt and shoot the girl at the same time. His shot echoes gobbled into the echoes of Tex Haven's shots. The bullet missed the girl.

Tex Haven flicked his guns at the man.

A fourth man came into the garden fifty yards away. It was Horst. He lifted a long-barreled revolver deliberately.

Tex Haven saw Horst aiming and suddenly flattened. The man Haven had been about to shoot ran away. Tex Haven let him go; Haven seemed to have more respect for Horst's marksmanship than desire for the life of the running man.

More men came into the garden. The place began to convulse with ripping shot crashes.

Tex and Rhoda Haven crawled slowly and carefully. Old Tex kept his gun ready. Neither seemed particular excited, and each dragged one of the suitcases. They got behind a fountain which was spouting three streams of water into a concrete bowl that overflowed into a fake brook, that trickled across the garden and eventually vanished into a sewer through a grille. Tex and Rhoda Haven got into the brook, were very wet by the time they reached the grille.

Horst and his men had lost track of them. When the Havens came up, they had the advantage of surprise. Horst had climbed on a garden bench, was staring. He had nerve, at least. But he flung himself off the bench when old Tex Haven leaped up and fired.

Shot sound again slammed through the garden. Bullets knocked red dust off bricks, broke two windows, frightened the pigeons anew.

Tex and Rhoda Haven dived into a narrow passage that led to the back street. They ran down the street.

Inside the apartment house, residents were very quiet, although occasionally one stole a furtive look from a window. A woman had been screaming, but had stopped. The snarling sirens of police cars were already approaching.

The Havens got into a subway and took a southbound train.

THERE was no trace of excitement in the manner of Tex Haven or his daughter. Sitting beside her suitcase, the girl idly contemplated the allurements of a tooth paste as set forth by a car poster, and old Tex Haven even purchased a tabloid newspaper from a newsboy who was working the subway train, and calmly scanned it.

Once Tex Haven said in a low voice, "Nobody 'cept Jep Dee knowed we was livin' at them Tower Apartments."

"Jep never told Horst," Rhoda Haven said quickly.

"Betcher life he didn't. Horst likely learned from that letter. He 'peared to know a piece of shark skin was in it."

They changed subway trains three times, shifted to taxicabs and used four different cabs.

The hotel to which they went eventually was small and respectable, had a proprietor notable for the size of his stomach and the proportions of his black mustache, who nearly fell over when he saw his guests, then exploded a delighted, "Tex Haven, you old bobcat in a rabbit skin!"

"Professor Smith and daughter be the names," Tex Haven said mildly.

"Oh, ho! So you're charming snakes again?"

"Bein' charmed, more like."

The Havens were shown to a suite of two small rooms, which were on the upper floor so the windows could not be shot into conveniently, and which had a handy fire escape.

Tex Haven called his daughter's attention to an item in the tabloid newspaper which he had bought in the subway.

"Be a mite clearer, you read this," he said.

Datelined Key West, Florida, the newspaper item told of the mysterious man named Jep Dee, who had been found, a torture victim, on an uninhabited coral island.

"Poor Jep," Rhoda Haven said in a low voice.

"Looks as if," Tex Haven said, "they ketched Jep Dee."

He got out his corncob pipe and filled it with fragments of poisonous-looking black Scotch tobacco which he tore, with difficulty, from a plug that was about the shape of a fountain pen, and fully as black and hard. Then he leaned back in a chair and let out clouds of smoke that smelled as if it came from a fumigator's smudge pot. Later, he cleaned and reloaded his guns carefully. There were five of the guns, of assorted sizes, and carried in different places about his long person.

By that time he appeared to have finished his thinking.

"Jep Dee found what him an' us are after, figures as if," he said.

"Yes," said Rhoda Haven.

"They kotched Jep, an' treated him sort of poorly. We don't know why they treated him that way, but we might smack a guess."

"They were trying to make Jep tell them where they could find us," the girl said.

"I'd smack the same guess," old Tex Haven stated mildly.

Tex dragged several seething, acid-tinted puffs of smoke from his pipe, then took the corncob out of his teeth and contemplated it lovingly.

"Such industry needs reward, strikes me," he said.

His daughter eyed him sharply. "What do you mean?"

"Ever hear of Doc Savage?"

"Doc Savage?"

"Yep.

RHODA HAVEN took hold of her lower lip with neat white teeth. She got up, went to the window, passed a hand over her forehead, then came back. Her mouth was grim.

"Look," she said, "when you defied the Japanese army and they chased us all over Manchuria, I didn't object."

"Come to think of it," old Tex Haven admitted mildly, "you didn't."

"And when you dared the German and Italian navy and landed a shipload of guns in Spain, I still didn't object."

"There for a while, I was kinda wishin' you had."

"The point," the girl said, "is that you could arrange for us to stage a single-handed duel with the U.S. marines and I would string along with you."

"You're tryin' to say—"

"Haven't you ever *heard* about this Doc Savage?"

"In certain circles," Tex Haven said dryly, "more people've heard of Doc Savage than know about Mussolini and Hitler."

"I don't doubt it."

"Strikes me," Tex Haven said, "that in two hundred years from now, there'll be more in the school books about Doc Savage than there'll be about Mussolini and Hitler."

"Maybe."

"Will, if civilization advances any. Times I doubt if it's gonna."

Rhoda Haven stamped a foot.

"Quit beating around the bush," she snapped, "and tell me what you've got up your sleeve."

"We're going," Tex Haven said, "to do Horst and Señor Steel a dirty trick."

"Dirty trick?"

"We're going to sick Doc Savage onto 'em. Give 'em somethin' to do besides devil us." Old Tex Haven looked at his daughter and assumed the expression of a gaunt tomcat surrounded by canary feathers. "Right pert idea, don't you think?"

"Which one of us is going to sick Doc Savage onto Horst and Señor Steel?" Rhoda Haven demanded.

"You, I reckon. Deceivin' a man is a woman's work."

Rhoda Haven frowned. "If I tell Doc Savage the truth, he will be likely to cut loose on *us,* instead of Horst and Steel."

Old Tex Haven grinned.

"There won't," he said, "be a splinter of truth in anything you tell Doc Savage."

Chapter IV
THE MISSING MAN

ABOUT an hour later, Rhoda Haven stood on the sidewalk in front of one of New York's highest buildings. By tilting her head back and straining her eyes, she could just discern the topmost—the eighty-sixth floor—windows, partially enveloped in a low-hanging cloud. Quite a number of people, she imagined, knew that behind those windows was Doc Savage's headquarters. She, herself, had known the fact for some months.

She knew that Doc Savage was an unusual man whose occupation was righting wrongs and punishing evildoers, frequently traveling to the world's far places to do so. She had heard that Doc Savage, sometimes called the "Man of Bronze," had been trained scientifically from childhood for his career, trained so successfully that he was an almost super-human combination of inventive genius, mental wizard and physical giant.

Personally, Rhoda Haven doubted a great many things she had heard about Doc Savage. He seemed too perfect, too much of a superman. She suspected a good deal of that was hokum.

It was also reported that Doc Savage took no pay for punishing the evildoers and righting the wrongs, and Rhoda Haven doubted that, too. It did not seem sensible. It was all right for men named Galahad and Lancelot to ride around in medieval literature doing such things, because they possibly never did actually exist. In real life, people expected to get paid for what they did.

Rhoda Haven compressed her lips.

"Still," she remarked, "where there is smoke, you generally find a fire."

By smoke, she meant the reputation of this Doc Savage, a reputation that gave nightmares to crooks, international or otherwise, whenever the name of the Man of Bronze was mentioned. She knew that mention of Doc Savage really scared certain kinds of people. She had seen it happen.

Rhoda Haven entered the skyscraper lobby, which was as vast as the interior of some cathedrals, and took an elevator that traveled upward so swiftly that she had to swallow wildly to equalize the pressure against her eardrums. She found herself standing in a corridor which had one door, an unobtrusive, bronze-colored panel lettered simply:

CLARK SAVAGE, Jr.

"At least," Rhoda Haven said with some approval, "he doesn't put on much of a show."

As a matter of fact, she had heard that Doc Savage dodged newspaper publicity so assiduously that it was almost impossible for a reporter to get an interview with him.

"I wonder," she added, "if he believes female lies?"

She knocked on the door.

The door was opened by a man who bore a striking likeness to an extremely long skeleton coated with some sunburned hide.

"Consociative accolades," he remarked.

"I hope," Rhoda Haven said, "that *you're* not Doc Savage!"

"An apocryphal hermeneutic," said the long string of bones.

"Eh?"

"A corrigendum."

Rhoda Haven narrowed one eye.

"I must have got off on the wrong floor," she said. "I wasn't looking for a walking dictionary."

With some evidence of reluctance, the string of bones lapsed into ordinary words.

"I am trying to explain that you have made a mistake," he said. "I am not Doc Savage. I am William Harper Littlejohn."

"And what else," Rhoda Haven inquired, "might you be?"

"One of Doc Savage's associates, or assistants, or whatever you would call the five of us who work with the bronze man."

WILLIAM HARPER LITTLEJOHN stood back politely for the young woman to enter, and she did so. The room into which she came was equipped with a large inlaid table, a very big safe, and a scattering of comfortable leather-upholstered furniture. It appeared to be a reception room.

The room was not as interesting as the man who had opened the door. Rhoda Haven stared at him.

"Revelatory peroration is ultrapropitious," he stated.

Rhoda Haven blinked.

"When they made you," she said, "they must not have had any materials left but bones and big words."

"A deleterious—"

"Whoa!" said Rhoda Haven. "What do I do to persuade you to use little words?"

"You just explain who you are," William Harper Littlejohn said, again reluctantly using small words, "and state your business."

"My name is Mary Morse," said Rhoda Haven.

"And—"

"I came here to see Doc Savage."

"Why?"

"That," the girl said, "is something I will only tell to Doc Savage."

"I see. Well, goodbye."

"What do you mean—goodbye?"

"Doc Savage isn't available. He is missing. He frequently becomes missing, and none of us know where he is. It happens often enough that we do not get alarmed. Furthermore, when he isn't here, he just isn't here; and we have no way of getting in touch with him."

Having ridded himself of this explanation with an air of injury at having to use such small words, William Harper Littlejohn turned to the inlaid table and picked up a massive book titled, "Influence of Lepidoptera on Ancient Decorative Design," which he appeared to have been reading.

Rhoda Haven said, "I need help."

"Eh?"

"My life is in danger."

William Harper Littlejohn put down the large book.

"Why didn't you," he said, "say so in the first place?" He took the girl's arm, led her to a chair. It was a very massive chair, and apparently extremely heavy. At least, it would not budge when the girl hitched at the chair to move it. She let the chair remain where it was.

"What is the trouble?" asked William Harper Littlejohn.

"Some men are trying to kill me and my father," Rhoda Haven said.

"Why?"

"We don't know."

"Who are the men who want you dead?"

"We don't have any idea," Rhoda Haven said, and looked as if she were telling the truth.

William Harper Littlejohn wore, attached to his coat lapel by a dark ribbon, a monocle. He never put this in his eye, and a second glance would disclose that the monocle was really a strong magnifying glass. Now he absent-mindedly whirled the monocle around by its ribbon.

"Just a moment," he said.

He passed through another door. This admitted him to the Doc Savage library, a large room crowded with cases that were in turn jammed with books, most of them scientific tomes.

William Harper Littlejohn made sure the girl was remaining behind. Then he went close to a large bookcase, which was really a panel that could be swung outward and reveal a niche in which a man might remain comfortably seated without his presence being suspected by anyone who might pass through the library.

"Doc?" said William Harper Littlejohn in a low voice.

THE voice which answered from inside the hidden niche was deep, and although controlled down to a whisper, it gave an impression of remarkable power.

"Yes, Johnny," it said.

Johnny used small words—he always used small

ones when talking to Doc Savage, for some reason or other—and asked, "I had our visitor sit down in the chair that's wired up with our new lie detector. Is the gadget working all right? You're watching the various indicator dials in there, aren't you?"

"It seems to be working," replied the striking voice of the man inside the niche.

"Has the girl told the truth?"

"Only once," Doc Savage said. "And that was when she said some men were trying to kill herself and her father."

"Do you want to go in and talk to her, Doc?"

"No. You do that."

"But—"

"And if she thinks she needs help, you might as well help her."

Johnny asked, "Shall I call in Monk and Ham? They're the only two members of our gang that are in town. Renny and Long Tom are in Czechoslovakia trying to build a dam and electrify it."

"Monk and Ham would want you to call them."

"I'll say they would. But I hate to think about the way they'll squabble. This girl is pretty. Every time she smiles at Monk, he'll have to fight Ham, and vice versa"

"Call them, anyway."

"All right," Johnny said. "But what are you going to be doing?"

"I will try," Doc Savage explained, "to think of something."

WILLIAM HARPER LITTLEJOHN rejoined Rhoda Haven in the reception room with a big smile and the request, "Call me Johnny. Everyone does."

"I will," the girl said, "if you promise to use small words."

"Now just what has happened to make you think your life is in danger?"

"Some men," Rhoda Haven explained, "attacked us in our rooms at the Tower Apartments. We escaped down the fire escape. There was a shooting affray in the garden where they tried to head us off, but we got away."

"I'm superamalgamated if I—I mean, I don't see why you didn't go to the police."

Rhoda Haven knotted and unknotted her handkerchief, and worked her mouth, looking very scared. For a girl who had behaved in her calm fashion during the gun fight, she looked very frightened indeed.

"I'm afraid," she said, "that one or more of our attackers were killed in the garden."

"They were?"

"Yes. The police would put us in jail for it, we were afraid."

"And you don't deserve to go to jail?"

"Oh, no indeed."

"In that case," Johnny said, "I'll have to help you."

He got up—he had been in shirt sleeves—and put on his coat, which fit him with about the same effect as a flag draped about the top of a flagpole on a windless day. He looked almost completely like a scarecrow. Certainly he did not resemble one of the most eminent living authorities on the subjects of archaeology and geology. He gave his monocle-magnifier a flourish, bowed low—pretty girls were not without their effect upon him—to Rhoda Haven, and escorted the young lady to the street.

"Primigenously, we colligate ancillary—"

"You promised," Rhoda Haven said, "to stop using such words."

Johnny nodded reluctantly.

"First," he said, "we collect help in the shape of Monk and Ham."

"I never heard of Monk and Ham."

"Most people," Johnny said, "have trouble keeping from hearing them."

They got into a taxicab and drove off.

A man who had been standing on the sidewalk, taking candid-camera shots of pedestrians and passing out coupons which entitled the receiver to a picture providing the coupon and twenty-five cents were mailed in, came to sudden life. He was a short, swarthy man, rather well-dressed for an itinerant photographer.

He ran to a parked car which had another dark man at the wheel.

"Follow that cab!" he barked.

"The girl—"

"She went to Doc Savage. Horst must be a mind reader."

The car—it was a rent-a-car sedan—snooped downtown after the cab, and the two swarthy occupants of the machine watched William Harper Littlejohn and Rhoda Haven enter a tall office building near the Wall Street district.

"Better call Horst," one said.

The other man got out of the car, hurried to a telephone. He said, "Horst, what in the devil ever made you suspect the Haven girl would go to Doc Savage?"

Horst swore. "Did she?"

"Nothing else but."

Horst swore some more, said, "I figured old Tex Haven was fox enough to try to sick somebody else's dog onto us. And this Doc Savage was the logical dog. For a long time, we've been afraid someone would set him on us."

"You mean this Doc Savage is tough?"

"Haven't you heard of him, you fool?"

"I . . . uh—"

"Where is the girl now?"

"She came out of the building with the longest and skinniest guy you ever saw—"

"That one is Johnny Littlejohn, who is famous for archaeology, geology and big words."

"And they went downtown and entered an office building—"

"What address?"

The man furnished Horst with the address.

Horst cursed a third time, said, "There is where Monk Mayfair, the chemist of Doc Savage's organization, has his lab. They've gone to get Monk."

"What do we do?"

"Get them. Take them prisoners. I don't care how you do it, but get it done."

"How," the man asked, "will I know this Monk Mayfair?"

"Just look at him," Horst snarled.

Chapter V
IMPULSIVE MR. HENRY PEACE

ANDREW   BLODGETT—MONK—MAY-FAIR was never mistaken for any other person. Upon occasion, when Monk was seen in dark alleys and other spots where visibility was poor—there had been one particular occasion when he was swimming nude in a tropical river—he had been mistaken for an ape. So definite was the resemblance that, on the swimming-in-the-jungle instance, a specimen-collecting naturalist had shot at him repeatedly with a rifle that fired mercy bullets.

Monk's face was fabulously homely, but fortunately it was a pleasant kind of homeliness. Dogs wagged tails at him, and children, who logically could have been expected to be frightened to death at sight of such a face, chuckled in delight. Babies always cooed and wanted to smack Monk's nose with their little fists, although much larger fists had already knocked the nose rather flat, as well as made some permanent changes in the shapes of Monk's ears.

Furthermore, there was some quality about the face that seemed to fascinate pretty girls. By grinning, smirking and crinkling his small eyes, Monk imagined he could increase his appeal.

He grinned, smirked and crinkled for Rhoda Haven.

The display moved Brigadier General Theodore Marley—Ham—Brooks to make a remark.

"The more I see of you," Ham said, "the more I'm reminded of a famous scientist."

"Who?"

"Darwin," Ham said.

Monk bloated indignantly. "Say, that's the guy who thought men came from monkeys."

The pair scowled at each other.

Ham Brooks was a wiry man, wide-shouldered, with an orator's large mouth, a high forehead—a man who was as completely Monk's opposite as one could be. He carried an innocent-looking, dark sword cane. He dressed always—he changed clothes a dozen times daily, if necessary, to be properly garbed for each different occasion or activity—in the most expensive and correct of attire fashioned by the most famous tailors. In fact, tailors had been known to furtively follow him down a street, just to watch clothes being worn as they should be.

Ham Brooks looked what he was, one of the most astute lawyers Harvard had ever produced—in contrast to Monk, who was one of the greatest living industrial chemists, and didn't look it at all.

"Who," Rhoda Haven asked Ham, "are you?"

Monk said, "He's an overdressed shyster lawyer named Ham Brooks, and while I hate to be disagreeably frank to another man's face, you want to watch him. He comes from a long line of ancestors who were not to be trusted. They were lawyers."

"Listen," Ham snapped, "my family springs from the best stock around Boston."

"My family never sprang from anybody!" Monk said. "They sprang at 'em!"

WHILE Monk and Ham halved their time impartially between scowling, giving each other man-eating glares, and smiling with utmost pleasantness at Rhoda Haven, the girl told the same story which she had earlier given to Johnny. The story from which much truth was missing. The tale about persons unidentified attacking her and her father at Tower Apartments for reasons unknown. She lied nicely throughout.

Johnny said, "The thing for us to do is go to Tower Apartments and see if we can pick up the assailants' trail."

"You're very nice to help me," Rhoda Haven said delightedly.

They had held the conference in Monk's penthouse, which was also his chemical laboratory, as well as an example of what a garish imagination could do with modernistic decoration.

"Wait'll I get my pig," Monk said, and called, "Habeas! Habeas Corpus!"

Habeas Corpus was a shoat with long legs, wing-sized ears, and a snout built for inquiring into the bottoms of tin cans. Habeas was an Arabian hog, of indefinite age, who probably would never get any larger than he was—about the proportions of an average-sized bulldog. He was Monk's pet.

Habeas appeared, accompanied by Chemistry, who was Ham's pet.

Monk didn't care for Chemistry, probably

They ran in different directions, but blindly, bumping into things.

"Let us," Johnny said, "extravasate."

Monk translated, "He means let's go to the Tower Apartments."

They extravasated to the penthouse elevator and eventually out on the sidewalk.

"We'll take a taxicab," Ham said.

While they were looking for a taxicab to flag, a man approached.

The man wore overalls, carried a huge paper-wrapped package on one shoulder. His face was soiled. A closer scrutiny would have shown that he was the same man who had been taking sidewalk photographs in front of Doc Savage's headquarters skyscraper. Unfortunately, no one gave him the closer scrutiny.

because Chemistry was a chimpanzee—if not a chimp, then some member of the baboon family—which bore a disquieting likeness to Monk himself. Seen far apart, so that they could not be distinguished by size—Chemistry came little above Monk's knees —there was likely to be confusion of identity.

Monk quarreled continually with Ham; Habeas Corpus squabbled perpetually with Chemistry.

The man fell down. Flat on his face, he flopped. Directly in front of Monk, Ham, Johnny and Rhoda Haven. The man hit the sidewalk hard, and the box he was carrying hit even harder.

The box burst. Fumes came out. The vapor was the color of the insides of rotten eggs.

The fallen man took told of his mouth and nose with both hands and pinched, so he could not breathe.

Monk, Ham, Johnny, Rhoda Haven—all stared in astonishment until the fumes came up and enveloped them and were breathed into their lungs, when they realized what was happening—knew that the vapr was gas—after which they ran in different directions, but blindly, bumping into things.

From assorted hiding places nearby came four men who wore gas masks and carried blackjacks, and a fifth man who drove a bakery delivery truck.

The gas-masked men with the blackjacks slugged Monk, Ham, Johnny and Rhoda Haven to the sidewalk. They loaded the senseless forms into the bakery truck.

By that time, there was a good deal of excitement around about, what with pedestrians who had walked into the tear gas, and people yelling for cops. But the bakery truck got away.

WHEN Monk was able to sit up, he felt of his left eye, and having had black eyes before, he knew its condition.

"Gave you a black eye," Ham said.

"They must have," Monk admitted. "I don't remember fighting for it."

"That tear gas was a nice trick."

"Nice enough," Monk snarled, "that I'm gonna pull some legs and arms off some bodies."

"Don't be impulsive," advised one of the four men who had worn gas masks.

The vanlike inside of the bakery truck was larger than a casual exterior glance indicated. The four former gas-mask wearers stood in strategic corners holding large and unquestionably efficient revolvers.

The man who had dropped the gas package sat on the floor near the prisoners and rubbed his leaking eyes. Monk gave him a kick. The man yelped, whipped out a knife, stabbed the floor where Monk's leg had been an instant before.

Monk howled disagreeably—his fights were always noisy—and took the knife-wielder by the throat with a pair of rusty-haired hands that could straighten horseshoes.

A man stepped forward, smacked a revolver down on Monk's bullet-shaped head. Monk dropped.

"Hell, shoot him if he cuts up again," another

man advised. "People will think the motor backfired."

There was silence, and no action except the jumping around of the truck as it moved fast. Judging from the lack of traffic noises, they were outside the city, and on a country road not too well maintained. Only twice did cars pass them, one of these blowing several times for a share of the road, which must have been narrow, judging from the swearing their drivers did. Finally the car stopped.

One of the men got out.

Five minutes later, he put his head back in the truck.

"Old homestead sure gone to hell since I was raised here," he said. "But nobody ain't ever filled up the old cistern."

"Cistern?" Ham said.

"Deep, lined with old brick, and easy to cave in," said the man. "With large green toads in the bottom."

"Any water?" another man asked.

"Hell, don't need water. We can use a knife on them first."

The prisoners were now tied with white cotton rope, while the men stood by with ready guns.

They were dragged out of the bakery truck, whereupon they saw a very seedy-looking farm, the principal crop on which seemed to be five-foot-high weeds. The house, two stories, was leaning southward, and the barn had apparently laid down years ago. Both buildings were minus about everything that could be pried off.

The man had removed old rotting boards from the top of the cistern. The captives were dragged close enough that they could smell odor—probably of unfortunately curious rabbits—that came out of the depths.

"YOU'VE got," growled the man who seemed to be spokesman, "one chance to eat dinner tonight."

"What's that?" Ham asked.

"Prove to us that there's no need of killing you."

Ham looked at the man indignantly. "How do you expect us to prove something we don't know? We never saw you thugs before. We have no idea why you seized us."

"You haven't?"

"No."

"It was because you were with this girl," the man explained. "Now that we're being frank, suppose you answer a question for me."

"Shoot."

"How much do you know? How much has old Tex Haven and the girl here found out? How much has Jep Dee told them?"

Ham said, "Who is Jep Dee?"

"Is that your answer?"

"The answer," Ham snapped, "is that we're completely puzzled. The girl just said mysterious men were trying to kill her and her father, and she wanted us to protect her."

Rhoda Haven said disgustedly, "And you can see how much protecting they did."

The girl, considering their situation, was remarkably calm. Much more so, in fact, than either Ham, Monk or Johnny; and they were accustomed to danger, having faced it with spasmodic frequency during the time they had been associated with Doc Savage. They also liked excitement, it probably being the strongest bond which held them to Doc Savage, next to an intense admiration for the capacity and character of the Man of Bronze. But they had an embarrassed suspicion that the girl was the calmest of them all.

They were beginning to see that Rhoda was a very remarkable girl.

"They don't know anything," the questioning captor decided suddenly. "The girl didn't tell them the truth. It's like Horst figured. She and old Tex Haven just tried to sick Doc Savage onto us."

"So now we do what?"

"Into the cistern with them."

"We could just as well have taken a machine gun to them when they came out of that office building near Wall Street."

"Hell, we had to learn how much they knew, didn't we? Give a hand."

They darted for Monk first, probably because he had made the most trouble. They had enough respect for Monk's fighting potentialities that all of them gathered around for the task of throwing him into the well.

The big red-haired stranger must have decided this was his opportunity. Because now he came out of the weeds. He did not make much noise.

The red-haired newcomer had two men disarmed practically before they knew he was with them. After that, there was no doubt about his presence.

THE fiery-haired stranger dived into the cluster of men surrounding Monk. Blow sounds, bleats of pain, profane yells, ripping clothes noise jumped out of what soon became a large ball of arms and legs and dust.

The stranger was big, much bigger than any man in the group. His shoulders were wide; his hips were lean. His strength seemed to flow as lightning. His actions were as flaming as the red of his hair.

His grin was big and cheerful through all. If he laughed once during the fray, he laughed a dozen times. Which meant that he laughed often, because it did not last long.

His eyes were blue. His teeth were white. His nose had a few freckles. His red hair needed cutting, and was tousled this way and that on his head.

When he waded out of the mêlée, walking on two stupefied faces as he did so, he carried all their guns. His hands were very large, but the guns made almost more than handfuls, even hanging on his fingers by the trigger guards.

He aimed at a man and shot.

Certainly he was no gunman. He was terrible. He missed a man he could almost have hit with his fist. His target got up and ran. He shot again and missed that man, too, and the fellow got up and ran, making dog-yelp sounds of terror as he went away.

The red-headed stranger did some more shooting, and his untouched targets did more running. By the time he had emptied one gun—hitting nobody—all Horst's men had departed like shot-at rabbits into the tall weeds.

The fiery-haired giant kept on pointing guns which banged loudly and futilely.

"Drab nab it!" said the redhead cheerfully. "I keep missin' 'em."

Rhoda Haven made whizzing sounds of disgust. "Such shooting!"

"I ain't so hot at puttin' holes in guys," said the red-headed young man.

"You couldn't," said the girl, "hit the side of a barn!"

"I sure like to hit 'em with my fists, however," the redhead advised.

The big stranger's attack, the routing of Horst's men, had happened so fast that the dust had not settled. But now the dust blew away and Monk, who had partly served as a platform for the fight, stopped howling and groaning. He sat up. His small eyes batted at the stranger.

"Who are you?" Monk demanded.

"Henry Peace."

"Peace?"

"Don't," said the redhead, "let the name mislead you."

"WHAT are you doing here?" Monk rapped.

"That might be *my* business."

"Huh?"

"If you had kept that nose out of other people's business," said Henry Peace, "it might not look so funny."

"What's the matter with my nose?" Monk yelled.

"Looks like something the cat gnawed on," Henry Peace said. "And don't yell at me."

Monk was a man who formed sudden and violent likes and dislikes. Apparently he had acquired a large, instantaneous dislike for Henry Peace.

"If somebody will take these ropes off me," Monk bellowed, "I'll show you that I can yell at anybody, and they'll like it!"

The exhibition that followed, under the circumstances, was probably childish; under other circumstances it might conceivably have been comical. Henry Peace untied Monk. Monk got up, squared off with his fists, and was promptly knocked flat on his back by Henry Peace.

Henry Peace then picked Monk up with remarkable ease and hurled him into the most convenient clump of weeds. Monk lay there, howled, kicked, tried to get breath back.

Henry Peace looked at Ham and Johnny.

"I don't like you guys, either!" he said.

He untied Ham, examined Ham's perfectly tailored coat with disapproval, then took hold of the coat tails and tore it up the back. Ham screamed rage.

Ham was a skilled boxer of the stand-off-and-jab-'em-blind school. He started to use his technique on Henry Peace. A split-second later, to his bewilderment, he was sprawled in the weeds near Monk.

Henry Peace untied William Harper Littlejohn, picked him up and threw him in the weeds, before Johnny could get organized.

"I'll be superamalgamated!" Johnny gasped.

"That's a good word to run away with," Henry Peace said.

Monk got up, showed renewed fight intentions.

"Drag it," Henry Peace ordered. "Vamoose! Beat it! Scram! Make tracks!"

The old cistern had been surrounded with a coping of bricks, and this had disintegrated with the years, so that a number of bricks were scattered handily. Henry Peace began picking up this Irish confetti and heaving it at Monk, Ham and Johnny.

Having narrowly escaped being hit by several bricks, Ham and Johnny took their flight. Monk reluctantly followed them.

"I can throw a brickbat," they heard Henry Peace say proudly, "straighter than I can shoot a gun."

Having reached safety some distance away in the weeds, Monk, Ham and Johnny held a conference.

"When I get hold of that red-headed guy," Monk growled, "I'm gonna massacre him!"

"You already had hold of him once," Ham reminded.

Monk glared.

Johnny, big words apparently knocked out of him, said, "I think we better try to trail those guys who were going to throw us in the cistern."

"But the girl—"

"If that red-headed guy can't protect her, nobody can," Johnny stated. "Anyway, if we go back there, we'll just waste time fighting him."

"Henry Peace," Ham admitted, "didn't seem to like us."

They wandered off through the weeds, seeking the trail of Horst's men.

Chapter VI
THE NOSE BUMPER

HENRY PEACE stood with a brick in each hand and peered at the weeds hopefully.

"Looks like the excitement's played out," he said in a regretful tone.

Rhoda Haven, still tied on the ground, looked as if she wanted to forcibly relieve her rescuer of a fistful of red hair.

"Does it occur to you," she said violently, "to untie me?"

"Sure. That occurred to me back near Wall Street."

"Near Wall Street?"

"Yep. When I seen you grabbed. I was lookin' at you when that fellow fell down on purpose and broke the tear-gas bottle in his package. I seen 'em grab you. So, thinks I, as long as I'm not doing nothing, I might as well pitch in and rescue you."

"I see."

"Anyway, I was in love with you."

"You *what?*" Rhoda Haven gasped.

"Smitten. Bit. By the love-bug." The red-headed young man's grin wrinkled his freckled nose. "Soon as I saw you."

Rhoda Haven squirmed, snapped, "Untie these ropes!"

"Don't you think I done me a nice job trailin' them fellows?" Henry Peace asked. "Lucky I had me a car handy."

"Are you, or aren't you—"

"Sure, sure. Keep your jaw still a minute, and I will."

Rhoda Haven held her tongue with some effort while the large young man took his time untying her. The frankly admiring way in which he looked her over caused her teeth to make faint grinding noises.

"Say, I've got good taste, don't you think?" Henry Peace asked cheerfully.

"What do you mean?"

"In picking you to fall in love with."

Rhoda Haven knotted small fists.

"You affect me," she said, "like the ocean."

"You mean because I'm awe-inspiring, and toss things around?" said Henry Peace.

"No. You make me sick."

Big Henry Peace's freckled grin remained undisturbed. "You'll change for the better. I grow on people."

Rhoda Haven looked him up and down frostily, made a half-admiring mental note that if he grew much more, they would have to start making doors wider at shoulder height. She kept any trace of admiration off her patrician features, however.

"Just who are you?" she asked.

"Henry Peace. But don't let the name fool—"

"You said that once. I don't care anything about your name. What is your business?"

"Right now, it's rescuing you."

"And after that?"

A big grin came over Henry Peace's sunny face. "Marrying you," he said.

Rhoda Haven controlled an impulse to see how hard she could hit him in the eye.

"How do you make a living?" she asked, holding to her patience.

"Sometimes I don't," Henry Peace admitted cheerfully. "I'm a guy with a hobby instead of an occupation. The hobby is hanging black eyes on people I don't like."

Rhoda Haven considered for a moment.

"Am I," she inquired, "going to be infested by you?"

"You ain't gonna get rid of me, if that's what you mean."

Rhoda Haven sighed, shrugged her shoulders, nodded—all three gestures indicating that she had surrendered to the inevitable.

Next, the young woman walked over to the cistern, looked into the depths—emitted a strangled cry of horror. She drew back from the cistern mouth, trembling. Her whole manner radiated horror.

Henry Peace, rushing forward, said, "Don't get the shakes! Nobody's going to throw you in there now."

Rhoda Haven, trembling more than before, pointed at the cistern.

There were gasps between her words. "There's already someone . . . down there!" she choked.

Henry Peace rushed to the cistern, looked, and because it was dark in the depths, got down on all fours the better to peer.

Rhoda Haven put a foot against the handiest portion of his anatomy and shoved. Henry Peace managed to turn, clutch the edge of the cistern with his hands, hang there. Rhoda Haven calmly kicked his fingers loose.

Henry Peace fell into the cistern, which was not very deep. Judging from the volume of the young man's indignant roars, he was unharmed.

"We're going to see," Rhoda Haven said grimly, "who gets rid of who."

WHEN Rhoda Haven walked into the small hotel where she and her father had established themselves, old Tex Haven got away from the fire escape near which he had been standing. He wore his smoking jacket, a heavily brocaded, very elaborate Chinese mandarin's robe which had been in his possession for years—in fact had been given to him by the Korean emperor before the Japanese took possession of that country. He was particularly satisfied with his corncob pipe, and fumes from the thing had the hotel suite smelling as if a poison-gas shell had exploded.

"Reckon you made out right pert at sickin' Doc Savage and his men on Horst and Señor Steel?" he asked.

Rhoda Haven went to a mirror, with feminine concern over her appearance, and examined herself. Then she went over and dropped in a chair.

"When I was a kid," she said, "I took a stick and poked it in a hornets' nest."

"There's smarter things to do," old Tex Haven said.

"What we've done today," his daughter told him, "amounts to the same thing."

"Eh?"

She told him what had happened. Her voice was disgusted when she explained that Horst had been clever enough to divine that they would attempt to involve Doc Savage. When she came to the appearance of Henry Peace, she crackled rage.

"The big red-headed hooligan," she said, "seemed to expect me to fall on his neck."

"Can't blame him."

"Well, I didn't care for his manner."

"'Pears you're a mite prejudiced. Mind explainin' what was wrong with his manner?"

"He wanted to marry me."

"That," said old Tex Haven, "sure don't prove he was crazy."

"Yes, but he told me his intentions thirty seconds after he met me."

"Reckon you never seen a sparrow after a bug," Tex Haven said. "A sparrow don't waste no time."

"I'm the bug, eh?"

Tex Haven took his pipe out of his teeth, contemplated it, rubbed his jaw.

"Last you seed of Doc Savage's men, they was bein' run into the weeds by this Henry Peace?" he asked.

"Yes."

"Likely as not, they'll start followin' Horst's men."

"They're fools if they don't. Horst's men were going to kill them."

Old Tex Haven took a long, luxuriant drag of vile smoke out of his corncob pipe, released it to further befoul the air of the room, and smacked his lips.

"We came out all right, figures as if," he said.

"We hankered for Doc Savage to take after Horst. He's after 'im."

"His men are."

"Same thing."

"Which brings us around," Rhoda Haven said grimly, "to what we do next, whatever it is."

Tex Haven went to the window shade and pulled it down. The bit of shark skin, which had been rolled up in the shade, fluttered out. He caught it.

"Jep Dee sent us this for a reason, strikes me," he said. "Jep Dee ain't the boy to do things without reason."

His daughter took the piece of dry, freckled-looking hide and scrutinized it thoughtfully. She felt of it, held it up to the light, shook her head.

"Beats me," she said.

There was a knock on the door.

Tex Haven blinked, muttered, "Last time somebody knocked on the door, hell broke loose."

He hastily rolled the bit of freckled shark skin up inside the window shade.

Then he looked at his daughter.

"You positive," he asked, "that nobody could've followed you back from that place where they was gonna throw you in the cistern?"

"Positive," Rhoda Haven said firmly.

The room was L-shaped. Old Tex Haven got at the angle of the L, stood there where his hands could get at his guns freely. He knew, from the construction of the hotel, that there was a steel beam at the angle of the L, which would stop bullets.

Rhoda Haven got out on the fire escape.

The knuckles banged the door again.

"Come in," Tex Haven called.

Henry Peace brought his big, freckled grin into the room.

OLD Tex Haven was standing slack-shouldered and sleepy—his deadliest attitude, incidentally. His long jaw sagged, his corncob fell out of his teeth, and one of his palms cupped instinctively and caught it.

"Drat it!" he said.

Henry Peace squinted at him. "What's the idea? Ain't I welcome?"

Old Tex Haven swallowed, apparently could think of nothing to say.

"Where's my fiancée?" asked Henry Peace.

"Your what?"

"My future wife—your daughter," Henry Peace explained.

Rhoda Haven came in from her hiding place, her heels tapping the floor angrily.

"I'm getting tired of that wife stuff!" she snapped. "The more I see of you, the less I can stomach you. In fact, you distinctly irritate me."

"Them pains you feel," Henry Peace assured her, "are probably the sprouting of a great love."

Rhoda Haven turned angrily to her father. Knowing old Tex as she did, she thought it might be a good idea to explain again that she felt that it was impossible for Henry Peace to have followed her here.

She said, "This air-minded tramp couldn't—"

"Air-minded—nothing!" Henry Peace interrupted. "I hate airplanes."

"What I meant is that you have air where a mind should be," the girl explained carefully.

Henry Peace looked so indignant that old Tex Haven chuckled gently. That chuckle turned out to be an error—it distracted his attention. Too, he hadn't expected Henry Peace to jump him, which was what happened. They hit the floor. Tex Haven's bony frame made a sound somewhat as if an arm-load of stove wood had been dropped.

Tex wrapped long, bony arms and legs, octopus fashion, around Henry Peace.

"I sure hates," he said, "to embarrass a young lad who thinks he's handy."

He tightened the grip, his ropy old muscles rolling something like a jungle snake starting to swallow a pig.

Henry Peace at once emitted several yelps of pain.

Old Tex Haven had at one time spent some months in a Japanese prison, and his cellmate had been a Japanese strangler who, as jujitsu expert, was probably the greatest ever to live. The Jap strangler would have been world-famous, except for a failing for getting into fights in which he choked his opponents to death. From the Nipponese, Tex Haven had learned about all that could be learned of the art of administering agony.

Also, age had not weakened the wirelike ropes that served Tex as muscles. The years, if anything, had improved them.

The two men went around and around on the floor. A table upset. Henry Peace gave more pain yips.

Then Henry Peace began taking hold of old Tex Haven in various strange ways. Tex started squawking like a sage hen. Tex had been showing great willingness to mix it with the large, red-headed young man.

Now Tex showed great willingness to let loose of Henry Peace. He had, he was discovering, caught a Tartar.

The two suddenly separated and got up, scowled at each other with mutual respect. Henry Peace had possession of all Tex Haven's guns.

"Standin' there, all ready to shoot, when I came in, wasn't you?" Henry Peace asked. "I didn't like that none."

Rhoda Haven frowned at her bony parent, said, "You must be slipping, dad."

**Tex and Peace
hit the floor.**

"Not slippin'," Tex denied. "I just got me a hold on a right tolerable man."

"He's a clown!" Rhoda said, and sniffed.

Henry Peace, having rubbed various parts of his anatomy which probably hurt, grinned cheerfully at the Havens.

"I'm beginnin' to think you're gonna make a better daddy-in-law than I expected," he said.

HAVING ridded himself of that declaration, Henry Peace pulled down his sleeves, straightened his coat and felt of one of his ears again to be sure it had not been pulled off. Then he gravely shook hands with old Tex and his daughter. The latter showed no enthusiasm.

"What's the idea of this hand-shaking?" Tex Haven asked.

"You were shaking the hand," Henry Peace explained, "of your new partner."

Tex jumped.

"What?" he yelled.

Henry Peace grinned at the gaunt old hell-raiser and soldier of fortune. "I've heard plenty about you."

"You heared of me?" Tex asked dubiously. "Warn't nothin' degradin', if war true."

"I've heard," said Henry Peace, "that you and this daughter of yours—my future breakfast companion—make yourselves about over a million dollars a year, one way or another. I heard, too, that you always turn right around and lose it. That's where I'm goin' to be different. I ain't gonna lose my share."

Old Tex Haven got out his corncob pipe and looked at it as if it had betrayed him.

"And what would you calculate your share?" he asked mildly.

"One third."

"Third of what?"

"That is what you can now tell me," Henry Peace said.

Old Tex Haven made faces and snorting sounds, and continued to eye his corncob pipe as if it had suddenly poisoned him.

"Ain't nothin' to tell," he said.

"You mean," said Henry Peace skeptically, "that you're entirely innocent of schemes?"

"Yep."

"You ain't doin' nothin' that you wouldn't describe to a policeman?"

"Nope."

"About that, we'll see."

Henry Peace went to a window and lifted it. The tops of trees were thick outside, but through them he could see a policeman standing on the sidewalk at the end of the block. Henry Peace raised his voice. The policeman looked as if he were having a dull afternoon.

"Help, help," yelled Henry Peace. "Police! Help! Murder! Bandits!"

The cop jumped. But his jump was nothing to the one Tex Haven gave.

"You durn fool!" Tex yelled.

"He's crazy!" snapped Rhoda Haven. "I told you so. Remember?"

Henry Peace stood still, grinned big.

The Havens flung a glance at the window shade which held the shark skin. They glared at Henry Peace.

The young man with the red hair and the freckles showed no inclination to do anything except stand and grin.

The Havens snatched their ready-packed suitcases, rushed for a back-window fire escape. They vanished down the fire escape.

When they were out of sight, Henry Peace went to the window, pulled the shade down and caught the bit of shark skin when it fluttered out. He pocketed the shark skin.

Chapter VII
FLORIDA RACE

HENRY PEACE went to the window that faced the street—the same window through which he had yelled for help and the police—and watched the cop charging into the front door of the little hotel.

The street below was one of the few in New York that had remained tree-lined through the years. The trees were large; some of them had branches as thick as elephant legs.

As soon as the cop disappeared, Henry Peace climbed on the windowsill, crouched, sprang out into space. Fifty feet or so below was the sidewalk, of hard concrete.

Doubled slightly—something like a high-diver with a jackknife half completed—Henry Peace plummeted into the top of a tree. He let two or three smaller branches whisk past, then his hands clamped a limb. The bough bent; disturbed leaves went *swoosh!*

Then Henry Peace was dangling safe, swaying slightly. He swung like a trapeze artist, sailed a few feet and fastened his hands to another branch. With ease and agility that could have been bettered very little by an experienced ape, Henry Peace dropped through the tree to the sidewalk.

He dusted off his hands, straightened his coat, and sauntered away. In his pockets were the many guns which he had taken from old Tex Haven, and these clinked together.

Henry Peace's sauntering gait was deceptive; he did not seem in a hurry, but in a short time he was in the wake of old Tex Haven and his daughter.

Tex Haven and Rhoda hurried down side streets, leaving the vicinity.

They rode uptown in a bus, and Henry Peace was perched on the rear bumper, wrinkling his freckled nose at the exhaust fumes.

Tex and his daughter engaged adjoining rooms in a small theatrical hotel. There was a discussion with the clerk over the selection of the rooms, Tex insisting he had a deathly fear of burning to death and must be near a fire escape.

Henry Peace came into the lobby—he had found a back door—and stood intently watching the hotel clerk's lips.

"Rooms 912 and 914 are exactly what you want," the clerk said. "Near a fire escape."

Henry Peace was apparently a lip reader, on top of his other accomplishments. He took to the stairs until he found Room 912.

The hotel owner probably thought his door locks were thief-proof, but the one on the door of Room 912 delayed Henry Peace no more than thirty seconds. Henry used his key ring, which he straightened out.

Henry Peace stood in a clothes closet until the Havens were installed. He heard Tex Haven say, "Waal, we're finally shut of that red-headed idiot."

"He isn't an idiot!" Rhoda Haven retorted unexpectedly.

"Eh?"

"Henry Peace," said the young woman perversely, "struck me as being rather clever."

Tex Haven snorted. "Women are the cussed-mindedest creatures."

Henry Peace came out of the closet. "That may be," he said, "but one woman is showing good judgment."

HENRY PEACE'S unexpected appearance caused Tex Haven to give a wild jump and grab successively for three or four of his guns, forgetting they were no longer in his possession. Then he recovered from his surprise, sidled to a chair, collapsed upon it, and looked at Henry Peace much as a rabbit might inspect a dog which had chased it into a hole.

"Now what do you want?"

Henry Peace put large freckled fists on his thin, capable hips and thrust out his lower lip. "The same thing as before. I want to be your partner."

Old Tex Haven rubbed his leathery jaw and squinted one eye at his daughter, who walked over and kicked her suitcase.

"I guess we're licked," she said in a resigned tone.

Tex asked, "You mean let him hang around?"

"Have you noticed us stopping him?"

Henry Peace grinned at them. "Now that I'm officially one of your gadgets," he said, "what are we all mixed up in?"

Tex Haven stuffed his pipe with black tobacco and applied a match.

"Try to figure it out by yourself," he suggested. "Be right helpful exercise for that handful of fleas you call a mind."

Tex put on a wide-brimmed black hat which he habitually wore, a hat that made him resemble an undertaker who depressed his profession.

He drew his daughter aside. "Calculate I better go back an' get that shark skin," he explained. "Dern thing don't make sense, but it's important, or Jep Dee wouldn't have sent it."

The girl nodded. "Good idea."

She watched her father leave the hotel. Then she inspected Henry Peace with no approval.

"You," she said, "are going to regret haunting us."

"There's two sides to every question," Henry Peace pointed out. "Why don't you be reasonable?"

"There's two sides to fly paper, too," the girl said grimly. "But it's important to the fly which side he lights on."

Henry Peace opened his mouth, but no word came out; so he shut it. This was the starting point for half an hour of deep silence.

When Tex Haven came back, he was galloping. Apparently he also had been running.

"Gone!" he yelled.

Rhoda gasped. "The shark skin was gone from the window shade?"

"Hide an' hair."

"What are you talkin' about?" Henry Peace asked innocently.

The Havens ignored both question and the author.

Rhoda Haven compressed her lips.

"Horst?" she said grimly.

"Maybe he's the one got it," said old Tex. "And maybe he didn't."

Rhoda said, "Two things we can do. Hunt Horst, take the shark skin away from him. Or head for Key West and get the straight story from Jep Dee."

"Yep."

"Key West sound best to you?"

"Yep," said Tex promptly.

The Havens grabbed their suitcases and rushed for the door.

Henry Peace exclaimed, "Wait for me!" and trotted after them.

Tex Haven stopped. He took Henry Peace by the necktie and pulled their faces close together.

"You know how much is involved in this?" Tex snarled.

"No. I—"

"The lives of thirty-one or thirty-two people—"

"But—"

"And maybe between forty and fifty million dollars."

Henry Peace's jaw sagged and remained down. "Uh—"

Tex finished, "You throw in with us, and eleven chances out of ten you get your head shot out from between your ears. Take your choice."

Henry Peace swallowed several times, mumbled something almost unintelligible about fifty million dollars and the lives of thirty-one or thirty-two people.

"Why, blast it!" he said. "You couldn't keep me away from this kind of mystery and excitement."

They hurried out and got in a taxicab. The cab ran several blocks.

"You reckon," Henry Peace asked, "that I better make my will?"

"Be a farish idea," Tex said.

"Stop the car!" Henry Peace barked abruptly. "There's a post office. I'm goin' in, write out my will, and mail it to the executor."

Somewhat unwillingly, the Havens halted the taxi and Henry Peace went into the post office.

"Drat that red-headed feller," grumbled Tex. "For triflin' little, I'd drive off an' let 'im hunt for us."

Rhoda Haven smiled slightly. "Don't," she said. "I think the young man is going to be interesting."

"Interestin'? Heck, what we've got on our hands is interestin' enough."

"He can fight, too," Rhoda reminded.

Henry Peace, in the post office, was doing something interesting. He was *not* writing any will, however.

He was putting the piece of freckled shark skin in an envelope, and addressing the envelope, which he mailed with a flourish.

He went back to the Havens.

"Get your will taken care of?" asked Tex.

"All taken care of," Henry Peace said.

NEW YORK postal service is fast. Henry Peace mailed the bit of freckled shark skin at five o'clock in the afternoon, and at six thirty it arrived in the central post office at Thirty-second Street and Eighth Avenue, where a postal clerk picked it up and noted the name to which it was addressed. The name meant something to the clerk. He walked quickly to a special pneumatic mailing tube, shoved the letter into a bullet-shaped container.

Another postal clerk came over.

"That marked important, or something?" he asked.

"The letter," explained the first clerk, "was addressed in the most unusual handwriting I ever saw. The writing was machine perfect, like script."

"A lot of queer mail goes into that special tube."

"Boy, don't it!"

"I guess still queerer things happen as a result of the mail."

"Yeah, from the rumors that get out. Still, you don't read much about him in the newspapers lately. Maybe he doesn't follow his queer profession any longer."

"Don't let that fool you. He avoids publicity. But every crook in the world is still scared of him."

"Ever seen him?"

"Once. When this special mail tube was installed in his headquarters."

"What does he look like?"

"Doc Savage," said the second clerk, "has the strangest flake-gold eyes. His skin is bronze, hair a little darker bronze. There's a silent way about him that—well, once you see him, you never forget him."

Air pressure whisked Henry Peace's letter through the pneumatic tube, under streets and sidewalks, then up vertically for eighty-six stories in a skyscraper, and it landed in a container, which caused a signal light to flash.

"An ultramontaneous anacoluthon," remarked gaunt William Harper Littlejohn solemnly.

Monk was the only other human occupant of the room. The two pets, Habeas Corpus and Chemistry, sat on the floor and looked at each other in an unkind way.

The two animals had been rescued from the Wall Street district where Horst's men had worked the gas trick.

Monk turned around and glared.

"Stop talkin' that foreign language!" he shouted.

"That's English," Johnny explained with dignity. "Anyway, what are you so touchy about?"

"Ham." Monk took his bullet-shaped head in his hands. "For hours now, we haven't heard from Ham."

"Ham is all right."

"How do we know he's all right?" Monk groaned.

"Well, he is trailing the Horst gang. We figured one man could trail them with less chance of being noticed, and we matched for the job, and Ham won."

"I'm worried," Monk muttered.

His homely face was a battleground for various kinds of concern.

Johnny snorted. "Earlier in the day, I heard you promise to knock all of Ham's teeth out and use them for marbles. Now you're worried."

"Ham is the best friend I've got in the world," Monk said emphatically.

Johnny, having opened the newly arrived letter, emitted a startled grunt. He held the fragment of freckled shark skin up for inspection.

"An acromatical involucrum," he muttered.

"Eh?"

"A puzzling piece of hide," Johnny said, using small words.

Monk examined the shark skin. "What makes you think it's hide?"

"Ratiocination."

"Eh?"

"A little common sense."

"If you don't stop using them words on me when I'm worried, I'm going to make you into something longer and thinner than you are," Monk said disagreeably. "Probably I'll just strew you out."

The homely chemist picked up the sheet of paper which had accompanied the shark skin fragment in the letter. There were words on the paper, saying:

THIS PIECE OF SHARK SKIN SEEMS TO BE THE KEY TO THE WHOLE MYSTERY. SEE IF YOU CAN SOLVE IT.

There was no signature on the note.

"Heck, you read this first, and that's how you knew it was a piece of hide," Monk complained. "What are these spots on it?"

"Look like freckles."

"There ain't no such thing as a freckled shark," Monk pointed out.

THE question of whether or not there was such a thing as a freckled shark had gotten to the stage of consulting the encyclopedia when a green light flashed.

"Probably Ham!" Monk exploded.

The green light was attached to a shortwave radio receiving set—hooked up through a sensitive relay which operated when a certain combination of clicking noises were received—and announced that they were being called by another radio. The green light served the same purpose as the bell on a telephone. To make it function, the operator of a sending set merely switched on his apparatus and, with his fingers close to the microphone, made the proper combination of snapping noises.

Monk reached the radio and cut in the loudspeaker.

Ham's voice said, *"Boy, you better move fast! They're headed somewhere."*

"Why didn't you tell us where you had been, you rattle-brained shyster!" Monk yelled indignantly.

"You oaf! Don't start yelling at me," Ham said over the radio. *"I was busy trailing that Horst gang. They're out on Long Island."*

"Where on Long Island?"

"The airport. The one that last transatlantic flier crashed on. Remember?"

"What are they doing?"

"Hear that plane motor warming up? They're getting in it."

"In ten minutes," Monk said, "we'll be out there."

The congested city location of Doc Savage's skyscraper headquarters had its inconveniences. One drawback was the fact that traffic made it difficult to leave the city quickly in an emergency. However, Doc Savage had largely overcome that handicap by installing what Monk called the "flea run."

Monk and Johnny got into the bullet-shaped cartridge of the flea run. Monk had grabbed Habeas by one wing-sized ear, his habitual manner of carrying the pig. He also made a grab for Chemistry, the ape, but the latter dodged away distrustfully. At the last minute, Chemistry ran and jumped into the cartridge.

Monk jerked a lever. There was a sound as if an elephant had coughed through his trunk, and the cartridge gave a terrific jump. The bullet-shaped car, which was so small that even two of them crowded it, traveled through a metal tube at a speed of considerably over a hundred miles an hour, driven by pneumatic pressure. It swayed, shook, and the noise was deafening. When it stopped at the other end, the shock rendered the occupants breathless.

"That blasted thing," Monk complained, "is worse than a mole's nightmare!"

They were now in Doc Savage's waterfront hangar—a huge, grimy brick building with a sign across the front that said "HIDALGO TRADING COMPANY"—where the bronze man kept his planes and such boats as he had occasion to use.

They took a plane that had practically no wings and twice the usual amount of motor.

The ship was a seaplane equipped with retractable landing gear for use on land. The wheels up, the craft lunged across the surface of the Hudson, and climbed like a big bumblebee into the sky.

DOC SAVAGE and his associates used a shortwave radio habitually. All their planes were equipped with transmitters and receivers. Monk switched on the one in the speed ship.

"We're on our way," Monk said.

Ham said, *"I see that the sky looks kind of funny over in that direction."*

"That," Monk said, "isn't a good gag."

The plane bored on up into the sky and dived into low-hanging clouds.

So fast was the ship that almost at once it was circling toward the airport, but at some distance.

Ham's voice came over the radio again.

"Something funny about this," he said.

Johnny said, "Hermeneuticalize."

Ham, who understood such words, knew that Johnny merely wanted an explanation.

"Horst's men," Ham said, *"apparently followed somebody out here."*

"Followed somebody?"

"Well, not exactly. What I mean is that they seem to have had somebody watching the airport, and they rushed out here when the fellow called them. They chartered a plane."

"Are they there now?" Monk asked.

"No. Horst and all his men left in the plane about three minutes ago."

Monk was flying the speed ship. He slanted it down, bumped the wheels on the tarmac, and braked to a stop near the administration building, which was small.

An old man in rags came out to meet them. The small old man had whiskers that looked like soiled angora goat wool, and spectacles that magnified his eyes into ostrich eggs. He looked as if his home were behind an ash can in some alley.

This was Ham in disguise.

Ham said, "I think I found out why Horst and his men rushed out here and took off in a plane."

"Why?" Monk demanded.

"Come over here and listen to a greaseball tell it."

The mechanic wore greasy overalls, had a distributor in one hand and an insulating screwdriver in the other. Apparently, he also had an observing nature; likewise an eye for profit, because it took two dollars to loosen his tongue.

He referred to Horst's men as "them last guys."

"Them last guys," he said, "took off to follow another plane that left earlier. The other plane belonged to a long, drawly old guy, and he's been keeping it here some time. Sweet ship, too."

"Was there anybody with the long old guy?" Ham asked.

"Boy, there was a honey!"

He described the "honey," and it was obvious that she was Rhoda Haven. The mechanic also described a large young man with freckles, red hair, and an impulsive disposition.

"When I catch that last one, I'm gonna take a souvenir off him," Monk said. "One of his legs or something."

Ham snapped, "We're killing time. We had better follow them."

They ran back to their speed ship. It took the air.

"They went south," Ham stated.

It took them something like forty minutes to pick up a dot in the sky ahead. Ham used powerful binoculars, said, "That's the Horst plane."

Monk sent the speed ship into the clouds, and after that dropped down only occasionally to spot the craft ahead. It became dark soon and they could see the flying lights of the plane ahead, which simplified the trailing. They merely extinguished their own lights and flew a mile or so in the wake of the other plane.

HORST was flying a rented ship. He was handling the controls himself, and doing an experienced job. It was a cabin craft, and there were seven men with him. One of the seven came forward to the cabin pit.

"Be tough if anybody reports we're flying south," the man said. "We told the guy who we rented this crate from that we were mining engineers, and that we were going up to Canada."

"Who's going to report anything? Airplanes aren't news any more."

"Well, I just thought of it."

Horst scowled. In the subdued light glow from the instrument panel, he looked like an intent satan. He gave the throttle an angry bat with his palm, but the thing was already wide open.

"Damn it!" he snarled. "We've got to overhaul old Tex Haven."

"Tex's ship is fast."

"Don't I know it!"

Horst looked so enraged that his followers saw the need of placating the chief with a little praise.

"You made a darn smart move, Horst," someone said, "in putting a man to watch old Tex Haven's plane. The old hell-raiser had given us the slip entirely. If you hadn't thought of watching the plane, we probably wouldn't have got on the trail."

Horst was susceptible to praise. He showed his teeth appreciatively. "You know what I think?"

"What?"

"The Havens are on their way to Key West to get hold of Jep Dee."

"Then the thing for us to do is get Jep Dee first."

Horst swore. He could swear more profusely in Spanish, so he used that language.

"Thing for us to do," he snarled, "is shoot old Tex Haven's plane out of the sky. Tell 'em to get the machine guns ready."

"You got any idea who the new guy is?"

"You mean that lug with the red hair and the freckles?"

"Yes."

"I got no idea who he is," Horst said grimly, "but he is no more bulletproof than the next man."

"It's risky to pull killings here in the States."

Horst said, "There's enough at stake that nothing is too risky."

The man went back in the cabin. The craft was not soundproofed, and was very noisy, and he had to bellow in each man's ear the order Horst had given.

Their machine guns, dismantled, were in large suitcases. They got these out, put them together.

They were modern weapons, the size of the conventional submachine gun, but they fired a more high-powered bullet than the conventional sub gun of .45 caliber.

They flew five hours and picked up the riding lights of a plane. One of Horst's men had a marine telescope, through which he peered for some time.

"The Haven ship!" he said.

Horst said, "Get set, boys! It won't take long to finish this!"

Chapter VIII
BAT BRAWL

THE Haven plane was sleek from the tapered cowling of its air-cooled motor to the trailing edge of its stabilizer fins. It had been built in a European factory. Tex Haven flew it himself and complained frequently.

"Blasted foreign ship," he grumbled. "I keep thinkin' about havin' to land it. Landin' speed is damn near a hundred miles an hour."

Henry Peace said, "Why did you buy it, if you don't like it?"

"Didn't buy it. Stole it."

Rhoda Haven explained. "It was a personal ship of Señor Steel. We had to leave his country in a hurry."

Henry Peace scratched in his thatch of red hair, which seemed to be his habitual gesture when he wanted to think.

"There's a Señor Steel who is president of the South American republic of Blanca Grande," he remarked. "Any relation?"

"Same."

Small hard knots of jaw muscle gathered under each of Rhoda Haven's smooth cheeks. She suddenly looked more grim than Henry Peace had seen her before.

"He's no president!" she snapped. "He's a dictator. A tyrant."

Henry Peace eyed her.

"Offered a hundred thousand dollars for your head, didn't he?"

Rhoda Haven blinked. "How did you learn that?"

Henry Peace opened his mouth to answer—and gave a wild jump. Simultaneously, there was a snarling sound, somewhat as if a big bulldog had been turned loose. The plane trembled. A respectable collection of sievelike holes appeared in the plane cabin.

Tex Haven turned around, eyed the holes, yelled, "Looks like the ants have gone to work on us."

"Lead ones," Henry Peace agreed.

OLD Tex came back on the plane control stick.

The little foreign plane arched up, hung in the sky by its moaning nose.

The other ship, the one from which the storm of machine-gun lead had come, pointed up and stood on its tail not fifty yards away. The ships were probably climbing, but the illusion was that they stood still.

"That's Horst!" Tex Haven yelled.

For a split second, the planes hung motionless in easy stone-throw, but the force of their up-swoop held the occupants temporarily helpless.

Tex Haven drew his six-shooters—Henry Peace had given him back the guns—and tried to knock out one of the cabin windows so he could fight. The glass, nonshatter, would not break. Tex lowered a window.

By that time, the other plane had climbed above them, was sliding over and its cabin windows were opening, machine-gun muzzles protruding.

"Watch it!" Henry Peace yelled.

Tex Haven was "watching it." He stamped left rudder, rocked with the stick. The plane flipped around and dived like a hawk that had folded its wings and was making for a chicken on the ground. Passing wind moaned, then became a siren scream.

"You running away?" Henry Peace yelled.

"I ain't stackin' six-guns against machine guns," Tex shouted. "I tried that one time."

Speed-shriek lifted higher and higher. The night-smeared earth came up, seeming to bloat toward them.

Henry Peace looked at the air-speed meter. The needle stood close to five hundred.

"Five hundred—great blazes!" Henry Peace squalled. "We're goin' five hundred miles an hour. No plane ever went that fast before!"

"It's a foreign crate, so the air-speed dial is marked in kilometers, stupid," Rhoda Haven told him.

Their plane leveled out and streaked south. The earth was about a thousand feet below.

Eastward lay the sea, a vast expanse that was like dull, frosted glass; and somewhat nearer was the coast, a succession of small, buglike islands, each with a wide, white beach on the seaward side. Below the plane, there seemed to be swamp; the swamp was veined with creeks, and splotched here and there with a lake.

Henry Peace wiped his brow with first one forearm, then the other. "I'd give a lot to be safe on the ground," he muttered.

Tex scowled at him. "Getting scared?"

"I always have been of planes."

Old Tex Haven craned his neck and squinted, then began to do something which he rarely did, but which he could do well—curse. He swore steadily, none of his words particularly profane by themselves, but connectively producing a blood-curdling effect. Toward the last, he speeded up until he sounded like a tobacco auctioneer.

A single bullet hit the left wing of the plane. A moment later they saw ahead of the ship tiny stars that seemed to fly as if they were pursued by the craft, red sparks that raced ahead and vanished.

"Tracer bullets!" Tex growled.

Henry Peace took a look backward, said, "Hey, that plane is catching us! It's faster than we are!"

The other ship overhauled them, got below them. More bullets pounded the craft. Tex banked. The other ship banked also. Tex came up and over in an Immelmann turn, but as the ship turned level at the top of the half loop, the other craft was almost beside them.

"Tarnation!" Tex growled uneasily.

The other pilot could fly.

It became evident in the course of the next two or three minutes that the other ship could fly rings around the foreign craft. They could not outrun them on straightaway, could not outmaneuver them in dog fight.

Henry Peace said, "If this keeps up, we're gonna be shot to pieces!"

He started for the cockpit.

Old Tex Haven turned around and showed him the business end of a six-shooter. "You can't fly," Tex growled. "Don't you come up here and start telling me what to do."

Henry Peace retreated into the cabin, sank into a seat. He fished in a pocket, brought out a metal box the size of a tobacco can, but about half as high. From this he extracted what might have been a sponge. He put this in his mouth. In the can with the spongelike object was a small nose clip. Henry Peace closed his nostrils with this. The Havens had not noticed.

Out of another pocket, Henry Peace took a bottle. He uncorked it, splashed the contents on the cabin floor. The stuff was liquid and it vaporized to gas quickly.

After a little while, Rhoda Haven looked sleepy and sank to the cabin floor, and soon Tex Haven was lolling back in the cockpit seat, his eyes closed.

THE plane windows had been closed. Henry Peace opened them, letting the rush of air sweep out the gas which had been in the bottle he had uncorked. The nose-clip had kept the stuff from entering his nostrils. He had done the necessary breathing through the chemical-treated filter—the spongelike object which he had put in his mouth.

Henry Peace had said he could not fly.

He took the plane controls now and flew the craft. He did not go through aerobatics with the Horst plane. He sent the ship into a tailspin. It fell, turning over and over, toward the earth below. The chase had led inland somewhat. There were farms below now, hilly weed-grown farms, the red soil gullied, the fields edged with trees and bushes.

Henry Peace stabbed a thumb down on the landing light switch. One light had been shot out, but the other drove a white sheet.

Once what was below had been a cotton field; now it was eroded until it looked like the Dakota Sand Hills in miniature. There were level stretches, but not many. Henry Peace selected one.

Coming in, Henry Peace kicked rudder to throw the plane from side to side—fishtail it—until it all but stalled. With flying speed gone, but enough left for control, he sat down. The ship bucked, jumped, ran up a short and steep hill. It lost speed there, and Henry Peace locked wheel brakes.

The plane came to a stop under a tree that looked as big as a cloud sitting on the ground.

Henry Peace scooped Rhoda Haven up with an arm, clutched old Tex Haven's collar, got the two limp figures out of the plane, and ran with them. Raced for cover.

The Horst plane came down a moonbeam, as noisy as a rocket, exhaust stacks blowing sparks. Machine-gun muzzles stuck from its windows and gobbled.

Bullets broke clods and knocked up dust around burdened Henry Peace. Then he lost himself in the trees.

In landing the plane, Henry Peace had acted with flash decision and unhalting execution, as though the landing of the racy-looking but not-too-efficient foreign ship had been a simple matter.

It had not been simple.

It was feat enough that Horst flew over with landing lights throwing a racing glitter before his plane—and decided not to attempt it. His plane was larger, needed more room to sit down. And that field down there was small and rough.

Horst began flying around and around while his men tried to shoot the bushes and trees to pieces, hoping to riddle Henry Peace and the Havens.

Then the third plane came down in the sky—the Doc Savage ship.

HAM BROOKS—he was flying the Doc Savage craft—had been flying off to the west, and high, inside a cloud. Fortunately, he had dropped down out of the cloud in time to see the end of the air brawl. Had they remained in the cloud, they would have gone on and missed everything.

Monk yelled, leaned out of the plane window with a machine pistol. Monk liked to yell before a fight, as well as during it. He aimed carefully, caressed the trigger.

The machine pistol felt like a large bumblebee buzzing in his fist. The ejector fed out a streak of empty brass cartridges, and the gun itself made a moan like a huge bull-fiddle.

Every fourth bullet was a tracer; they stood in the sky in a red-hot wire, and the wire waved and touched the cabin of Horst's plane.

Gaunt Johnny reached, knocked Monk's arm, spoiled his aim.

"What's the idea?" Monk yelled.

Johnny used small words.

"You know blamed well Doc Savage has a rule against trying to kill anybody," he snapped.

"Doc wouldn't know anything about it," Monk said with cheerful reasonableness.

By that time Ham was upon the tail of the Horst craft. The tail of a commercial plane is its blind spot; these were commercial jobs.

Monk said, "If we're gotta be finicky, I'll just shoot some holes in his wings."

He proceeded to do this. He had charged with a drum of Thermit-type incendiary slugs. They splashed like drops of liquid fire on the wings of Horst's plane. Fortunately, the wings were of metal and while the incendiaries did not do the wings any good, the only real harm was a dozen or so melted holes. But the Horst party didn't like that.

For four or five minutes, there was dog fight in the sky. Horst found his ship hopelessly outclassed, himself completely outflown.

Then Horst arched his plane, pointed south, opened throttle. He was going to try a straight, running escape.

Ham said, "We'll make him think he's standing still!"

Monk had been hanging out of the windows so far that it seemed remarkable he hadn't spilled out. Now he jerked back, clamped hold of Ham with one hand, pointed with the other.

"That light is talking!" he barked.

The light he meant was on the dark earth, in the clearing where the Haven plane had landed. It seemed to be the landing lights of the Haven ship, switched off and on.

"Dots and dashes," Ham said, after looking.

Monk spelled out the message: *"H-e-l-p. I a-m m-a-n w-h-o m-a-i-l-e-d y-o-u s-h-a-r-k s-k-i-n. H-e-l-p."*

There was an astonished interval between Monk, Ham and Johnny.

"We better land," Ham said.

Monk yelled, "We can't let that Horst gang get away."

Ham ignored Monk, pointed their ship toward the earth in a long spiral.

The plane carrying Horst and his men droned off to the southward and escaped.

Chapter IX
SCRAMBLE FOR JEP DEE

HENRY PEACE, having observed that one of the two planes above was spiraling earthward, stopped jacking the light switch and sending out Morse code. He climbed out of the Haven plane cockpit and narrowed one eye at the sky.

"I hope," he muttered, "that the men in that plane are who I think they are."

Having put feeling into that remark, he tramped through the weeds toward the spot where he had left the Havens. En route, he was hooked by some bushes which had thorns. He examined these.

"Blackberries," he muttered. "Ripe."

Ripe blackberries gave him an idea and he gathered handfuls of them, squeezed them and got dark-red juice. He poured blackberry juice in his hair, smeared it down the side of his face, made rather a gory-looking mess.

"I've been shot!" he said in a loud, worried voice.

He wasn't surprised to find the Havens stirring, trying to sit up. The gas was rather harmless, producing unconsciousness which lasted only a short time.

The Havens sat up. Tex patted the ground and felt of it, apparently amazed to find the solid earth under him. Rhoda peered at Henry Peace until she made sure of his identity.

"You are shot!" she gasped.

"Ain't serious," Henry Peace told her.

"Let me see it!" Rhoda commanded.

Henry Peace withdrew hastily. "Ain't nothin'," he insisted. "A bullet just hit my head and careened into space."

"I suppose you got it out," the young woman said.

Henry Peace decided the remark meant she believed there was only space inside his head, so he grinned at her. The grin irritated the young woman.

Rhoda Haven tried to stand. The effect of the gas still had hold of her muscles and she failed to stay erect. Having slumped to the ground, she was even angrier.

"What happened?" she snapped.

"I don't know," Henry Peace lied cheerfully. "I was unconscious. I guess my prospective daddy-in-law here landed the plane."

"That's a lie," Tex barked. "Something put me to sleep."

"You must have done some flying in your sleep then," Henry Peace assured him.

There was a swooping roar, and the moon shadow of a plane passed low overhead. Its landing lights dived upon them like white monsters. Then the ship banked steeply, pointed down and the pilot began fishtailing it. It was going to land.

After taking one look at the smallness and roughness of the field, however, the pilot decided several more looks might be sensible. The plane zoomed up, circled again.

"That isn't Horst's plane," Rhoda Haven exclaimed.

Tex yelled, "I don't care whose it is. Can't have nobody grabbin' us now. Too much at stake!"

Henry Peace picked up both the Havens, galloped into the brush and reached a tree. It was huge and hung with Spanish moss. Carrying Rhoda Haven only, Henry Peace clambered into the tree. Perhaps fifteen feet up, he found a well-hidden cradle of boughs and put the girl there.

"Think you can hang on?"

"Yes," she said.

Henry Peace departed and a moment later returned with Tex, who, like his daughter, was still physically helpless from the effects of the gas. He left the Havens there in the tree. "Aren't likely to find you," he said.

"Reckon not," Tex admitted.

Henry Peace said, "Me, I'll try to see what I can do about the situation."

THE darkness then swallowed Henry Peace. He made very little noise, did not appear in the moonlight again, but shortly he was back at the Haven plane. He took a scrap of paper from his pocket, a pencil, and wrote on the paper:

> You will find something interesting in the big tree a hundred and ten yards southwest. Don't tell them about this note.

The tree described was the one in which he had left the Havens. He stuck the note in the edge of the plane door where it was not likely to escape notice.

The darkness swallowed him again. He made hardly more noise than was made by the occasional cloud shadows that passed. Lying among the weeds, he watched the Doc Savage plane swoop three times and rake the field with its floodlights, while the pilot decided upon the safest method of landing.

Then the plane came down, bumped the ground, rolled up the little hill, following exactly the same procedure that Henry Peace had used in landing the Haven craft. This ship was bigger, faster, but scientifically designed wing flaps gave it a much slower landing speed. It rolled to a stop thirty yards or so from the Haven ship.

Monk, Ham and Johnny dived out.

Ham leveled a machine pistol at the Haven plane, yelled, "Come out of there!"

"It's empty, you shyster," Monk told him.

They ran to the plane, found the note which Henry Peace had clamped in the door. They read this.

"Now what in blazes!" Monk exploded.

"Whoever the fellow is," Ham said, "he's trying to help us. Let's look in that tree."

They stalked cautiously through the brush. They carried small spring-generator-operated flashlights of a type which Doc Savage had developed, and these stuck whiskers of light through the underbrush.

Monk led with Ham crowding him, with Johnny having more trouble because his gaunt length kept getting tangled in the underbrush. They had a little trouble with their direction and missed the tree. They were standing in the thicket, pawing Spanish moss off their shoulders—the stuff was like cobwebs, except that it was as thick as baling wire—when the motor of their plane unexpectedly began banging.

Our ship!" Monk squawked.

They struck out wildly for the craft. Shrubs tripped them, boughs knocked against their heads and thorns hooked into their clothing. Monk got sidetracked in a blackberry thicket and stood there screaming and bellowing.

Their plane motors were hot, so the thief did not need to delay to warm them. He simply locked left wheel brake, revved right motor and snapped the plane half around. Exhaust stacks poured flame, the ship leaped forward, and the little hill threw it into the air almost like a catapult. Even then its wheels almost scuffed the tops of trees on the other side of the little field.

Monk and the others stood and gaped at their departing ship.

"Superebullitive!" Johnny exclaimed.

"This is no time for one of them words," Monk growled.

"We're in a fix!" Ham said.

THEY rushed back and removed enough ignition wiring from the Haven plane to make sure that no one would fly off with that one.

"You know what?" Monk growled.

"What?" Ham scowled at him.

"That note in the plane door was a trick. It sent us off looking for that tree so they could steal our plane."

"Then there's probably nothing in the tree," Ham said.

"We might make sure of that," Johnny suggested, using small words.

Five minutes later, they were holding their flashlight beams on the Havens. Tex and Rhoda Haven had not yet mastered enough physical strength to take flight, but there was nothing wrong with their voices; and old Tex had moved his hands enough to get them full of guns.

"Calculate you better start runnin'," Tex advised, "while you're able."

Monk muttered, "Say, that's the girl who came for us to help. Show her who we are."

They turned one of the lights upon themselves, giving the lens a twist so that it fanned a wide beam. Their appearance did not impress Tex Haven, because he had not seen them before. Rhoda grabbed one of her father's gun hands.

"Those are Doc Savage's men," she said. "Don't shoot!"

"I don't care who they are!" Tex brandished his guns as much as his muscular instability would allow. "I been messed with too much by different people!"

There was an argument between Monk, Ham and Johnny on the ground, and the two Havens up the tree. They compromised on the Havens remaining armed and suspicious, but climbing down out of the tree with the assistance of Monk, who had to show plainly that he carried no weapons. They all walked out onto the small field and stood in the brilliant moonlight.

Tex Haven peered at Monk suspiciously in the moon-glow.

"You send one of your gang ahead in your plane, chasing Horst?" he asked.

"No, blast it!" Monk said. "Somebody stole our plane."

"Eh?"

"We don't know who it was," Monk added.

Tex Haven felt of his pockets to make sure that his corncob pipe and stick of black Scotch tobacco had survived. Then he eyed his daughter.

"Henry Peace," he said, "ran off and left us."

His daughter kicked a clod indignantly.

"If he did," she said, "it wasn't because he was double-crossing us."

"He said he couldn't fly," Tex reminded her reasonably.

Rhoda Haven made several starting-to-say-something noises, but apparently could think of nothing satisfactory.

Tex continued, "You take the cussedest attitude toward this Henry Peace. When he's around, you act like he was flu germs. The minute he's out of sight, you start stickin' up for 'im."

Rhoda Haven said nothing to that. Monk, who had a great deal more brains than his appearance indicated, realized that this fellow named Henry Peace must have been making some headway with attractive Rhoda Haven. The idea did not appeal to Monk.

Monk said, "We found a note stuck in the door of the plane—*ouch!*"

Ham had kicked Monk's shin. "The note said not to mention it," the lawyer whispered.

"The fruit of the peanut bush to you and Henry Peace both," Monk said. He proceeded to tell the Havens about the note.

"Blast that Henry Peace," Tex Haven yelled indignantly. "He framed it so that we'd be caught by you fellows while he got away in your plane!"

Rhoda Haven went into a deeper silence. Monk assayed two or three casual remarks, intended to break the ice, but she did not seem appreciative of what he had told her about Henry Peace.

Habeas Corpus and Chemistry had been ranging the brush. They approached. Habeas, the pig, came up and rooted at Monk's leg. Monk picked the shoat up by an ear and exhibited him proudly.

"My pet," he explained.

Rhoda Haven remained silent.

"This hog," Monk announced, "couldn't love me more if I was an ear of corn."

That remark did not impress Rhoda Haven either. Monk was mildly disgusted.

"Let's get going," he said.

Tex Haven blinked. "Going where?"

"Why, we'll just keep on following them other two planes," Monk declared.

Chapter X
PEOPLE IN DUNGEONS

HENRY PEACE, the man who had said he could not fly a plane, made a perfect landing at Key West, Florida. It was also a remarkable landing, because it was on a golf course instead of an airport. The plane skipped a sand trap, rolled down a fairway, and came to a stop on a green, where its wing tip pushed a flag over.

Henry Peace had told a fib when he said he couldn't fly a plane. He had told large fibs about several things. He seemed to be enjoying it.

He vaulted out of the plane.

Henry Peace seemed to have a remarkable knowledge of the layout of Key West. As a matter of fact, his knowledge of other cities over which he had flown—Miami, Key West, Jacksonville, Charleston—had been just as complete, although there had been no occasion to exercise the knowledge.

The plane had landed less than a hundred yards from some palm trees. Behind the palms was the home of the best-posted detective in the Key West police department, the man who probably knew more about what went on in Key West than any other man.

Henry Peace walked to the detective's home, knocked, and the detective appeared in a nightshirt.

"Who the devil are you?" he asked. "What the blazes you want?"

Henry Peace walked in and took a comfortable chair.

His voice changed when he spoke. It took on a completely different personality.

He said, "You must be doing well. You've put on a little weight since the Albergold kidnapers were stuffing you in a canvas sack and tying it to a weight."

The detective jumped. He eyed Henry Peace, and his eyes flew wide. His mouth also fell open.

"Bless me!" he yelled. "You're—"

"Henry Peace is the name now," Henry Peace said.

The detective seized Henry Peace's hand and pumped it. He was profoundly moved. In fact, something happened to him that had not occurred in years—his eyes became damp with gratitude.

"Believe it or not," he said fervently, "I still get down on my knees and give thanks for your saving my life that time."

"Forget it."

"I wish I could forget the way those kidnapers tortured me before you appeared."

Henry Peace said, "Know anything about a man named Jep Dee?"

The detective nodded. "That's the fellow that a college boy found on an island. Jep Dee had been tortured. He refused to tell any kind of a story. For a while, he had a mania for keeping a piece of old rope tied around his neck. But one night he took the rope off; and that same night, Jep Dee had a fight in the post office with a cop because he thought the cop was trying to get a letter that Jep Dee had just mailed. We found out that the letter was addressed to someone named Rhoda Haven, in New York City. They took Jep Dee back to the hospital. He's blind, but the doctors seem to think he'll be all right eventually. The sun burned his eyes, or something, and he has nerve shock."

Having listened to this long speech in silence, Henry Peace was satisfied that he had the whole story briefly.

"Then Jep Dee is something of a mystery," he said.

"Very much so."

"What hospital?"

The detective told Henry Peace the hospital where he could find Jep Dee.

THE hospital must be busy, because there were many lighted windows, although this was a late night hour. On the seaward side was a pleasant shelf of a veranda, and interns and doctors came and stood on this frequently and smoked cigarettes or gossiped.

The Gulf Stream, that current of incredibly blue water fifty miles wide and a mile deep flowing past the tip of Florida, was quiet tonight. There were almost no waves—only swells—and these came in like fat, slow-moving blue elephants that turned to a yellow color as the water shoaled, and broke on the beach, each time sounding as if someone had stepped into a wastebasket full of paper.

A trailer stood on the beach. There was nothing unusual about that, parked trailers being found almost anywhere in Florida. This one was above high-water level, and had been there some days. Palm-tree shade made it rather dark.

It could have been a coincidence that the trailer stood in the spot from which the hospital could be watched most thoroughly.

Henry Peace appeared in the darkness beside the trailer. He had made absolutely no sound.

"Hello," he said.

The trailer tenant gave a violent jump. He had been sprawled in a canvas chair just inside the trailer door, where he could watch the hospital.

"What the hell!" he exploded.

He also reached into the pocket of his beach robe, where there was a gun.

Henry Peace said, "I came on ahead of Horst."

Which was more truthful than some of the statements he had made.

"Who're you? I ain't seen you before."

"Lots of things you ain't seen, maybe," Henry Peace said. "At least, I think I'm ahead of Horst. He in town yet?"

The trailer tenant was a small, dark, useless-looking fellow. He considered for a while before he answered.

"Horst's plane should be somewhere between here and Jacksonville," he said, "judging from the telephone call I got when they refueled in Jacksonville."

"You're watching Jep Dee?" hazarded Henry Peace.

"Sure. We're going to take him out of the hospital when Horst gets here."

"What room is he in?"

The man pointed, "Second floor, third from left. Room with storm shutters over the window."

Henry Peace did not comment. He was silent, thinking. There had been some excitement and action since he first contacted the Havens, and the mystery of Jep Dee. But he had not learned much, really. The mystery of Jep Dee was still just that—mystery.

Henry Peace assumed his most convincing tone.

"I'm a new man, just getting into this," he said. "You are supposed to give me the low-down."

"What low-down?"

"Everything. Explain it."

The other snorted. "Listen, bud, there's more millions of dollars involved in this than you can shake a stick at."

"Yeah, I heard the rumor—"

"And almost forty people have got to die. They won't, if things go wrong. In which case, our names will be mud."

"I heard that rumor, too, but—"

"But—nothing!" snarled the trailer tenant. "I ain't telling you a thing. The hell with you, partner! I don't even know you."

The man's manner was determined enough to show that he had made up his mind to talk no more.

Henry Peace held his fist in front of the man's nose.

"You see what's in this?" Henry Peace asked.

The man did the natural thing—peered at the fist.

"Hell, no, I don't see—"

Possibly he then saw stars. Or maybe it was just blackness. He lay down backward on the floor, hard enough to shake the whole trailer. Henry Peace blew on the right fist, with which he had hit the man.

"Carrying this Henry Peace character too far," he muttered. "Fool around and break my knuckles if not careful."

He tied his victim with the trailer clothesline, also gagged him. Then he consulted his watch.

"Better get Jep Dee before anything else," he decided.

Two policemen had been assigned to watch Jep Dee, on the possibility that he might try to leave the hospital again, also on the chance he might decide to talk. The two cops split each day in twelve-hour watches. It was considered a soft job.

Jep Dee had not been giving any trouble. In fact, he frequently seemed glad to have the officers around.

Furthermore, the hurricane shutter had been put up at Jep Dee's window. The shutter was constructed of steel, could be fastened from the outside. It made the room a jail, literally.

The hospital wall below the window—Jep Dee's room was on the second floor—was not considered climbable.

Henry Peace looked the wall over, then took off his shoes and socks. He had remarkably long toes, and they seemed to be trained, flexible, and incredibly strong.

He climbed the wall that was not considered climbable. Unfastening the hurricane shutter was merely a matter of sliding a bar.

He got into the room. Jep Dee slept. Henry Peace grabbed Jep Dee's mouth with one hand, the man's nose with the other, and lay on Jep Dee so he could not make a commotion.

"I'm helping the Havens!" Henry Peace said.

He said that several times.

Jep Dee was silent, except to take in a great rattling gulp of air, when he was released.

"Horst is coming to get you," Henry Peace said. Jep Dee said several words about Horst's character that should have made the air smell of brimstone.

"I've got to move you," Henry Peace explained.

Jep Dee said, "I'm willing."

Henry Peace scooped Jep Dee off the bed, went to the window, and in a moment stood poised on the ledge with his burden. The slick, silver bole of a palm tree slanted past a few feet from the window. Henry Peace jumped, clamped himself and his burden to the palm, and slid, not fast enough to friction-burn his long powerful legs, to the ground.

A few minutes later, he lowered Jep Dee in the shadow of the palms along the beach—but some distance from the trailer.

"Eyes improved any?" he asked.

"Not much," said Jep Dee. "Who the dickens are you, anyhow?"

Henry Peace now began talking. His tone was persuasive, and no one would have guessed from his words that he was anything but a lifelong acquaintance of old Tex Haven. Very casually, he mentioned anecdotes concerning Tex Haven's soldier-of-fortuning in China, Korea, Manchuria, Spain and South America.

"OF course," said Henry Peace, "I don't know much about what Tex has been doing in South America. He just took on my help unexpectedly."

"That must explain," muttered Jep Dee, "why I haven't heard Tex mention you."

"As a matter of fact," said Henry Peace, "Tex didn't have time to give me a full account of this present proposition. He said you'd do that."

"What shall I begin with?"

"Start off with that piece of shark skin. What does the thing mean?"

"You saw it?"

"Yes."

"Then I don't need to explain. It explained itself."

Henry Peace said, "I'm darned if it did."

The man lying on the sand put both hands to his eyes. He made an enraged snarling noise.

"If I could just see!" he gritted. "Boy, did they give me the works before I got away! And to think I put in weeks finding that island, while the Havens waited in New York!"

Henry Peace, suddenly alert, prompted, "Oh, yes, you looked for the island while the Havens waited in New York. Just what did you find on the island? Old Tex wants to know that."

"I think the place can be entered," Jep Dee muttered. "I imagine the pay-off would be over ten millions."

"Ten millions," said Henry Peace, "is a lot of money."

Peace grabbed his limp friends and ran for cover.

"My guess is that there are forty people in the dungeons. Some of them have been killed already. Most of the others undergo daily torture. Some of the dungeons are rigged up with the damnedest torture devices you ever saw. Did you know that rats will eat a man alive?"

"I don't believe," said Henry Peace, "that any rat would have nerve enough to eat a live man."

"Well, you're as wrong as a war. I saw 'em. They let me watch. They pulled off my fingernails and pulled out my eyelashes, then they took me down to watch the rats eat a man. They were letting them eat a little of the man each night."

Henry Peace was silent a moment. "That is too horrible. I don't believe it."

"Suit yourself."

"Suppose," said Henry Peace, "that we get the whole thing clear in my mind."

"How do you mean?"

Henry Peace suggested, "You go back to the first and explain the whole thing. Start at the beginning."

Jep Dee lay very quiet for a while.

"Hell with you!" he said.

Peace held his fist in front of the man's nose.

"But—"

"I'm wise to you now!" Jep Dee snapped. "You don't know the first thing about this mystery. You've been stringing me along. So the devil with you! I don't tell you anything more."

Henry Peace made a gesture of disgust

"That makes two of you," he said.

"Two?"

"The other one," Henry Peace explained, "is in a trailer."

A fight followed. Jep Dee had regained some of his strength in the hospital, and he put up an impressive scrap. He knew every vicious trick of hand-to-hand combat, and he used them all.

Henry Peace got Jep Dee flattened out in the sand and tied and gagged with strips of his own hospital nightgown. The strips took almost all the nightgown.

"You better stay here," advised Henry Peace, "because you're pretty naked, and it might embarrass somebody if you start wandering."

There was not much chance of Jep Dee leaving. About the only thing he could move was his ears.

Henry Peace walked back to the trailer with no more noise than a shadow.

The man was lying on the trailer floor, exactly where he had been left. Henry Peace bent over him.

The prisoner instantly reached up and took Henry Peace by the throat.

"C'mon, Horst!" he yelled.

Out of the back of the trailer, and out of the front, where they had been concealed, men came leaping. They piled upon Henry Peace. They had clubs, knives, ropes, all ready for the combat.

Henry Peace was hopelessly outnumbered.

Chapter XI
THE VIOLENT MR. PEACE

ANDREW BLODGETT—MONK—MAY-FAIR was walking down a Key West Street, closely trailed by his pet pig with the large ears and long legs. They both stopped.

"Listen!" Monk exploded.

They were close to the sea, so near that swells breaking on the beach frequently shoved out tentacles of white spray that reached almost to their feet. Palm trees around them were, in the night, like giants holding up hands with fingers distended.

The hospital where Jep Dee had been confined was over a hundred yards distant, and on the left. They had called at a morning newspaper office and learned the story of Jep Dee, as much of it as the newspapers knew. It had been a quick source of information; the trouble was that the newspaper now knew some Doc Savage aides were in town, and reporters would haunt them for stories.

The sounds seemed to come from a spot in front of the hospital. There were grunts, yells and thumping noises.

Long-bodied, long-worded Johnny cocked an ear.

"A tintamarrous bombilation!" he remarked.

"Sounds more like a fight to me," Monk muttered.

Ham said, "That, short-and-hairy, is what he meant."

Ham, who was noted for being suitably dressed for every occasion, was attired in what Monk termed the "tom-catting" suit. This was a black suit with black accessories—shirt, tie, socks, handkerchiefs, and hat, all black—which matched the harmless-looking black sword cane that he always carried. Chemistry, Ham's pet chimp, was rather dark by nature and matched his owner.

They stood there in the darkness, listening to the fight, debating what to do.

The fight seemed to be in progress around a trailer.

The Havens, father and daughter, kept a disgruntled silence. They weren't enthusiastic about being with Monk, Ham and Johnny, but they had not been able to do anything about that. They had been haunted by the Doc Savage associates since they had been found in the tree following the aerial dogfight.

Ham nudged old Tex. "Good time for you to tell us what all the scrambling is for."

"'Tain't, neither."

"Might save us all a lot of trouble if you explained the mystery."

"Rootin' under that log," said old Tex, "won't get you nothin'."

Monk was more than ever intrigued by the qualities of Rhoda Haven—not the least of these being her figure—and he was also convinced that he had a rival in the person of the missing Henry Peace. Monk had been making derogatory remarks about Henry Peace. He made another one now.

"Henry Peace," said Monk, "has disappeared, so he probably got scared and cleared out."

Rhoda bit her lip, snapped, "Listen, you robin-eyed—"

"Whatcha mean—robin-eyed?"

"Eyes that are always resting on limbs," the young woman said coolly. "Henry Peace is worth a squad of some of the people I've reluctantly become acquainted with."

Monk stood torn between two desires—the yen to make passes at a pretty girl, and his always-strong liking for a good fight. The fight yen won.

"C'mon!" Monk barked. "Let's see whether that scrap needs our attention."

THE bedlam at the trailer stopped suddenly.

Almost complete quiet followed. They could

hear the waves making the sounds that were like someone stepping into a wastebasket of paper. Their own feet crunched sand.

They came to the trailer, and blazed flashlight beams.

Johnny had a favorite word when he was astounded. He used it now.

"I'll be superamalgamated!" he exploded.

The door had burst off the trailer. Inside, the bunks had been torn loose, windows knocked out, dishes broken, pots and pans trampled out of shape. Everything that could be used to hit a man over the head apparently had been employed for that purpose.

Ham jumped around with his flashlight, counting the senseless men who were scattered about.

"Six!" he exclaimed.

Monk gazed at broken noses, scuffed faces, torn clothing.

"Brothers," he said, "a human hurricane sure went through here."

He took another look at the six victims.

"These are Horst lugs," he announced. "Some of them were with that gang who tried to throw us in a cistern on Long Island."

Old Tex Haven had been doing some eager inspecting for himself.

"But Horst ain't among 'em!" Tex said disgustedly. "Depend on the head skunk to be out of the den when the roof fell in."

"I'll bet," said Rhoda Haven triumphantly, "that Henry Peace did this."

"Humph!" Monk said.

They looked around the vicinity for some trace of the hurricane—Monk stated an unnecessary number of times that it couldn't be Henry Peace—that had done all the damage. They found no one.

A Horst thug stirred, groaned, sat up, wanted to know, "Where's that red-headed devil?"

"You see!" Rhoda Haven ejaculated triumphantly. "It *was* Henry Peace!"

"Rats!" Monk said grumpily.

Ham walked over to the hospital and entered. When he came out and joined them, he looked so downcast that Monk commented on the fact.

"You went in there like a lion and came out like a postage stamp," Monk said.

"Like a postage stamp?"

"Licked."

"This is no time for such cracks!" Ham snarled. *"Jep Dee is gone from that hospital!"*

THERE was a prompt rush for the hospital, where they put barrages of questions that got them no information of value. The visit to the hospital did, however, impress Rhoda Haven with a point. The information that Monk and others were associated with Doc Savage worked wonders with the hospital people. They fell over themselves to offer any service. There were comments of the highest character regarding Doc Savage's ability.

"This Doc Savage," Rhoda remarked when they were outside, "must be quite an individual."

Monk nodded violently. "For once, you're right in your judgment of somebody!"

Johnny rubbed his bony jaw.

"Perscrutination seems pragmatical," he stated.

"Put it in English," Rhoda Haven requested.

"I suggest," said Johnny stiffly, "that we now resort to asking questions of people—you included."

"I see."

"The questioning to be coupled with such persuasive violence as may be necessary," Johnny added.

"I see," Rhoda Haven repeated coolly.

A man walked up boldly in the darkness.

"You Doc Savage's men and party?" he asked.

"You said it," Monk told him.

"A guy named Henry Peace sent me," the stranger explained. "He said to tell you he'd taken somebody named Horst, and was waiting for you with a man named Jep Dee. He said for me to show you where he was waiting, and to bring you if you wanted to come."

Monk scowled blackly, said, "We don't want to come."

"Try not to be as simple-minded as usual," Ham advised the homely chemist. "Of course, we want to go."

Rhoda Haven turned a flashlight so Monk could see the triumphant expression on her attractive features.

"I notice," she remarked, "that most of the accomplishing around here seems to be done by Henry Peace."

Monk looked as if someone was feeding him worms. He did not say anything.

Ham and Johnny loaded unconscious Horst thugs into the trailer, tying them with bed sheets, fishing lines and anything else they could find.

"Inchoation is contiguitudinous," Johnny remarked.

"Eh?" said the messenger.

"Maybe he means," Monk suggested, "that now we start."

"Why didn't he just say so?"

"He only speaks English when he has to."

"Oh. One of them kind of guys, eh? I don't see why these foreigners who come over here can't speak American."

The car attached to the trailer was a shabby-looking old heap, but at the first traffic light, Ham sprang out to inspect the motor in amazement.

Instead of the wheezing four cylinders he had expected, he found sixteen polished ones that were snorting out at least two hundred horsepower.

Their guide was a rather hungry-looking fellow in overalls and a straw hat. He seemed somewhat dumb in almost every way.

He directed them to a lonesome, sandy road that led through some palmettos to a clump of lonesome-looking palms that stood up stark in the white moonlight. There he told them to stop.

The guide got out.

"There's five or six army machine guns covering you fools," he said. "You stopped your car over a buried case of TNT that's wired to explode when a switch over yonder is closed. If you want to get tough, just hop to it!"

Having delivered this news, he dived behind a convenient palm tree.

Chapter XII
THE BRONZE MAN

AFTER lightning strikes, there is usually a moment of everything-stopped silence. This one lasted about twenty seconds.

Then a machine gun stuck out a tongue of red flame from the palm thicket and gobbled ear-splittingly. In the next quarter minute, possibly two hundred bullets hit the car engine. The hood came loose, flopped, banged, and finally flew up and away and the big motor itself broke in places. Impact of the bullets shook the whole car until the occupants held to things.

When the bedlam stopped, Monk was yelling. He thought the others were being murdered wholesale, the bullets missing him by some miracle.

But shooting was only to put the car engine out of commission.

"Come outa there!" a voice rapped angrily. "That car being armored won't do you any good!"

That was the first they knew about the car being armored.

"Let's fight 'em!" Monk gritted.

The voice yelled, "We wasn't kiddin' about that TNT under you!"

"I don't think they are," Ham muttered.

Johnny, shocked into using small words, said, "They surely don't plan to kill us immediately, or they would have cut loose with the machine guns. We better surrender."

Monk growled, "What puzzles me is why they don't go ahead and try to kill us?"

They learned why after they left the car, after they stood with their arms in the air, and were relieved of weapons, and after the captors discovered that Monk, Ham and Johnny were wearing bulletproof undergarments of a chain mesh. These were torn off with some difficulty, leaving the late wearers almost embarrassingly unclothed. They learned the reason they had been kept alive when a captor barked:

"Where's Jep Dee?"

Monk looked around for some trace of Horst, but the mastermind did not seem to be in sight. The head skunk, Monk thought savagely, was staying out of sight whether the hole was falling in or not.

"C'mon!" the captor snarled. "Only reason you're alive is because you can tell us how to git hold of Jep Dee."

Monk began, "There is where you're mis—"

And Ham kicked his shin, hissed, "Want to make us dead, stupid? They find out we don't know where Jep Dee is, and they'll kill us."

Monk saw where it would be wise to let their captors think they knew where Jep Dee could be found, if they wanted to think that. He said no more. The others also clamped lips.

They were slapped and kicked and threatened for five minutes.

"This is gonna take time, so we better get 'em on the boats," a man growled. "No tellin' who might show up to investigate that shooting."

The sea was close, it now developed. The prisoners were led a short distance, then shoved through mangroves for fifty yards, coming out on the bank of a tidal creek on which floated four varnished dinghies.

"Whar might the head polecat be?" old Tex Haven inquired.

"Horst?" A man laughed. "Boy, he don't know what minute Doc Savage is going to turn up in this thing. He don't want to be around when that happens."

"He skeert of Doc Savage?" asked Tex.

"He ain't nothin' else!"

"He's not alone, either," another man muttered. "Right off, I can't think of anybody I'd be more scared of."

The prisoners were shoved close to the four dinghies, and after a grunted suggestion by one of their captors, it was decided to take them two dinghy loads at a time.

Monk, Johnny and Rhoda Haven were loaded in two of the dinghies, along with four captors, a pair to each little craft. The dinghies—twelve feet long, of light lapstreak construction, the wood varnished—were standard yacht tenders.

The two dinks paddled along the tidal creek, and the creek swung sharply left.

Just after the pair of small boats rounded the corner, the rearmost one—the boat containing Johnny and Monk—overturned.

IT happened suddenly. No warning. Before the

occupants could even yelp, they were in the briny creek water. It was too sudden and violent for any accident.

The men in the lead boat turned. One of them splashed a white flashlight beam.

They saw a swimmer making for them. He seemed to travel with fish speed. But there was more about the swimmer than speed.

And there was more about him than his giant size.

There was, probably most striking of all, his bronze complexion. Bronze was the swimming giant's color motif, his hair being a little darker bronze than his skin.

His eyes—when he was very close to the dinghy, the flashlight glare disclosed his amazing eyes— were a strange flake-gold tint. Flake gold that seemed stirred by tiny winds.

"Doc Savage!" a man yelled.

Doc Savage put hands on the dinghy rail. The hands were barred with sinew, the arms above them incredibly muscled. He jerked. The dinghy upset.

"Monk, Johnny—swim this way!" Doc Savage called.

The bronze man's voice had a crashing power, as arresting as lightning.

Rhoda Haven floundered in the water. Her wrists were lashed, as were the wrists of Monk and Johnny. A dropped flashlight was still glowing on the bottom of the creek, about eight feet down. The water was very clear, and the flash glow diffused and made them seem to swim in milk.

Rhoda saw Doc Savage dive swiftly. The next instant, she was seized, dragged beneath the surface. She had enough mind presence to hold her breath.

Doc Savage slashed her wrists free.

She did not, for an instant, realize what else the bronze giant was doing. He shoved a clip on her nose; it closed her nostrils tightly enough to hurt a little. Then he shoved a mouthpiece between her teeth, a mouthpiece to which was attached a rubberized pouch. She knew what it was, then.

She swallowed the salt water that was in her mouth, after which she was able to breathe, underwater, as long as she did not take deep breaths, with the mechanical "lung." Chemicals in the rubberized pouch, in the mouthpiece-filter, purified her breath and furnished oxygen.

By swimming downward, she kept on the creek bottom.

Doc Savage had already reached Monk and Johnny and struck at their wrists lashings with his knife. He merely jammed a mechanical lung into Monk's hands, another into Johnny's clutch. They knew what to do with them. Doc himself donned one of the lungs.

The three of them—Doc Savage, Monk and Johnny—sank beneath the surface together. They found Rhoda Haven, faintly discernible on the outskirts of the glow that came from the waterproofed flashlight on the creek bottom.

Monk seemed inclined to stay and drag some of their late captors below the surface.

Doc Savage jerked at Monk's arm, discouraging his ideas about lingering.

IT was probably fortunate that Monk did not stay. The other two dinghies rushed into view, foam at their bows, loaded down with men who had machine guns.

The swimming Horst followers were hauled aboard the newly arrived dinghies.

The submachine guns roared and mowed down surrounding mangrove thicket.

The men heaved hand grenades overside, which burst, causing the creek to vomit water high in the air; and dead fish began coming to the top and floating bellies-up, and a nurse shark that had been in the creek made an agony-maddened threshing.

Some distance down the creek, Doc Savage led the others out into the mangroves. They listened to grenades burst, and men swear.

"A tintinnabula," Johnny remarked.

Monk said, "If that means a devil of a noise, you said it!"

There was more moonlight around them than they cared for.

Rhoda Haven gripped Doc Savage's arm.

"You ... you are Doc Savage?" she breathed. "How on earth did you come to turn up now?"

Doc Savage did not answer that, because there was an interruption—Monk gave a great horrified start. The homely chemist had remembered his squabbling mate, Ham Brooks, was still a Horst prisoner.

"Ham—we've got to rescue Ham!" Monk gasped.

Rhoda Haven added something grim and imperative about saving her father, too.

"Crawl through the mangroves," Doc Savage said. "Keep going due south."

The bronze man then vanished. There was no commotion, no elaborate flourishing of arms or leaping into the tops of mangroves. The metallic giant merely walked a few paces—and suddenly could no longer be heard or seen.

"Doc's going after Ham and Tex Haven," Monk explained.

"Hadn't we better help him?" Rhoda Haven demanded.

Monk snorted.

"There's only twelve or fifteen of Horst's gang back there," the homely chemist said. "Doc won't need any help."

"Are you crazy?" Rhoda Haven asked incredulously.

"No, I've only seen Doc Savage in action," Monk explained.

They began creeping through the mangroves, heading south, as the strange bronze giant had directed. The mangroves were almost without leaves; none of them were more than ten feet high nor much thicker than Monk's thumb. They were as tough as iron. They grew in a solid mat, the boughs interlacing. There was usually about a foot of space between the lowermost branches and the mangrove swamp mud. Monk, Johnny and Rhoda Haven started mud-crawling southward.

ABOUT this time, the Horst men stopped shooting and throwing hand grenades into the mangrove creek.

"They got away!" growled the man in charge. "We better see they don't grab Ham Brooks and old Tex Haven from us!"

Both dinghies were paddled back furiously to where the other two prisoners had been left. The Horst men were frightened now.

They had seen Doc Savage finally, gotten a sample of the bronze man's work. Back in New York, when they had first learned they were pitted against the mysterious and almost legendary Doc Savage, they had been afflicted somewhat by the creeps. But as the hours passed, and Doc Savage in person did not appear, there had been a reaction; and they had been inclined to beat chests and say, "Hell, we ain't scared of this guy!"

Simply because the bronze man had not appeared, they had started to think what they hoped in their hearts was true—that the reputation of Doc Savage was a myth, a soap bubble blown by hot air from gossiping tongues.

But now the bubble had burst.

And there stood their personal devil, just as big and bronze as they'd heard he was.

With fright-driven haste, the Horst men seized Ham Brooks and drawly old Tex Haven, flung them into the dinghies, and rowed back down the mangrove creek.

They heaved hand grenades into the water as they progressed. The blasting grenades made concussions that would have killed any man, even Doc Savage, attempting to attack the boats by swimming below the surface.

Their flashlights raked the mangroves. Their machine guns lead-ripped every lump of dark shadow.

What saved them was their gas masks. They had donned these—all but the prisoners who had been in the trailer, and who naturally had been rescued. The latter had no masks.

The men without masks collapsed unexpectedly, every one of them. It happened at a point where the creek was narrow. The men with masks were terrified. Their machine guns ran out thunder and lead until the barrels turned red-hot. They heaved grenades as fast as they could dig them out of pouches.

Doc Savage—he had laid down the barrage by heaving small, marblelike capsules of gas from a distance—was forced to flatten in mud under mangroves. He was no more bulletproof than the next man.

The dinghies—carrying all of Horst's men and Ham and Tex Haven—got out of the mangrove creek. Digging oars drove them for the yacht.

THE yacht was sixty-five feet long. Also deceptive. From the waterline up, she was a two-masted schooner, with a clipper bow, a nice hull line, and a clean stern. Her sails were all jib-headed, and raised and lowered on neat tracks instead of the old-style mast hoops.

Outwardly, she looked like some moderately rich man's plaything, a schooner capable of a top speed of ten knots at the very most. Except that the masts were hinged like a Dutch canal boat, so they could be lowered.

If one got close to her when she rode in very clear water, and looked at the hull lines below the surface, the impression was a little different. The water-buried part of her was built like a Harmsworth trophy contender. More than half the boat was engine room, crammed with the newest high-speed Diesel equipment.

When the dinghies had been hooked to davits and yanked aboard, the yacht anchor came up, and the craft gathered speed until she was jumping from one wave to another.

An investigation showed that the gas victims seemed merely to be unconscious.

The man in charge went below and got on the shortwave radio. It was a very modern radio, equipped with a "scrambler"—a mechanical-electrical device which made it impossible for any listener-in to understand what was being said.

The man talked to someone on the radio for some time. Then he went on deck and made a speech to his men.

"We're going to the island," he said.

"But that will leave Doc Savage untouched," a man reminded him. "And it will leave Jep Dee running loose, somewhere. To say nothing of that Henry Peace, whoever he is."

"That's all right," said the man who had talked on the radio. "Something new has turned up."

"New?"

"Señor Steel is here."

The listeners, to a man, looked as if a cold wind had come down out of the north.

"Here—on this boat?" one croaked.

"No, no," said their informant impatiently. "Señor Steel is in Key West."

The news of the coming of Señor Steel seemed to have spread poison over the city of Key West, as far as they were concerned. Every man was obviously glad that the schooner-speedboat was leaving the vicinity.

Chapter XIII
SEÑOR STEEL

WHEN Johnny Littlejohn, Monk Mayfair and Rhoda Haven were convinced they had crawled ten miles through the mud and mangroves—it was probably a full half mile—they came to a road.

"Bivouacial quiescence," Johnny remarked.

"He means," Monk explained, "that here is a good place to rest."

They flopped down on the coral sand of the road. They had heard the powerful Diesel motors of the yacht and guessed what they were; but that sound was gone now. Enough of a breeze was blowing to rasp mangrove boughs together occasionally, a sound somewhat as if skeletons were being moved about.

No one said anything. They were too tight with strain, wondering what had happened to Ham Brooks, Tex Haven and Doc Savage, to feel like making words.

Suddenly, they heard a strange sound. It was a trilling, pitched low, and possessed of an exotic quality that made the nature of the sound difficult to define. It was weird, might have been the work of a vagrant wind in the naked mangroves and it had a ventriloquial quality that made it seem to come from everywhere.

Monk sprang up.

"I better go," Johnny said, using small words.

"Huh?" Monk said.

"I better go," Johnny repeated, more firmly.

Monk muttered something about going ahead if he was so danged anxious, and sank back to the road sand.

Rhoda Haven reached out and gripped Monk's arm, asked, "What was that strange noise?"

"It might be the wind," Monk told her, and was good enough a liar to make it sound truthful.

Johnny walked down the sandy road, taking quick steps with his long bony legs. He did not know from what direction the sound had come, but he did know it had been made by Doc Savage.

That weird, exotic trilling note was a characteristic of the man of bronze, a thing which he did unconsciously in moments of mental stress, and sometimes made deliberately to indicate his presence.

Having gone some distance, Johnny stopped. A moment later, without any noticeable sound, Doc Savage was a bronzed tower in the darkness beside the gaunt, big-worded archaeologist and geologist.

Doc Savage said, "They got away with Ham and Tex Haven. Boat. A fast boat."

Johnny said several small words. They were not profane words. They were just short words that showed how desperate and puzzling he considered the situation.

"I want," Doc Savage said, "your advice."

"My advice?"

"Do you think I had better let the girl know that Henry Peace and Doc Savage are the same persons?" the bronze man asked.

JOHNNY gave the query some consideration. He was by nature something of a psychologist, in contrast to Monk, who liked to bump people around with his fists, or Ham, who liked to sway people with his agile tongue and was not averse to bumping them with his fists or pricking them with his sword cane, either.

Johnny said, "You put on a disguise and called yourself Henry Peace in the first place because—"

"When Rhoda Haven came to us in New York, she did not tell the truth," Doc Savage explained quietly. "I hoped to take the personality of Henry Peace, just a knockdown-and-drag-out young soldier of fortune, and join Rhoda Haven and her father, and thus learn what it was all about."

"And—"

"It did not work," the bronze man said disgustedly.

"Maybe it's nearer to working than you think."

"What do you mean?"

"The girl," said Johnny, "is in love with you."

Doc Savage made a sound that was dubious.

"You're mistaken," he said. "Whenever I'm around, she acts as if ants were in her oatmeal."

"Yes, but when you're not there—"

"When I'm not there—what?" Doc demanded.

Johnny rubbed his long jaw. He found this situation interesting.

"Just the same," he said, "I think it would be advisable to turn into Henry Peace again and join us."

Doc Savage did not seem enthusiastic about that. "I doubt if she will tell Henry Peace anything."

"I'm betting she will."

"Well—" The bronze man changed feet uncomfortably. "Oh, all right. Henry Peace will turn up again, then."

"When Henry Peace shows up," Johnny said dryly, "he had better watch out for Monk."

"What's the matter with Monk?"

"He's acquired an elephant-sized dislike for Henry Peace."

"Maybe," Doc Savage said thoughtfully, "I had better tell him who Henry Peace is. I didn't tell him earlier because I knew that as long as the Henry Peace disguise had Monk fooled, it would fool anybody."

Johnny snorted.

"It would be more fun," he said, "if you didn't tell him."

This terminated the conversation, and Johnny went back to the other two. He found Monk telling Rhoda Haven what he thought of Henry Peace, which was practically nothing.

"When I get through with that Henry Peace," Monk said, "he'll be pounded down small enough to get lost in caterpillar fuzz."

After this promise, Monk drew Johnny aside. He knew, of course, that the long archaeologist had gone off in the darkness to consult with Doc Savage.

"They got Ham and Tex Haven," Johnny explained.

He did not add that Doc Savage had decided to go on being Henry Peace. Monk did not know that Doc Savage was Henry Peace. Monk detested Henry Peace. It was going to be interesting when Monk found out who Henry Peace really was. Ham Brooks, who had spent years squabbling with Monk, would like to see that.

Johnny shivered. He suspected that unless they did something drastic in a hurry, Ham Brooks might not live to see anything much.

Shortly, Doc Savage appeared. One moment there was moon-silvered darkness about; then the bronze man stood silent beside them.

"We have not much time to waste," he said quietly. "The Horst men will keep Ham and Tex Haven alive for a while and torture them in an effort to learn the whereabouts of Jep Dee. But they do not know where Jep Dee is, so they will eventually be killed."

RHODA HAVEN was a soldier of fortune's daughter. She had the temperament, the courage, the fatalism for her profession. She was something of an axman of fate; like her father, she could attack something gigantic and chop away at it, and when the terrible moments came—the moments when there was no telling where the giant would fall, or what it would crush—she could clamp her lips, put up her chin, and take what came, and know that what had happened would not have occurred if she had not used the ax.

"Do you know where they took my father?" she asked in a level voice.

"How could I know?" Doc Savage countered. "You did not tell my men the truth when you first came to us in New York. You have not told them much since."

"I have not told them many lies," the girl countered grimly.

Doc Savage came to the point. He put a blunt statement of facts.

"You and your father and Jep Dee are after something," he said. "Jep Dee hunted for it here in the Florida Keys, while you and your father waited in New York. Jep Dee must have found what you sought, but he was caught by Horst, and barely escaped with his life. He was delirious, and muttered stuff about thirty-some people being in imminent danger of death. He had a piece of freckled-looking shark skin on him when he was found. He mailed it to you and your father. Horst came to New York and tried to get the shark skin and kill you. You came to me and tried to get me and my men to chase Horst. Obviously, that was to keep Horst occupied while you and your father went ahead with your original plans to get something down here in the Florida Keys."

"You have," said Rhoda Haven levelly, "learned a lot."

Doc Savage put a question as blunt as his statement of facts.

"What is the something?" he asked. "What are you after?"

Rhoda Haven hesitated.

"You want to know what the piece of freckled shark skin is?" she asked.

"Yes."

"And you want to know what my father and I are after?"

"Yes."

"And about the thirty-some people who are going to die if something isn't done?"

"Exactly."

Rhoda Haven compressed her lips. She was thinking. She thought of all that she had heard of this remarkable man of bronze—things which she had thought fantastic when they first came to her ears, but which she was beginning to realize were true. Through her mind ran the legends of the feats he had performed, of his strange career of righting wrongs and punishing evildoers throughout the far corners of the earth.

These legends of the doings of Doc Savage were many, and some of them were fantastic, but all had one thing in common. Those who fought the bronze man with tremendous treasures at stake—always lost them. The bronze man's wealth was fabulous, she had heard, a great hoard piled up of the treasures, the great inventions, which he had taken in the course of his adventures.

The thought of losing everything that she and her father were fighting for settled on her mind an ice that froze any warm impulse she felt to confide in him. She was a fighter. She would continue fighting.

She said, "My father and I are fighting for tremendous stakes, part of which are rightfully ours. We knew the chances we were taking when we began."

"But—"

Rhoda Haven lifted a silencing hand.

"I'm going to do what dad would want me to do," she said. "I'm going to refuse to tell you anything."

"You—"

"We'll solve our own problems. We always have."

Doc Savage's strange, flake-gold eyes studied the young woman. "Mind telling me why?"

"Greed, maybe. When we risk our lives like we have—I'm referring to my father, Jep Dee and myself—we expect to get what we're after."

"At this stage of the game," Doc Savage reminded dryly, "you are almost licked."

That was true. The girl could think of no effective answer. Except one. A gesture of verbal defiance.

"Don't forget," she snapped, "that Henry Peace is still running around loose and doing things!"

AS a result of that remark, it was a perfectly natural move for Johnny Littlejohn to drop back alongside the bronze man after they had started along the road in the direction of Key West. Johnny made sure that neither Rhoda Haven nor Monk would overhear him.

"You see," Johnny told Doc Savage.

"See what?"

"She's that way about Henry Peace."

After this remark, Johnny watched the bronze man with interest. He could see that Doc was flustered. In fact, the bronze man stumbled over a rut and almost fell down.

"Blast it!" Doc said.

Johnny did not think he was referring to the rut.

"The thing for you to do," Johnny advised, "is to turn into Henry Peace again."

"Nonsense!" Doc said too promptly.

Johnny said grimly, "It's the only way we've got of maybe learning enough to save Ham."

Doc thought that over.

"You're probably right," he said, with somewhat the resigned air of a Christian about to be thrown to the lions. "I'll turn into Henry Peace."

Doc Savage walked on ahead of the party, to scout their course. The first street lights of Key West were not far ahead.

Johnny rejoined Monk and Rhoda Haven, and after glancing at the young lady, felt like sighing. Doc Savage might be a scientific genius, a mental wizard and a muscular phenomenon—but his knowledge of women put him in about the same category as a babe in arms. That was, of course, the result of the bronze man's determination to avoid feminine entanglements.

Doc Savage held the conviction that, if he ever fell in love, his enemies would strike at him through his sweetheart or wife.

Probably he was right, Johnny realized. So it was a good idea. But Johnny was also convinced that any good idea can be carried too far, and Doc had overdone this one. He'd had absolutely nothing to do with femininity. The result was that Doc had acquired an abysmal ignorance, Johnny believed, of the fair sex. Doc was also scared of them.

Doc Savage had protested a great reluctance for becoming Henry Peace again, and making passes at pretty Rhoda Haven.

Johnny secretly suspected that the bronze man really liked the idea. He did, or he wasn't entirely human. Johnny thought he was human.

They reached an avenue lined with palms. In the palm shadows, it was very dark. Doc was still leading.

Suddenly, from ahead, there came a yell.

"Get your hands up, dang you!"

It was Henry Peace's voice.

Blow sounds followed. A crash of palmettos, as if someone had been knocked into the vegetation under the palms. More blows. Then running feet hammered the ground.

Doc Savage's voice crashed out.

"It's Henry Peace!" Doc shouted. "He's running. Wait there!"

A crashing went away through the brush. It sounded very much like Doc Savage pursuing Henry Peace.

Monk snorted, for Rhoda Haven's benefit, said, "Your red-headed, freckle-faced hero bumped into a real man. And there he goes. Runnin' like a rabbit."

"Henry Peace," said Rhoda Haven indignantly, "will make this Doc Savage look tame before he's done!"

Monk snorted so loudly that he hurt his nose.

"All your bragging about Henry Peace," he said, "goes in one of my ears and out the other."

"That," Rhoda Haven said coolly, "is because there's nothing in between to stop it."

Henry Peace came out of the palm shadow into the moonlight. He had a revolver. He pointed the weapon at Monk. But he spoke to Rhoda Haven.

"After we're married," he said, "we're gonna lead a more peaceable life than this."

Rhoda Haven, in view of the way she had been holding up for Henry Peace, reacted in a strangely contrary fashion. She walked over and tried to slap Henry Peace. He caught her wrist and held her easily.

The young woman stamped a foot indignantly.

"I wish," she snapped, "that I had been made a man."

"You have," Henry Peace assured her cheerfully. "I'm him."

Doc Savage had put on the Henry Peace disguise while walking down the road ahead of them.

WHILE Rhoda Haven maintained an indignant silence, Monk and Henry Peace exchanged a few words. They did not swear, exactly, but there was enough acid in their tones to bleach the surrounding tropical vegetation.

"You do what I tell you!" Henry Peace warned Monk, waving his revolver.

"You can't hit the side of a barn with that!" Monk growled. "I saw a sample of your shooting on Long Island!"

"I should have let them throw you in the cistern that time!" Henry Peace told him.

Evidently Monk's confidence in Henry Peace's bad marksmanship was not as strong as he claimed, because he let himself be made a prisoner.

Henry Peace marched them off to the right, to a lonesome spot on a sandy beach. He bound Monk and Johnny, ankles and wrists, with their own belts. Then he addressed Rhoda Haven.

"About time," he told the young woman, "that you give me the truth on this mess."

She had been thinking over the situation. And she had reached some conclusion.

"You got Jep Dee out of the hospital?" she asked.

"Yep."

"Where is he?"

"Little place down the beach from here."

Rhoda Haven said, "Go get him."

"Why?"

"Jep Dee is the only one who can help us. He knows the meaning of that piece of freckled shark skin. He knows the whereabouts of the spot to which Horst's men probably took my father."

Henry Peace nodded grimly. "I'll bring Jep Dee. You watch these two Doc Savage men."

He walked off into the night.

The moment Henry Peace was out of sight, his way of carrying himself changed, and his stride altered—he became Doc Savage in everything but appearance. Acting the part of a personality as different as Henry Peace was a mental and physical strain, and he was glad to relax.

Henry Peace had not told the exact truth about where Jep Dee had been left. Henry Peace, in fact, did not stick exactly to the truth in a great many of his statements. This was in marked contrast to Doc Savage, who never told anything but the truth, even when a lie might be convenient to mislead an enemy.

Jep Dee was in a tourist cabin near the center of town.

Doc Savage was thoughtful as he walked. He was puzzled with himself. He was rather enjoying being Henry Peace. He didn't approve, exactly, because Henry Peace was an untruthful rascal who had a weakness for a pretty girl. Henry Peace was boastful, insolent, and made love at every opportunity.

It wouldn't do, Doc Savage decided uneasily, to play Henry Peace with too much enthusiasm.

It might become too pleasant.

To get his mind off the distressing idea that Doc Savage, the man of determination, might be tempted to really turn into an untruthful rascal named Henry Peace, the bronze man stopped and bought a morning newspaper. He wanted to learn how much commotion the events of the night had created in Key West.

He saw the advertisement at once. It was half a page, hence hardly to be missed. It said:

DOC SAVAGE

JOHN DOE WISHES YOUR HELP. THIS NEWSPAPER WILL TELL YOU HOW TO GET IN TOUCH WITH HIM.

Chapter XIV
HAVENS—CROOKS

INSTEAD of going on for Jep Dee—who would be safe enough where he was awhile—Doc Savage removed his Henry Peace disguise, then called the newspaper.

"The advertisement," he explained, having identified himself, "seemed rather imperative."

"I presume it is," said the voice at the newspaper. "John Doe is waiting at the Caribbean Hotel."

When Doc Savage looked it over, the Caribbean Hotel seemed a respectable hostelry of some size.

He spent twenty minutes going to different places around and in the hotel, standing and looking and listening. This satisfied him that, if it was a trap, the trap was inside the room.

"Mr. Doe," the hotel clerk said, "is in the penthouse suite."

"Thank you," Doc Savage said, "but I think it is rather late in the night to make a call."

He walked out, leaving the impression he would be back later. He went around to the back of the hotel, took out a small grapple attached to a silk cord, tossed it and snared the fire escape, to which he climbed. He took his time, made no noise, and reached the roof.

The roof was a garden. In the center stood a Spanish type of bungalow, rather small, very neat, very flamboyant, and probably stunningly expensive.

All the bungalow doors were closed. The bungalow itself was dark.

Doc Savage produced—from a vest which contained a number of pockets holding unusual gadgets—a contrivance which resembled a small bicycle pump, but which had a long needlelike spout.

He filled this oversized hypodermic from a non-breakable metal bottle which was also in the vest, and squirted the contents under a door. He refilled the hypo and squirted more fluid under all the other doors he could find.

He ambled over to the penthouse balcony and stood looking at the Gulf Stream. The sea was moon-kissed, stretched away and seemed to blend with the sky, and the riding lights of boats in the harbor were scattered sparks that bobbed a little.

When the gas he had squirted under the doors had had time to take effect, he put on the underwater lung, which was also a gas mask, walked to a door, took hold of the knob, and without much apparent physical effort, tore knob and lock out of the door. He walked in.

There was only one man there, so he must be John Doe.

John Doe would make a good football player, of the boy-he's-not-big-but-can-he-carry-that-ball type. Unquestionably, he was in good physical trim. He was senseless, but his muscles felt like truck tires, anyway.

His face was the color of good smoking tobacco. Doc opened his shirt and noted that his chest and the rest of him was the same color.

John Doe had been sitting in a chair, fully dressed, waiting in the dark. There was a long-nosed automatic on the floor at his feet, so probably he had been holding that in his hands.

Doc searched John Doe. Then he searched the penthouse. There was no baggage.

There were twenty-five cartridges for the automatic in John Doe's pockets, but absolutely nothing else. Not a thing to show who he was.

John Doe woke up after a while.

"I am Señor Steel," he said.

HE was not what Doc Savage had expected. In appearance, at least. He did not look like the kind of man that the newspapers had painted.

True, however, the newspapers had never printed Señor Steel's picture. It was said there were no photographs of him in existence. It was reported that there were X-ray machines planted to throw beams across every door in the palace of the dictator of Blanca Grande. The X rays would ruinously fog any films that photographers might try to carry in or out of the palace. As a matter of fact, Doc Savage used the same gag in his New York headquarters. The two men didn't want their pictures taken for similar reasons.

Both Doc Savage and Señor Steel had enemies who would gladly hand their pictures to hired killers.

The similarity stopped there, as far as Doc Savage knew. For the last year or two, many stories had spread concerning Señor Steel, dictator-president of the South American republic of Blanca Grande. He did not stand well with the American government—for one thing, he had followed the example of others in appropriating the property of United States oil companies. And there were other stories, not wholesome.

Señor Steel looked young. Except that there was grimness around his mouth and eyes.

"You are Doc Savage," he said quietly.

"Yes."

"I will not waste time," Señor Steel stated bluntly. "Here are the facts: I am president of Blanca Grande. I do not have a good reputation."

Doc nodded, said nothing.

"My reputation is bad," said Señor Steel, "because lies have been spread about me. Political lies."

He waited for that to soak in, then went on. "Stories have been told of my imprisoning and shooting numbers of political enemies. People, prominent and good people of Blanca Grande, have vanished, and I was given the credit both at home and abroad. The truth is that I had nothing to do with those people disappearing."

Doc Savage looked interested.

Señor Steel said, "One of my political enemies is responsible. This enemy is a professional soldier of fortune. He helped me with the revolution by which I gained the presidency of Blanca Grande. I found out that this soldier of fortune was a bloodthirsty rascal who expected to loot the treasury. I ran him out of the country. Since then, he has schemed against me."

"The soldier of fortune's name—"

"Tex Haven."

Doc said, "You claim that Tex Haven is a crook?"

"Exactly. He is aided by his daughter. Also by another rascal named Jep Dee. And by a villainous group of men headed by a man known as Horst."

"Horst is working for Tex Haven?" Doc asked.

"He was."

"What do you mean—was?"

"They have fallen out. Quarreled. Now they are fighting over the loot."

Doc inquired, "What loot?"

"The Tex Haven gang has stolen a lot of money from Blanca Grande," Señor Steel explained grimly. "They have seized prominent people and are holding them somewhere for ransom. That is the loot."

"I see," Doc said.

"I want you," Señor Steel told Doc Savage, "to help me wipe out the Havens, Jep Dee and Horst."

"My services are never for hire," Doc Savage explained.

"I know that. My government will donate a million dollars to any charity you wish to name."

Doc Savage considered what had been said. It sounded truthful. It was all reasonable, too, since the more violent kind of modern politicians had been known to do such things. And Señor Steel's voice certainly had a ring of truth.

"Care to go with me?" Doc Savage asked.

"Of course."

THIRTY minutes later, Doc Savage cautiously approached the spot where Rhoda Haven was guarding Monk and Johnny during the absence of Henry Peace, who, as far as the girl knew, was still on his trip to fetch Jep Dee. Neither Doc nor Señor Steel showed themselves, at the bronze man's suggestion.

Monk was doing some loud talking, probably in hopes of attracting help. It was sure he was not getting enough information to pay him for the breath he was wasting.

"Let us loose!" Monk yelled.

"Not so much noise!" Rhoda Haven ordered grimly.

"Who is this Henry Peace?" Monk persisted in a loud voice. "I don't know who he is. Doc Savage don't know. Who is he, anyway?"

Rhoda Haven came over and poured a palmful of sand in Monk's large mouth. This discouraged his noise.

Doc Savage touched Señor Steel's hard-muscled arm, and they withdrew in the night until they were out of earshot.

"I don't understand," Señor Steel said. "Those prisoners are two of your men, Monk and Johnny."

Doc explained, "They are being Rhoda Haven's prisoners deliberately in hopes of learning something of importance."

Señor Steel thought that over. He chuckled suddenly.

"The real identity of this Henry Peace is a mystery?" he asked.

"Somewhat," Doc said.

Which was the truth—somewhat.

The bronze man now explained quietly that they would go and get Jep Dee, adding that they would then return to this spot and seize Rhoda Haven, after which he hoped they would be fortunate enough to clear up the entire affair.

They went to the tourist cabin where Jep Dee lay.

"Do not speak," Doc warned Señor Steel. "Jep Dee must not hear your voice. He might recognize it."

Jep Dee was stronger. He was sitting up in a chair, and replacing the bandage across his eyes, a painful operation because of his nailless fingertips.

Doc Savage said, "I'm the man who got you out of the hospital. We were none too soon. Horst's men arrived soon afterward."

Jep Dee was satisfied.

"I can't see," he said. "I took the bandage off my eyes, and I can't see."

"It is night," Doc reminded him.

"I know. I found a match and struck it. I could just see a faint glow. Damn! Did my eyes hurt!"

Señor Steel went to an open window, looked out, shrugged to indicate there was no one in sight. He remained at the window, leaning out frequently, on sentinel duty.

"Who's that?" Jep Dee demanded.

"Fellow helping us."

"Oh."

Doc Savage said, "Horst and his men have seized Tex Haven and carried him away on a boat. Do you have any idea where they would take him?"

"To the island, probably," Jep Dee said grimly. "To that hell-hole."

"Where is the island?"

Jep Dee's expression showed plainly that he was not going to answer that. But he thought it over for a moment.

"You say you're working with Rhoda Haven?" he asked.

"Yes."

"I'll tell *her* where the island is."

"You—"

"I'll tell Rhoda," Jep Dee said emphatically. "Nobody else."

"All right," Doc told him. "We'll join Rhoda Haven."

Señor Steel arose from the sill of the open window, where he had been sitting. They left the tourist camp and headed for the spot where Rhoda Haven was guarding Monk and Johnny.

Doc Savage had reached a decision. He was going to get the whole group together, disclose the fact that Henry Peace was really himself, Doc Savage. He had an idea that was the best way. Jep Dee, he believed, would then reveal the location of the island to which Tex Haven and Ham had been taken. Jep Dee might give that information freely. If he didn't, there was such a thing as truth serum.

But they met Monk Mayfair running wildly along the beach.

"Horst himself!" Monk yelled. "He grabbed Rhoda Haven and Johnny! I got away!"

Chapter XV
SHARK WITH FRECKLES

IT was impossible. Horst could not have known the whereabouts of Rhoda Haven, Johnny and Monk. Or maybe he had. Maybe—

Doc Savage made, for a brief moment, his low, exotic trilling sound, and this time it was an unconscious reaction to mental shock. Shock because of the impact of a suspicion that he had been duped, had overlooked an important possibility. He did not do that often. He had lived through many dangers in the past because he made it a practice to overlook no possibilities, to prepare against every eventuality.

Monk was explaining how it had happened—an unexpected rush out of the darkness, a furious fight in the night. And he, Monk, had escaped only because he had previously succeeded in loosening his bonds.

"And it was just after Habeas Corpus and Chemistry came around," Monk finished. "Two pets must have trailed us."

The pig and the chimp had come up in the darkness. Chemistry chattered uneasily a time or two, and Habeas emitted one forlorn grunt.

They left Jep Dee for the moment, and moved quickly, the three of them, back to the spot where Rhoda Haven and Johnny had been seized. There was no trace of them; only a trail that led to a road some distance away, and in the sand that had blown over the road, tracks of a car.

Monk looked at Señor Steel. "Who's this?"

Señor Steel told who he was. He also repeated the story about the Havens and Horst and Jep Dee all stealing loot and kidnaping in Blanca Grande, then falling out among themselves.

"We've still got this Jep Dee!" Monk snarled. "Where's he?"

Doc Savage warned, "Make Jep Dee think we are working with him, so he will tell us the location of the island."

They went back to Jep Dee.

"Did Horst really get Rhoda, too?" Jep Dee asked grimly.

"Yes."

Jep Dee wasted no more words.

"The quickest way to that island," he said, "is by plane."

"We have a plane," Doc told him.

Jep Dee growled, "That piece of shark skin had a map showing the location of the island, also the spot on the island where the cache is situated."

Monk snapped, "There was nothin' on that shark skin! Just freckles!"

"Who is this squeaky-voiced guy?" Jep Dee demanded.

"Another man helping us," Doc said.

Jep Dee, satisfied, went back to the subject of the bit of shark skin. "You say there was no map on it?"

"You were in the water after you drew the map?" Doc asked.

"Yes," Jep Dee admitted. "I swam for hours, escaping from that island."

"Then the map must have washed off the shark skin, except for spots which resembled freckles," Doc suggested.

"Why—sure! Sure, that's what happened! The water washed the berry-juice ink I used off the shark skin. I've been blind as a bat since I was picked up, so of course I didn't know the drawing had soaked off."

THIRTY minutes later, Doc Savage's fast little plane—the craft which he, as Henry Peace, had stolen from Monk, Ham and Johnny on the way south—sent a roaring sound over the golf course where the bronze man had landed when he came to Key West. The little craft picked up its tail, angled past a sand trap, took the air. Doc handled the controls. He cut the exhaust into the efficient mufflers, and the plane became a dark ghost that hissed.

Jep Dee resumed talking, went on describing, as best a blind man could, the location of the island.

Monk listened intently, poked a pencil point speculatively at a chart that showed the myriads of islands composing the Florida Keys.

Señor Steel remained silent in one of the cabin seats. He had not spoken at any time, had given Jep Dee no chance to identify the Señor Steel voice.

The sky in the east was faintly promising sun. But on the plane there was still nothing but moonlight, and below it, silver moonbeams that crested the beach surf with lactescence. The sea was a dark infinity, the islands darker spots like moss.

"We haven't long until daylight," Doc said gravely.

"But the island isn't far," Jep Dee said.

The plane rocketed on, in a direction generally northward. It was climbing; Doc Savage intended to have plenty of altitude, and then coast down silently when they came near the island.

Already below them were the keys, some of the strangest islands in the world. First, the water was shallow, so shallow that it was possible to step out of a boat in some places and wade, if one felt so inclined, as much as fifty miles; and in only a few places would the sea be more than neck-deep. The islands themselves were low. Hurricanes swept over some of them at times. Few of them had white beaches; shores of naked, mud-colored coral were more frequent. From the high night-flying plane, of course, it was impossible to tell just how grim and unpleasant the islands were.

Monk gave flying directions in a low voice.

Finally, "How much farther?" Doc Savage asked.

"If this is an island I've got my pencil on, about fifteen miles," Monk said. "If it's a fly speck on the map—I don't know."

Doc Savage used night glasses—binoculars with lenses of extremely wide field, so that they gathered much light—on the sea below. Shortly, he saw a boat.

"We'll drop down a little," he said, "with the motors muffled."

The plane sank in the sky. The engines were expertly silenced, the propeller of a special design to eliminate much of its natural roar. Doc examined the boat.

"Two-masted schooner," he said, "running faster than any conventional schooner could run."

"Recognize it?" Monk asked.

Doc Savage said, "That is the boat on which Ham and Tex Haven were taken."

Jep Dee stirred impatiently, demanded, "Who is Ham?"

"Another man who is helping us," Doc explained.

A bit later, Monk leveled a hairy beam of an arm.

"There she be," he said.

IT was not a mile long. It was not half a mile wide. It somewhat resembled a green doughnut out of which someone had taken a bite.

Doc Savage said, "We might as well land in the lagoon."

The lagoon, of course, was the water in the center, the hole in the green doughnut.

Jep Dee said, "Come in from the north. They're on the south side."

"The lagoon safe?"

"Nothing is safe down there," Jep Dee said grimly. "But they won't be watching the lagoon. It's mostly shoal, not more than a foot or two of water. Do you have to come in through the entrance?"

"No."

"That's good," Jep Dee said. "They've got one of those electric eyes set across the entrance. That's what caught me. Can't even a rowboat come into that lagoon without breaking the electric-eye beam and giving an alarm."

Monk said, "They must have the place all fixed up."

"Fixed up is right!" Jep Dee swore for a little while. "Wait until you see the cache!"

Doc Savage cut the plane motor, set the ship gliding at as slow a speed as possible, to keep down wind noise from its flying wires. He nosed it in to the island from the north.

Spray sheeted from under the floats when they touched; then the plane settled. The lagoon was glass-smooth; there seemed to be no wind whatever.

"Break out the paddles," Doc directed.

They were regular canoe paddles, capable of driving the small plane after a fashion. But before they paddled far, they discovered that it was simpler to drop off in the water, hardly more than knee-deep, and shove the plane.

They pushed the plane to the mangroves, found a small indentation, backed the craft into that and tied it there, poised with its nose toward the open lagoon, where it could be unlashed quickly for flight.

Jep Dee muttered, "What about me? I don't want to give the idea that I'm a coward, but I don't like the idea of being left alone in this plane. I can't fly it, even if I wasn't blind."

"We will leave you in the mangroves," Doc told him.

They left him concealed among high mangrove roots, with an emergency kit of blankets and food from the plane. Before they left him, he asked a question.

"What's the matter with this other guy with us?" Jep Dee demanded peevishly. "Why ain't he said nothin'?"

Monk said, "He got smacked in the neck with a fist, and it hurts him to talk."

Jep Dee seemed satisfied.

Doc Savage led Monk and Señor Steel into the mangroves.

"The schooner will be here soon," the bronze man explained. "When they take the prisoners off, we might as well follow them. Be a simple way to find the cache."

Señor Steel spoke quickly. "I can think of a better way."

Doc studied the man in the moonlight. "Better way?"

"The cache," said Señor Steel, "is located on the very southern tip of the island, where there is high ground and some palm trees. It will save us time to make directly for it."

Doc Savage said, "You seem to know a great deal about the island."

"One of my agents reached it, and got away, without finding out the exact location. He stowed away on Horst's schooner speedboat."

"Agent?"

"You seem to have met him," Señor Steel said.

Doc made his voice puzzled. "I have met one of your agents?" he asked.

"Henry Peace," said Señor Steel.

"Henry Peace is one of your agents?"

"Exactly."

Chapter XVI
MUD

AT first, there was mangrove swamp around them, the earth being boggy and in some places covered with water. It was tidal flat that flooded at high tide, and the tide was out now; so that the mangroves, for a foot or so above the mud, were slimy and slick. They heard, occasionally, small sharks make splashing sounds in the pools, and crawfish sometimes fled with furious skittering noises in the shallow water.

Once Monk slipped off a mangrove stem, landed on his head in mud which was semiliquld and about three feet deep. He had to have Doc's help to extract himself.

"Brothers," he said, "some day I'm gonna give up this hero business and settle down to a peaceful life of finding out what's in test tubes."

They reached the path shortly after that. It was on higher ground, where there were palms, palmettos and a few trees of the tropical evergreen variety.

"Boy, here's easier going!" Monk gasped gratefully.

He would have started along the path, but Doc gripped his arm, stopped him.

"Let me examine your machine pistol," the bronze man requested.

"It's in working order," Monk said.

"We are going into action," Doc reminded him. "Let's be sure."

Monk drew his machine pistol and passed it to the bronze man. They stood close to the high palmettos and shrubbery that lined the path. The shadows were like blobs of oil smoke that were standing still.

Faint clicking noises indicated Doc Savage was unclipping the ammunition drum from Monk's pistol and scrutinizing it.

"All right," he said. "You have plenty of spare ammo drums?"

Monk's pockets were full of mud.

"The drums are probably muddy as blazes," he said, and felt of his pockets.

He gave a great, dismayed start.

"Gleeps!" he exploded. "I haven't got a single spare ammo drum!"

Doc Savage said, "You probably lost them when you fell into the mud."

Monk made mutterings of disgust, took his machine pistol when Doc Savage handed it back to him.

The bronze man now spoke quietly.

"You and Señor Steel will remain here," he directed. "You need a breathing spell, after going through those mangroves. Too, we should scout this path. It would be poor strategy for all of us to do that—if there should be a trap, we would all fall into it."

"That is true," Señor Steel said in a rather strange tone.

"Wait here," Doc repeated.

The bronze man vanished in the shadows.

HE went quietly. He followed the path about twenty yards, turned off, headed back toward where they had left the plane.

Monk, who'd had so much painful trouble with the mangroves, would have been amazed at the speed of the bronze man's movements across the swamp. Probably he would not have been surprised —he knew all about the bronze giant's almost uncanny muscular agility.

Jep Dee crouched where he had been left.

"Easy does it," Doc told him quietly. "I decided to move you."

"Why?" Jep Dee asked.

"Rigging up a little surprise party," the bronze man explained cryptically.

He moved Jep Dee a considerable distance from where he had been located, and left him on higher ground, lying in a trench in the sand which was quickly scooped out by hand.

"Be back in a minute," Doc said.

He went to his plane. Still intact in the baggage compartment were equipment cases—a standard outfit of gadgets which the bronze man and his aides always took with them when setting out on an adventure. Gas masks and the little anaesthetic gas grenades were a part of the equipment.

Doc Savage distributed gas grenades about the plane, placing them so that the ship could hardly be approached without the gas being released.

On the handles of the cabin door, on the controls themselves, the bronze man smeared a sticky liquid which was hardly noticeable. The liquid was an anaesthetic, too, that penetrated the pores of the hands; and while anyone handling the plane controls might not get enough of the stuff to cause unconsciousness, it was sure to deaden their arms, make them feel very ill, and create a good deal of worry.

He smeared more of the sticky liquid on the surrounding brush, on the plane guy lines.

Then he went back to Jep Dee.

Giving Jep Dee a gas mask, Doc Savage explained about throwing the anaesthetic gas grenades. He put a supply close to Jep Dee's hand.

"If anybody comes, how'll I tell whether they are enemies?" Jep Dee asked. "I can't see."

"They will say, *'The sand is green,'*" Doc Savage explained. "That will be the password. Unless they give it, cut loose with the grenades. But put on the gas mask first."

He gave Jep Dee a gas mask and showed him how it worked.

Then he made a round of Jep Dee's hiding place and distributed more of the sticky liquid on the mangroves, where anyone trying to creep close to the spot would be fairly sure to get into it.

When the bronze man approached Monk and Señor Steel, he could tell that they were getting impatient. He did not show himself, did not let them know he was near.

"About time Doc was gettin' back," Monk said uneasily.

Doc Savage now began his examination of the path. He went very slowly, searched with the utmost care, for he distrusted almost everything upon this island.

The death trap that he found was ingenious.

It functioned if one did not carry some kind of a projector that turned strong ultraviolet light upon the receiving cell of an electric eye. There was an electric-eye beam across the path; if the beam was interrupted, a machine gun began firing at once, swinging a little as it fired, to rake the path thoroughly.

Doc got acquainted with the whole grisly trap.

He put his hand over the electric eye, from a safe spot.

The machine gun cut loose deafeningly, and its lead mowed down mangroves. It fired perhaps two hundred shots. Then it stopped, empty.

Doc Savage went out in the path and lay down where he might have fallen if shot. He carried a fountain pen with red ink, and he spread the ink on his face and clothing in realistic splotches.

MONK MAYFAIR heard the machine-gun roar, jumped to his feet.

"Doc!" he gasped. "Something has happened—"

He did not finish, because Señor Steel hit him. Señor Steel used his fist, and he set himself carefully, because he could see that Monk had an iron jaw. The blow sounded like an axman's first hard cut at a tree.

Monk jerked very stiff and rigid and fell, as the tree would fall, backward.

Señor Steel did not have a gun. He'd had a gun at the hotel penthouse in Key West, but he'd been able to find no trace of it after he regained consciousness there, with Doc Savage in the same room.

So Señor Steel took Monk's machine pistol. He fumbled with the thing until he found how it operated.

He fired a short burst at Monk's chest.

Then Señor Steel wheeled and ran—not toward Doc Savage, but in the opposite direction, along the path—until he came to a sandy beach.

Far out to sea, barely distinguishable in the moonlight, was the approaching schooner. Señor Steel ignored it.

He pulled a tangle of vines aside and disclosed a buried, wooden box with only the hinged lid showing. There were several lanterns in this—strange, square lanterns with lenses that seemed to be made of black glass. When Señor Steel switched the lantern on, it still gave no light.

It was an ultraviolet lantern that would keep the electric-eye death traps from functioning.

Señor Steel carried the lantern back along the path until he found Doc Savage's prone form.

He laughed once, then. A rather terribly gleeful laugh. And he fired a burst from the machine pistol at Doc Savage's chest.

Señor Steel then picked up Doc Savage and the bronze giant was limp. He carried the big form into the jungle, to a creek in the mangroves that had a mud bottom.

He threw Doc Savage into the creek. Then he stepped upon the bronze giant's body, and jumped around until he had trampled Doc's form some two feet in the mud.

"Good place for them both," he told himself.

He went back and got Monk. Monk seemed to be breathing, it dawned on Señor Steel when he had carried the apish chemist to the mudhole, so he shot him again.

After he had dumped Monk in the mud, he stood on him until the homely chemist was deep in the mire. Then he got out and wiped his shoes on weeds.

"We question the prisoners to see if Doc Savage left any record of what he learned," he remarked to himself. "Then we bump them, and this thing is settled!"

He walked away.

Doc Savage came out of the adjacent darkness, waded swiftly into the mud, groped for Monk, and dragged the unfortunate chemist out on dry ground.

Monk had regained consciousness under the mud. He was not very pleased with the situation.

Chapter XVII
HORROR CACHE

DOC SAVAGE had two things to do at once. First, he had to keep track of Señor Steel, to be sure the man did not evade him. And secondly, he must keep Monk from making a noise that would betray the fact that they were both alive.

Keeping Monk quiet was the big problem. Monk wanted to make a noise, a lot of noise. He had mud to get out of his mouth, and a lot of words, all sulphur-coated, that he wanted to release. Doc Savage held the homely chemist's mouth and nose, shook him, pounded on him, and otherwise conveyed the need for silence.

After Monk got the situation straightened out, he was quiet. He cleaned out his mouth and nose, wiped his eyes, and scraped off his face as best he could.

"Somebody is gonna pay for this!" he snarled. "Somebody is sure gonna!"

"Let us hope so," Doc whispered grimly. "Do not make too much noise."

The bronze man did not follow Señor Steel immediately. Instead, he ran back to the cache—the hinged box in the ground under the vines—from which Señor Steel had taken an ultraviolet lantern. There were other lanterns, and Doc Savage got one of them.

He had previously followed Señor Steel to the spot, interrupting his operation of playing dead to do so.

The bronze man carried one of the lanterns, hurried along the path.

"Quiet," he warned.

Monk could walk now. He had been thinking, and the more he thought, the madder he became.

"That Señor Steel slugged me!" he gritted. "He's a crook."

"A large one," Doc admitted.

"He the head of this thing, by any chance?" Monk demanded.

"My guess is that he is."

They crept along in silence—there was still no sign of Señor Steel ahead—while Monk did some more thinking.

Doc Savage breathed: "Here are the ammunition drums you thought you lost. Also a spare machine pistol."

"Huh?"

"I slipped them out of your pockets the first time you fell in the mud. Later, when I examined your gun, I substituted blank cartridges."

Monk muttered, "I don't get this!"

"It was to prevent Señor Steel killing you with your own weapon," Doc Savage explained. "He shot you a number of times while you were unconscious. He didn't know he was shooting blanks. Then he threw you in the mud and tramped you under. He thinks we are both dead."

"Both? He do that to you, too?"

"Yes."

"Hm-m-m."

"His idea that we are dead," Doc Savage said grimly, "is going to make it much simpler for us to fight him. He won't be expecting much."

Monk rubbed his hard knuckles together fiercely.

"When I get hold of that guy," he said, "he's gonna think there's a blasted violent spook around!"

SEÑOR STEEL was taking his time. The path—there were a number of the electric-eye death traps along it—forked in the approximate center of the island, and one arm led over to the deep water along the south side of the island. Here was an anchorage, protected by a hook of reefs offshore, where a craft could lie with safety in anything short of a full gale.

It was into this anchorage that the schooner came, two searchlights sticking out like long white whiskers from her bow to pick up the channel range-markers. She rounded the stake that marked deep water, and the anchor rattled down. A dinghy was put overside.

Ham Brooks and Tex Haven were dumped into the dinghy, and the craft was rowed ashore.

Señor Steel's appearance on the shore got sudden gasps. They were not happy gasps, either. The men became uneasy. It was evident that they feared Señor Steel. They stood about with uneasiness in their manner. When Señor Steel did not say anything, they grew more worried.

"We've been doing the best we could, your highness," a man mumbled nervously.

Señor Steel said, "You've done excellently."

His voice was cold, but it was evidently warmer than the men had expected. They brightened perceptibly.

"What do you wish done with the prisoners?"

"Hold them here a minute," Señor Steel directed. "Horst should be showing up in the plane."

"Horst has Rhoda Haven and the Doc Savage assistant named Johnny," a man told him.

"I know that, you fool!"

The men withdrew to a respectable—and safe—distance. In all their minds were the things they knew about this Señor Steel. The diabolic cleverness of the man, his cold and almost insane rages when things went wrong. The fact that he was so unpredictable. He might, and on occasion did, do anything.

They were afraid to work for this Señor Steel, and they were afraid not to work for him. That summarized it.

The plane came shortly. It was a fast and modern job, with every appliance for safety and speed. The cabin fittings were the utmost in luxury—leather from Morocco, rare tapestry from Gobelins, a painting by an old master that had cost a hundred thousand dollars, in one end of the cabin. Señor Steel had wanted solid gold fittings. But gold was too heavy, so the handles and window cranks and such were only gold-plated.

It was the personal plane of Señor Steel, president-dictator of Blanca Grande, which was a very unfortunate South American republic.

It landed and unloaded Johnny and Rhoda Haven. Also Horst.

Horst was as scared of Señor Steel as the others.

"This Doc Savage," he said, "is a devil. I haven't been able to do anything with him."

Señor Steel showed his white teeth. "I have. He is dead."

He told about tramping the bodies of Doc Savage and Monk deep into the soft swamp mud. They were dead, he said. He sounded very pleased.

"The only thing left," he added, "is to question the prisoners and make sure Doc Savage left no written record of what he learned."

"What about Henry Peace?"

"Well, what about him?"

"He's a mystery to everybody," said Horst.

"Some soldier-of-fortune tramp. Forget him."

MONK MAYFAIR gripped Doc Savage's arm, said, "We could jump them now," in a low whisper.

"Not now," Doc breathed.

The palmettos were thick around them, for shrubbery grew with luxuriance close to the beach. The sand was soft, and had muffled their footsteps.

Monk whispered, "I know we're outnumbered, but—"

"Let them lead us to this thing they call the cache," Doc said.

"Oh!" Monk understood, even if he was itching for a fight and didn't want to wait.

The march along the island path started. At this end, too, there was a cache of the ultraviolet lanterns that prevented the path death traps from working. They took no chances on one lantern protecting the whole group. They carried four.

They walked to the fork where the two paths joined, continued along the one that led to higher ground—higher ground being such only in comparison with the rest of the island. The greatest altitude was probably no more than twenty feet, and there were plenty of evidences that high hurricane water had swept over during the past.

They came to a hut.

It was not a hut that would attract anyone's interest. It might arouse a little pity, perhaps. It was very squalid. The old man who occupied the hut sat outside.

The old man had a beard, rather a remarkable beard, one that a family of nest-hunting mice could have envied. He also had wrinkles, such wrinkles that it was hard to tell which one was his mouth.

"Hell's fire!" he said. "Ain't I ever gonna get to go to bed tonight?"

He said that before he saw Señor Steel. Then he saw Señor Steel and got down on his knees and began protesting that he hadn't known his highness was along.

They went into the shack, lifted a trapdoor. There was sand. They scraped away the sand, and

there was a wooden lid. They lifted the lid, and there was a box full of gimcracks—rifle, revolver, knife, a good suit, a purse containing some money—such as an old man who was afraid of thieves might hide under his house. They took these out and opened the bottom of the box. This disclosed what seemed to be an ordinary abandoned well. Into the well they put a rope ladder which the old man of the hut produced.

They climbed down into the well, which was walled with brick, and pushed on certain of the brick, and finally stepped through a trapdoor into the cache.

It was lighted with electric bulbs, and it did not smell pleasant. It smelled, in fact, nauseating.

"They must be burning one of them now," Señor Steel said.

"Yes," a man told him. "Old Goncez, who hid all his gold somewhere before we got him. I think that tonight he'll tell where it is."

It was about this time that Doc Savage walked out of the darkness outside the shack and took the old man with the beard by the throat.

DOC SAVAGE had moved quickly, and the old man was taken by surprise.

Doc was also a master of certain methods of inflicting pressure on the spinal nerve centers so as to induce instantaneous paralysis. After he had pressed awhile, the old man became helpless, and could not cry out. Eventually, if certain readjustments were made, osteopathic fashion, on the nerve centers, he would be none the worse. But until then he could not move nor talk.

"You oughta let me biff him one!" Monk said.

"You'll get plenty of chances to biff people, I'm afraid," Doc advised grimly.

The elaborately secret entrance to the underground cache had been left open. Descending the ladder, they could not help grimacing. Even the swamp mud had a rather pleasant aroma by comparison.

Monk suddenly gripped Doc's arm, breathed anxiously, "Could this smell be gas?"

"It's burned flesh," the bronze man explained.

The corridor, concrete-walled, was narrow for perhaps ten feet. Then there were steps, twenty or so. After that the passage widened.

It seemed to be a long subterranean corridor, off which opened various steel doors. The electric lights were brilliant, and some of the doors stood open.

When feet stirred ahead, Doc Savage quickly drew Monk through one of the doors that was dark.

Men approached, and Señor Steel's voice sounded. He spoke in a cold, clipped fashion, describing the exact location of Doc Savage's plane, and particularly the spot where Jep Dee had been left.

"Get Jep Dee," Señor Steel ordered. "Shoot him on the spot. The plane is not so important. We will fly it out to sea somewhere and sink it."

Six men strode past in the party that was going after Jep Dee.

Doc Savage produced a handful of glass bottles which he had taken from the equipment case on his plane. He gave these to Monk.

"Gas?" the homely chemist whispered.

"You have to be careful with this stuff," Doc warned. "It works through the pores of the skin, and it's pretty bad. If you have to throw it, get away from the stuff. Don't let it touch you, or you won't feel much like fighting."

Monk said, "There won't nothin' make me feel like not fightin', the mood I'm in!"

THEY listened, finally thrust their heads into the lighted corridor. There was no one in sight. But voices came from what seemed to be a larger room fifty feet or so distant.

The door of that room was not open. But there was a barred aperture in the steel panel.

Doc Savage went forward silently, took a chance, and looked through the opening. It seemed to be safe enough. No one inside was interested in the door.

It was a large room of naked concrete, like a great basement. On the far side was a circular door of steel—a vault door. Every eye was on this.

Señor Steel was working on the combination of the vault. He got that door open. Inside that was another door, locked by key; and centrally located in that, a round lid.

Yanking the lid open quickly, Señor Steel popped a large bottle through. They could hear the bottle break. Señor Steel closed the lid instantly.

Monk, close to Doc Savage's ear, breathed, "A gas chamber on the vault."

Monk's chemistry knowledge had told him that. There was a chamber between doors of the vault, an air-tight one, probably filled with some form of deadly gas; and the bottle of chemical which Señor Steel had broken in the chamber would neutralize the gas, render it harmless, so that the vault could be entered.

After a while, Señor Steel opened the other vault doors, three of them.

"Give me the stuff I sent up recently," he ordered.

The "stuff" was jewels. Several hundred thousand dollars' worth, judging from the scintillating cascade that poured from Señor Steel's hand when he dipped into the small casket which was handed him.

He walked into the vault with the jewels, and they had a brief glimpse of an array, seemingly hundreds, of yellow metal bars in neat stacks.

"Looks like the inside of a mint!" Monk breathed.

Señor Steel came out and locked the vault, operated levers which probably charged the chamber again with gas.

"Get old man Goncez off the slab," Señor Steel snapped. "We'll put one of Doc Savage's men on. This overdressed one with the big mouth."

He meant Ham.

Chapter XVIII
WHEN DEAD MEN FIGHT

THE slab was of iron, and there were iron bands to hold ankles, and others to hold arms. It stood on four legs in the center of the large concrete room. Steam pipes made a mattress on the iron slab, and these led to a gas boiler which stood to the left. The boiler burned gas of the ordinary steel-bottled kitchen variety; and it was making heat now with a low moaning sound.

Old Goncez was perhaps seventy. It was doubtful if he would live. He looked as if he had been scalped, but probably that had been done with red-hot irons. There was a place in the boiler for heating irons.

Goncez could not move when they tossed him aside. He was not tied, and no one told him not to move; he was just past doing anything.

Rhoda Haven was in the room, and Ham, Johnny, Tex Haven.

They seized Ham.

Rhoda Haven made a gasping sound of horror and jumped forward. They grabbed her, and there was a short struggle. Then Rhoda Haven began talking. Not exactly screaming, but almost.

"We'll give up!" she cried. "We'll stop. We won't bother you—"

Old Tex Haven said savagely, "Like hell we'll stop!"

The girl paid no attention to her father.

"We won't bother you again!" she went on crying at Señor Steel. "Let us go and we won't come near this cache again, or ever try to make trouble for you. You know us—you know we keep promises."

Señor Steel said coldly, "I don't know anybody well enough to take their word."

The girl said: "You used a million dollars of our money. We financed and managed the revolution that put you in power. We'll forget that. Won't that satisfy you?"

Tex Haven said, snarling: "Won't nothin' satisfy the skunk. We was goin' to run Blanca Grande with an honest government and develop the country, and we'd have made millions and not harmed anybody, and made work for plenty of people. But Señor

Steel wasn't satisfied with that. He had to run us out and start grabbing everything in Blanca Grande. Look at the country now. Half the population starving. More misery in Blanca Grande right today than in any ten other countries."

Señor Steel laughed.

Then he jerked his head at the strong room where he had put the jewels.

"But look at the profit," he said. "Over eighteen millions."

"Heard it was fifty," Tex snapped.

"Exaggerated."

Old Tex Haven showed his teeth in an unpleasant way. They had taken his corncob pipe away from him, and that had not helped his mood.

He said: "The skunk that was your father must have crossed with a fox. You're slick. You had eighteen million dollars you had looted from Blanca Grande, and you had to keep it somewhere. You couldn't keep it in European banks."

"No," Señor Steel agreed cheerfully, "I couldn't keep it in European banks. They've made it against the law to take money out of most of those European countries. Anyway, their currencies aren't stable."

Tex said: "And you couldn't use American banks because the United States government figures you should pay for some of the American oil companies your government confiscated."

Señor Steel laughed.

Tex continued: "It was slick of you to pick an island inside United States waters, like this one. You knew no foreign government would be seizing it for an air base or something."

Señor Steel shrugged. This was praise. He was pleased.

Tex Haven said: "You brought a lot of your political prisoners here, you polecat. Old Goncez, here, is an example. I hear you've got almost forty more in the dungeons. Well, that's going to be your undoing. You can't torture people on that scale and get away with it. Matter of fact, you've slipped. Jep Dee found this island. Others will find it."

This wasn't praise. Señor Steel did not care for it. He pointed at Ham.

"Go ahead and torture that fellow," he ordered.

Tex Haven finished, "If I've got to watch a torture, how about giving me back my pipe?"

Someone came over and slapped him several times, great long-armed slaps that made loud noises.

RHODA HAVEN put her chin up and made her mouth tight. She had been shaken for a moment, when she tried to plead their way free, but now she had hold of herself, would take her medicine. Like old Tex Haven, she was made of human oak and human steel, and she had picked her career of soldier-of-fortuning, had liked it, knowing always what the wages might sometime be, and now she would accept the end.

Tex Haven shook with rage, but could do nothing. He wanted his pipe.

Johnny and Ham were calm, if not happy. They had been in tight spots before, not that practice made them any the less susceptible to fright—but previous danger had taught them that the thing to do in a case such as this was keep the mind so busy trying to figure a way out, that it would have no time to dwell on what seemed certain to happen. Death, in this case. Señor Steel would order them killed eventually, of course. Now, he was just worried about written records that Doc Savage might have left.

Monk was scared. He wasn't even in danger—yet. But he was more worried than anybody. His arms were trembling, and he had to keep his teeth clamped to prevent their chattering.

Monk was terrified for Ham. They were about to put Ham on that steam-torture horror.

The homely chemist's skin seemed to get as tight as a drumhead.

"We gotta go in there!" he gritted.

"Yes," Doc agreed, "we better."

The bronze man reached up and unscrewed one of the light bulbs that illuminated the corridor. He had his pocketknife ready the instant the bulb came out, and he plunged the blade into the socket.

A small devil of blue-green fire popped and hissed as the blade short-circuited the socket, and molten metal fell like jewels. Fuses blew.

There was darkness, blacker than it seemed any darkness could be.

Doc Savage and Monk Mayfair went into the concrete torture vault.

And screaming started somewhere else in the cache—weird screams by many voices, as if there were fear of darkness.

THE bronze man did not start fighting. Monk had sense enough not to cut loose with his fists, either, which was a remarkable piece of self-control for Monk, wanting to fight as he did.

The men in the vault would not know an enemy was attacking. Not for a moment or two. They would think the lights had failed.

While they were thinking the lights had only gone bad, Doc Savage cut Johnny and Ham loose. He bumped into people, of course. They swore at him, cursed each other. There began to be some noise in the place.

"Stop this racket!" Señor Steel yelled. "One of you fools light a flashlight. Where's the idiot responsible for keeping these lights operating?"

His tone promised something unpleasant for the idiot who tended the lights.

The grisly wailing from elsewhere in the cache was louder.

Doc Savage found Rhoda Haven. She was close to her father. They were trying to free each other.

The bronze man said, low-voiced, "It's Doc Savage. I'm cutting you loose. Make for the door."

He had told Ham and Johnny the same thing, and no one else had heard. He did not intend to be heard this time. But Horst was close. He caught the words.

"Doc Savage!" Horst screeched. "Doc Savage is in here!"

Señor Steel spoke rippingly.

"Shut up!" he rapped. "Doc Savage is dead!"

For a dead man, Doc Savage began to do a good deal of damage. He found Horst, struck him, knocked him against a wall. He hit another man.

Two more men got Doc's ankles, and he went down, but did not stay down. He broke someone's arm before he got up, and the arm owner started screaming steadily in a high, yip-yipping voice, like a dog.

His shrieks were a flutelike accompaniment for the wails somewhere else in the cache.

Doc got to the door.

"Out?" he asked.

Ham, Johnny and the Havens, he learned, were in the corridor. Only Monk was still in the big room.

"Monk!" Doc rapped loudly. "Get out of there! I want to use gas!"

Monk didn't hear. Or he didn't want to hear. From the sounds—knuckles crushing flesh, a bone popping now and then, and screams—he was having the fight he'd wanted for hours.

"Lock the door!" Monk howled. "Don't let any of 'em get away from me!"

There were at least a dozen men in the room. Monk, the optimist, didn't want any of *them* to get away.

"The big dope!" Ham gasped anxiously.

Ham thought as much of Monk as Monk thought of him, but the only time he'd ever admitted it was once during an operation, when he was under anaesthetic; and he'd claimed he was not responsible at the time.

Doc heaved bottles of gas into the room—the stuff that worked through the skin pores. Masks would not protect against it. It was not fatal, but it would be very uncomfortable.

The gas went to work in the room almost at once, and there was screaming, so much screaming that it sounded like a great chorus singing the climax of an opera.

Monk's yelling was the loudest of all.

There was a stout fastener on the outside of the door. Doc secured that.

And more men came running and attacked them in the corridor.

THE new attack was not entirely a surprise. They had realized there must be other men in the cache. There had to be a generator room at some spot to supply the electric current. And the prisoners—they were somewhere.

It was very dark, but one of the new attackers had a flashlight. Doc Savage threw his pocketknife, the blades closed. He was fairly close to the flashlight, threw the knife very hard. He missed the light, but hit the hand that held it. The man dropped the light.

Doc plunged in, and there was a short and furious fight over the light on the corridor floor. The bronze man got it and used it to blind their assailants.

None of the newcomers seemed to have guns. But they did have wrenches, and one of them a wood chisel that could split a skull. They were obviously the men who maintained the cache.

They retreated, took flight soon. They were outnumbered.

Doc Savage, flinging after fugitives, began passing barred, cell-like doors.

The wailing from elsewhere that they had heard—it came from these cells. There was not as much of it as had seemed; only four or five voices. Voices of the prisoners. Of people who had been confined and tortured and threatened until everything was gone from their bodies but fear.

On past the cells, the flight went. It ended in the generator room, where flight was no longer possible. Cornered, the men turned and fought.

The last fight did not last long—Ham and Johnny and Tex Haven did most of it with their fists, while Doc Savage blinded men with the flashlight.

They went back past the wailing cell occupants to the big concrete torture room.

Only one man was yelling in there now. It was Monk. The apish chemist was tougher than any of the others, for the pore-penetrating gas had made all but Monk unconscious. Monk was standing in the middle of the room and roaring.

They let him out. He'd been right when he predicted the gas would not take the fight out of *him*. He wanted to fight more than ever.

"Who turned that gas loose on me?" he bellowed. "I was lickin' all them guys, and somebody ruined it!"

He bounced up and down and squalled.

"Who did it?" he screeched.

"Henry Peace," gaunt Johnny said dryly.

They let time enough elapse for the gas to become ineffective in the torture room—the vapor lost its potency after the elapse of ten minutes or so—before they went in to count their victims and make sure all were there.

"We better tie up Horst and Señor Steel first," Ham said grimly.

But Horst and Señor Steel were not in the concrete torture room.

THERE remained, too, the group of Horst-Steel men who had been sent after Jep Dee.

Tex Haven, Monk, Ham and Johnny went after those. It was almost an hour before they returned.

They brought Jep Dee along.

"What's this all about?" Jep Dee demanded.

"We'd've been back sooner," Ham explained, "only we had to tie them up. We found the party that went after Jep Dee. They got gassed when they tried to get into the plane."

By that time, Doc Savage had given the prisoners in the cells a brief, general examination. He had released about twenty of them. The others were pretty bad, in no mental condition to be released now.

There were at least four cases of stark insanity among the prisoners. Complete mental collapse brought on by the unspeakable tortures to which they had been subjected. Those would need treatment.

"No sign of Señor Steel or Horst?" Doc asked.

"No trace," Monk grated.

Doc Savage suggested arrangements for the cache prisoners requiring medical treatment. They would be taken to Key West hospitals, where Doc himself would attend to their care, for greatest of this strange bronze man's skills was his ability as a surgeon and physician.

His quick-formed opinion—he did not express it at the moment—was that most of the Horst-Steel political prisoners could be led to recovery.

Doc Savage went to Rhoda Haven and her father.

"Have you any demands to make," the bronze man asked, "regarding the hoard of gold and jewels in the vault, which we incidentally haven't opened yet?"

The Havens must have talked that over. Their answer was prompt.

"No comment," old Tex Haven said dryly.

"What do you mean by that?" Doc asked.

Tex Haven had found his corncob pipe somewhere, and he had stuffed it, was filling the surrounding air with fumes so vile that Monk insisted he preferred poison gas.

"When I went to you in the first place," Tex said slowly, "I figured that you might come out on top, wind up in possession of Señor Steel's stolen wealth. To tell the truth, I didn't really mind that. I don't mind it now. It's yours."

"Mine?"

"I know enough about you," Tex said, "to be sure that you will put that money back where it belongs—to benefit the people of Blanca Grande, from whom it was taken."

Doc Savage considered that.

"Would you take over the managing of a commission to use this money to build factories and develop other means of permanently employing and benefiting Blanca Grande?" he asked.

"Me?" Tex was surprised.

"Yes."

Tex grinned. "I'll do it, of course. On condition that you put one of your men down there to watch me and my daughter. I don't want any suspicion of dishonesty."

Johnny, glancing at pretty Rhoda Haven, put in, "Monk would like that watching job."

Monk manifestly would like it, his expression indicated.

Monk's smug expression apparently irritated Rhoda Haven.

"I wish," she said, "that we could find a young man named Henry Peace."

"That big loud-mouth!" Monk said disgustedly.

Rhoda Haven's eyes snapped.

"I intend," she said angrily, "to marry Henry Peace. He proposed several times, you know."

Tex Haven snorted, said, "He proposed every time he saw you."

Doc Savage swallowed several times and turned red. A bit later, he got Ham and Johnny aside.

"Don't you ever let her find out who Henry Peace was," he warned grimly. "Monk still doesn't know, and see that he never does. You hear?"

The bronze man sounded so deathly serious that Johnny and Ham doubled over laughing. It was the first time they had ever laughed *at* Doc Savage.

THE next day, they opened the treasure vault. Monk did the opening, fully equipped with gas mask and a gas-proof rubber suit—it was an ordinary diver's suit which they had flown up from Key West during the morning—for safety's sake.

Monk came rushing out of the vault.

"During that fight," he yelled, "two of them tried to get into the vault through that gas chamber. They didn't make it. They're both dead in there. I stumbled over the bodies."

Monk was a bloodthirsty soul at times. He acted as if this was one time he was glad to stumble over two bodies.

"Who are they?" Ham demanded.

"Horst and Señor Steel," Monk said. "Who'd you think?"

THE END

KING OF THE PULPS by Will Murray

Many men have been dubbed the "King of the Pulps." The super-prolific Frederick Faust, better known as "Max Brand," was the writer who best exemplified that illustrious accolade. For several years Faust had a story or serial in every weekly issue of Street & Smith's *Western Story Magazine*—often several per number under many pen names. The publishing house of Street & Smith itself was sometimes described as the "King of the Pulps."

Two artists were also hailed as the King of the Pulps. Dry-brush illustrator Nick Eggenhofer was the first. Walter Martin Baumhofer inherited the title during the Great Depression. Both specialized in Western art, but Baumhofer expanded into virtually all genres during his decade or so painting for Hersey, Clayton, Popular and of course Street & Smith.

Born November 1, 1904, in Brooklyn, Baumhofer gravitated to art early in life. "It was in high school that I first discovered what a pencil was really for," he later recounted. "Although it took me a while to decide it was better used in illustrating other people's stories than in writing more of the sort of fiction I perpetrated on the school magazine."

Baumhofer had the good fortune to go to the only high school in the metropolitan New York area with a top-shelf art department. The career-making turning point came when, as he later put it, "a cross-eyed art teacher named Paternak hauled me up in front of the class and told me I could draw if I tried."

Baumhofer attended the Pratt Institute on a four-year scholarship, graduating in 1925, in the same class as future pulp cover artist Rudolph Belarski and the woman Baumhofer would later marry, Alureda Moore Leach.

Like Nick Eggenhofer, Baumhofer started off doing interior illustrations. That summer, Baumhofer took some samples to *Adventure*—itself known as the "King of the Pulps." He was given the entire December 20, 1925 issue to letter and illustrate, which he recalled "was rather like having a gold nugget fall right into your pocket."

At the suggestion of H. Winfield Scott, Baumhofer switched from dry brush to oils, carving out a career during the latter 1920s working for pulp publishers like William Clayton and Harold Hersey, both then flying high but doomed to crash with the Stock Market implosion of 1929. His first pulp cover was for Clayton's *Danger Trails,* which the artist once described as "a crummy imitation of *Adventure."*

In 1930, oblivious to the gathering economic storm, Walter Baumhofer married fellow artist, Alureda Leach. Affectionately known as "Pete," she often posed for his covers. They set up housekeeping on Waverly Place in Greenwich Village, within walking distance of Street & Smith.

Walter M. Baumhofer

Baumhofer recalled this pivotal point in his career. "My wife and I left on a long honeymoon all through the West to find that, on our return, the Great Depression had set in earnest."

Times were tough. Pulp chains were shrinking or going out of business at an alarming clip. Baumhofer tried to make a go of it doing Western covers, but found his research trip was getting in the way. "Almost lost my pulp popularity, when, during my honeymoon spent in the West, I finally saw a genuine, dyed-in-the-sagebrush cowboy," he later related. "After considerable argument with editors, finally put back the bright red shirt instead of the lovely sun-faded colors I had just discovered."

Times continued to be bleak. "After a year, we had exactly a hundred bucks between us. Instead of paying the rent I blew $30 of our little hoard on a speculation cover for S&S and they were crazy about it. This was for model hire at the then current rate of one dollar an hour. The painting was done in a rather more detailed manner than was then being used...single figure of a Western holdup man, in a yellow slicker, holding a Winchester, black background with slants of rain."

It appeared on S&S's *Western Story Magazine,* September 3, 1933. Street & Smith wanted more of the same. In fact, they put him under contract.

The timing was perfect. Doc Savage was then in the planning stages.

When Baumhofer received his first Doc Savage assignment from S&S art director W. Heighton "Will" James, it came with a simple description for the new pulp hero: "A Man of Bronze—known as Doc, who looks very much like Clark Gable. He is so well built that the impression is not of size, but of power."

Baumhofer wisely ignored the directive to make Doc look like the reigning Hollywood box-office star of 1932, instead hiring a man named Bill Cuff to pose for Doc Savage. The artist recalled Cuff as "...the absolute antithesis of a model's image... his hair had retreated pretty far back on his head, his eyes were too small...and he had rather a lump, almost, on his upper back… but, the best hands I've ever had the good fortune to draw from."

For that classic first cover, Baumhofer depicted Doc Savage in a ripped shirt, "to show his bronze chest," as he later explained.

Doc Savage Magazine took off. "That pretty much ended the Depression for me," Baumhofer allowed.

With the fourth issue, the artist replaced Cuff with Carl Hewitt, a much superior choice. Baumhofer met Hewitt at Sag Harbor, Long Island, where he spent the summer of 1933, and was impressed by his

athletic physique. "Carl was the perfect type for Doc, beautifully muscled, with not a hair on his body, apparently... and what a tan! Real 'Man of Bronze'. His shortcoming, if you can forgive an inadvertent pun, was that he was quite short, which of course, I took care of in the painting."

Thanks to Baumhofer's painterly skills, readers never noticed the new improved Man of Bronze. Hewitt lived with the Baumhofers for two years, sometimes modeling for other artists. In return, the artist taught Hewitt how to letter.

But Cuff was not cut loose in favor of Hewitt. Baumhofer continued to use Cuff's hands for Doc Savage's. As 1933 progressed, Street & Smith launched a new Western title, *Pete Rice*. Again, Baumhofer landed that assignment, as part of his S&S contract, which required him to paint fifty covers a year.

"As far as I can remember," said Baumhofer, "Bill Cuff posed for Pete Rice and his pals, Misery and Teeny, too. He also posed for Doc's aides, I think."

Cuff frequently did double duty as an outlaw on numerous Western covers. From time to time, Baumhofer used his own father as a cover subject.

Over the 1933-34 period, Walter Baumhofer produced 84 pulp covers—not all of them for Street & Smith! For Popular Publications, he painted the cover to the first issue of *The Spider,* as well as a flock of *Dime Detective* and *Dime Mystery* covers. Baumhofer was glad to leave *The Spider* after one *Shadow*-style cover. The art director wanted him to paint a multitude of figures on every cover.

"I doubt if anybody did as many pulp covers as I did in the '30s," Baumhofer remarked. "It staggers me now just to think about it."

Before he could go to work for Street & Smith rival Popular Publications, even though he was a freelancer, Baumhofer had to clear it with Will James.

"James was very decent about it and said, 'Sure, as long as you work in a different style,' which I did somewhat less detailed and splashier and looser than for Street & Smith," Baumhofer allowed. His contract with Popular was very specific. It required that all work "…will equal the quality of the pictures you are now doing for *Doc Savage* covers."

The workload meant the artist had no time for

Walter Baumhofer's first cover for Street & Smith

nonessential research. "It may seem a shocking confession, but I rarely if ever got a chance to read any of the Doc Savage stories," Baumhofer admitted. "I was usually handed a short synopsis, not even of the story, but of the incident to be shown on the cover. As a matter of fact, I had little chance to do any reading…" He focused all of his attention on his compositions and achieving certain effects designed to sell magazines.

"It was a splendid training ground," Baumhofer recalled. "No more critical audience ever existed than that which read the old pulps. Any lapse from authenticity, and BOOM, a letter to the editor!"

The artist's formula for a *Doc Savage* cover was something he could reduce to four simple words: Show Doc under stress.

"Also," he revealed, "my better half 'Pete' did indeed pose for Pat Savage, as well as most of the women I painted at that time. Anything to save a buck!"

Busy painting some of Street & Smith's top magazine heroes, the artist got confused one month.

"This multiplicity of heroes led me to a rather embarrassing situation," Baumhofer revealed. "In addition to the *Doc Savage* and *Pete Rice* covers, I was doing a lot of covers for Street and Smith's *Wild West Weekly,* with a number of repeat heroes —one in particular, Silver Jack Steele. In my rush to get the work out, I never noticed, but one month

Doc, Pete and Silver Jack bore a remarkable resemblance to each other. It was a good thing Silver Jack had a streak of white in his hair—he at least was distinguished thereby from the other two. Street and Smith were pretty nice about it—only a mild admonition—But I never made that particular mistake again."

In 1936, Walter M. Baumhofer abandoned the pulp field for the higher paying and more prestigious slick magazines, starting with *Liberty.* He never looked back, and enjoyed a long career in advertising, calendar art and his favorite, nature scenes. In 1939, his poster for the classic film *Gone with the Wind* was one of the finalists. "The King of the Pulps" had become the "King of the Slicks." There seemed no mountain he could not climb.

His secret? "I like sincerity and authenticity in pictures," he explained.

Baumhofer remained a magazine illustrator until photographers began replacing artists in the slick magazines of the 1950s. He believed it was a mistake.

"Magazines lost something when they switched from illustrators to photographers. A photographer snaps a fisherman when he's holding up the fish. An artist takes the moment before that, before you know if the fish gets hooked or the deer gets snagged. It was a tease thing."

Baumhofer may well have been correct. By the 1960s, the slicks had gone the way of the pulps. He had seen two distinct eras of art pass away, pulp and slick, and had conquered both. "We had the best of it" was his assessment.

Baumhofer estimated that he painted some 500 canvases for the pulps alone, during a period of a decade. His final *Doc Savage* cover was *Cold Death,* showing the Man of Bronze using his famous nerve-pressure technique to subdue a criminal. In all, he painted 43 memorable *Doc Savage* covers.

Ironically, Bantam Books briefly considered hiring the artist to paint the new covers for their Doc Savage reprint series, which kicked off in 1964, but ultimately decided that they wanted a different look than Baumhofer's naturalistic style. While James Bama reinterpreted the Man of Bronze, at times he discovered that Baumhofer's original depictions could not be improved upon and executed his own takes on those classic compositions.

Walter Baumhofer died in 1986. Looking back over his indelible career, he observed, "Those were good, exciting times. I've always felt fortunate in that I've been able to do something I really enjoyed all my life... These works represent my whole life. They bring back so many memories—memories of times long past, of models, assignments, stories, editors, and long hours of work; of days when illustration was alive and vigorous." •